Wedding bells are ringing for these happy couples—except t

Marriages of Convenience!

But if the bride and groom can let each other know they want more than just a paper marriage—a lifetime of happiness awaits…

*First published in Great Britain 2001
by Harlequin Mills & Boon Limited,
Eton House, 18-24 Paradise Road,
Richmond, Surrey TW9 1SR*

TEMPORARY WIFE © Joan Kilby 1999
MOTIVE FOR MARRIAGE © Linda Markowiak 1997

ISBN 0 373 04814 9

20-1101

*Printed and bound in Spain
by Litografia Rosés S.A., Barcelona*

TEMPORARY WIFE

Joan Kilby

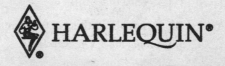

TORONTO • NEW YORK • LONDON
AMSTERDAM • PARIS • SYDNEY • HAMBURG
STOCKHOLM • ATHENS • TOKYO • MILAN • MADRID
PRAGUE • WARSAW • BUDAPEST • AUCKLAND

To Michael,
who knows 'the Secret'
with love and gratitude.

ACKNOWLEDGEMENTS

I would like to thank Nieve Jones and the crew at Optus Local Vision; Janna M Dieleman and colleagues at Delta Cable TV; and Lawrence McDonald for providing information and insight into the world of television.

Thanks to Fraser Valley potato grower Robert Swenson, and to Ruby Friesen for interviewing him. Thanks also to John Friesen, whose pursuits include farming as well as sailing, for information and inspiration.

Joan Hunt told me all about the trials of broken hips, and Cheryl, from the Department of Customs and Immigration, explained the intricacies of work permits and immigration.

Special thanks to Ghislaine Jauselon for correcting my French, and for sharing colourful stories of life in Tahiti.

Any technical errors in this book are mine.

CHAPTER ONE

MONDAY MORNING AND Burton O'Rourke had a lot on his mind. Just when he'd thought his life couldn't get any better, it had suddenly turned very, very bad.

Torrential rain drummed on Vancouver's gray and soggy downtown core, beating an unrelenting tattoo on Burton's big black umbrella and hampering his long-legged stride down Burrard Street. Although the weather matched his mood, it was incidental to his problems.

Roughly forty-eight hours ago, his maternal grandfather, the person he loved most in the world after his mother, had been alive and feeding his flock of prize-winning Rhode Island Reds. Sometime before lunch on Saturday, Granddad's heart had seized while he was lifting a heavy piece of lumber. And he was gone, just like that. Slumped on the sagging steps of the farmhouse he'd built with his own hands almost sixty years ago.

Burton sidestepped a puddle, bumping umbrellas with a faceless passerby. He stepped up his already-brisk pace amid the stream of workers hurrying to their dry, well-lit offices and shops. Pointless, futile anger—directed at himself as much as at fate—drew a spontaneous muttered curse from him. He should have been there to carry that lumber. Because of him, perhaps, Granddad had been cheated out of seeing another spring turn to summer, seeing his crops grow and ripen.

Granddad's death also left question marks around Burton's half-finished documentary about the history and future of farming in the Fraser Valley. He had a nasty feeling Murphy would come up with an answer. One he wouldn't like.

Burton ducked out of the rain and into the Channel Seven television station. Granddad hadn't lived to see the dramatization of his life's work, but by God, Burton would make sure the old man was remembered.

He shook out his umbrella in the doorway, and collapsed it into clammy nylon folds as he crossed to reception. Halfway there, he did a double-take. Lillian Spencer, the station's attractive elderly receptionist, had changed her hair. Normally fluffy and white, curled in a fashion befitting a grandmother ten times over, it was now cut in a youthful, spiky style.

"Good morning, Burton," Lillian said, glancing up from her computer to greet him with a smile. "Still raining, I see."

"A morning fit only for ducks and native Vancouverites," he said as he balanced his briefcase on his knee and popped the latches. Removing a single stem of yellow freesia, he added it to the vase bursting with spring flowers on Lillian's desk. He kept the vase full by adding one flower every day. Rain or shine. Life or death. "You've had your hair done."

Lillian pulled the freesia toward her and inhaled. "You're a darling, Burton." Straightening, she gingerly touched her hair. "Do you like it? My grandniece is going to hairdressing school. I think it makes a change from my plain old-lady style."

"Nobody would ever call you plain, Lillian," he said, hoping she wouldn't notice he hadn't answered her question.

He shrugged out of his coat and slung it over his arm. The cuffs of his long-sleeved navy cotton sweater and his black denim pants were damp, as were the socks inside his black Rockports. He ran a hand through his short hair and flattened the annoying cowlick that curved over his right brow.

"Is Murphy in yet?" Grief, briefly suspended, resurfaced in a frown. He hated having to deal with this now, but he couldn't rest while the future of his documentary was uncertain.

"He just went up." Lillian peered at Burton over the rims of her half-glasses, her gray wisps of eyebrows knitting in concern. "Is something wrong?"

There was no reason to keep Granddad's death a secret, except that it hurt like hell to talk about it, and Lillian had an attentive way about her that drew a person out. "My grandfather died on Saturday."

"Oh, Burton. I'm so sorry." Lillian discreetly punched a button to save the spreadsheet on her computer screen.

"Thanks, Lil, it's okay—" He stopped, wiping a hand across his eyes. "Actually, it's not okay, but I can't do anything about it." Intentions, good or bad, never did anything.

Lillian shook her head gently, watching his face. "Very upsetting. Was it unexpected?"

"Yes." His voice sounded harsh and suddenly he found he couldn't talk about it, after all.

Lillian's gift lay in knowing when to offer sympathy and when to offer a distraction. She touched his hand. "Ernest has arrived."

"Ernest?"

"Your new production assistant. He's setting up his desk in Jim's old spot."

"Good. I'll see him in a few minutes. First I've got to talk to Murphy."

"Yes, of course. *Lost Harvest.*" Lillian had instantly understood the ramifications of his grandfather's death.

Burton nodded, one hand clenching into a fist. Everyone at the station knew how much this project meant to him. Maybe some didn't know it was a tribute to the man who'd been his greatest influence, but they were aware it would be the first piece he'd written, as well as produced.

The phone rang.

"Good morning, Channel Seven," Lillian said in her well-modulated telephone voice. She listened a moment, then glanced up at Burton. "Your mother," she whispered, a hand over the receiver. "I'll put her on line one."

Burton nodded and started down the corridor. He could hear Lillian gently murmuring her regrets over his mother's recent loss. He was worried about Mother; she and Granddad had been very close. Her grief, like Burton's, was as fresh and deep as a newly dug grave.

The key ready in his hand, he unlocked his office door and swung it open in one motion. The space was a scant ten-by-twelve, mostly taken up by shelves lined with rows of boxed videotapes. The file cabinet in the corner was stacked high with more videos. Three walls were covered with photos, mostly black and white, relics of his early years as a photojournalist. On the fourth wall was a window that overlooked a parking lot. Burton didn't care about the view, or lack of it. He had a highly developed inner vision that lent color and shape to his world, and provided him with abundant mental images. Sometimes more than he could cope with.

Kicking the door shut, he rounded the desk, scooped up the telephone receiver and punched line one. "Hello, Mother," he said, sinking into his chair. "How are you this morning?"

"I'm fine, Burtie dear," Catherine O'Rourke replied, her voice clear and high. "Just fine."

Anyone else would think she sounded like her normal cheerful self. But Burton heard the note of strain, knew she was barely hanging on to her control. He took a leaf from Lillian's book. "I arranged with Granddad's neighbors to look after the dog until we can figure out what to do with him. They'll feed the chickens and collect the eggs, as well.''

''That's nice of them. Did you...cancel the phone and the electricity?''

He understood her hesitation. Mundane details like a name in a phone book or on a hydro bill gave a certain solidity to life, provided proof of existence. And when they were cut off for good... It had been the same when Dad had died five years ago and they'd had to cancel his car insurance and credit cards. It was hard to let go.

''Let's keep the utilities going for a while,'' Burton replied. ''At least until you've sorted through his things. Until *we've* sorted through them,'' he amended, knowing how hard it would be for her to do it alone.

''All right. Thank you.''

''How is it going with the funeral arrangements? Can I do anything?''

''No, I'm fine. I like to keep busy. It takes my mind off...things.'' The quaver in her voice was now clearly audible. ''I just wish I'd been there when he died. I wish...''

Burton's throat thickened with his own intertwining of grief and guilt. The image of Granddad as he'd found him replayed itself before his mind's eye as it had done countless times over the past two days. For months he'd been meaning to get out there and help fix the front steps of the farmhouse. Why hadn't he made the time to just go and do it? When he finally had gone, it was too late.

Old Doc Perkins had insisted that at Granddad's age, cardiac arrest could have come at any time. Sure, Burton thought. One could also argue that death was inevitable, a fact of nature, a peaceful end to a full life. But no matter which rationalization he applied, William Armstrong's death still felt like his fault. Granddad had always taught Burton the meaning of responsibility. Death was the final lesson.

"We're reading the will tonight," Catherine said. "You'll be there, won't you?"

Burton covered his face with his hand and swore silently.

"Burton? Did you hear me? I said—"

"I heard you." He cleared his throat. "What time? It's going to be chaos around here today—" He broke off. Every day was chaos, a battle to stay ahead of a breakneck schedule constantly being undermined by the unexpected.

"Eight o'clock. Now, Burton..." Rather than reproach him, her tone implied she expected him to do the right thing.

Burton flipped open his daily planner to the ribbon that marked last Friday's date, April 30. He turned the pages forward to Monday, May 3.

Every time slot until seven-thirty at night had something penciled in. Snatching a pen out of the bamboo holder on his desk, he made a slash through tonight's seven-thirty entry. And wished for the zillionth time there were forty-eight hours in every day. "Don't worry, Mother. I'll be there. I'll come straight from the station since I'll be working late."

Catherine sighed. "When are you not? You're so much like your grandfather."

Burton's gaze moved to the opposite wall, to a photo he now realized he'd been avoiding looking at since he entered the office. Sandwiched between the stark images of a Belfast bomb blast and a group of Israeli soldiers bristling with Uzis, was a color portrait of Granddad.

William Armstrong's weathered brow was almost as stern and unyielding as the soldiers'. But his sense of humor, honed as fine and dry as the prairies from whence he'd come, was evident in the curving lines around his strong mouth. His hair, once a dark copper like Burton's, had turned to a thick shock of white, but his eyes, the same brilliant blue he'd passed on to his grandson, had barely dimmed with age.

"I'll take that as a compliment." Burton pressed his thumb and forefingers to the inner corners of his eyes. "I imagine whatever he had will go to you as his only child, but if his chess set isn't spoken for, I'd really like it to remember him by."

"I know he would want you to have it," Catherine said, her voice warming. "You were only nine when he taught you how to play. The pair of you used to sit under that horse chestnut tree in the side yard, brooding over the game for hours."

Burton remembered it well—the old man's quiet chuckle as he applauded Burton's first unassisted checkmate, his own bursting pride at his grandfather's approval. The silence on the line stretched. Burton felt the sting of tears. He reached into his pocket for a handkerchief.

"He was a great guy," he said at last. "I have to go," he added, tucking the handkerchief back in his pocket. "Call me if you need anything."

"I will. And don't forget—eight o'clock at Mr. Bingham's house."

Burton wrote down the address of his grandfather's lawyer and said goodbye. Then he strode back down the hall to the elevator, and jabbed the button for the fifth floor There had to be a way to keep the project going.

The elevator inched upward, past Research and Public Relations, past the cafeteria and whole floors of offices. Burton shut his eyes and tried to visualize Murphy waving aside the objections and difficulties inherent in continuing a show whose main character had died.

The elevator jolted to a stop, the doors opened with a *ping,* and the image of a benevolent and risk-taking Murphy disappeared in a puff of mental smoke.

At the outer desk, Sylvia murmured into the telephone receiver cradled between her neck and shoulder while her long lacquered nails tap-danced across the computer keyboard. She glanced up, her cinnamon-colored mouth a startled "O" as Burton walked past her, knocked once on the double oak doors and pushed his way into the plush-carpeted corner office.

Odd. The air, usually so full of cigar smoke that breathing was a health hazard, smelled conspicuously fresh this morning. "Excuse me, Murph, can I have a word?"

Ponderous and bulky, Ed Murphy leaned back in his leather swivel chair and grunted acquiescence. "What's up, O'Rourke?"

Burton pulled out one of the guest chairs in front of Murphy's big oak desk and leaned forward with his elbows on his knees. "It's *Lost Harvest*. Something's happened. Something that'll affect the show."

"Get to the point," Murphy demanded in his cigar-stoked growl. He took a swig from a giant-size mug printed with a black silhouette of the Vancouver skyline.

Impelled back to his feet by a sudden tightening in his chest, Burton said, "My grandfather died. On Saturday."

Murphy's responding grunt contained sympathetic overtones. "Sorry to hear that. You want a day or two off, you got it."

"Thanks, but that's not what I need right now." Burton paced restlessly across the room, unimpeded by furniture or implements of work. At the far side he turned and faced his boss. "I want to keep going on *Lost Harvest*."

Murphy's fleshy face settled into a scowl. He reached a thick hand across his desk to extract a handful of jelly beans from the brass humidor that, until recently, had contained the finest Cuban cigars. "How the hell you going to manage that?" he barked, popping a bright purple bean into his mouth.

Burton strode back to Murphy's desk. "I've got hours of taped interviews—Granddad in his kitchen, out in the barn. I've got interviews with local marketing boards, the minister of agriculture—''

"A bunch of talking heads. What you need are shots of your grandfather on a tractor. A farming documentary needs to show him planting, harvesting…all those things farmers do.''

"I've been waiting for the weather to cooperate.'' Burton rubbed his jaw with the frustration of it all. Granddad had been held up by the rain, too. One hundred acres were plowed and ready to plant with potatoes. Both he and Granddad had thought they had plenty of time. "I'll just have to find another farm to use for location shots. No big deal.''

"I dunno, O'Rourke. This project was supposed to be finished weeks ago. Channel Seven is about entertainment. I had a helluva time convincing the board to take a chance on a documentary in the first place. It's going to be damn near impossible to get them to agree to another delay.''

Burton moved to the plate-glass window and gazed out at the rain-soaked corner of Burrard and Comox. "The Fraser Valley has some of the richest soil on earth, and our farmers are being forced out of production by high taxes, cheap imports and the demand for further development. We should be growing food, not houses.''

"Spare me the rhetoric, O'Rourke. And sit down. You make me nervous always moving around like that.'' Murphy popped the rest of the jelly beans he was holding into his mouth. Then he flicked the flame on the silver cigarette lighter shaped like an ocean liner that plied the sea of papers on his desk.

Burton looked at the jelly-bean-filled humidor. "You've quit smoking again. No wonder you're in a foul mood.''

"Don't be a smart-ass,'' Murphy said. "Cut your losses, O'Rourke. It's not as though you don't have anything else on your plate.''

"This is my grandfather's *life* we're talking about.''

"That's exactly what I never liked about this project." Murphy jabbed a pudgy finger at him. "You're too involved. No disrespect to your grandfather intended, but it's a waste of time to carry on. You've had a tough break, but don't let it affect your judgment."

Burton resumed pacing. "There's nothing wrong with my judgment. You want entertainment? *Lost Harvest* is a show that's informative, interesting and suitable for the whole family. It has human interest coming out its ears. Old farmers retiring, younger family members reluctant to take on a way of life that provides little financial incentive and a ton of hard work. Loss of heritage, the changing identity of a region. Give me a week. I'll find one of Granddad's cronies. We'll redo the entire show."

"Stop talking, goddamn it, before you start making sense. This project is going back on the shelf. It's been a ratings risk all along, and the odds just went up. We have a responsibility to our sponsors. Hell, we won't *have* any sponsors if we don't come up with the goods."

"And just who are these sponsors?" Burton demanded. "California tomato growers? Housing developers? People who have a vested interest in seeing a show like this fail?"

"Fact one," Murphy said, ignoring Burton's question, "Channel Seven is in a slump. Sponsors are getting nervous, and that means tighter purse strings. Fact two, the board of directors wants something fresh and exciting. They came up with some suggestions at their meeting last week." He leaned over to pull open a side drawer and rummage through the files. "Why the hell they pay me to be vice president of programming, I don't know," he muttered. "Here we go," he said, pulling out a file folder and opening it. "One of their ideas is not half-bad—a cooking show."

Burton stared in disbelief. "A cooking show?"

"You betcherlife. And you're going to produce it."

Burton gave a short, mirthless laugh. "What I know

about cooking wouldn't fill a measuring cup. Get Trudy to do it.''

Murphy grunted. "You're lucky it was me who heard that sexist remark and not the lady in question."

Burton gestured impatiently. "I only meant because she likes cooking shows. She told me she watches them all the time."

"Trudy is booked up. You've got a hole to fill. Summer's coming and it's always slow what with reruns and fill-ins. We've got to give the ratings a kick up the backside."

"You think a cooking show is the answer? Come on, Murph."

"You'll make it happen."

Burton pushed a hand through his hair. "I'm not a miracle worker. The documentary was at least something I could get my teeth into."

"Don't be so quick to write off cooking shows. Trudy isn't the only one who watches them. This food craze is even bigger than exercise. In these lean, mean times, people want comfort, and comfort means food." Murphy popped another half-dozen jelly beans into his mouth and sat back to chew.

Burton resumed pacing. "I've got the crew assembled for *Lost Harvest*. The schedule is finalized. Everything's done but the final shooting. All I need is the green light from you."

"Save your breath, O'Rourke. I'm giving you the cooking show because it's important, and because you're the best damn producer I've got. So quit your bellyachin' and get on with it."

Burton snorted and furrowed a hand through his hair. "I'm beyond cooking shows, Murph, and you know it. I've done game shows, news, sports, soaps..." He turned and pointed a finger at Murphy. "Remember the miniseries I did last year that got picked up by CBS? And what about that L.A. production company that's been sounding me out to do a movie-of-the-week?''

"What about it?"

"I could go elsewhere," Burton said quietly.

Burton held Murphy's gaze for a full five seconds. Then he started for the door. It was a heavy bluff, and he wasn't at all certain it would succeed, but he was desperate. He was almost through the double portal and starting to sweat when Murphy cleared his throat with a phlegmy rumble.

"Don't go off like a cheap firecracker, O'Rourke," he grumbled. "I didn't say you couldn't ever do your blasted documentary. Make this cooking series a success—and by that I mean a significant jump in the ratings—then, if you find yourself another farmer, you can have the resources to finish *Lost Harvest*."

Burton broke his stride. If he'd learned anything in seven years of television, it was to recognize a final offer when he heard one. Keeping his expression carefully neutral, he turned and held his ground. "A cooking show would have to be prime time to earn a jump in the ratings."

Murphy waved a pudgy hand. "We'll move things around if we have to."

Burton stepped back into the office. "And the budget? I can't raise ratings on a shoestring."

"You'll have a budget appropriate for a half-hour prime-time slot." Murphy leaned back in his leather swivel chair and belched. "That'll have to be good enough."

Burton put his hands on his hips and stared at the floor. A cooking show was beneath his experience and talent. But prime time was not. It might work. Damn it, he'd make it work. *Lost Harvest*—and Granddad's memory—depended on it.

"I want this deal in writing," he said, lifting his head. "Shooting of *Lost Harvest* has to start no later than August first if we're going to get enough outdoor shots with sun in them.''

Murphy's face creased into a bulldog grin. ''Maybe you should take yourself to Hollywood, O'Rourke, where the sun always shines.''

Burton grinned back. ''Maybe I will.''

But he knew he wouldn't. His career was important, and he was working for the day he'd be able to pick and choose his projects. But he loved Vancouver, rain and all, and besides, now that Granddad was gone, his mother had no family but him.

Murphy scowled again, but Burton knew this time it was purely for effect. He and Murph tussled on a regular basis; it didn't stop them from being friends.

''You've set yourself a helluva schedule, O'Rourke,'' Murphy said. ''You're the only guy I know who comes in here and demands to be overworked.''

Burton shrugged. As his career had progressed from camera work to directing to producing, the demands of his job had tightened around him. He'd tied the knots himself, every rope the challenge of a new project he couldn't back away from. That was the way he liked it.

He strolled over to Murphy's desk to lift the lid on the humidor. ''I see you don't like licorice.''

Murphy gave a wheezy chuckle. ''Help yourself. Then get outta here. And next time, knock before you barge into my office.''

''You got it.'' Burton popped a black jelly bean into his mouth. Then he carefully moved the guest chair back to its proper position. Before he shut the double oak doors behind him, he poked his head back through. ''Thanks, boss. Give my regards to Mrs. Murphy.''

Out in the reception area, Sylvia's glossy mouth was now busily chewing gum, her lacquered nails drumming the desktop as she waited for a printout.

''Morning, Sylvia,'' Burton said as he went past.

"Morning, Burton." She flicked her shining fall of chestnut hair behind her shoulders and gave him a parting smile.

Burton bypassed the elevator and took the fire stairs to the first floor.

Lillian glanced up as he pushed through the heavy door. "How did it go?"

"Do you like cooking shows, Lil?"

"Love them. Why?"

"Because that's what's replacing *Lost Harvest*."

Her kindly face twisted sympathetically. "I'm so sorry, Burton."

He shrugged. "That's show biz. What I need now are fresh troops. Send in my new assistant, please."

THE ALARM CLOCK RANG, long and shrill. Bleary-eyed, Veronique Dutot peered over her hot-pink comforter at the window. Rain sheeted down the pane and drummed on the roof, dripping steadily from the eaves. Did it never stop raining in this horrible country?

With a groan, she hit the off button, fully intending to go back to sleep.

A sneeze took her by surprise. *Mais, non!* Not a cold. She snuggled under the covers and tried to recapture the dreamscape of a white coral beach fringed with palm trees and lapped by crystal-clear turquoise water.

The telephone rang.

Veronique snuggled deeper, but the phone was not as easily silenced as the clock. Muttering in French, she sneezed again, then snaked an arm up through the bed-clothes to drag the receiver into the muffled warmth of the down-filled quilt. *"Allo?"*

"Veronique! *C'est moi,* Ghislaine!"

"Ghis!" Veronique sat upright, her chill forgotten in the excitement of speaking to her sister, half a world away in the South Pacific. She answered her in French, glad to use her native tongue. "I didn't expect you to call. Nothing's wrong, I hope?"

"I just wanted to talk," Ghislaine replied. "How are you? What are you doing?"

"Wishing I was in Tahiti with you." Veronique sighed, her mind filling with images of the island—the color and bustling heat of Papeete harbor, the heady scent of frangipani filling the air at dusk, the chickens pecking at coconuts in her sister's yard....

"How is Donaldo?" she went on. "And Coralie? And *le petit* Hugo?" She'd never met her baby nephew, but on top of the refinished walnut dresser opposite her bed stood a photo of him—a wisp of hair and a gummy grin—cradled in his three-year-old sister's arms.

"Everyone's fine. Coralie asks about you all the time—when is Veronique coming again? And Hugo is growing a tooth."

"A tooth! Already! You better send a new photo. Tell me, did you get the part-time job at the bank?"

"No, they wanted someone with more qualifications."

"Too bad—"

"Poof! Who wants to be all buttoned up, anyway? I'm better off sticking with the airline for now. Yesterday Donaldo and I took our sailboards and windsurfed halfway to Moorea." She paused. "I wish you were here, Vero. Remember how we used to windsurf for miles, nothing but the wind and the sea and the sky? Listen, can you hear that?"

Veronique listened hard. She heard a soft rushing sound that rose and fell rhythmically. It called to something deep in her soul. Something fundamental, like the relaxation of the mind that came only from conversing in her native tongue. "What is it?" she whispered.

"Have you forgotten the sound of the ocean already?"

Veronique flopped back on her pillow with a groan. "Don't torture me!"

"Oh, Vero, I know you hate it in that cold, wet country. Donaldo's cousin, Jean-Paul, is building a floating-restaurant at the marina. He's looking for a head chef and asked if you were available. Head chef, Veronique!"

Head chef! Her dream was to someday have her own restaurant, but for now... She could go home, be among her family and friends. "What did you tell him?"

"I said I would talk to you." She paused, then said, "Your husband, that horrible Graham Gerritson, is dead. Why don't you come home?"

"I want to. I will—soon. Marion is getting out more. She went to the library last week, and I've almost convinced her to join a bridge club."

Ghislaine gave an impatient snort. "I don't understand why you concern yourself with your ex-mother-in-law."

"She's lonely, Ghis, and that's something I understand." Veronique tugged the duvet up around her neck. "She and Stan moved here from Toronto just to be near Graham and me. Since Stan and Graham died in the plane crash six months ago, she has no other family or friends. She used to be so fun-loving, and now she doesn't want to do anything. But she's very kind. When I first came here, she was the only one who even tried to speak to me in French. Not more than a badly mangled word or two, but she tried."

"Come home, Vero."

The warm, enveloping sound of her sister's voice tightened the gossamer threads that bound Veronique's heart to a place thousands of ocean miles away, making it ache with an almost physical need to rejoin her family. "Soon," she said. "I promise."

Tears trickled from the corners of Veronique's eyes and seeped into the pillow. The tremor in her sister's voice was echoed in hers as they said goodbye.

Veronique lay on her back and stared at the damp patch on the ceiling where the rain had soaked through a leak in the roof. Was it really less than a year since she'd left Tahiti?

The tiny island had been her home since the age of ten. She'd gone back to France once, to cooking school in Paris. On her return she'd taken a job at the Club Med, working her way up to sous chef. Five or six years went by and she'd become bored and restless.

Bored? Ha! If only she'd known then how much she would yearn for her old life. But she'd longed for change. Any change. And fate had sent her a brown-haired, blue-eyed Canadian businessman on holiday. His looks had been more intriguing than handsome, but the physical chemistry...*oh la la.* He'd charmed her with passionate glances and long-stemmed red roses. Where he'd found roses in the tropics she couldn't guess. Nor could she ask. Unable to speak more than a few words of English, she'd simply smiled, dazzled by his romantic gesture.

They hadn't needed words to snorkel on the tropical reef or to lie in each other's arms on the beach in the moonlight. And all the English she'd needed was *yes* for him to whisk her away from her beloved home to this foreign country, foolishly believing his perfect manners and charming smile were the reflection of a beautiful soul. Foolishly thinking, too, that a change of scenery would banish her ennui. Only she found she'd exchanged one tiny problem for a set of massive ones.

Veronique pushed back the comforter and crawled naked out of bed. She'd taken this apartment on the third floor of an old house because the heater was set permanently at eighty-five degrees to allow heat to reach the basement suite. Even so, her flesh rose in goose bumps as soon as she left the warmth of her down comforter. She dressed hurriedly, pulling on stockings and a straight skirt the color of black coffee and then buttoning a cream silk blouse over her bare breasts. She slipped a chocolate-colored cashmere sweater over her head, tugging the cuffs down till a thin line of cream silk showed below the brown. The cheval mirror by the old-fashioned wardrobe reflected the warmth of the apricot walls, a profusion of greenery on the windowsill, and a short, slender woman dressed in bargain-basement chic. Pursing her lips, Veronique turned to study the back view. Okay, she would do.

Her sheepskin slippers didn't match the elegance of the rest of her outfit, but they shielded her feet from the cold tiled floor of the bathroom. While the water ran from cold to hot, she used her fingers to untangle her thick, wavy hair. Shoulder-length was impractical for a chef, but she couldn't bring herself to cut off the sun-bleached tips of her honey-dark curls. They were the last tangible reminder of her life in Tahiti.

Veronique's fingers stilled as she stared at the sad sack reflected in the mirror. Loneliness hung around her like the leaden clouds that clung to the coastal mountains. What she hadn't told Ghislaine was that Marion was *her* only friend, as well. Her attempt at a smile turned into a grimace, and she had a sudden, terrifying mental image of her *self* being washed away by the endless rain.

She could not spend another winter in this cold, damp country where the sun disappeared for months at a time. She needed warmth and sunlight, friends and family, people who shared her language and her culture. People who understood her and loved her for who she was.

She needed to go home.

Veronique splashed warm water on her face. With her eyes shut she could almost imagine it was the tropical ocean.

She would go home.

The possibility of happiness unfolded inside her like the *tiaré* flower after the rain. This afternoon she would give notice at Le Soupçon. This morning she would tell Marion of her plans.

Her excitement withered at the thought of how the older

woman would be affected by her news. Since the deaths of their husbands, they had become closer, relying on each other for company. Perhaps too much so. She suspected that some weeks she was the only person Marion spoke to other than the mailman or the grocery clerk.

Veronique made herself coffee and toast in the small kitchen, which was hung with copper-bottomed pots and strings of garlic and chili peppers from the market. Then, with professional efficiency, she whipped up Marion's favorite cake. When it had baked and cooled, she packed it into a wicker basket along with a book of crossword puzzles. Outside her Kitsilano apartment, she caught a bus that carried her over the bridge, through the city and over another bridge to her mother-in-law's house perched high on the edge of a cliff in West Vancouver.

Veronique stepped off the bus. Head down, shoulders hunched against the rain, she jogged the short distance to Marion's gate. Rain-soaked pansies lined the path to the bright red front door, but Veronique didn't spare their drooping velvet heads more than a glance. Huddled under the gabled overhang, she lifted the brass knocker and tapped three times.

CHAPTER TWO

THE DOOR OPENED A CRACK, and one gray-blue eye peered over the chain. "Is that you, Veronica?"

"*Bonjour,* Marion. Yes, it is me, Veronique." As always, she emphasized the correct pronunciation of her name, but she did so with a good-humored smile.

The door shut. Veronique heard the chain slide back, then Marion, well-groomed as usual in a tailored maroon shirtdress, swung the door wide to welcome her in.

"Hello, my dear." Marion smoothed her carefully styled gray hair and adjusted the belt of her dress. "You shouldn't have come all this way in the rain just to see me."

"Poof! The bus, he goes practically door-to-door." Veronique breezed inside and lightly kissed Marion on both cheeks. The first time she'd done that Marion had recoiled in surprise, but now she seemed used to what she once regarded as Veronique's excesses.

Marion frowned in concern. "Your voice sounds odd, Ronnie. Are you all right?"

"I think I am coming up with a cold." Veronique sneezed twice, rapidly.

"Coming *down* with a cold. I don't know how you can catch a cold when your apartment is as hot as Hades. It's a wonder you're not sick!"

"I *am* sick." Sniffing, Veronique unbuttoned her soggy wool coat and peeled it off. "Yesterday I miss my bus and was caught in the rain, hopping mad like a wet cat. My dress, she stick to me, and the water it pours down my back... *Attention!*" She shook her head like a Saint Bernard, and Marion stepped back quickly, away from the spray.

"You need to dress for the weather, my dear." Marion took Veronique's coat and hung it over the open door of the hall closet to dry. "And find a place to live that doesn't leak. I don't know why you sold your house after Graham passed away." She paused. "You could move in here with me. This house is far too big for one person, and goodness knows I could use the company."

Oh la la. Veronique twisted the gold bangle on her wrist. Selling Graham's house had been the first step toward going home. Here was the perfect opportunity to tell Marion she was returning to Tahiti. She just wished it hadn't come up so soon. "That is very kind of you, but—"

Marion cut her off with a self-deprecating laugh and a flutter of her blunt-fingered hand. "Oh, I know you wouldn't want to live way out here with an old woman."

Veronique captured her hand and gave it a squeeze. "Just look what I've brought." She lifted her basket up and peeled back the blue-and-white gingham. "Your favorite, almond torte."

Marion leaned over the basket and inhaled with obvious pleasure. "Oh, and a new book of crosswords, too. You're so sweet, Ronnie."

Veronique shrugged. "It is nothing."

"You're always so thoughtful and kind. When I think what a good wife you were to Graham, it's all I can do not to weep." Marion tucked her bottom lip tightly beneath the top one. "Such a short time together. It's so...s-sad."

Veronique knew from experience Marion would dissolve into tears unless she acted quickly. "You mustn't upset yourself over me," she said, pulling Marion into a hug. "I am fine. No, don't cry, *chère* Marion. Think how puffy your eyes will get. Is that coffee I smell?"

She didn't want to talk about Graham and feign a grief she didn't feel. He'd been controlling, manipulative and cruelly unsympathetic to her feelings of isolation. All this she might have borne if it hadn't been for... Her mind skittered away from bad memories. She'd been packing her bags to leave him when she'd received the hysterical phone call from Marion telling her that the light plane carrying Graham and Stan to a remote fishing lodge had crashed in the wilderness of northern British Columbia. She couldn't bring herself to disillusion Marion about her only son, so she'd kept quiet, but Marion's peace of mind had come at a price. If Graham was the one thing they had in common, he was also the barrier to her and Marion becoming true confidants.

"It's French roast," Marion replied, dabbing at her eyes. "Your favorite. But first, I have something for you."

She led Veronique into the living room with its sofa and chairs in a matching floral print and wooden lamps with the plastic still protecting their shades. Folded on top of a knitting caddy beside the couch was what appeared to be a sweater made of ivory-colored silk wool.

Marion handed it to Veronique. "I hope it's not too big. I wanted it to be a surprise, so I had to guess at the size."

Veronique held the sweater out in front of her, admiring the simple lines, then put it to her cheek to feel the caress of its slippery softness. "Silk! It is beautiful! *Merci, merci.* So warm, so soft. You did not have to do this, *chère* Marion." She reached up to kiss her again.

Marion's cheeks flushed. "It's just something to do while I watch TV. I'm glad you like it. Now, come and have some coffee." Her head a little higher, she led the way down the hall to the spotless and gleaming kitchen.

Veronique draped her new sweater over the back of a chair and placed her basket on the counter. She carefully removed the plate with the almond torte while Marion poured cream into a dainty floral creamer.

"After we have coffee, perhaps we go to the seniors' center," Veronique suggested. "As the bus passed I saw a notice saying the bridge club meets today. You play bridge, *non?*"

"Yes, but... Oh, my dear, I don't know. I'm not a joiner. Never have been. Stan was all I ever needed. Why, he and I—"

"Marion." Veronique took a step to lay a gentle hand on the older woman's arm. "Stan is gone. You need to get on with your life. You need to make friends. Everyone needs friends. Especially when they have no family."

"I have you. We've got each other." Marion's wistful smile went straight to Veronique's heart.

"Yes," she agreed quietly, and dropped her arm. "We have each other."

Veronique cut the cake while Marion poured coffee into Royal Albert china cups and set the creamer and matching sugar bowl on the lace tablecloth in the dining room.

When they were both seated, cup and cake before them, Veronique put her hand over Marion's. Her mother-in-law's long, thin fingers felt cool and papery. Her solemn gray-blue eyes looked a question. On the mantelpiece, a small ormolu clock ticked quietly.

"I'm going home, Marion."

Marion gave an almost inaudible gasp, then glanced away. "You mean, to your apartment? Did you forget something?"

Veronique noted the pink in Marion's powdered cheek. She'd glimpsed the shock in her eyes. Marion hadn't misunderstood.

"No, I mean to my real home—Tahiti. I can't stay here any longer. I'm sorry. I will miss you. I hope you will come and visit me. It is very beautiful there...."

"It's beautiful here, too." Marion gazed into her coffee.

Veronique watched helplessly as a large tear rolled down the older woman's cheek and dropped into her cup, spreading ripples in the dark, creamy liquid.

"Do you really miss it so badly?" Marion asked softly. "Your parents don't even live there, you said."

"They went back to Bordeaux, it's true. But my sister and her family live there. And my parents spend the winter there every year since they retired. It's my home. I did most of my growing up there."

"I grew up in Toronto—I guess we're both out of our element," Marion said a little too brightly.

Perhaps. But Marion didn't know what it was like to be in a place where no one spoke your native tongue. No one she knew, anyway. Even when she'd learned the language, she'd still felt like a stranger in a strange land. Especially living with a husband who hated everything foreign about her.

A husband who'd left her a sizable sum of money she didn't want to touch.

"Before I go, I want to sign over to you the money Graham left." She held up a hand when Marion started to object. "*Non,* I insist. I have saved all my wages from the restaurant...."

Marion shook her head. "With Stan's estate and the insurance money, I have all I could possibly need."

Veronique sighed. Perhaps if she explained why she didn't want the money... But she couldn't. She wanted to be completely free of Graham, but without hurting Marion.

"I have Sunday off," she said, squeezing Marion's hand. "Why don't we go somewhere interesting? The museum? The art gallery? Perhaps a walk in the park if it's not raining."

Marion drew herself up and dabbed at her eyes with a tiny paper napkin. "You know I don't go anywhere on Sundays," she scolded with a brave smile. "My favorite program is on in the afternoon."

"*Strange Lovers*? You could tape it."

"*Lovers and Strangers,*" Marion corrected her with a laugh. "Oh, I never could work out how to use that thing. Stan always did that."

"I'll show you." Veronique wasn't sure how to do it, either, since she didn't own a TV, but it couldn't be that hard to figure out.

"I was also going to take down the drapes in the living room on Sunday. They need to be dry-cleaned."

"But no!" Veronique exclaimed with an alarmed glance at the nine-foot ceilings. "How will you reach? It is too dangerous."

Marion gave a tinkling laugh, as though confident in her ability to take care of her home, if nothing else. "I've got a stepladder. I've done this sort of thing before."

"Okay," Veronique said dubiously. "If you're sure you can manage." She paused, thinking about how she might still get Marion out of the house. "I know. You could drop the drapes off at the cleaners on your way to my place."

"Or," Marion replied, "since you're not doing anything that day, you could come over and watch *Lovers and Strangers* with me, then take the drapes with you when you go. If you don't mind, that is."

Veronique laughed. "All right, Marion. Unless I develop pneumonia or become swept away by the flood, I will come. Be careful on the stepladder. Maybe you'd better wait till I get here, so I can help you."

"Oh, don't worry about me. I'll be fine."

"WELL, ERNIE, I THINK that about covers the general routine around the station." Burton leafed through the papers on his desk for the list of shows he was currently producing. "How's your work space? Okay?"

Ernie sat on the edge of the guest chair with the eager air of a puppy. Behind his round, wire-rimmed glasses, his myopic gaze was fixed expectantly on Burton. "Yessir. It's fine."

"Ah." Burton pulled a sheet of paper out from under a chunk of the Berlin Wall he used as a paperweight and handed it to Ernie. "Familiarize yourself with this schedule." He frowned. "Scratch that bottom item and add 'cooking series.' We'll call it…oh, I don't know… *Flavors*. Dumb name for a dumb show."

"Sounds good to me, Mr. O'Rourke." Ernie pushed his glasses up his nose and scanned the list.

"Call me Burton. The cooking show is a last-minute item, but it's top priority. Preproduction tasks we normally do in months, we'll have to accomplish in weeks." Burton tapped his pen against his temple. "I'm thinking we'll do it live-to-tape in front of a studio audience."

"Live-to-tape?" Ernie repeated, his voice cracking slightly. "I know I haven't been around long, but isn't that kind of risky for a cooking show?"

"It is unusual," Burton admitted, "but we need something out of the ordinary to warrant prime-time exposure. Graham Kerr did it successfully in Seattle. If it worked for him, we can make it work for us."

Excess energy propelled him to his feet. In spite of himself, he was getting enthused—as he always did when planning a new show. No doubt Murphy had counted on that.

"Get straight onto Research," he continued. "Ask for everything they've got on the top chefs in Vancouver. I want James Barber or Susan Mendelson—someone well-known who can draw an audience. The ratings have got to go through the roof on this one. All right, off you go."

Ernie jumped up. "Yessir. Right away."

Burton smiled. The boy reminded him of himself as a cadet reporter at the *Vancouver Sun* almost fifteen years ago—eager to learn and desperate to make good. "Relax,

Ernie. This isn't the army. If I'm sometimes abrupt, well, it's just the way I am. Don't take it personally.''

Two hours later Burton was striding down the carpeted corridor toward studio one, where taping of his weekly soap opera, *Lovers and Strangers,* was due to start in ten minutes. Ernie trailed behind, his short legs working to keep up.

"What big-name chef did you come up with, Ernie?" Burton said over his shoulder.

"None, Burt."

Burton froze in his tracks. Burt? Ernie? Pivoting on his heel, he saw Ernie's moon-shaped face gazing up at him with complete innocence. "Don't call me that again or I'll have to fire you."

"But you just hired me!" Then comprehension sparked behind his round glasses. Ernie chuckled. "Oh, I get it. Burt and Ernie. Say, that's pretty good, Burt."

"Ernest," Burton growled in warning. If he didn't nip this in the bud, it would be all over the station. He could already hear the comments around the water cooler.

"Okay, boss, I'll try to remember."

"Good. So who have we got?"

Ernie shrugged his plaid-flannel-covered shoulders. "I told you. No one."

"You tried Barber and Mendelson? How about Umberto?"

Ernie shook his head. "No, no and no. They all have commitments for the next six months at least. You can't get chefs like that on short notice."

Burton snapped his fingers, thinking hard. This show had to work or he'd never get *Lost Harvest* off the ground. "Okay, forget the big names. We need someone new, fresh, innovative. Get me a list of the hottest restaurants in town with bios on all their chefs."

"Male or female?"

"Doesn't matter." Burton resumed his long-legged

charge toward the studio. "Attractive wouldn't hurt, but it's not essential. Spark is what sells."

"Say, Bur—Burton," Ernie amended hastily. "There's this great Greek restaurant Rita and I go to near my place in Surrey…"

Burton glanced at him with interest. "Rita? Not by any chance the same Rita who works here in makeup?"

Ernie blushed.

"Come on, why the big mystery?"

"You know office gossip. We didn't want everyone to know we're going together." Ernie's smile was shy but proud. "Don't tell anyone, but we're engaged."

"That was quick work," Burton said. "You've only been here half a day."

"We met at a dog show last fall," Ernie explained. "She's got a standard poodle—you know, one of the big ones. Took first prize over my dog. She was really nice about it."

"I'm sure she was. What kind of dog do you have?" Burton's interest was piqued at the idea of Ernie and his canine companion pursuing romance with the diminutive Rita and her giant poodle. He pictured the two of them occupying the basement suite of a Vancouver special, raising a clutch of tiny, timid Ritas and shy little Ernies. Dog shows on Saturday and roast beef at the in-laws on Sunday…

"Border collie. Smart as a tack. As I was saying," Ernie continued, "the chef at Stavros is a real character and—"

"We're talking prime time," Burton cut in, not unkindly. "We can't use some never-been from the burbs."

"Why not?" Ernie said, puffing a little in his effort to keep up with Burton. "He does unbelievable things with grape leaves."

The sign above the studio door flashed Five Minutes to Air. Burton gripped the doorknob and gazed down at his assistant. He liked the boy's doggedness, but he was a little wet behind the ears.

"Stuff the grape leaves, Ernie."

Ernie's round eyes widened. "That's what Tony does—"

Burton bit back a smile. "Greek food is old hat. I want *Nouveau*—something or other. And I want it quick."

"Okeydokey, boss, I'll get on to it right away."

Ernie turned to leave, but Burton reached out and clapped a hand on his shoulder, gently steering him through the studio door. "After lunch, hotshot. Right now we've got a show to do. Get the talent out of their dressing rooms and onto the set. It's vital we stick to our schedules, Ernie. He who comes in under budget survives to produce another day. Remember that."

BURTON RIFFLED THROUGH the file Ernie had put together while his assistant put a tape into the VCR in the second-floor screening room. It was late afternoon and the building was relatively quiet, a brief hiatus between the taping of a kids' game show and the evening news.

"Good work, Ernie," he said, scanning the contents. "Smart thinking to include cooking instructors, as well as restaurant chefs."

Ernie's face glowed. "Wait till you see the tapes. I got Research to pull all the interviews the station's done with local chefs over the past three years." He clicked the button to start, then backed up two steps to pull up a seat beside Burton. "First up is Bud Perry, seafood king."

"Sounds good." Burton settled back in his chair as the monitor came to life.

Five minutes later he was stifling a yawn. "Forget it, Ernie. Bud has a delivery like a sea cucumber on Valium. Next!"

Between tape changes he scanned the newspaper clippings of restaurant reviews, discarding most while putting aside a small pile for a closer look. The stack of tapes dwindled without a single chef striking him as having television potential.

"What is this obsession people have with food?" Burton grumbled half an hour later.

"Gee, Burt. You have to eat to live."

"These people seem to live to ea—" He froze and glanced up. "What did you call me?"

Ernie cleared his throat. "Burton?" It came out as a squeak.

"I sincerely hope so, Ernie. Is that all?" He glanced at his watch and started to rise.

"Wait. This is the last interview." Ernie removed his glasses and polished them on his shirt, an anxious smile on his homely face.

Burton resumed his seat, but with little hope. While Ernie fast-forwarded through the host's introduction, he flicked through the rest of the file. Hmm, he thought, pausing at an ad for a cooking class led by an elegant-looking Englishwoman. Possible, possible.

Then he heard the Voice—French, female and throaty. His gaze flashed upward, his attention instantly riveted by the woman on screen. Her face was animated, her hand gestures dramatic, her body movements fluid and graceful.

"Stop the tape. Stop right there."

Ernie pushed the pause button, freezing the frame just as the woman chef turned to gaze directly into the camera. Burton leaned forward to study the face beneath the thick, curling mass of caramel-colored hair.

Her nose was a bit too big, her mouth too small, but there was a light in her vivid green eyes and a sparkle in her dimpled smile that made such deficiencies seem trivial.

"Hit Play," Burton urged, keen to hear her voice again.

And what a voice, he thought, as the tape rolled forward. Blithely ignorant of the rules of English grammar, she was laughing and assertive, seductive and mischievous. The lively, wildly exotic purr of a tiger kitten. Charisma with a capital *C*.

"She's perfect!" Burton jumped to his feet. The file folder spilled off his lap onto the floor, scattering contents that had lost all relevance. Mesmerized, he touched the TV screen with splayed fingers, as if he could feel the silk of her blouse, the soft curve of her hip through the glass.

"Absolutely perfect," he repeated softly. He turned to Ernie. "Who is she?"

"Veronique Dutot," Ernie replied, reading from his notepad. "Second chef at Le Soupçon on Granville Island."

Burton paced the tiny room, able to take only two steps in either direction. "Nouvelle cuisine, no doubt. No one stays that slender on cream sauce and filet mignon."

He reached for the telephone on the desk and punched in a number. "Lillian! Get me Veronique Dutot at Le Soupçon restaurant."

Unable to sit still and wait, Burton headed for the stairs. Ernie ran after him. When they arrived at reception, Lillian was making sympathetic noises into the receiver. Burton stood over her, jingling the change in his pocket. At last she put the phone down.

"Well?" he demanded.

Lillian gazed up at him. "It seems she gave her notice this afternoon. Her boss sounded pretty annoyed."

Burton frowned. "What does this mean? Is she available? Or is she going to another restaurant?"

Lillian shook her spiky head. "Apparently she's from some French island in the South Pacific and is going back there to live."

"Damn!" Burton spun on his heel to pace the lobby, then strode back to Lillian. "Make me a reservation at Le Soupçon for eight o'clock, please. No," he said, remembering his grandfather's will, "better make it nine-thirty."

A GENTLY CRACKLING FIRE warmed the lawyer's book-lined study. Old Mr. Bingham droned on in legalese.

Burton's head drooped. His day had started fourteen hours earlier and it was far from over.

As he'd expected, his mother inherited what little money Granddad had left after taxes had eaten away at it over the years. There would be worse to come now that Granddad had died. The old man used to say the government stayed up nights thinking of ways to squeeze farmers off the land.

Burton had no expectations for himself and no desires other than the chess set. His main purpose in being here was to provide moral support for his mother. She had lots of friends, but times like this made him realize it was family that was important. Catherine sat beside him, a tall, trim figure in black, dark hair swept off a face whose natural humor had been subdued by grief. One hand clutched her leather handbag, the other clasped his.

He was starting to drift off when the sound of his own name made his eyes snap open.

"And to my beloved grandson, Burton William O'Rourke, I bequeath my two-hundred-acre property in Langley, including the farmhouse, the outbuildings and all of its chattels."

THE RAIN HAD SLOWED to a steady drizzle by the time Burton parked on a side street on Granville Island, a small plot of land in False Creek. Located next to Vancouver's business district, it was home to theaters, markets, restaurants and trendy shops.

Ducking through the glass doors of Le Soupçon, he entered a foyer of dark wood, gleaming brass and luxuriant green foliage. The coat-check girl took his damp raincoat with an inviting smile. Burton returned her smile and under other circumstances might have asked her name, but tonight he was a man on a mission. He needed a chef-presenter, and Veronique Dutot was his last, best hope.

He bribed the maître d' to give him a table near the

kitchen, then ordered a Scotch straight up from a young man with a stubby blond ponytail and a three-day beard.

The swinging doors of the kitchen were hidden by a potted ficus, but as the waiters went to and fro he heard snatches of muffled orders interspersed with the faint clang of pots and pans. In the center of the dining room, a pianist tinkled out soft jazz, which mingled with the muted conversation of diners. The walls were hung with Gauguin prints, visual promises of tropical paradise in warm, bright colors and languid women with bare, brown skin. Burton sipped his drink and felt it settle in a pool of heat in his empty stomach. Tahiti was an inviting thought on a cold, wet night in the town they called the "village on the edge of a rain forest."

He swirled the Scotch in his glass. Hard liquor wasn't his usual indulgence, but he was still reeling from the shock of inheriting the farm. He was touched and honored Granddad had entrusted it to him. A thousand good memories were attached to the two-story farmhouse with its orchards and acres of rolling pasture and cropland.

But what on earth was he going to do with it? Plenty of people commuted to Vancouver from the Fraser Valley, but with the long hours he worked, he needed the convenience of his West End apartment. Nor could he afford to keep up both residences. A farm required maintenance. Granddad had done his best these past years, and Burton had helped out when he could, but the barn needed painting, and the fences...well, the fences didn't bear thinking about.

Dinner came, and he put his worries away to concentrate on an excellent fresh halibut in a delicate sauce spiced with curry and something else he couldn't identify. He'd just run the last forkful of fish through the last drop of sauce and placed it in his mouth when the sudden crash of breaking dishes made him glance toward the kitchen. Somewhere out of sight, a woman exclaimed loudly in French, her words followed by a burst of throaty laughter.

Veronique Dutot. Her voice conjured up the after-dinner delights of strong French coffee laced with Benedictine.

The crash of dishes was possibly not a good sign, but his photographer's eye had appreciated the color and presentation of his dinner. It had tasted fantastic and was exotic enough to appeal to an audience weaned on fresh ginger and cilantro.

"That was great," Burton said when his waiter had taken his plate and returned with a cappuccino. "Who's the chef?"

Blond Ponytail scratched his jaw under its layer of peach fuzz. "Veronique is on fish tonight. Veronique Dutot. Was there anything else you wanted?"

"Just the bill. And if I may, I'd like to give Ms. Dutot my compliments in person."

"I'll let her know," the waiter assured him, and hurried off.

Burton lingered over his coffee. Fifteen minutes passed and she still didn't appear. He ran his fingers through his hair and his tongue over his teeth, and tried to feel charming and persuasive, instead of annoyed and desperate. Each time the kitchen door swung open, his heart sped up. And each time, he had to remind himself the anticipation he felt was strictly business. For distraction, he pulled out his pocket calculator and juggled numbers to see how far he could stretch the programming budget to entice Veronique to stay in Canada.

His head was down, his pen scribbling over a notepad, when the doors to the kitchen swung open. A variegated blond head and one angular shoulder clothed in starched white linen poked through.

Veronique paused to scan her apron front for spillage, then hissed over her shoulder to Glenn, the waiter, "Which table did you say?"

"Forty-two," Glenn said, layering loaded plates across his left arm. "Over in the corner. A guy on his own. I think he's about to leave."

Bon. Veronique was not averse to compliments on her cuisine, but tonight she just wanted to get home and nurse her cold in a long, hot bath. Stepping around the potted plant, she entered the dining room.

At that moment, the man at table forty-two glanced up and looked straight at her.

Her heart stopped. Blood drained from her face, her fingers went cold and her breath stuck in her paralyzed lungs. *Mon Dieu!* It was Graham. Impossible. He was dead. But...the hair, the eyes, the shape of the nose, the slant of the jaw...all exactly the same.

And it was just like this she'd met her husband, coming out of the Club Med kitchen to accept a compliment.... Déjà vu washed over her in sickening waves.

He'd seen her! He was getting up.

Panicking, she backed into the kitchen, yanking furiously at her apron ties. "Louis! I am leaving," she called in French to the master chef.

Glenn, his arms laden with soiled plates, stepped out of her way. "Hey, did you talk to that guy?" he asked.

"I cannot!" she cried distractedly, conscious only of an overpowering need to escape. Tossing her apron into the basket of dirty linen in the corner, she ran from the kitchen, grabbed her coat and small leather backpack from the locker room and dashed out the back door. Picking her way through puddles, she rounded the corner of the building and followed the path to the street.

CHAPTER THREE

BURTON WATCHED VERONIQUE'S hasty retreat in astonishment. He checked his shirt for curry sauce, glanced behind him… Nothing seemed out of the ordinary.

Blond Ponytail went by with a load of desserts.

"Excuse me," Burton called.

"Be right there," the harried waiter called back.

He returned in a few minutes with the bill enclosed in a discreet black folder and placed it on the table.

"Did Ms. Dutot say when she'd be out?" Burton asked, reaching for the bill. "I thought I saw her, and then she disappeared."

Ponytail grimaced. "Uh, sorry. She just left."

"What!" Burton pushed back from the table, causing his empty cappuccino cup to clatter onto its side in the saucer. This was the only address the station had for her. If he didn't catch her here, he might not find her again. "Did you tell her I wanted to speak to her?"

"Yeah, but she wasn't feeling well."

"Thanks, anyway." Burton pulled out a couple of twenties, threw them on the table and dashed out of the restaurant.

His gaze swept the length of the brightly lit, rain-soaked street. Pedestrians dotted the sidewalk. Umbrellas jostled for position in a queue outside the Granville Island Theatre. Cars swooshed by on pavements glistening with rain and reflected light.

A half block away, he spotted a small, dark figure hurrying along, shoulders hunched against the rain. Her hair, coiled and frizzing in the moist air, gleamed as she passed beneath a streetlight. It had to be her; everyone else on the street seemed to be in pairs or groups.

Burton ran, dodging pedestrians, till he drew up beside her. "Excuse me, Veronique Dutot?"

She cast a startled glance sideways at him, the way a woman does when approached by a stranger. Instead of softening to cautious curiosity, her expression turned to shock—eyes wide, mouth open in a silent scream.

He backed off a step. "I didn't mean to startle you...."

But she wasn't listening.

She blinked hard, rubbed her eyes with her fists. Stared. Then abruptly dropped her gaze. With a shaky hand, she sketched the sign of the cross over her breast, and low, mumbled words seemed to spill directly from her heart.

For once in his silver-tongued life Burton had no idea what to say. "I'm Burton O'Rourke," he managed to say at last, and held out his business card. "Producer at Channel Seven Television."

She squinted at the small print, which was rapidly becoming blurred by raindrops. In the light of the streetlamp, her eyes were dark and her face as pale as a ghost's. "Who are you?" she whispered.

"Burton O'Rourke," he repeated. "I asked to see you in the restaurant.... Is something wrong, Ms. Dutot? Are you ill?"

Instead of answering, she tugged her collar higher around her neck and, with one last wild-eyed glance at him, hurried away.

What the hell? Burton shoved his card back into his pocket and started after her. "Wait. Please. I just want to talk."

The mist coalesced into drizzle and trickled under his collar. Damn. He'd forgotten to get his raincoat from the coat check. Ignoring the cold drops snaking down the back of his neck, he lengthened his stride.

"Ms. Dutot?" he said when he'd caught up with her again.

She sneezed violently. "Go away!"

"I didn't mean to frighten you. I won't hurt you. I'd just like a chance to tell you more about the cooking show before you make up your mind."

Slowing a little, she cast a white-faced glance at his chest. "Cooking show?"

"Yes." He slowed to a halt to keep her in one place, thankful she seemed to be comprehending at last. "My secretary talked to your boss about it this morning. Can we talk?"

"*Non.* In two weeks, I will be gone from this country." She flung her hand out in a dismissive gesture, then again hurried away.

A gust of wind buffeted his back and a sudden cloud-burst drenched him with chilling rain. Burton turned his face into the deluge. *Anything else you'd like to hit me with, Big Guy?*

Ahead, a bus pulled around the corner. Veronique picked up her pace, boot heels clicking on the pavement.

"Fine," Burton called out, throwing up his hands. "But if you change your mind and want to talk, call me. Okay?"

She broke into a run.

He watched, mentally calculating the speed of the bus, the speed of the woman and the angle of their respective trajectories. He knew the race was futile even before she shook her fist in a gesture of despair and defeat. Belching diesel fumes, the bus rumbled past the empty stop.

Her arm fell to her side. Her shoulders slumped under her black woolen coat. Even her curls seemed to have lost their spring.

She covered the few yards to the bus shelter, which offered little protection from the gusty, wet wind that blew in off the Pacific. Burton saw her shoulders hunch and heard the muffled sound of a series of explosive sneezes. She reached into her pockets. Her hands come away empty.

He didn't want to harass the woman. He ought to just leave her alone.

But she needed him.

Burton walked to the shelter and approached her cautiously, as if confronting a frightened, wild animal. She looked pathetic—and appealing. From an inside pocket he produced a clean cotton handkerchief and silently held it out to her.

She looked at it suspiciously, then slowly reached out. Her fingers were surprisingly long and tapered, her nails short and very clean. A Band-Aid, not a wedding ring, circled the third finger of her left hand. Not that he was interested in her marital status.

"Merci," she said in her husky voice. She blew noisily, then looked uncertainly at the handkerchief.

"Keep it," Burton said. "I've got plenty. My mother drummed certain things into me as a child. Always carry a clean hankie, never go to bed with wet hair and—"

Miraculously the corners of her lips curved upward. "My mother told me that, too."

Burton smiled back, encouraged, even though her gaze had yet to rise higher than the second button on his jacket.

"Do I look like an ax murderer? Is that it?" he said humorously. "Because, you know, if you don't like my face, I could change it."

Her smile vanished. "You look like my late husband. Exactly like him."

Burton spun away in a quick double-take. No wonder she'd acted as if she'd seen a ghost. "I'm sorry. I had no idea."

"You could not know."

She stared at his feet. He stared at her pinched white face. "You missed your bus."

She glanced at her watch. "There will be another in twenty minutes."

The drizzle had turned to steady rain. "Can I buy you a cup of coffee?"

"Thank you, n—" She broke off as a sneeze convulsed her body.

"You really ought to get out of the rain."

She hesitated, glancing at her watch again.

"Look, there's a coffee shop across the street. You can watch for your bus from there."

She sniffed, then sighed. "Okay."

At the all-night coffee shop, pink neon winked in the window and a Formica counter ran parallel to a row of booths upholstered in red vinyl. An old man nursed a cup of coffee at the counter, and a young couple dressed completely in black were engaged in a passionate discussion in one of the booths.

"Two coffees, please," Burton said to the waitress filling napkin dispensers behind the counter. He slid onto the bench seat opposite Veronique at one of the booths.

She shrugged off her coat and with her fingers shook the water out of her hair. The rain had darkened it to amber, and her skin looked pale in the harsh fluorescent lighting. Her face wasn't any more beautiful in person than on tape, but she had a certain something that snagged his attention and wouldn't let go. That something would catch the attention of the viewing audience, too.

"Ahhh—" she pressed the hankie to her nose "—chieu!"

"Bless you." Burton couldn't help smiling. She even sneezed with a French accent. "That's a very bad cold."

Her eyes pressed shut, and she massaged her temples. "It is this awful weather."

"You should be at home in bed, instead of running around the streets on such a wet night."

Veronique's fingers froze. *Mon Dieu.* That sounded exactly like something Graham would say. Who was this man, and what was she doing having coffee with him?

Once again she tried looking at his face, but her gaze jumped away automatically, as though physically repelled. She stared, instead, at the crumpled wet cotton in her hands with its monogrammed *B* in one corner. Graham had not used cotton handkerchiefs. He'd kept a little plastic pack of tissues in his briefcase, and a box in the car, plus one in the bathroom. In Tahiti she didn't get colds. Here, it seemed, she got one a month.

The waitress brought their coffee, steam rising from thick white mugs. No caffe lattes or cappuccinos in this establishment. Across the table from her, the man's long, blunt fingers tore open a sugar sachet. "When you say I look like your late husband, what exactly do you mean?"

Oh la la. What a question! Her heart beat fast as she remembered the moment she'd spotted him across the dining room. This man Burton had the same downward slant to his mouth, the same long nose and pugnacious jaw. The same short hair—although more coppery than Graham's—and the same intense blue eyes.

Veronique's covert glance across the scarred Formica table confirmed what her rational mind knew must be true—he wasn't Graham. Her husband had had a mole on his left cheek. This man had none. Between Graham's eyebrows a pair of fine lines had frequently deepened in disapproval. There were no such lines on Burton. Perhaps she simply hadn't encountered them yet. He seemed kind, but then, so had Graham at first.

Veronique took a sip of her coffee, strong and black, and it bolstered her enough to answer. "Your *visage*...your face, is very similar. Although he did not have this curl—what-you-call-it?—on top of the head."

"Cowlick."

In her peripheral vision she glimpsed dark eyebrows angled in a frown, then his firm voice became comically lamenting. "I've tried barrettes, but they're just not me."

It was so unexpected, she laughed.

"My hairdresser suggested using a gel," he continued, "and then I had three cowlicks instead of one."

In spite of herself, she chuckled again. Graham, although charming when he wanted to be, had taken himself too seriously. The thought of her dead husband sent a wave of cold anxiety washing over her, and she reached to the back of her neck to twine a long curl around her index finger. *Non!* She would not think about Graham, not ever again.

"I must go," she said, and started to rise.

"I really enjoyed the halibut."

It was probably the only thing he could have said that would have made her pause. She knew her cooking was good, but direct feedback was rare. *"Merci."* She cast a brief smile in his direction, then reached for her backpack.

"The curry I detected right away," he added as though she wasn't putting on her coat and preparing to leave. "But there was something else, almost a licorice flavor." He leaned toward her over the table. "What's the secret ingredient? I promise not to tell a soul. I won't even make it myself, since I'm completely hopeless in the kitchen. Please, just satisfy my curiosity."

She knew exactly what he was doing of course. But this recipe was her newest creation. How could she resist? Slowly, she sat down again, although she didn't remove her coat. "Fennel. You chop the bulb very fine and sauté in just a little butter before puréeing."

"Ahh. I don't know much about cooking, but I know what I like." He paused. "And I would really like you to consider doing this cooking show."

She focused on the gold pen peeking out from a breast

pocket behind the vee of his pullover. "*Monsieur,* I do not know if you have noticed, but I cannot even look at you. How could I possibly work with you?"

"I could hardly not notice," he said, sipping his coffee. "It's the worst blow to my male ego since Sissy Jamieson wrote 'Burton is a blockhead' all over the bathroom wall in grade four. But I got over that, and I'll get over this. The question is," he finished gently, "would you?"

Would she? Could she? Or would she remember the pain and humiliation of her life with Graham every time she looked at Burton O'Rourke? She pushed her hands into her hair, unable to answer.

"Has it been very long since…?"

"Six months."

"Oh. I'm sorry." His voice was filled with compassion. "I guess the sight of me would be painful."

Not in the way he obviously thought. She hesitated on the brink of telling him she'd hated, not loved, her late husband. But explanations would only cause her pain, not to mention be irrelevant to him. "I am not over him," she conceded.

"I know how hard it is to lose someone close to you." Pain hid behind the sympathy in his voice.

"You do?"

This time, he looked away. When he spoke it was to his rain-streaked reflection in the window. "My grandfather."

Veronique studied the taut line of his jaw. "I'm sorry."

He shrugged.

The waitress came by and refilled their cups. She dropped a handful of creamers onto the plate between them and moved on.

Burton picked up a creamer and peeled back the plastic lid. In silence he tipped the tiny container over the rim of the cup and cream swirled through the black. "I saw the interview you did with Rafe Corrigan on the morning program," he said after a pause. "You looked great in front of the camera. I think you'd enjoy this cooking series we're putting together. It'll be prime time, live audience...."

Veronique's nerves stood on end. Live audience? He thought that would entice her? Before the *Vancouver AM* interview—which Louis had arranged—no one had mentioned the terrifying sound of hundreds of pairs of hands clapping in the darkness. Or how petrified she would feel being the object of scrutiny for rows upon rows of total strangers.

"If the show is so special, why do you ask me? Why not someone like Susan Mendelson?"

"All the well-known chefs are committed for the next six months and beyond," he admitted. "But that's good," he added quickly. "I've decided I want someone fresh."

He really knew nothing about her, yet he was eager to take her on. Again, like Graham. What kind of man proposed after knowing someone only a few weeks? What kind of woman accepted? She had learned a lesson from her impulsiveness. Granted, this man wanted her as the presenter for his TV show, not as his wife. But still.

"And...colorful?" Veronique asked, sipping her coffee. "I suppose you think I'm colorful." At first, Graham had thought she was wonderfully colorful. Then, later on, too colorful. Like a Hawaiian shirt he'd bought on holiday only to find it didn't fit in with his urban executive wardrobe.

Burton shrugged. "*Colorful* is probably not a word I would apply to anyone other than a member of a mariachi band, but I would say you're definitely photogenic."

She heard the admiration in his voice, and like everything else, it reminded her of Graham, whose admiration hadn't lasted. Maybe her antagonism toward Burton was unreasonable, but his appearance recalled memories she'd rather forget. Like Graham ridiculing her poor English, yet not wanting her to take a night course to learn to speak better. Or turning off the French radio so he wouldn't have to listen to that "gobbledygook." Or badgering her to hang up whenever she talked on the phone to Ghislaine. He couldn't bear not knowing what she was saying. Couldn't bear not being in total control.

"I'm going back to Tahiti soon," she reminded Burton.

"There's only thirteen segments. The whole thing will take no more than a couple of months," he said persuasively. "We'd be finished taping by July. You could enjoy the summer here and be back in the South Pacific come fall."

"I know the summer here," she said dryly. "I don't enjoy the rain."

"This summer will be good," he assured her, not having given it a thought before now. He sipped at his coffee. "How long have you been in Canada?"

"Eleven months, ten days and—" she checked her watch "—forty-two minutes. I must go."

Burton glanced out the window at the bus stop across the street. "Relax. There's not a bus in sight. You speak English very well, considering you've been here less than a year. Why are you in such a hurry to leave?"

"I work very hard to learn English. I only come because my husband have a business here. His home is here, so my home is here. Now he's dead, I go." She pushed her cup away and got to her feet. "I really must go."

Burton slid along the bench and followed her up. "I'll drive you. I haven't even mentioned the perks of the job like, like…free publicity and, uh, extra money for location work—"

"No. Thank you." She wound a black woolen scarf around her neck and slung her leather backpack over her shoulder. At the doorway, she paused. "Goodbye, Monsieur…"

He fished his card out of his pocket and, before she could protest, tucked it into a side pocket on her backpack.

"O'Rourke. Burton O'Rourke. Just think about the show, okay?"

A bus swung around the corner and this time slowed to a halt in front of the stop to pick up a pair of teenagers. Without answering him, Veronique ran outside to the bus and up the steps. The doors closed behind her with a clang.

Burton had followed her out and he watched until the bus pulled away. His last view of her was of a white face pressed against the window, as though only from the safety of distance and a glass barrier could she bring herself to look at him.

She must have really loved the guy. Head down, Burton walked back to the restaurant to retrieve his coat. He felt hollow and deflated, as though he'd somehow missed out on something good. And it wasn't just a presenter for his cooking program.

A WELCOME BLAST OF WARM air hit Veronique when she opened her apartment door. She shrugged out of her damp coat, kicked off her boots and slipped into the sheepskin slippers that waited by the door like a faithful pooch. By the light of a single table lamp, she crossed the worn Persian carpet to the built-in teak shelving next to the mantelpiece. She'd given Graham's CD player to Marion, but she'd kept the cassette player, scorned by him, for herself. She touched a few buttons, and a moment later Piaf's throaty voice purred out a torch song.

On a side table, the answering machine's red light blinked. Ignoring it, she crouched low to open the bottom drawer of an old wooden file cabinet she'd bought at an auction, much to Graham's disgust. He'd tried to stop her, but she'd persisted. Once she'd sanded it down and applied new varnish, it looked better to her than his brand-new metal cabinets.

She leafed through the hanging folders and soon found what she was looking for—her work permit. Burton's mention of the approaching months had made her curious. The expiry date on the permit was June 2—less than four weeks away. With Graham's death, her application for immigrant status had been automatically canceled. Without it, she couldn't renew her work visa.

Veronique slid the folder back into place and shut the drawer. Well, no matter. In two weeks, she would be going home.

Rising to her feet, she went to the kitchen and filled a copper watering can from the tap. Caring for her collection of tropical plants was a ritual she never tired of. She murmured sweet nothings to each as she moved around the apartment, dreaming of the garden she would grow one day soon in Tahiti.

"How are you tonight, my lovely?" she murmured to her favorite, a sweetly scented gardenia with glossy leaves and waxy white flowers. "Graham said I would never get you to grow, but he was wrong, wasn't he? He didn't know what a little love can do for a hothouse flower."

Graham. Burton. She shivered despite the warmth of the room and clutched the watering can to her chest. How was it possible another man could look so much like her late husband?

At least she could walk away from Burton without repercussions. Knowing she would never see him again gave her a sense of freedom. Freedom from the confused mix of anger, resentment and bitterness Graham had ultimately inspired in her. Feelings Burton had so unexpectedly caused to well to the surface.

Did those feelings include attraction? Desire? The thought startled her. It had been so long since she'd even thought about love. But after all, it had been Graham's physical type that had drawn her in the first place.

Veronique stood very still, eyes closed, and plumbed her first reaction at seeing Burton O'Rourke. That swift rush of adrenaline, the way her heart raced and her palms had grown suddenly damp… No. Not desire, surely. Simply a response to being startled. And a reminder of the unhappy past.

Opening her eyes, she released her breath and moved again among the rows of plants banked against the bay window. Her head brushed a mobile of brightly painted wooden fish, which twisted and swam as though trying to break free of their vertical school.

"Non, je ne regrette rien…" she crooned along with Piaf. Then sighed. If only it was true that she regretted nothing. But she had many regrets. Worst of all was the loss of that brief, glorious fraction of time when she'd believed herself and Graham to be truly in love.

Veronique passed the answering machine on her way to refill the watering can. The red light blinked reproachfully. *Oh la la.* She ought at least to listen to it.

The usual series of clicks and whirs sounded when she punched the replay button. After a moment, her travel agent came on to confirm Veronique's flight to Papeete with stopovers in Los Angeles and Hawaii.

Oui! Veronique spun around, hugging herself. She was going home at last!

Another series of clicks and beeps indicated someone had called but not left a message. Veronique started to move away. Then came another abrupt click. She heard Marion's voice. It was fraught with fear and pain.

"Veronica? Are you there? I need you, dear." Marion gasped, a soft, raspy sound barely audible above the static on the tape.

Veronique walked back to the machine and stared at it, goose bumps rising on her arms.

"Ronnie? Where are you? I thought you'd be home by now." Marion's voice was high-pitched, ready to crack. "I was taking down the drapes…the stepladder…I reached too far…it fell. I fell.'' A sob, tightly held in check, then, "I think I've broken something, Ronnie. It's quite…painful. I called 911, but can you come? Please come, Ronnie. Please. I can't move.''

CHAPTER FOUR

IN THE CONTROL BOOTH high above the studio floor, Burton donned his headset. He scanned the bank of monitors that relayed shots of the kitchen from each of the three cameras set up at different angles. A fourth, "to air" monitor, displayed the scene viewers at home would see, an ever-changing composition he would create as taping progressed. Burton had a chair, but he preferred to stand and pace while directing the technicians in the booth or conferring with Vince, the floor manager. He glanced at his schedule, then at the digital chronometer on the table, which ticked away the time in hundredths of a second.

"Ready one," he said clearly but quietly, alerting Mario, the vision switcher, and Bill, head camera operator, to begin with camera one. "Pan up…left. Whoa. Good."

Next to Mario sat Kate, the audio technician, who watched the needles on a series of dials and adjusted the sound level by sliding buttons around on a large panel.

Burton spoke into his headset again. "Stand by." Down in the studio, Vince held up a sign reading 30 Seconds to the chef behind the makeshift kitchen counter.

Three weeks had passed since the night Burton had had coffee with Veronique. Since she hadn't contacted him or shown up for the advertised auditions, he presumed she'd gone back to Tahiti. Well, so what? he thought for the twentieth time, trying to banish her image from his memory banks. He would cast Emily Harper-Smythe, a poised and efficient Englishwoman who'd auditioned the day before. A cooking instructor of some repute with experience on cable TV, she filled the bill to perfection—if only she had a little more pizzazz.

"Roll tape," Burton announced, and Vince began his countdown.

The final chef to audition was a hulking man with hairy black knuckles. Burton watched him prepare his first dish with growing impatience. Chef Wareneki mumbled into his mustache, and the chef's hat he'd insisted on wearing kept slipping forward and obscuring his face. The audience, a mix of retired folk, housewives and the underemployed, was getting restless. So was Burton.

"Cut!" Burton barked into his headset to Vince. Then he burst out of the control booth and skimmed down the sharply spiraled staircase to the set. Murphy and his damn cooking shows!

Camera operators and stage hands parted as he crossed to the kitchen. "Take five, everyone." He went up to the chef. "Mr. Wareneki, we need to talk."

One hand resting on the chef's burly shoulder, Burton steered him aside where they couldn't be overheard. "I'm sorry, but we're running out of airtime."

Chef Wareneki's thick black eyebrows disappeared beneath the starched white brim of his chef's hat. "But I still have to demonstrate my individual chocolate soufflés. They are already in the oven to bring out later."

"Don't worry about that. I've got enough on tape to make my decision."

A movement near the bleachers snagged at his peripheral vision. Another person leaving? He turned. And his heart leaped.

Veronique. She wore a black, long-sleeved dress that hugged her slender, curvy figure. The burnished tips of her softly curling hair spilled over elegant, angular shoulders. Plain, simple, undeniably chic. Her bright green eyes glanced in his direction, then quickly away.

Adrenaline sent his pulse into high gear and nearly had him striding across the studio floor toward her. Then he caught himself. He already had his chef.

Anyway, Ernie was taking care of her.

He turned back to Wareneki with a consoling remark, all the while keeping his eye on what was happening across the room. Veronique had rested one slim hand on Ernie's arm and was gesticulating with the other as she spoke. Hmm. Ernie's gaze was riveted on Veronique as though she were Mata Hari, the Virgin Mary and Marilyn Monroe all rolled into one. His chest was puffed out, and somehow he seemed to have grown taller.

"Excuse me," Burton said to Wareneki, and headed over. Master Ernest was far too impressionable to be left alone with Veronique. Before he could say "bouillabaisse" she would have him wrapped around her little finger.

"What's the problem, Ernie?" he said, clapping a friendly hand on his assistant's shoulder.

"No problem." Ernie didn't take his eyes off Veronique. "Your chef has arrived."

"My chef!" He glanced at Veronique. Her gaze darted between Ernie and the studio floor. Anywhere but at him.

"Ernie, go help Mr. Wareneki organize his stuff to leave." He turned back to Veronique, arms crossed over his chest. "My assistant was out of line just now. The successful candidates were chosen last week to do a live audition this week. I'll be choosing my presenter from among them."

"But I have changed my mind," she said, gripping the strap of her leather backpack. "I want to do the series."

And God help him, he still wanted her to do the series, too. Emily Harper-Smythe might be poised, but Veronique was dynamic. Where the Englishwoman was pleasant-looking, Veronique was magnetic. She might not be able to look him in the face for more than a split second, but he couldn't keep his eyes off her. And he knew the audience would feel the same.

But he wasn't ready to let her know that. He had to be sure that if he hired her, she wouldn't let him down. Why was she here now? And how badly did she want the job?

"Well, now, I don't know," he said, uncrossing his arms to scratch his jaw. "Wareneki was the last to audition. The boys will be wanting to pack up the set."

"But you offered me the series."

Was that desperation in her voice? "You turned it down."

She shrugged, a fascinating, complicated gesture that involved not only her shoulders, but her head and all her features—the eyebrows raised, lids lowered, mouth pursed.

"I did not say I didn't want to do it. I said I could not."

She held her elbows in tight to her sides. Talking to Ernie, she'd been fluid and unconsciously graceful. With him, she was all angles and nervous energy. He found himself wanting to change that.

"I've made my decision." He added a dash of regret to his voice.

"Not Monsieur Wareneki, surely." She sounded deeply offended.

"No, Emily Harper-Smythe. Englishwoman, very elegant."

Her hand flipped up, and a thin gold bangle slid over black cashmere. "Poof! The English do not know how to cook." But her lightning glance at his face held a trace of uncertainty. "Was she any good?"

Burton smiled cheerfully. "Terrific. Very professional. Her Thai vegetable curry was delicious." He patted his stomach at the memory.

Veronique straightened her shoulders. Two small spots of red burned in her cheeks, enhancing her vivid hair and brilliant green eyes.

"It is only right you give me a chance to prove myself,"

she said, glaring at his chest. "You beg me to do the show. I come all the way down here to tell you I will consider it, only to find you have hired someone else!" One hand swept dramatically skyward, and she burst into a torrent of excited French.

God, she was gorgeous. And if she would only look him in the eye, she'd know he thought so. She'd also know he'd give her whatever she wanted, including an audition.

Ernie was at his sleeve. "Hey, Burt. The guys want to know—"

He spun around. "'Burton,' you dolt!" He stopped short and took a deep breath. "Tell Vince to hang tough for a while."

He took another breath and turned back to Veronique. "One—I never beg. Two—I haven't hired anyone yet—"

"You should not talk to him like that." Veronique's frowning gaze followed Ernie. "He is a sensitive young man."

Burton gritted his teeth. "Tell me, what made you change your mind about doing the show?"

Again that hint of desperation in the ragged, in-drawn breath, and the shaky hand through tangled curls. "My mother-in-law, she break her hip. She must stay in hospital for some weeks. She have no one to help her but me. Already I quit my job at the restaurant, and there is nothing else available, so…" She trailed off, looking embarrassed.

"So you thought you'd fill in the time with my cooking show." *Look at me.*

"We help each other, I think." She stared fixedly at his shirtfront. A tiny twitch started at the corner of her nostril.

Behind him, Ernie cleared his throat. Burton started. "What is it now, Ern?"

"She could fill in the rest of Wareneki's time slot. You know, sort of a minishow. One dish."

"Thanks for the suggestion." His dry tone went right over Ernie's head.

"Any time, boss." Ernie smiled at Veronique.

Veronique beamed back at Ernie. *"Merci."*

Burton felt an uncomfortable twinge somewhere in mid-chest. Him, jealous of Ernie? No way.

"All right," he said to Veronique. "Since Wareneki's out of the running, you can finish his segment. Ernie, go tell Vince we'll shoot one more set. Let's get moving before we lose the rest of the audience."

Veronique glanced at the bleachers, and a shiver skittered through her. She'd come to the studio today expecting a brief chat to negotiate money and menus. Now her sure thing hinged on a public performance. "But I have nothing to prepare!"

Burton's chest, and the arms crossed in front of it, looked unsympathetic. "You can prepare whatever Wareneki was going to make. Chocolate soufflé, I think he said."

Veronique didn't respond. Maybe it wasn't too late to call Louis and ask for her old job back. Though in truth, she'd been glad to leave Le Soupçon. Louis had hands like an octopus and the morals of an alley cat.

"Chocolate soufflé," Burton repeated. "Can you make it?"

Her head snapped up. "But of course. Every apprentice chef knows how to make that." But her mind went blank even as she mentally reviewed the recipe. How many eggs, exactly? How much cream?

Then Burton was leading her across the floor. She'd meant to tell him right away about her work visa running out, thinking maybe he could help. Now it was too late. Everything was happening too fast. People were all around them, Burton issuing orders as they went. So many cameras and wires and lights…

"Nervous?" Burton murmured.

"Not at all." Never would she admit such a thing!

"Don't worry. You'll be fine. Just remember to look directly into the camera. Don't look at the audience."

They stepped onto the set. The floorboards sounded hollow beneath her feet. The "kitchen" looked like a department-store display. There was a fake window with a light behind it and some fake plants hanging from the fake ceiling. She felt like a fake herself.

"But these people are right in front of me, watching what I do," she protested in a low voice. "How can I not speak to them?"

"Trust me on this. Your real audience is the people at home in front of their television sets."

She glanced around the kitchen and wiped her palms down her dress. Everything looked so small. So unfamiliar. "Go on," she said.

"The ingredients are in the fridge. The pots and pans in the cupboards—"

"I am a chef. These things I know."

A white apron with a bib hung on a hook beside the stove. She took it down, inspected it for cleanliness and put it on. Then took a deep breath. "I am ready."

"Great. In just a few minutes the floor manager…that's Vince there with the red baseball cap…will begin the countdown, at first out loud, then like so—" He broke off with an exasperated sigh. "Veronique, you're simply going to have to look at me!"

Taking another big breath, she raised her eyes—and exhaled in relief. All she was expected to look at was his hand. He counted down the seconds by folding his fingers back one by one.

"When he claps the board together—" Burton illustrated that, too "—you're on." He moved around the set as he spoke, straightening some pots, whisking a dirty cloth out of sight. He stopped in front of her to tuck a strand of hair behind her ears, his fingers cool and impersonal. She tensed, remembering touches that had nothing to do with Burton. Her confused senses wanted to attach the scent of English Leather to him, but all she could smell was the merest whiff of sandalwood. And chocolate soufflé.

Veronique swallowed. "He does not say 'action'?"

He laughed, a warm, melting chuckle. "That's only when making movies. You've got twelve minutes to complete the segment. I'll be in the control booth." He indicated a glass-fronted room high on the opposite wall. Then he walked off the set and disappeared into the crowd of camera operators and assorted others whose position and function she had no idea about.

Twelve minutes! *Oh la la.* Self-consciously, Veronique began to assemble the utensils she would need to create a soufflé. In her nervousness, she banged the top of a double boiler into its base with a clang. Chocolate soufflé! She did not want to do someone else's dish. That would not show Monsieur Burton what she could do.

"Thirty seconds to air," announced an unsmiling man with headset and clipboard.

Banks of bright lights flared on, making her squint. Three cameras were positioned, to her right, left and dead center. Her stomach flip-flopped like a lobster in a pot of boiling water.

"Ten…nine…eight…"

This was even worse than preparing *choux* pastry in front of Maître Chef Duxelles at the Cordon Bleu in Paris.

The floor manager's voice stopped. She saw his hand go up, fingers outstretched.

"Five…four…"

Blank. Her mind was completely blank.

"Two…*one.*"

She gazed into the camera directly in front of her. It seemed to engulf her, sucking her down the round black hole into a tortuous maze of shutters and lenses. Veronique stared into the unseeing eye, paralyzed.

Was that herself reflected in the dark glass? It reminded her of Marion, small and pathetic in her high hospital bed. Marion needed her. She, Veronique, needed this job. She hadn't wanted it, but now she had to do it.

"Bonjour."

Merde. She'd croaked like a frog! Swallowing hard, she cleared her throat and spoke again. "My name is Veronique Dutot. I am to prepare a soufflé."

She could not speak to the camera; it was too alien. Her gaze went to a woman in the front row who wore her hair in a similar style to her aunt in Bordeaux.

"The soufflé is a very special dish," she confided to the woman, and imagined Tante Hélène nodding in agreement. "With all that cream and eggs the soufflé can be very heavy, but no, she must be light as a cloud. And she is very versatile. You can make dessert soufflé. *Par example,* chocolate. But I don't care so much for chocolate soufflé. Let's see what else we have in the refrigerator."

With a silent prayer, she opened the fridge door. Thank heaven! On the otherwise bare shelves were several plastic-wrapped parcels of vegetables. They must have been left over from the Thai curry. *Pah!* She could do better than the Englishwoman, even with leftovers.

Transferring her bounty to the kitchen counter, Veronique beamed at the audience. "This is the test of a true cook—to make a delicious meal out of whatever you happen to have in the cupboard. Today I will show you how to make…ah, spinach soufflé."

A movement caught her eye, and her gaze flicked up to the control booth. Burton was at the window, frantically making a cutting motion with his hand. *Mon Dieu,* but he made her nervous. Raising the bunch of spinach, she blocked him out of her vision.

"Come closer. Please…" She waved her arm at the scattered groups high in the bleachers. "Come where you can experience the colors, and the aroma of the cooking."

She didn't wait to see if they would follow her directions but quickly unwrapped the vegetables and placed them on the chopping board. With nothing prepared in advance, she had no time to waste.

"Okay, first the garlic. Lots of garlic." Her hands flew, smashing the cloves, ripping the skins off and chopping furiously. "Onions..." She peeled and sliced faster than she ever had before. "Into the pot with them..." Bits and pieces flew everywhere. *"Oop, et là!"*

"I never cook on TV before," she confided to the audience with a laugh. "Okay, add a big knob of butter...." She turned on the gas flame under the pot, and the garlic and onions began to sizzle. "What a beautiful aroma. *C'est fantastique, non?*

"Now some flour, stir it around.... This is called a r-r-roux." She rolled the *r* till it swallowed the vowels.

This might be fun, after all, she thought. If only she wasn't so conscious of Burton O'Rourke watching from on high. She wouldn't look at him again. Glowering like that, he was sure to make her forget some crucial ingredient.

"Now, we need eggs. Maybe six eggs yolks, and nine or eight eggs whites." With one hand, she separated the eggs into two bowls while with the other, she stirred the roux. The familiar movements helped to relax her.

"You know why the best chefs are women?" she asked the audience with a grin. "Because they can do more than one thing at a time. If I had a baby under my arm, I would look just like my mama when I was a little girl in France, and she cook for me and my three sisters and Papa."

She glanced into the pot. *"Alors.* Now we add milk to make a thick béchamel sauce—about a cup...." She poured straight from the carton. "A little at first, so it do not go lumpy. Stir hard. Then more...*oop, et là!* Too much. Never mind. Let it thicken, turn the heat down...now, to the spinach.

"Wash it well...chop it roughly...put it in the pan and turn up the heat." She shook the pan vigorously. "Wonderful food, spinach. Make you strong like Popeye."

From the corner of her eye, she caught a glimpse of someone to the left of the stage signaling to her. She glanced at the control booth. Burton wasn't there so that meant... Yes, it *was* him. His short, coppery hair was tossed like a salad, and he held up one hand, fingers outstretched. What did that mean? Surely not "five minutes." She still had so far to go, and a soufflé could not be rushed.

Steam billowed out of the spinach pan when she lifted the lid. "Done!" she proclaimed, and scraped the wilted greens into the pot with the sauce.

"Now to beat the eggs whites. A copper bowl is best—" she glanced around "—but this will do." She grabbed a stainless steel basin.

She poured in the egg whites and picked up a large wire whisk. "You can use an electric beater, but beating by hand is better even though it is slower." She heard a groan from the darkened sidelines and ignored it. "Start slowly to beat, breaking the whites, making them foam. Then, a little faster, then very fast." She glanced up at the audience. "Who needs the dumbbells, *hein?*"

Chuckles rose from the blackness beyond the lights and gave her heart.

"To fold the eggs whites into the sauce require a light touch," she explained, holding the bowl up so the audience could see. "A big spoonful at first, mix lightly, then fold the rest in carefully. Now to prepare the soufflé dish.

"Dishes," she amended, catching sight of a half-dozen small ramekins. "Normally, I make this in one large dish. But—" she shrugged "—we make do. Always we make do. Grease them with butter and dust with grated Parmesan...."

Veronique searched the fridge. No cheese. "Never mind," she said cheerfully, "just remember to add the

Parmesan when you make it at home. Mushrooms or ham are also good with spinach. Now, plop, plop, into the little dishes it goes. *Et voilà,* they are ready to go in the oven.''

Veronique loaded the soufflés onto a baking tray and carried it to the oven. "About thirty minutes in a moderate to hot oven and…" She removed another pan of ramekins containing barely risen chocolate soufflés, and held them up for the audience to see.

"These are…not what one expects from a spinach soufflé. But—" she beamed a smile to the audience "—if you follow my instructions, your soufflé will be high and puffy, like white clouds on a sunny day.''

Through the shadows behind the set, she sensed Burton coming closer.

"If I had a few minutes more, I could show you some simple garnishes…"

"Cut!"

The overhead banks of lights switched out with a series of loud thuds. Veronique leaned against the counter and wiped a dishcloth across her damp forehead. It had been terrifying, but she'd done it. Done it? *Mon Dieu,* she had triumphed!

"Well," she said, turning to smile at Burton's left shoulder as he strode onto the set, "what do you think?''

"What do I think?" he repeated, his eyes round and harried. "I'll tell you what I think. You don't follow instructions. You can't stick to a schedule. And you talk way too much!''

Her hopes collapsed like Wareneki's pathetic soufflés. Eyes burning, she stared at his chest in silence. She would have to go back to Louis the Octopus. And beg.

"Burt, hey Burt." Ernie tugged on Burton's elbow.

"Ernest!''

"Sorry, Burton. But look!" Ernie pointed to the audience.

The scattered groups of people had voted with their feet,

gathering into one enthusiastic knot in the front two rows. Contrary to Burton's opinion, the majority was over-whelmingly in favor of Veronique.

"Oh, great," he muttered, pushing a hand through his hair. "Exactly what I'd hoped for."

Veronique saw it, too. Exhilaration bubbled unexpectedly through her. They liked her.

BURTON HAD BARELY BEEN home from work twenty minutes when the doorbell rang. It was his mother, with a large paper bag containing something that gave off a delicious savory aroma. As always, Catherine O'Rourke was stylishly dressed, in black jacket and pants. Burton was relieved to see she'd recovered some of her bounce. Maybe too much bounce, he thought darkly as she sailed through the front door and headed straight for the galley kitchen at the back of his one-bedroom apartment.

Catherine cast a pitying glance at his half-eaten plate of baked beans on toast. "I brought you some homemade chicken soup. You can still get a cold this late in the season, you know."

Burton took the bag from her hands and placed it on the counter. He drew her into a hug. "Thanks, but I'm thirty-four—much too old to be receiving care packages from my mother. You just look after yourself."

She eased out of his arms and gestured to his open briefcase and the stack of papers spilled across the two-person table. "Why are you still working at this hour?"

"I've got scripts to approve for tomorrow." Burton sat down again and scooted his chair in.

Catherine shed her damp trench coat and sat down opposite him, crossing one leg over the other. "Honestly, Burton," she said, flicking a wisp of dark hair off her forehead. "What's to become of you? You're all work and no play. How long has it been since you've done anything for fun? Taken any photos? And what's happening in your sex life?''

''Mother!''

Catherine carried on, unperturbed. ''Have you called Beth's daughter for a date yet?''

''No, and I don't intend to. Beth is your friend, not mine.'' He took a mouthful of beans and toast.

''I want grandchildren, Burton, while I'm still young enough to enjoy them.''

Swallowing, Burton raised a warning finger. ''Don't start.'' Then, to distract her, he leaned forward confidingly. ''I've got a new PA at the station. His name is Ernie and he keeps calling me Burt.''

Catherine laughed and flapped a well-manicured hand. ''Oh, that's too funny. Burt and Ernie. Is he short?''

Burton nodded, grinning. ''And he's got a round head with fuzzy dark hair that sticks out in tufts over his ears.''

''He doesn't!''

''Well, not quite. His hair is light brown and slightly wavy, although he does have a round head. He's a good kid. He's going to do fine.''

Catherine laid an elbow along the back of her chair and rested her jaw on her knuckles. ''So tell me, have you found a chef for your cooking show?''

His smile faded. Burton sliced savagely into his beans and toast. He didn't want to be reminded of Veronique. The audience had responded to her exactly as he'd expected, but what he hadn't expected was…was… He didn't even know what to call the crazy way she made him feel.

''Burtie!''

His head came up with a jerk. ''I beg your pardon?''

''You're woolgathering.''

''Woolgathering?'' His eyebrows rose. ''Have you been reading Jane Austen again?''

The mixture of irritation and motherly indulgence on

Catherine O'Rourke's face disappeared abruptly. She looked down at her well-manicured hands. "It's the only thing that completely absorbs my mind," she said, her voice quavery.

Burton understood; photography did the same thing for him, though it had been ages since he'd taken his camera out. Just one more thing he never had time for anymore. He reached for her hand and gave it a squeeze. "Sorry."

"It's okay." She straightened with a shaky but determined smile. "You were telling me about your new chef."

Burton scowled. "The test audience was riveted. Ernie was practically in a swoon—and he's supposedly engaged to be married. Even Murphy thought she was—"

"She?"

Burton swore he could see antennae rise out of his mother's sleek pageboy hairdo. "Murphy," he said, stressing the name with a warning frown that told her to keep any further remarks about his love life, or lack of it, to herself, "thought she was a corker. He actually used that word. The entire camera crew is completely infatuated."

"And you're not?" Catherine cast him a shrewd glance.

"Definitely not. She didn't listen to a word I said. She had no concept of time— Wait a minute, I'll show you what I mean. I've got a tape of her audition." He pushed back his chair. "Come on."

"What about your dinner?" she said, jumping up to follow him into the living room.

"It'll keep." Burton plugged the tape into his state-of-the-art video player and sat on a stool to fast-forward to Veronique's segment. Catherine sat on one of the two chairs of vaguely Swedish design that made up the only large furniture in the room.

"There, that's her," he said, stopping the tape. "The one with the hair and the voice."

"You mean the woman in the chef's apron, behind the stove?" Catherine remarked dryly.

They watched for a moment in silence. Behind Veronique's charm, Burton could see a woman clinging to the edge of control. She'd held it together, he had to give her that, but it had been a close thing. He glanced at his mother to check her reaction and was surprised to see her leaning forward with a smile that blossomed every now and then into a chuckle.

The taped segment ended, and the small audience broke into enthusiastic applause.

"Burton, she's wonderful!" Catherine said, turning to him. "So full of life. So confident—"

"Confident? She was terrified."

His mother waved this away with a flick of her perfectly manicured fingers. "She has terrific rapport with the audience. And she made do wonderfully with what she had. Women can relate to that."

Burton jumped to his feet and began to pace the small living room. "She didn't have to 'make do'! That's not the way a TV cooking show works. Everything is planned, prepared and premeasured to ensure nothing goes wrong."

"Nothing did go wrong," Catherine insisted.

"That depends on your point of view. The show has a tight schedule, an even tighter budget. Plus, it'll be taped before a live audience. There's no room for retakes if she screws up. If I don't make this work, Murphy will scuttle my plans for *Lost Harvest*."

Catherine twisted in her chair to look at him. "You took risks with *Lovers and Strangers*. Look how well that paid off."

"Going on location for a daytime soap is a far cry from letting a deranged Frenchwoman loose in front of a live audience."

Laughing and shaking her head, Catherine got to her feet. "Sounds to me like this is more personal than professional. Are you sure you're not just a little interested in her?"

Burton glanced away. Mothers and their sixth sense. "I hardly know the woman. I was ticked off when she turned down my first offer to appear on the show. Now I'm wishing she hadn't changed her mind. People like her are hell to work with. I'm responsible for bringing the show in under budget. It's me who has to fix things if they go wrong."

"It was only an audition. She'll learn."

Burton leaned over and pushed the eject button to retrieve the tape. "Maybe. She's coming in tomorrow to talk it over."

Catherine handed him the cover. "If you really feel she won't work out, I'm sure you can persuade Ed Murphy you should hire someone else."

Burton shook his head. "That's the trouble. She's got style, she's got pizzazz, she's warm and human and funny. She'll be really popular and the ratings will go through the roof."

"Then you should count your blessings."

"I'll be counting them from a padded cell in the loony bin before this is over," he replied gloomily. "If it wasn't for the documentary, I'd chuck it all in right now."

"You know you don't mean that." She glanced at her watch. "I'd better be going. Put that soup in the freezer if you're not going to eat it right away."

"Sure," he replied automatically. "I'm sorry I haven't been able to get out to the farm yet to help go through Granddad's stuff. This cooking show has been sucking up every spare minute. Have you got much done?"

"Not really," Catherine said, walking back to the kitchen where she'd left her coat and purse. "I cleaned out the fridge and took whatever was perishable from the pantry. His clothes I put in a bag for the Salvation Army. Oh, and I brought Rufus home with me. I didn't think it fair to leave him with the neighbors for too long."

"You brought Rufus to the city?" Burton leaned on the

doorjamb in the entrance to the kitchen. "Do you think he'll be happy there?"

She shrugged. "He seemed glad to see me, poor thing. Over at the Vandermeres he has to sleep outside and share rations with their two dogs. He's fine in the backyard, and now that summer's coming I can take him for a walk every day."

"Still."

"I know."

Their eyes met, and Burton knew Catherine was thinking the same thing he was—Granddad's absence was a tangible thing. Like a boulder in midstream, it created ripples and eddies downstream in time.

Catherine blinked bright eyes and reached for her coat. "Have you thought about what you're going to do with the farm?"

Burton heaved a sigh. "I think about it all the time, but I've yet to come to any brilliant conclusions. Living out there isn't practical, and I hate the idea of renting it out to strangers. Tomorrow I'm meeting a real estate agent to go over the property and give me an idea of its market value."

"You're not thinking of selling!" Catherine's voice rose in alarm.

Burton led the way down the short hallway to the front door. "I don't want to, but at the moment it's looking more and more like a white elephant."

"It's your inheritance, Burton. You'll marry someday, I hope. The country is a wonderful place to raise children."

He perched on the edge of the hall table. "You told me you hated living out in the sticks when you were a teenager. It was so isolated you couldn't even go to the movies."

"Things are different now. There's more development out that way. More activities for young people."

"True, but it's not the life for me," Burton argued.

"I'm no farmer. I don't have time to plant crops even if I wanted to. On the other hand, it would be wrong to let the land lie fallow, even worse to sell to developers. It's a real bind."

Catherine set her purse on the table beside Burton so she could put on her coat. "I could rent out my place and live at the farm until it suits you."

Burton pushed away from the table and held her coat while she slipped her arms into the sleeves. "And shovel half a mile of driveway every winter? What about your aerobics class? And your book club? I can't see you being happy out there, either."

"I guess not. But please, Burton, don't put it on the market without telling me."

"Sure."

She turned to face him, eyes alight with newly hatching schemes. "Why don't I get Melissa to call you?"

"Melissa? Who's Melissa?"

"Why, Beth's daughter, of course."

"Forget it, Mother." He gently steered her toward the door. "I'm not interested in meeting anyone right now. And when I am, I'll find my own dates. Thanks, anyway."

"Or what about that Frenchwoman?" she said, doing up her buttons. "What's her name?"

"Veronique?" he said. "Don't even think about it."

"She's not terribly pretty, I know, but she's got something." Catherine peered intently at him the way she used to when he was a teenager coming home late from a party. "Don't you think so?"

"I think it's time you went home and badgered the dog for a change." Burton reached around her to open the door. "Oh, by the way, did you happen to bring the chess set?"

Frowning, Catherine tied the belt around her coat. "That's the oddest thing. I looked for it, but it wasn't there."

"Not there! Did you look in the cabinet in the living room where he always kept the games?"

"Of course. The Monopoly and the Scrabble games were there, but not the chess set."

Burton scratched his jaw. "How could that be? I know he sometimes took it out to play against himself, but he was always so careful about putting it back."

Catherine slung the strap of her black leather purse over her shoulder. "I know. That's why it's so odd. I hope…" An anxious frown slanted her carefully shaped eyebrows.

"What?"

She glanced away. "Nothing."

"Come on, Mother, what were you going to say?"

"Nothing." She leaned up to kiss him on the cheek. "I'm sure it will turn up. Goodbye, Burtie darling. See you soon."

"Bye." He gave her a hug and shut the door behind her. The chess set was missing. Another loss, one that left him anxious and uneasy. But Mother had been intent on other things and probably more than a little distraught. He'd have a look for the set tomorrow, after his appointment with Veronique. It had to be there somewhere.

CHAPTER FIVE

VERONIQUE ROSE ON TIPTOES to peer through the small high window into the hospital ward where Marion lay with her broken hip. Her move to the rehab center had been postponed when a secondary infection had set in around the pins holding her brittle bones together. The delay seemed to have set her back emotionally, as well as physically. The curtains were shut, the lights were off, and Marion's eyes were open, staring at nothing.

Veronique dropped back to her heels. She twined a long curl around and around one finger. *She is giving up, I can see it happening. She will need me, and need me, and need me, forever.*

Never before in her life had friendship come with such a huge responsibility. A letter from the Department of Immigration sat in her backpack, weighing her down like a chunk of lead. She hadn't found the courage to open it yet, because she knew what it would say. The implications for herself—and for Marion—were frightening. Only a week left before her work visa expired and she would have to leave the country. But she couldn't tell Marion and add that to all her other worries.

Veronique took another peek through the window at Marion's drawn face, and her heart contracted at seeing her timid, good-hearted friend further diminished. *Pauvre* Marion. She had no one else.

With a sigh, she leaned on the door and went in.

"*Bonjour,* Marion." She spoke softly but cheerfully as

she approached the bed and set her leather backpack on the floor. "How are you feeling today?"

Marion slowly turned her head. Her eyelids fluttered as she focused on Veronique. "Not very well." It seemed an effort for her even to talk.

She has aged, Veronique thought, dismayed. Her hair color was in need of renewal and the skin on her thin hands resting on the pale green coverlet looked almost transparent. "It's only been a few weeks. Give yourself time. Did you see the doctor today?"

Marion nodded weakly. "She says I'll be ready to move to the rehab center of the hospital next week. While I'm there I'll have physiotherapy to get my joints working and learn how to walk again." Tears moistened her sparse gray lashes. "I wish Stan were here. I still can't believe he's gone forever."

She closed her eyes and the tears seeped out from beneath her lids to trickle down her pale cheek. "I'm sorry, Veronique. I know I'm a burden."

Veronique fought back a flutter of panic. "You are not a burden, Marion, but you must be brave." She spoke firmly. "This is not the end. You will grow strong again. Stronger than ever."

"What if I don't?" Marion cried in a feeble outburst of passion. "What if I have to use a walker for the rest of my life? What if I never go home? Tell me one good thing that could ever come from this."

Veronique gave her an affectionate smile. "It got you out of the house."

She walked around the bed to the window and snapped open the curtains. A dozen stories below, sunlight reflected off car windows as traffic backed up along Burrard Street. "Ah, that's better," she said. "The sun is good, no? It brightens the spirit."

Marion squinted at her, one hand raised to protect her

eyes from a shaft of sunlight. "I'm not a brave person, Ronnie. I never have been."

"Nonsense. People are not born brave...."

"They have courage thrust upon them," Marion finished in a dismal monotone.

Veronique laughed and pulled up a hard-backed chair to the bed. "There now, I was going to say the same thing, but with three times as many words. And what happens after the rehab center? Can you go home?"

"Yes, but even then I won't be able to look after myself. The nurse told me I'll be on crutches for weeks, maybe months. I won't be able to dress, or cook for myself. I'll have to get a home help."

"I will move in and look after you until you are better," she said, pushing aside worries about the uncertainty of her own immediate future. She put on a smile and teased. "Better the tyrant you know than the tyrant you don't."

Marion hitched herself higher on the pillow. "But how can you do that if you're going back to Tahiti?"

"I'm not going right away." Veronique got up to help Marion adjust her pillows more comfortably. When she'd seated herself again, she said, "I auditioned to be a chef on a TV cooking show. Maybe I will get the job. The audience liked me." She curled a lock of hair around her finger. "But I don't think he liked me."

"Who could possibly not like you, my dear?" Marion said.

"Burton O'Rourke. The producer."

"Burton O'Rourke?" Marion's eyebrows pinched together. "That sounds familiar."

"He also produces your favorite show—what do you call it—*Loving Stranger*?"

"*Lovers and Strangers*. Oh, Ronnie, how exciting!" Two spots of pink appeared in her sallow cheeks.

"I don't know. He's a very uptight man. At first I thought he was kind even though he look like—" She broke off and rose to walk around the foot of Marion's bed. "During the audition he went berserk. He didn't like that I talk to the audience. Or that I change the menu. And everything have to be timed right down to a fifth of a second," she said, tapping the face of her wristwatch. "No time to chat, or joke, or think about what is coming next. He will drive me crazy!"

Marion shifted in her bed to watch Veronique. "Give him a chance, poor man. He must have so much on his mind. So many people to organize. When do you start?"

Veronique shrugged, her mouth pursed in speculation. "I don't know yet if I have the job! His assistant seem to think I do, but *Monsieur* O'Rourke, he does not say yes or no. He just tell me to come to his office tomorrow. Today, that is."

Marion's mouth dropped open. "Goodness' sake, girl! What are you doing here? Get along to the television studio and find out."

Veronique smiled. A little vicarious excitement had brightened Marion's spirits better than comfort and kind words. "Don't worry. The appointment is for two o'clock, and the studio is right next door to the hospital."

She reached for her backpack. "Before I go, I brought you some chocolate. And a new book. I hope you haven't read it already."

"Ooh, a romance." Marion reached for her reading glasses and glanced at the title before flipping it over to read the back cover. "No, I haven't. Thank you, dear. And Ronnie…?"

Veronique glanced up from fastening the thongs on her backpack. "Yes?"

"I know you're not very happy here," Marion said, her gray-blue eyes uncertain. "You're not staying because of me, are you?"

Veronique rocked her head from side to side. "When I

got the chance at the cooking show I decided I could stay a little longer."

Marion was silent a moment. "How much longer?"

"Until the end of summer. I'll leave before the rains come."

"Oh, you and the rain. Weather's not everything, you know."

Veronique smiled a little sadly. Weather was actually quite a lot when it was all you had. True, she had Marion, but although she was very fond of her, it wasn't enough. After Graham she needed love, and nurturing—preferably in a warm climate.

"I'm very glad you're staying longer, but…" Marion's voice shook, and she paused to clear her throat. "I will get a home help. I don't want to be a burden to you."

"You are not a burden, Marion—"

"Don't argue, Ronnie," Marion said with surprising firmness. "I am grateful for everything you do for me, but you're not going to bury yourself way over on the North Shore with an invalid old woman."

"We shall see," Veronique said, rising. "Wish me luck."

She put on a confident smile, but the butterflies in her stomach were already taking wing. She didn't know which would be worse—if she got the job, or if she didn't.

VERONIQUE FOLLOWED the Channel Seven receptionist down a wide corridor, admiring her spiky white hair. They stopped in front of a closed door, and the older woman knocked.

"Come in."

Lillian opened the door. "Ms. Dutot is here to see you." With an encouraging smile, she said to Veronique, "Good luck."

Veronique returned her smile and went in. She got a quick impression of wall-to-wall photos and shelves of videocassettes before her gaze lit upon Burton, who was scowling over some business papers. For one horrible second she felt as though she'd stumbled through a time warp and come across her husband seated at his desk at home. She gulped in a deep breath and pressed a hand to her chest as her heart leaped into high gear.

Then he glanced up, and it was not her husband at all, but Burton who rose to extend his hand. His palm was warm and dry, and his fingers enclosed hers completely. Her stomach flipped over, and her heart raced faster, leaving her even more confused.

"Have a seat," he said, releasing her hand to glance at his watch. He frowned. "I've only got about five minutes though before I have to leave for another appointment. If you're going to work in television, you've got to learn to be on time."

Startled, Veronique checked her watch. "It's not yet two o'clock. I'm five minutes early."

Burton frowned. "I asked you to come at one o'clock."

"I am sure you said two o'clock."

"My life revolves around schedules. I don't think I would be mistaken." He flipped his desk diary around so she could see it. "Right here," he said, tapping an entry midway down the page. "One o'clock."

Veronique leaned over the desk to look. Her name was indeed opposite the time he'd indicated.

"It cannot be right." She glanced up. Straight into deep blue eyes framed with dark, coppery lashes. Then immediately down to an argumentative jaw so close she could see the glint of coppery stubble.

"I will show you," she said, breathless. Digging into her backpack, she whipped out the envelope on which she'd scribbled the time of their appointment. The return address, the federal Department of Immigration, surfaced under Burton's nose. Quickly she flipped it over. "*Voilà*. Two o'clock."

"Proves nothing. This," he said, tapping his diary again, "is official."

Veronique stuffed the envelope back inside her pack without revealing its contents as she'd originally intended. There was no point introducing that complication until she was offered the job, which at the moment seemed unlikely.

"Your assistant was there—he can tell you," she said to Burton's left shoulder. Her English wasn't perfect, but she could hear the difference between "one" and "two."

She got an impression of dark eyebrows pulling together. "Never mind about Ernie," he growled. "We're wasting time arguing. How about coming with me? We can talk about the show while we're driving."

"Driving? Where to?"

"Langley." Burton picked up a file—one with her name on it—and thrust it, along with a stapled sheaf of papers, into a black leather briefcase. "I have an appointment at three at my grandfather's farm." He tossed a calculator into his briefcase, snapped it shut and strode to the door. "It's a nice drive. The whole thing won't take more than a couple of hours. I've got the contract with me, so if we come to an agreement—"

"Stop!" she cried, throwing up her hands. "You are rushing me. I need to think if I am free."

In truth, she didn't have to think more than a few seconds to know she was completely, utterly, depressingly free. Le Soupçon was history. Marion was being well looked after. Graham's friends never called anymore. And for the past five months she'd been careful not to make any new friends whom she would regret leaving. On the other hand, Burton was a busy man. If she left now, who knew when she'd get another appointment? Or if he'd call the Englishwoman, instead.

"I will come," she said, slinging her backpack over her shoulder. "But I must be back by six o'clock."

"No problem." He swung his coat over his arm. "Big date?"

"Ah...something like that." A date to talk to her sister halfway around the world. A date she wouldn't miss for anything.

They picked up his car, a silver Tercel, from the underground parking lot and within minutes were heading east on Georgia Street, zipping in and out of traffic like a ricocheting bullet. The sun that had briefly brightened Marion's hospital room had been enveloped by thick, dark clouds. Fat drops of rain began to splat against the windshield. Burton turned on the wipers and pressed the defog button. Two clear patches formed on the bottom of the windshield and slowly spread upward.

Jumbled thoughts and confused feelings held Veronique's tongue. She listened to the rhythmic swish of the blades and the hiss of tires on the wet road. Swept away again. No, it was not the same. Her heart was not involved, or if it was, then only to the extent she was doing this for Marion. She glanced sideways. It was easier to look at his profile than his full face, but harder to accept he wasn't Graham when she couldn't see his eyes.

"Have you seen much of the Fraser Valley?" Burton said, shifting down for a red light. His hands and feet moved in tandem, quickly, efficiently.

She watched his rapid movements and intense gaze on the road ahead. Could she work with a man so speedy and nervy? "Once we went to Harrison Hot Springs for a convention, but Graham preferred the city, where his business contacts and his friends were."

"What about you? Are you a city girl?" He shifted gears again, muscles and sinew moving under the tracings of dark hair on his lightly tanned forearm.

"I'm an island girl. A bit of city, a bit of country. But always a garden, the ocean and the sun. Freedom to wan-

der—and a home to come back to.'' A home that was
waiting for her now.

They'd left the city streets for the freeway. Veronique
cracked open the window on the passenger side and inhaled deeply of the towering evergreens that lined the
roadside. Houses and trees, fields dotted with horses, all
zipped past as Burton picked up speed.

"I've always lived in the city," Burton said, "but when
I was a kid I spent most of my summers at my grandfather's farm, where we're going now. He died recently, as
I think I told you, and left it to me.'' He sighed and tapped
his fingers on the steering wheel. "I used to travel a lot
as a photojournalist, but I don't have time for trips these
days.''

"You should make time. You are like the—what do you
call them? The skinny dogs that race?''

"Greyhounds?''

"*Exactement.* Always running and running, faster and
faster after the bunny.'' She made paws of her hands and
paddled through the air.

He laughed. "The difference is,'' he said, "I get the
bunny in the end.''

"My husband worked much overtime. He became vice
president of a chain of travel agencies—the week before
he died.''

Burton's smile faded. "Heart attack?''

"Plane crash.'' Her gaze dropped. Although she didn't
feel a speck of grief or loss, she couldn't be happy that
even a rat like Graham had died.

"I'm sorry.'' His voice was low, consoling. "At least
he achieved something.''

Veronique made a dismissive gesture. "What good is
that when you're gone?''

"Who knows how far a good man's influence will extend? If everyone stopped to smell the roses, there'd be no
one to tend the garden.''

"Je m'excuse?" Her mind struggled with the unfamiliar expression. She tried to recall if she'd seen anything like it in the book of sayings she'd picked up to study colloquial English.

"I mean—"

"I think I know what you mean. I was not suggesting—" she waved a hand uncertainly "—that. All I said was, you, *Monsieur* O'Rourke, are too speedy. You should relax."

"I do relax." He frowned, as if trying to remember the last time he *had* relaxed. Then he slanted her a brief smile. "If you have to judge me, I'd rather you just admired my stamina."

Veronique quickly turned to the window to hide her smile. At times he could be quite charming.

"So, are you interested in doing the show?" He came up close behind a semitrailer going under the speed limit.

"Are you offering it to me?"

"Yes." His gaze flicked from the side to the rearview mirror and back. Then his car shot sideways into the other lane and roared past the truck.

Mon Dieu! Veronique thought, clinging to the armrest. "What about the menu? Can I choose what I want to cook?"

"Yes, within certain guidelines. Whatever you plan, you'll have to run by me."

"But I am the chef." Consultation she didn't object to so much as working one-on-one with him.

"Television is a collaborative effort. Nobody gets one hundred percent say in what they do. I'm giving you plenty of leeway as it is, considering you're an unknown quantity. Emily Harper-Smythe has put out two cookbooks, you know."

If he gave the show to the Englishwoman, she, Veronique Dutot, could end up flipping burgers in a fast-food joint. She shuddered. "When I cook I have a vision in my brain,'' she said, tapping her temple. ''Certain dishes complement each other. I cannot have you insist on...on...chocolate cake when I wish to concoct a mango mousse to finish a dinner of tropical origin.''

''Let's not get technical. I'll be directing, as well as producing, because I like to retain creative control. But basically, all I'm interested in is appearance and timing. For television we need dishes that are colorful and quick to prepare. The details of what goes with what, I'll leave to you.''

''That's okay, then,'' she said, appeased.

''If you do come on board,'' he said, flicking on his indicator and changing back into the left lane, ''we'll get started right away on preproduction tasks—research, scripting, set design, menus and so on. Once those are complete we'll be shooting two, possibly three segments a day for one or two weeks, depending on how much studio time we can get. Do you think you can handle that?''

Her nose tilted up. ''If I can handle entrées for a five-star restaurant with seating for three hundred, I am sure I can handle an hour or two of television work a day.''

He swung onto the exit ramp signposted for Langley. ''The show is only a half hour, but each segment takes two hours or more to tape. I can't stress enough how important it is we stick to schedule.''

''I can do it.''

His fingers gripped the steering wheel as they took the sharp corner on the exit ramp at ten miles an hour over the speed limit. ''It's important you're totally committed to doing this series. If not, I need to know now.''

Veronique made a sweeping gesture with her hand. ''I cannot commit myself until I know hours, pay, conditions... What are you offering?''

The salary he named was, she suspected, lower than he was prepared to go. She responded with a tiny toss of her head. ''I made more at Le Soupçon.''

They negotiated upward until they reached a deal both were happy with. Under the circumstances, money was of secondary importance to Veronique, but she was too practical and had too much self-esteem to sell herself short.

Burton turned onto a secondary road edged by deep ditches and sprawling blackberry bushes. Metal mailboxes on posts appeared at intervals beside gravel driveways leading to farm buildings set well back from the road. The land was gently undulating, broken by long rows of poplars acting as windbreaks.

They rounded a bend in the road, and Burton slowed to turn into a driveway flanked by two big maple trees. He geared down again for the steep incline, and as they wound up the hill between grassy verges dotted with wildflowers, Veronique found herself craning forward for a first glimpse of the farmhouse he'd inherited.

The fitful rain had stopped, and the clouds parted, revealing tantalizing glimpses of clear blue sky. They came to an orchard, row upon row of apple, cherry and plum trees, whose rain-sparkled leaves dripped onto lush green grass. A two-story Victorian farmhouse came into view, faded yet dignified, with a wide veranda and fancy cutout trim. Sunlight glinted off its big front window and the smaller gabled windows on the second floor. It faced south over rolling farmland, past the mudflats of Boundary Bay, across the American border to where a white-peaked Mount Baker floated above the blue horizon.

It was more beautiful than she could have imagined.

Burton pulled up in front of the house and turned off the ignition, aware suddenly of a strange reluctance to be here.

His first impression as he walked toward the house was that it looked the same as always: wisteria just about to bloom around the veranda, white-painted wooden siding, green filigreed trim....

And the front step that still sagged.

The sight of it stopped him cold. He looked again. Everything was different. The windowpanes looked starkly blank and empty. The chimney didn't curl with smoke. The front door didn't stand open in welcome.

Granddad was gone.

Burton tested the broken step with his foot, and the board gave under his weight. He heard the crunch of gravel as Veronique came up behind him on the path.

"You should fix that," she said, "or someone will get hurt."

He had to clench his jaw to stop his face from contorting. He jammed his hands in the back pockets of his jeans and took a couple of deep breaths, striving for control.

"Burton?"

She didn't know how Granddad had died. "Yes?" He turned a falsely bright questioning look her way.

She frowned, and her gaze slid away. "Nothing."

He took one of the large rocks lining the flower bed and shoved it beneath the broken board as a temporary prop. Then he climbed up to the porch and pulled on the metal handle of the screen door. It opened with a creak, reminding him that as a kid he'd called it the "scream" door. Gram had laughed every time, and he'd gone on saying it long after he'd learned the correct word, just to make her happy. The memory made him chuckle and, surprisingly, eased some of his pain.

Propping the screen door open with his hip, he fished in his pocket for a ring with two keys on it and inserted one in the lock. He glanced back at Veronique. "Coming?"

She made that funny twist of her shoulders and head that expressed so much, and so little—restrained acquiescence, a kind of Gallic fatalism—and started to climb the stairs.

The door opened to shadows, a quiet hallway and the musty smell of no one home. Yet it still smelled like

Granddad's house. Memories came back in a rush, tumbling in his head. Himself as a child, as a teenager, as an adult. Warmth, love, a haven from the trials of ordinary life. Gram baking bread, Granddad stoking the wood-burning stove. Then just Granddad, but still a second home.

He turned left, drawn to the big country kitchen where he'd spent so many happy hours. He and Granddad had played chess at the large kitchen table while Gram kneaded dough and rolled it into soft, round balls which she'd cover with clean tea towels and leave to rise. As the chessboard emptied, the room would fill with their moist, yeasty scent.

He paused on the threshold, his gaze sweeping the scarred red counters, tall white-painted cupboards and round-edged appliances—forty years old if they were a day. Thick oak beams crossed the high ceiling where Gram used to hang strings of onions and garlic, and in the fall, a ham. At the head of the wide pine table was Granddad's chair, the one he'd made himself, with wooden arms and a padded, fabric-covered base that rocked on hand-carved rockers. For an instant he saw Granddad, seated before the laid-out chess set, his work-roughened hand outstretched in welcome. Heat pricked the backs of his eyes. Homecoming held a bittersweet edge.

Silently Veronique slipped past him into the room. She crossed the worn lino to push back yellow-flowered curtains, and through the big picture window he could see apple trees blooming with pink blossoms. He knew their branches and their hollows, the knots to use as steps on the way up, the best places to perch.

She glanced over her shoulder and, just for a second, looked him square in the face. "There was much love here. I can feel it."

The warmth of her tone made him confide, "One of the reasons I came out here today was to look for my grandfather's chess set. It holds a lot of special memories."

She tied back the curtains, letting in the sun. "Is it missing?"

"It's not where it's supposed to be. I'm going to search for it before the agent arrives."

"Do you mind if I explore a little? I promise I don't touch anything."

"Go ahead." He wanted to be alone for a bit, anyway.

He left her peering into the walk-in pantry and went through the arched doorway to the dining room, where ceramic ducks flew across an eggshell-blue wall above Gram's rack of souvenir teaspoons, and on into the living room.

The "games room," as Granddad jokingly called the cherrywood cabinet that held the chess set, was beside the fireplace. On the mantelpiece, dust had collected on his high-school graduation photo, Gram's Royal Doulton shepherdess and on Granddad's pipe resting in the lumpy clay ashtray Burton had made in grade two.

A huge chunk of his life was in this house. His parents had moved five times while he was growing up—this was the one constant. How on earth was he going to part with it? Or replace it?

He skirted Granddad's recliner, Gram's armless rocker where she'd spent her evenings knitting and the big comfy sofa where he'd sprawled with a book as a child or stretched out for a nap after Gram's Sunday roast. Crouching in front of the cabinet, he turned the old-fashioned key in the lock.

He hadn't really expected a miraculous reappearance, but the empty space where the chess set should have been was a blow, anyway. He ran a hand over the bare shelf. It was gone, all right. But where?

Rising, he crossed to the dining room and stood on a chair to peer on top of the oak sideboard. Nope. Not in the cupboards, either. Long, prowling steps took him back through the hall to the bookshelf in the spare downstairs bedroom. The shelves were crammed with Raymond Chandler and Jean Plaidy, copies of the *Farmer's Almanac* and back issues of *Better Homes and Gardens,* but no chess set.

He carried on down the hall to Granddad's room, his footsteps sounding too loud on the hardwood floor. He hesitated an instant, then pushed open the door and stepped inside, feeling like a kid entering off-limits territory. Quiet pervaded the monastic room. There was the old-fashioned wardrobe, the white dresser and matching bedside tables supporting family photos and a couple of paperback mysteries. The brass bedstead was covered with the patchwork quilt Gram had hand-sewn as a bride. So much he'd taken for granted. Not just the chess set had value.

There was a sound in the hallway, and Veronique's bright head poked around the door. "Did you find it?"

"Not yet." He opened the door to the mahogany wardrobe and gave a start at the reflection of his tense face in the full-length mirror on the back of the door. His gaze bounced away, skimming the bare shelves and sagging rod where a few hangers dangled empty. One hanger lay on the floor.

Conscious of Veronique's watchful gaze, he left the wardrobe to pull out every drawer in the dresser. He checked underneath, then went back to the wardrobe to probe the dusty top surface. Nothing.

"Upstairs," he muttered, brushing past Veronique in the doorway. The faint floral scent of her perfume followed him down the hall to the staircase near the front door.

The three upstairs bedrooms had lain empty for a lifetime, waiting for the large family that had never eventuated. They were still empty of all that mattered. Veronique followed behind, silently double-checking his efforts. When Burton found himself poking through neat piles of towels and sheets in the linen closet, he gave up the search. Granddad had been occasionally absentminded, not senile.

Burton clumped down the stairs and slumped onto the third step from the bottom. The chess set was really gone. He'd never considered himself particularly sentimental, but the crack that had opened in his heart when Granddad died became a little wider.

Veronique sidled past and stood at the base of the stairs, her slender fingers curving around the newel post. "Do not worry. It will turn up. Is there an attic?"

"No, but there's a basement, although I can't believe it could have found its way down there. I'll look later," he said, glancing at his watch. "The real estate agent is due any minute."

Her green eyes grew round. "Real estate agent? Is that who you've come to meet? Don't tell me you're going to sell this wonderful farm!"

Burton shoved a hand through his hair. "What else am I going to do with it? I can't farm it, and anything else would be a waste." He was getting tired of explaining the obvious.

Veronique threw both hands in the air. "Don't give me this logic! Even I, a stranger, can see that you love this place. What would your grandfather think? He entrusted you with his home to cherish and to pass on to your children."

"How can you possibly know that?" Ignited by frustration, his temper flared. "Maybe he was just giving me a nest egg. This is a valuable piece of property."

"Of course it is valuable, but it is not worth half as much to anyone else as it is to you!" Agitated, she paced a few steps away before turning back. "How can you throw away what your grandfather worked so hard to build? Something this special doesn't come your way more than once in a lifetime. Here you can find the *tranquillité* you need."

"I haven't had a moment's peace since I inherited it." Burton got to his feet. God, he hated this. He didn't even sound like himself. The fact that she was right only made him feel worse. But why was she so het up about it?

With an upward slashing motion of one hand, Veronique turned away. "It is none of my business. What do I care what you do?"

The sound of a car crunching up the gravel drive came through the screen door.

Burton pushed it open and stepped onto the porch. A cherry-red BMW came to a stop behind his Tercel. Acid ate at his stomach, reminding him he'd missed lunch. "Here he is now."

CHAPTER SIX

A WELL-GROOMED MAN in his fifties emerged from the car, buttoning his navy jacket with one hand while he extended the other to Burton. "Afternoon, Mr. O'Rourke. Don Chetwynd, Valley Real Estate."

As Burton shook his hand, his mental VCR fast-forwarded to images of the agent bringing strangers through his grandparents' house. The sick feeling in his stomach intensified.

"Nice piece of property you got here, Mr. O'Rourke. I was real sorry to hear about your grandfather."

"Did you know him?" Burton turned and led the way back up to the house. "Watch that first step."

Don Chetwynd chuckled. "I went to school with your mom. I've been out a few times more recently trying to convince William to put this place on the market. The way housing prices are going up, this farm would bring in a tidy sum if developed properly."

Burton kept his expression cool and neutral. "This is prime farmland, Mr. Chetwynd."

"Call me, Don. Hello-o-o," he added, seeing Veronique in the doorway.

She stared back at him, unsmiling. *"Bonjour."*

Burton made the introductions, then led the agent into the house. As the screen door shut behind him he saw Veronique wander off around the house in the direction of the orchard.

They toured the farmhouse, and Burton could tell Don

Chetwynd wasn't seeing a lifetime of memories or even the beautifully proportioned, high-ceilinged rooms. He was seeing a cleared lot that would make way for new houses. He was seeing dollar signs and billboards that read Mountain View.

They went out the back way, through the kitchen and the back porch, which housed the washing machine and dryer. Behind the house, plowed fields were bordered on one side by a row of poplars, separating it from the Vandermeres' farm, and on the other by towering cedars. A creek-cum-drainage ditch ran from a small wood at the top of the hill down through the cedars.

Big red hens fluffed their feathers and scattered clucking as they walked through the farmyard, reminding Burton he ought to thank Hank and Mary Vandermere for taking care of Granddad's flock. He ought to just *give* them the chickens. Maybe he would.

"The barn needs painting," he said coming toward the old wooden structure. "I'll get that done before the place goes on the market." The words were out before he realized what he was saying. When had he made the decision to put the farm up for sale?

"I wouldn't bother if I were you," Chetwynd replied. "Whoever buys will just rip it down, anyway. Drake Developments is actively looking for land in this area. You say the word, and I'll bet my license you'll have an offer you can't refuse within the week."

Burton paused outside the double barn door. "My grandfather wasn't interested in selling to developers, Mr. Chetwynd, and neither am I. If you want to see the place so you know what to tell prospective farmers who come looking, then we'll continue. If not, we might as well call it quits right now."

Chetwynd laughed. "Just as stubborn as your grandfather. The thing about the future is, you never know quite how it'll turn out. Or how you'll feel in, say, three months' time.'' He gestured with a hand weighed down by chunky gold. ''But by all means, let's continue.''

Burton pushed open one of the tall doors and stepped back to allow Chetwynd to precede him into the cool, cavernous interior. Straw rustled beneath their shoes. Mice scurried. Then silence. Dust motes swam in the sunlight shafting through the high window over the hayloft.

Memories washed over him like clips from old movies—himself leaping from the cross beams into hillocks of loose hay, searching the nooks and crannies for stray eggs with Gram, watching Granddad tinker with the diesel engine on his old John Deere tractor, which was still parked to one side on the rough dirt floor. Granddad never had gotten around to building a separate machine shed.

In spite of Burton's admonitions, Chetwynd started explaining local zoning regulations. Burton ignored him and walked slowly around the barn, his thoughts puzzling over a vague notion that something about the place seemed wrong. He couldn't put his finger on it, but it felt like something was missing....

He stopped suddenly and turned, his gaze sweeping from the ancient harnesses hanging from one wall to the long-disused horse stalls lining the other, as if he could catch whatever it was in the corner of his mind's eye. Nothing. He shook his head. He must be getting fanciful. All that was missing was Granddad.

The horse stalls were filled with seed potatoes, and his mind flipped back to the acres of freshly plowed fields that rolled into the distance behind the house. It was June. Granddad had been getting ready to plant the fall crop. The magnitude of his responsibility grew, accompanied by a burst of anger. How the hell had Granddad expected him to take proper care of the farm? What did he know about sowing and harvesting?

His anger subsided as quickly as it had come. It wasn't only Granddad's fault. They all—he and Mother included—had acted as though the old man would live forever. Why had they never talked about what would happen after he was gone?

"Guess you won't be needing those this year, eh?" Chetwynd put his hands in his pockets and rocked back on his heels.

Burton's jaw tightened. "What makes you say that?"

"Hell, why plant when you're going to sell? Even your granddad wouldn't see the sense in that."

Burton had had a gutful of Don Chetwynd. "I'm not putting the farm on the market right away," he snapped, making the decision on the spot. "Since I talked to you last, a family heirloom has gone missing, and I can't sell until it's found."

Chetwynd smoothed his lacquered hair. "I'm sorry to hear that. But if someone comes along who's interested in farming, I'll give you a call."

Burton was about to tell him not to bother, then shrugged. The chess set might turn up today for all he knew. "Just don't count on me being ready to sell."

FROM THE ORCHARD, VERONIQUE watched the real estate agent drive away. She didn't know why she'd gotten so angry at Burton, only that there was something about this unpretentious yet dignified farmhouse with its lopsided front steps, chickens scratching in the dirt and flowering trees that reminded her of home.

Ridiculous, really, when her home was so totally different.

She pushed away from the tree she was leaning on. They could delay no longer the decision on whether or not she was to do the cooking show. Burton might think he had his answer already, but he didn't know about the letter.

When she came around the side of the house, he was standing beside a picnic table of thick cedar. Above him spread the massive limbs of the horsechestnut tree, its spiky cones thick with frilly white-and-pink blossoms.

Her footsteps slowed. There was a contemplative droop to his mouth, and his fingers splayed across the wood as if he wished he could read his fate in its lines, like the palm of a hand. His motionless stance contrasted sharply with his earlier restless, nervous energy.

Alors, he had a quiet side. Perhaps he was not completely impossible. She wished she could bring herself to offer whatever comfort a stranger could give, a squeeze of the hand, a consoling word, but it would feel like she was offering comfort to Graham, a laughable concept. Burton wasn't Graham. She knew that, but she didn't feel it.

He turned and saw her watching him. "He's gone."

Her gaze shifted away from his face, although her attention was still focused squarely on him. "I am sorry I was angry before. I had no right."

"It's okay. Granddad taught me to play chess at this picnic table the summer I turned nine," he said. "We'd sit out here all afternoon. Gram would bring us Kool-Aid and cookies."

She wandered closer. "Kool-Aid? What is that?"

Burton's mouth twisted in part grimace, part smile. "A sweet, flavored drink for kids, but Granddad drank it, too. I took it for granted at the time that he liked it, but I suppose he was just keeping me company."

He sat and leaned his elbows on the table. Veronique sat on the other side, not directly opposite, but a little way down. The heavy planks of yellowed cedar felt as solid and unmovable as the earth beneath her feet. From the corner of her eye, she glimpsed Burton's features in the filtered green light of the horsechestnut. He was lost in the past.

She plucked a long strand of grass and crushed the sweet, juicy stem between her teeth. "You miss him."

"And her. But mostly Granddad. I was closest to him. We spent so much time together over chess."

"Perhaps he gave the set away?"

Burton shook his head. "Granddad would never do that. He promised it to me years ago when I was a teenager. Besides, it was an antique. It was valuable."

Lightly she brushed the feathery end of the grass once across the back of his hand. "It will turn up."

"I hope so," he said, his gaze following the stalk of grass. "I can't sell the farm until it does."

"Do you mean that?" she asked, slightly disbelieving.

"The chess set is the only thing of his I ever wanted. It *is* him." The sincerity in Burton's intense blue eyes matched his words. "I won't let the farm go without finding it."

"I see." She believed him.

With a whispered plop, a blossom dropped from the tree above and landed in her hair. Before she could remove it, Burton reached over and pulled it from her springy curls. His fingertips brushed her palm as he presented it back to her with a tiny smile.

"Merci." Eyes downcast, she studied the frilly confection of cream and pink. The air seemed to grow stiller, heavier.

"Will you do the series, Veronique?"

Miracle of miracles, he pronounced her name correctly. At least, as correctly as an *Anglais* could.

"Yes." She nodded. "Yes, I will like to do it."

And at this moment, she couldn't even remember why she'd been so worried it wouldn't work out. Ah, yes, the menu. She smiled. What a small thing to fret about. She would create splendid food and he would adore it.

The pleasant glow of anticipation lasted only seconds before the recollection of government regulations crushed it. She tugged apart the thongs on her backpack and pulled out the letter she'd been so careful to hide from him earlier. "Perhaps you'd better read this before we sign a contract."

Burton glanced at the return address, frowned and turned the envelope over in his hand. "It hasn't been opened."

"I know what it says," she replied. "Go on. Read it."

She tucked her hands up into her sleeves while he inserted a forefinger beneath the sealed flap and tore it open. One stiff sheet unfolded in his hands. He silently skimmed the page, then glanced up at her. "What does this mean?"

"My work visa expires in a week." She explained quickly to get it out in the open and over with. "My husband's death automatically canceled my application for landed immigrant status. Without that, I cannot get another work visa. I was hoping, if you offered me the job, you could do something, call someone." Now that she said it aloud she realized how unrealistic it sounded. She wouldn't blame him if he was angry with her. "I'm sorry I have wasted your time. I wanted to help my mother-in-law, so I grab at the straws. You must find another chef. And I will have to leave the country."

"Hold on," Burton said, scanning the letter a second time. "Don't give up so easily. Could you get some sort of reprieve on the basis of caring for your mother-in-law?"

"I have already written to them, explained the situation. They refuse to give me even a little more time."

Burton folded the letter and tucked it into his pocket. "Leave it with me. I'll see what I can do to square it with Immigration."

Mon Dieu. He sounded so confident. Graham had been like that. Nothing was a problem he couldn't fix. Except for her.

Burton went to his car and came back with his briefcase. Veronique watched while he riffled through a stapled sheaf of papers, making a notation here and there in blue ink. His hands weren't like Graham's; Burton's were longer and leaner. And bare of the chunky rings Graham had had in common with Don Chetwynd.

Finally he slid the papers and the pen toward her. She paged slowly through to the end, pretending to read, rather than admit her ability to read English was so poor she couldn't understand more than one word in three. She was working on it, but she hadn't graduated from the children's books she checked out of the library, and she certainly wasn't up to legalese.

"And the menus?" she asked, hoping it wasn't spelled out in black and white.

"You'll have input, but I get the final say." He held out a pen.

Instead of taking it, Veronique wrapped her arms around her waist. All she'd wanted to do was go back to Tahiti, yet every day, every hour, led her deeper and deeper into this other new life. She was *fatigué*. Burned-out. But Marion was depending on her. And it wasn't as if she expected to *enjoy* the next two months. Happiness was just a vague promise for the future.

Burton cleared his throat, and his fingers began to drum discreetly. Not allowing herself to think about it any longer, she took the pen and wrote her signature in her squiggly, up-and-down hand, ending with a sharp dot at the end of Dutot. *"Voilà,"* she said, and pushed the pages back across the table. "We have the deal." She tried to smile, but it wouldn't come.

ERNIE HURRIED DOWN to reception to greet Veronique on her first working day at the station. She and Burton were going to plan the menus, and Burton had asked Ernie to come along and take notes. There she was, chatting to Lillian. His heart rate picked up and he lengthened his steps.

Her hair was wet with rain, and her paisley jacket drenched and dark over the shoulders, but the smile she flashed him was pure sunshine. He tugged self-consciously at the tie around his neck and wondered guiltily when he'd last dressed to impress Rita. He pushed the thought aside. Veronique was way out of his league, and nothing was ever going to happen between them. But he wanted to look his best when it didn't.

"Ms. Dutot—er, Veronique. Welcome."

"*Bonjour,* Ernie. What a nice tie." Smiling, she adjusted the knot, leaving him breathless. "Look, it is paisley, like my jacket. I just knew we were going to be simpatico."

Ernie blushed and pretended not to see Lillian's look of mild amusement. "If you'd like to come with me..." He turned quickly to hide the heat in his cheeks and led the way down the hall toward Burton's office while Veronique told him about her bus ride to the station.

"A great furry dog leaped onto the bus and put his big muddy paws on the driver," she said. "The man, he was so mad, but the dog, he was laughing."

Ernie stopped outside Burton's office. "You like dogs?"

"They are wonderful," she said warmly. "So faithful and loving."

"I like them, too," he said, smiling at her over his shoulder as he knocked. The door, which had been ajar, pushed open. "Excuse me, Burt—" He leaned around the door. No one there.

"He must have gotten tied up with something," Ernie said. "Have a seat. Can I get you some coffee?"

"Thank you, yes." She slung her backpack over the arm of one of the two guest chairs and sat down.

Ernie hustled down to the coffee room, anxiously wondering if there'd be anything left of the fresh pot he'd put on to brew earlier. Just as he came through the door, Murphy poured the last of the coffee into his giant-size mug.

Until today, he'd never encountered the vice president

of programming without Burton around to do the talking. Ernie sidled warily over to the coffee machine. The old man's temper since he'd quit smoking was already a legend.

"How are you making out, Ernie?"

The jovial tone startled him. "G-great. I mean, I'm doing okay, I think."

He slid the pot off the burner and rinsed out the dregs, his mind racing. Should he put the coffee on and go back to Veronique, then run back in five minutes when the coffee was done? Or should he wait for it and leave her wondering where he'd disappeared to? Darn that Murphy and his big mug, anyway. He ripped open a fresh packet of ground coffee.

"O'Rourke working you hard, boy?"

Ernie's hand shook, and coffee spilled across the counter. "I'm l-learning a lot. It's a little different from cable TV." Cripes, why had he gone and said that? Murphy would think he didn't know what he was doing.

Murphy uttered a sharp grunt, presumably his opinion of cable TV. "Saw Burton rushing off a moment ago to Props. The kitchen just arrived for this new cooking show. You're working on that, aren't you, lad?"

Something about the way Murphy growled the question made Ernie wonder if the big boss thought checking out the kitchen was the production assistant's job. But Burton had asked him to meet Veronique.... Unless Burton hadn't trusted him to make sure the kitchen checked out okay. Sometimes it seemed like Burton thought he was the only one who could get things done.

"You can learn a few things from O'Rourke," Murphy added, slurping loudly from his cup. "He's the best in the business."

"I will. I mean, I do, sir." Perspiration formed at Ernie's hairline. He had to get out of here, fast. Fill the jug, pour it in, switch it on...

Darn. Murphy was leaning against the counter as though he was settling in for a chat.

"So what do you think of the Vancouver Canadians' chance at the pennant this year, Ernie? You a baseball fan?"

"You b-bet I am, Mr. Murphy." He loved baseball and usually he liked nothing better than to discuss it. But Veronique was waiting.

"The station has a couple of season tickets. Fans around here get to a game or two." A phlegmy cough rumbled from Murphy's chest.

"That sounds great," Ernie said over the hacking that seemed to go on and on. He filled two cups, grabbed a handful of creams and sugars and had started to back away when he noticed Murphy looking apoplectic. "Are you going to be all right, Mr. Murphy?" he said, alarmed. "Should I call someone?"

Murphy, red-faced and eyes bulging with the strain, stopped coughing long enough to gasp on a breath. "I'm fine." He waved him away. "Go."

"Okay." Ernie turned, and shamelessly ran.

Veronique was gazing at the photos on Burton's wall when Ernie returned with the coffee. With luck he'd have a few minutes with her before Burton showed up.

"Sorry I took so long," he said. "Had to make a new pot." He set the cups on the edge of the desk. The cream and sugar spilled from his hand and fell to the floor. Flustered, he crouched to pick them up. "I didn't know what you liked in your coffee so I just brought lots of everything."

"It looks wonderful. *Merci*, Ernie."

Her voice did something weird to his insides, like going down the first big hill on the roller coaster. He removed his glasses and polished the steamy edges on his tie, taking deep breaths to control his breathing. "I was just chatting with Murphy, vice president of programming," he said casually, as though he and Ed got together every morning to chew the fat. "Burton was called down to Props. Apparently—"

"The kitchen just arrived." Burton strode through the door, and instantly all attention turned to him. "Morning, Veronique. Morning, Ernie. Ah, coffee. Any more where that came from, Ern?"

Ernie sighed. "Sure thing, boss." He slipped back out the door, hoping like hell Murphy had gone back to his office.

Burton waited until Ernie had left the room before he pulled Veronique's letter from the Immigration Department out of his briefcase. He normally wouldn't send Ernie out for coffee, but the fewer people who knew about her work visa problem, the better.

"I talked to this Ms. Papazian at the Immigration Department—boy, was she a grouch." He passed the envelope across his desk to Veronique, and her face fell. "I haven't given up. Last night I wrote half a dozen letters—to my member of Parliament, to the Human Rights Commission…you name it—explaining the situation. Stressing, of course, the importance of your ex-mother-in-law's well-being rather than the show."

"Of course. I would not be here if not for Marion."

"My plan," Burton continued, "is for my letters to initiate an investigation. And for the various government departments to get so tangled up in their own red tape that by the time they've made a decision, Marion will be well enough to cope on her own and taping of *Flavors* will be complete."

Her smile was brief and skeptical. "Thank you for trying," she said politely.

He sat back in his swivel chair and spread his hands apologetically. "I wish I could have gotten you a temporary work visa, but for now this is the best I can do."

Ernie returned with another cup of coffee.

"Thanks, Ernie. Just set it down and have a seat." Burton located the file labeled *Flavors* from among those on his desk and flipped through it. "Okay, we've got the kitchen being assembled—" He broke off to glance at Veronique. "You're going to love it—granite countertops, washed-oak cupboards, top of the line appliances." He turned to Ernie. "We can use most of the same crew as *Lost Harvest*. Did you ask Carly to start working on a script?"

Ernie nodded. "She said she'd have something ready this afternoon for you to look at."

"Excuse me," Veronique interrupted. "Why do I need a script? I am not an actor."

Burton glanced up, and as usual, her gaze slid away. A guy could get a complex about this. "While you're cooking you can ad-lib, but we need set lines for you to say at the beginning, to cue commercial breaks and to wrap up the show. You'll soon know it by heart. The biggest bit is the intro, and once we have that taped we'll just splice it into every segment."

"Oh, if that is all…" She sneezed and pulled out a hankie.

His hankie. Burton's eyebrows rose. Well, well. He was touched that she'd kept it all this time. He noticed her damp hair that was drying into tight curls, and the wet jacket hanging over the back of her chair. "Ever consider getting an umbrella?"

She shrugged. "I lose umbrellas. Are we going to talk about the menu? I have written down some ideas." She reached for her backpack and pulled out a spiral-bound notebook.

"Great." Burton noticed his untouched coffee and took a sip. "I'm a dab hand at opening cans, but what I know about cooking would fit on the back of a soup label. On the other hand," he said, rising from his chair, "I know what we need in terms of producing this sucker."

He paced the tiny space behind his desk. When his brain got active, his feet wanted to move. "I want a show that's fast-paced and colorful. With recipes that can be completely prepared and cooked within the time allotted. Minimal use of electric appliances—they're too noisy. Let's go through your list of recipes, Veronique, and decide what will work and what won't."

He paused, noticing Ernie had his head down and was scribbling industriously. "You're not taking minutes, Ern," he said in an undertone. "Just get the main points." What the hell was the kid wearing a tie for?

"Oh. Okay." Ernie blinked behind his round glasses.

Veronique consulted her notebook. "First, I thought I would like to do a risotto."

"Risotto's good," Burton said. "It's quiet." Then he frowned. "But not very colorful."

"Pumpkin risotto is very beautiful with the dark orange against the creamy rice."

"How fast is it to prepare?"

She pursed her lips. "That depend on what exactly you mean by fast."

"Say, five to ten minutes?" he suggested hopefully.

She laughed her low, throaty laugh. "First you must prepare the pumpkin. Then the rice, he must be stirred for twenty minutes—"

"That's way too long," Burton said, cutting her off. He planted his hands on his desk and leaned over it. "What about using, say, carrots, instead? Maybe stir-fry them to speed things up. Stir-fry is perfect for TV."

Veronique drew herself up, chin high in the air. "I cook haute cuisine, not TV dinners."

Burton continued to pace; two steps one way, two steps back. "I'm not suggesting you lower your standards, God no. Just…experiment a little with alternative ingredients."

"I experiment all the time. I change this, I change that," Veronique said, waving a hand to illustrate. "But the changes, they has to make sense. Pumpkin is very different texture from carrot—it is creamy like the rice, not crunchy. You cannot change one for the other because it is convenient. It would be like using pineapple, instead of corn, just because they were both yellow." She turned to Ernie. "That wouldn't be right, would it?"

Ernie cast a desperate glance at Burton. With a judicious lift of his eyebrows, Burton let him know just whose hand was feeding him. "Gee, Veronique," Ernie said, "I guess not, but—"

"Nobody's trying to make you put pineapple into a stew," Burton said in the most placating tone he could achieve between gritted teeth. "But I don't see the big difference between carrot and pumpkin. They're both savory, and both orange—since you seem to be stuck on the color thing."

She half rose in her seat. "It is not I who am stuck on the color."

Ernie cleared his throat. "E-excuse me, B-Burton, Veronique. I'll bet Veronique plans to, you know, cook the pumpkin beforehand and then just toss it into the risotto. That way it's even faster than carrots. Isn't that right, Veronique?"

Smiling, she touched him on the shoulder. "But of course that is how I would do it!"

Burton stared at Ernie. The boy surprised him sometimes. To Veronique he said, "It might have been helpful if you'd mentioned that in the first place."

Veronique shrugged. "It was obvious."

For the next four hours they worked their way through the list, stopping once for more coffee and for Ernie to order in sandwiches. Burton tossed some recipes out, bullied Veronique into modifying a few and accepted her judgment on still others. Together, they organized, estimated and calculated until every dish had been planned down to the last detail, each segment timed to the minute.

Finally Burton stood behind his chair and stretched. "Well," he said, bringing his arms back to his sides, "at least that's settled." He leaned forward on the back of his chair and studied Veronique. "Your hair. It's a pretty color, but…"

"But what?" A frown appeared.

"Would you consider getting it styled? Nothing radically different, just a trim."

Her index finger curled through the long tresses at the back of her neck and tugged. "No."

Burton frowned. That multicolored mop didn't fit with the sophisticated way she dressed. He made a closer inspection of her blouse and skirt, which he was able to do because her gaze was resting on his knuckles. Maybe her clothes weren't as expensive as he'd first thought, just well put together. "Will you think about it?"

"Non."

"Okay, it was just a thought. We'll look on it as part of your exotic and eccentric personality that's going to make this show a hit."

She glanced up at him then, her face growing pale. When she spoke, it was with quiet intensity, from some place deep and hurting. "I hope your taste for the exotic does not fade before the series is over."

He blinked. What was *that* about? In the silence that followed, he could hear rain drumming on the roofs of the cars in the parking lot outside his window. "How about we go check out the kitchen? Then, Veronique, you can make a list of the utensils you'll need."

She rose, slinging her backpack over her shoulder. "I have my own set of knives."

"Great." He ushered her out with a quick prayer she wouldn't end up using them on him.

"Coming, Ernie?" He threw his arm across his assistant's shoulders as they followed Veronique out of the office. "Good suggestion back there," he said in a low voice. "You're a real diplomat."

Ernie smoothed the beginnings of a frown into a smile and made an effort not to let his annoyance show. Burton was just trying to make him feel good. But why did tall people always think they could throw their arms across the shoulders of shorter people, like they were some kind of public leaning post? Just because he was young and less experienced didn't mean he shouldn't be taken seriously. And just because he was short didn't mean he could be patronized.

CHAPTER SEVEN

SPITTING RAIN HAD DAMPENED the sidewalk when Veronique alighted from the bus across the street from the hospital. She had an hour to spend with Marion before going to the market to buy groceries for the first day of taping tomorrow. Yesterday she and Ernie had gone shopping for pots and pans and other dishes. It had been fun and Ernie had been so sweet, trailing after her loaded down with her parcels. She had to be careful not to encourage him—that wouldn't be fair. But he was such fun to tease, like the little brother she never had.

Veronique hurried through the hospital to Marion's new room in the rehabilitation center located in another wing. Marion was moving around on crutches, but she still had too much time to think and tended to fret when Veronique was late.

"*Bonjour,* Marion," Veronique sang out as she strode through the open door into the semiprivate ward.

"Hi, Ronnie," Marion whispered. She put a finger to her lips, and pointed to the next bed.

Someone new had arrived in the night. The woman occupying the other bed looked roughly Marion's age. She was thin, with long dark hair. Her eyes were shut, but the arms lying on top of the covers seemed tense and rigid, giving Veronique the impression she was only pretending to sleep.

She lowered her voice to a whisper, anyway. "*Voilà,*

Marion," she said, pulling a package of hair color out of her bag. "Today you are going to the beauty parlor."

Marion struggled to sit up. "You really shouldn't have bothered, Ronnie. No one's going to see me in here."

Veronique wasn't fooled by Marion's protest. She could see the gleam of interest in her mother-in-law's eyes and rejoiced at the progress. "Nonsense. You are doing it for yourself."

Marion glanced at her roommate, whose face had taken on an almost imperceptible frown. Marion beckoned Veronique closer and whispered in her ear. "She was in a temper last night when they brought her in. She's had surgery. I don't know what it was, she wouldn't say, but you should have heard her snap at the nurses."

"Perhaps she was in great pain," Veronique whispered back. "Come, let us go. We can talk better in the washroom."

Veronique pushed the wheelchair over to the bed and helped Marion into it. Placing a folded towel across Marion's lap, she wheeled her down the hall to the communal wash and laundry room where there was a wide sink and a nozzle attachment.

Veronique adjusted the temperature and directed the spray onto Marion's bent head, wetting her hair thoroughly.

"Tell me about the studio," Marion asked over the noise of the water. "Have you started taping yet?"

"Tomorrow. I am so nervous my hands shake just to think of it. At least we have agreed on the menu."

"It must be so exciting working in a television studio. Did you see *Lovers and Strangers* yesterday? I can't believe how mean that awful Tiffany is to Reilly. He really loves her, even if she is quite a bit older."

Veronique laughed uneasily as she helped Marion sit upright so she could towel-dry her hair. "You really must get out more. Tiffany and Reilly are not real people."

"Oh, I know that." Marion adjusted the belt of her dressing gown and shifted her leg on the bit of the wheelchair that held it out straight. "What's it like working for an important producer? Is he nice?"

Scary was the word that came to mind. She was always afraid she'd forget and call him Graham. Afraid of remembering the past; afraid of not remembering and repeating it. Briefly she contemplated telling Marion that Burton resembled Graham. No, that would only get her started talking about Graham.

"He wants me to cut my hair!" She reached for the package of hair color and flipped the instruction sheet over to the French side. Thank heaven for a bilingual country, at least in theory.

Marion eyed her in the mirror. "It's time you got rid of those blond ends."

"Not yet." Veronique snapped one bottle into the base of the other and shook. "We will do the whole head at once, eh? It has been so long we don't need to do the roots separately."

"Whatever you think, dear."

Veronique arranged the towel around Marion's shoulders to protect her robe from spills, then pulled on the plastic gloves and squeezed a stream of gel onto Marion's hair.

Marion's eyes were shut, showing thin blue veins on her eyelids. Her hands were folded in her lap, relaxed. "You know, Ronnie, maybe you just need a holiday."

Oui. Tahiti. "Mmm-hmm."

"I mean, you haven't been away since Graham took you to San Francisco."

Veronique's hands stilled, knuckle-deep in foamy goo. "Pardon?"

"Don't you remember? It was the second weekend in February. He called to wish me happy birthday and to explain why you two wouldn't be over for dinner. I didn't speak to you, but I could hear you laughing in the background.''

Ah. Now, she remembered. How like Graham to cover his tracks so carefully. She'd spent that weekend watching old movies while he'd flown to San Francisco on a sudden business trip. Marion had heard a female voice, but it hadn't been hers. Back then Veronique had suspected he was seeing someone else, although she hadn't realized he'd gone away with the woman that particular weekend.

It wasn't the worst thing he was capable of.

"I'm sorry we missed your birthday dinner." She hoped her voice didn't sound too strained.

"Oh, that doesn't matter now, Ronnie."

Veronique's fingers trembled as she worked the color through Marion's hair. Sometimes she awoke in the night and wondered whether Graham would have arranged that last-minute fishing trip if she hadn't confronted him about that other woman and told him she was leaving. She always pushed the thought away, angry with herself for feeling even remotely responsible for his death.

"Ronnie?" Marion's voice called her back. "Are you all right?"

"I'm fine. It's just…San Francisco wasn't so very fun for me." She washed her hands and arranged a plastic shower cap over Marion's hair—the type of plastic cap you got free at a nice hotel. She supposed one didn't wear plastic caps while showering with a lover. You brought them home as a souvenir for your wife.

"*Bon,*" she said, with a sigh, and set the small kitchen timer she'd brought in her backpack. Then she took out a deck of cards, and Marion wheeled herself over to a small table for folding laundry. They played the twenty minutes away, keeping score of their crib hands in the margins of the hair-color instructions.

"I won again," Marion announced, gathering in the

loose cards. "You're not paying attention today, Ronnie. Something on your mind?"

Veronique was saved from answering by the timer going off. "Time to see the new you."

She rinsed and shampooed, then blow-dried, doing her best to style Marion's hair. "Life is strange, eh, Marion? A few weeks ago I was only a chef. Now I'm a TV star and a hairdresser." She poked a curl, fragrant with chemicals, into place. "Well, maybe not a hairdresser. When you get out of here, you must get this done properly."

"It's wonderful, Ronnie. Thank you." But at the mention of leaving the hospital, an anxious look crossed Marion's face.

Veronique said casually, "The nurse told me about the bridge club. They meet tonight, *non?*"

"Oh, Ronnie, I keep telling you, it's too soon after Stan's passing for me to socialize."

"Nobody's asking you to marry again. It's just a friendly game of bridge." Veronique came around the front of the wheelchair and crouched at eye level. "Please, Marion, for me?"

"For you?" Marion looked confused.

"When I go back to Tahiti..." She grasped Marion's hand as the other woman's mouth tightened. "When I go back, I want to know that you have other friends. You don't want me to worry or feel bad that I am abandoning you, do you?"

Marion smiled sadly and squeezed Veronique's hand. "Of course not. I just don't know what I'm going to do without you."

"When the time comes, you will be strong in mind and healthy in body—you will see. I talked to the head nurse here about getting you a home help. You will let me pay for it from the money Graham left— *Non,* I will not take no for the answer."

"*An* answer. Ronnie, we've settled this. Graham left that money to you."

From down the corridor came the squeak and clatter of the meal trolley. The aroma of overdone roast beef and packet gravy drifted through the open door. "Dinnertime," Veronique announced. "We'd better get you back before the new girl eats your meal."

She tossed the used hair-color box into the garbage, gathered up Marion's towel and wiped down the sink. Then she took hold of the handles and pushed the wheel-chair back to Marion's room. Her roommate's bed was empty, and sounds of running water came from the bath-room. Veronique helped Marion back into bed and ad-justed the pillows so she could sit upright.

"Do you think…?" Marion began, then stopped. "No, forget it."

"What?" Veronique took her jacket from the back of the chair and picked up her backpack.

"It's too much to ask.…"

"Just tell me, Marion. I'll let you know if it is too much."

"I just wondered if I could possibly come down to the studio and watch *Lovers and Strangers* being taped some-time. When my hip is a bit better, I mean. And if they allow outsiders in."

Outsiders were allowed in. Friends and relatives of the crew came along frequently. Sometimes students from the film school.Veronique imagined introducing Marion to Burton, and Marion fainting or bursting into tears at the spitting image of her dead son. And what of her feelings? Would seeing Marion with Burton make him appear more like Graham, or less?

Veronique gazed at Marion's eager, wistful face. Mar-ion, who had so little to look forward to. "Yes, I think so," she said.

Marion smiled the biggest smile Veronique had seen

since before Stan and Graham had died. "Oh, Ronnie. Thank you so much."

BURTON PUSHED THROUGH the doors to Channel Seven. It was Wednesday morning, and with taping on *Flavors* starting today he had a lot on his mind.

He dropped his umbrella in the stand and started across the lobby to where Sylvia was leaning over Lillian's desk, inspecting a fistful of long purple fingernails. "...this guy I met at a computer course. I woulda gone out with him, but then he started going on about his hard drive." She cracked her gum. "So-o-o-o cute, but he's, like, such a techie."

"What a pity," Lillian murmured, out of sight behind Sylvia's shapely backside.

"Morning, ladies."

Sylvia straightened away from Lillian's desk to waggle her fingertips at him. "Hi, Burton."

Burton jerked to a halt. Lillian's snowy white hair was shot through at the temple with neon streaks of lime and purple. Hair whose soaring gelled spikes had abandoned all pretension to fluffiness. "I see your grandniece has advanced to hair color, Lillian."

She beamed up at him from behind the desk, patting her hair proudly. "Good morning, Burton. Yes, Sandy's been practicing again. Don't you just love it?"

"I've, ah, never seen anything quite like it on...uh..."

One gray eyebrow lifted as Lillian gazed steadily back and waited for him to finish floundering.

Burton took a big breath and forced himself to look, really look at Lillian. To disassociate himself from his prejudices about appropriate hairstyles for grandmothers. When he did, to his surprise, he saw an attractive woman having fun experimenting with her appearance.

With a genuinely admiring smile, he dropped a hot-pink

carnation into her vase. "Actually, Lillian, I think it's great."

Ernie came scurrying toward the desk, frowning down at his clipboard. "Is Burton in yet, Lillian?"

"Right in front of you, big fella," Burton said. "How's it going? Everything ready to start taping?" He clapped an arm around his assistant's shoulder and steered him toward his office. For a second he thought he felt Ernie tense under his friendly hand. Nah, couldn't be.

"The electricians have finished wiring the set," Ernie said. "Bill and the guys are setting up their cameras. We should be ready to go as soon as Veronique gets here."

"Great, Ern. With a presenter as, shall we say, unpredictable as Veronique, it's nice to know I've got a PA who can get things happening and keep everyone in line when I'm not around." He held Ernie's mild brown gaze to impress upon the boy that although expectations were high and the tasks arduous, he had every confidence Ernie would rise to the occasion.

Ernie passed the back of his hand across his forehead, which was covered with a faint sheen of perspiration. "Gee, th-thanks, Burt. I mean, Burton. I'll do my best."

From reception came the sound of throaty laughter and a melodious French accent. Burton turned. "Ah, there she is now."

Ironic that her first day on the set should be June the second, the date her work visa expired. So far he'd had no luck getting the Immigration Department to change their collective mind. He'd only succeeded in raising bureaucratic interest in her case to the point where they'd started asking him a lot of sticky questions. Like, why wasn't he hiring a French-Canadian chef, eh? Just his bad luck that the official who'd responded to his inquiries had been born in Trois Rivières, Quebec.

Veronique approached, her averted gaze skimming the framed stills from various television shows that lined the walls. How could he get her to look at him? It wasn't just his ego at stake, but the success of *Flavors* and, ultimately, his documentary.

She came closer. Ernie's eyes glazed over. Burton had a brainwave.

"Ernie, show Veronique to the dressing room and then take her to Makeup. I have to get something from Props. I'll meet you in the studio." He lifted a hand in greeting to Veronique before hurrying into his office to drop off his briefcase.

When he emerged, Veronique had caught up with Ernie and was bussing him on both cheeks. *"Bonjour, bonjour. Ça va?"*

Burton quickly turned down a secondary corridor and ran up a flight of stairs. Okay, the dual peck on the cheeks was a French custom, but she never greeted him like that. When had she started treating Ernie like a friend, as well as a colleague? Would she ever see him that way? Would she ever see him at all?

Ernie, meanwhile, was awash in body heat and Chanel No. 5. But by the time he'd figured out what Veronique was doing it was too late to press his lips against her cheek. She'd already drawn back, digging in her backpack for something and chattering about the bus, which was late, and her stocking, which had torn.

Ernie forced another image into his clouded brain. Rita. Lovely Rita, with her smooth dark hair bobbed under her pointed chin. Rita, whom he suspected of being too good for him, but who had consented to marry him, anyway.

"Uh, g-good morning, V-Veronique." He whipped off his fogged-up glasses and polished them on his shirttail. No ties today. Not even for Veronique would he wear a noose every day. "You can put your stuff in the dressing room, and after you get done in Makeup, we'll meet Burton in the studio." Makeup. The thought of taking Veronique to meet Rita made the perspiration stand out on his brow.

"Bon." With a flourish she produced from her bag a large, ripe mango. She handed it to Ernie, then pulled out a cucumber, a tomato, some green onions and a bouquet of fresh cilantro, and piled them into his unwilling hands already burdened by a clipboard and pen.

"I knew something was missing from the menu the other day when we were planning the grilled pork Polynesian," she said. "Mango salsa. The grilled pork, he must have mango salsa."

"Oh, no," Ernie said, alarmed. "Burton's not going to like adding another dish at the last minute."

"Poof. He will love it—it's colorful and quick, and low-fat, too. It has absolutely no effect on the waistline."

"It'll have a big effect on the schedule. At rehearsal yesterday, we just squeaked in on the timing." Almost dropping the cucumber, Ernie clutched the mass of fruit and vegetables tighter to his flannel-clad chest. A paper fell out of his clipboard and fluttered to the floor. "You can't add things at the last minute, Veronique. Burton won't allow it. Sure, he's a bit of a stickler, but that's why he's the best—"

She cut him off with a conspiratorial smile that made his stomach drop. "Er-r-rnie," she purred. "We will just have to surprise him. We will show him how well it works."

"Veronique!" he pleaded. He didn't like the sound of that "we."

"Don't worry, Ernie. It will be fine. The mango salsa takes just two minutes to make. Chop, chop, chop, and it's done."

Burton thought he was reliable. Burton was counting on him to keep Veronique in line. Ernie drew himself up a little taller, made his voice a little deeper. "Veronique, I forbid you to make mango salsa."

She laughed and pushed his chest lightly, dislodging the mango. Despite his desperate effort to catch it with his elbow, it fell. Veronique reached for it, trapping it against his upper thigh. "*Oop, et là.* Mustn't bruise the fruit." She glanced up at him with a sly lift of her eyebrows.

Ernie's cheeks flamed. She was flirting with him. He was gonna mess up his career. And his engagement. And he was only twenty-two. Oh God, oh God, oh God.

"Here, take these back." Ernie shoved the produce into her open backpack as if it was stolen goods, his gaze darting from side to side. The corridor was empty, but with microphones in every second room, the walls had ears. No, that was paranoid. Ernie picked up his dropped schedule and mopped his forehead. "Don't do it, Veronique. I beg you."

"Such a worry warp, Ernie." She smiled her dimpled, dazzling smile. "Now, don't tell Burton. I'm counting on you." She slung her pack over a shoulder, causing her cream silk blouse to strain across one curving breast, sublimely unaware of the havoc she was creating in his conscience-control center. "Which way to Makeup?"

Sweating profusely, Ernie led her to the dressing room where she hung up her jacket, then to Makeup. The door was open and Rita was at the counter arranging her cosmetics and brushes. Oh God. She would take one look at his guilty face and know instantly Veronique had kissed him.

"Hi, Rita." His voice cracked.

Her face lit up at the sight of him. "Hi, Ernie." Blushing, she pushed a strand of straight brown hair behind her ear and shyly braided her hands together in front of her rose-colored sweater.

His smile instinctively took on warmth. Then he quickly frowned so she wouldn't think him overly warm and get suspicious. Flustered, he motioned Veronique forward. "This is Veronique, the chef on *Flavors*. Veronique, this is Rita.'' He turned to Rita. "Taping starts in twenty minutes. Can you get her ready, please?''

"Sure. Hi, Veronique. What beautiful hair you have.''

"Bonjour. Merci.'' She smiled at Rita. "Where should I sit?''

"Right here.'' Rita spun the high swivel seat around and held it while Veronique climbed onto it. Then she tied a pink plastic cape around Veronique's neck and arranged it to protect her clothes.

All right, Ernie thought, as Rita made styling suggestions while Veronique nodded into the mirror. He smiled smugly at how well he'd handled the situation. They hardly noticed he was there.

"Shall I put your backpack someplace safe?'' he suggested to Veronique. Anything to get that mango away from her.

Smiling, she waggled a finger at him through the mirror. "You naughty boy. You know I need that backpack.'' She glanced up at Rita. "He's so sweet and helpful, *non?*''

Rita nodded, but a tiny frown appeared between her eyebrows. Uh-oh. Time to scram. He bade Veronique a hasty goodbye and left Rita with whispered instructions not to get talked into anything. Then he raced back to the studio where the crew was assembled, and doing last-minute checks on the sound and light equipment. Burton would know how to handle Veronique. Where the heck was he?

Someone called his name and he turned to see Vince, the floor manager, coming toward him. Vince was six foot four and sported a black handlebar mustache and a Vancouver Canadians baseball cap. When he stopped in front of Ernie, Ernie felt like a midget.

"Say, Ernie, where's Burton? And Veronique? We've got to get our asses in gear. The studio's booked for another show after lunch.''

"I know.'' Ernie checked his watch. "Veronique's in Makeup. I'm sure Burton'll be along any minute.''

Vince lifted his cap, stroked a hand over his receding hairline and slid the cap back in place. "Okay. We're ready whenever the man shows." He returned to where the camera crew were positioned around the set.

Pausing outside the studio door, Veronique cautiously touched her hair. Rita had fluffed her thick mat of curls into a spiraling mass of blond and bronze, which gave her height and accentuated her cheekbones. The makeup she'd smoothed over her face and neck felt unfamiliar and made her feel somehow unreal, almost like an actor on TV. *Mon Dieu,* but that's exactly what she was. Her palms grew damp. This was the moment.

She pushed open the door at the back of the set. On the other side of the studio, beyond the cameras, the audience filled twenty rows on either side of a center aisle. Near the edge of the set, she saw Ernie consulting his clipboard and hurried over to him.

"Ernie. How much time do I have?"

"Hi, Veronique. Hey, you look great." He checked his watch. "You've got about five minutes till airtime. Burton hasn't arrived yet."

"I go arrange myself in the kitchen, then. I am so nervous, Ernie."

"Me, too," he blurted unexpectedly.

"You? Never," she declared. "You look so professional with your clipboard and your headset."

Suddenly the chatter from the crew stilled. For two endless seconds there was total silence. Then the buzz started again, twice as loud, like crickets in a heat wave.

"Morning, gang," Burton called in the brisk voice he used when he was in high gear. "We're running late, so let's get going."

Zut alors! Veronique blinked and looked again. She recognized him by his long legs and the black vest he'd been wearing over a white shirt, but what was that on his head? And his face!

He had on black plastic glasses with a big nose and a villainous mustache that stopped just short of hiding his mouth. Covering his short coppery hair was a multicolored wig that looked as if he'd put his finger in an electrical socket. Her hand went to her mouth to cover an unladylike snort of laughter.

Calmly he walked over, put up his hand and with a straight face asked, "How many fingers am I holding up?"

Still giggling, she said, "F-f-four."

Beneath the black plastic mustache, his mouth curved. "Good. That's how many minutes you have before we start taping."

Funny, she'd never noticed before that his smile was higher on one side than the other. Or that fine laugh lines bracketed his lips. She felt herself warm to him. He'd played the fool to ease her discomfort. It was just a trick to get her to pay attention to his instructions, but his approach was to persuade rather than coerce. Unlike the other man she'd known with eyes like his.

He touched her shoulder and his voice softened. "Are you ready?"

Swallowing a sudden lump in her throat, she nodded. Then she looked at his bulbous plastic nose and started to laugh again. Burton made a movement of his head that suggested an exaggerated rolling of the eyes and gave her a gentle push toward the kitchen.

As she moved off, Ernie came forward, his smile giving way to an anxious frown. "Excuse me, Burt...on, b-b-but—"

She glanced back. *Oh la la.* Was he going to give her away?

Luckily for her, Vince had come up to confer, and Bill, the head camera operator, stood a pace away, awaiting final instructions. Burton said, "Just a sec, Ern."

Veronique scurried off to the kitchen to quickly unload the vegetable contents of her backpack into the fridge. She kept a watchful eye out, but by the time Burton had finished with the others, Ernie was caught up in some crisis concerning the electrical lead to one of the cameras. With some relief, she saw Burton disappear up the spiral staircase to the control booth while Ernie remained on the studio floor.

Burton paced behind Kate and Mario, giving last-minute instructions, while mentally playing around with different camera angles, planning the composition of shots that would be sent "to air." He spoke into his headset. "Let's have a sound check, Vince, Kate."

On the monitors, three images of Veronique stood behind three teal granite counters, showing close-ups in right profile, left profile and straight on. Through his headset, he heard Vince tell her to say something in a normal speaking voice. She looked nervous and vulnerable and brave.

"A snitch in time saves nine," she recited. "Birds of a feather talk together."

Laughing at the way she mangled the old sayings, Burton glanced at Kate, who gave him a thumbs-up. "That'll do," he told Vince. "Okay, Bill, pull focus."

Bill zoomed camera one in on Veronique, adjusting the focus on the most sharply resolved part of the human body, the eyes. Closer, closer, till her face, then just her eyes filled the screen.

Burton knew Veronique was simply looking into the lens the way Vince had told her to, but he had the oddest sensation she was gazing directly at him. Her eyes were wide emerald prisms, fringed with dark-gold lashes. They grew large, larger, drawing him in further, deeper, till she was only a blink away. Till the dark and mysterious center silently spoke secrets meant for his eyes only.

"Burton?"

Someone was talking. Vince. With a start, Burton glanced up. Then Bill's camera zoomed out and Veronique's face grew small again. He let out a breath and spoke through his headset to the floor manager. "Stand by."

Veronique touched the back of one hand to her damp temple. Her other hand gripped the edge of the granite counter. Just for a moment, when she'd looked into the camera lens, Burton's face had flashed before her eyes. Not Graham's, not a blurry mixture of the two men. Just Burton—staring into her eyes as if he was seeing her soul.

In the darkness beyond the floodlights she could just make out the shadowy shapes of the front row of the audience. She picked an elderly man as her talking target. Then Vince held up a sign—thirty seconds.

She licked her lips. Vince made a hand motion that meant she was to get into her presentation position. Shoulders back, head high, big smile…

Her gaze flicked to the control-booth window high above the studio floor. Between the monitors, she glimpsed Burton watching her onscreen and speaking into his headset. A smile lifted the corners of her mouth. He was still wearing those silly glasses and wig.

Vince held up another sign. Ten seconds. Banks of lights blazed down, hotter than the Tahitian sun.

Oh la la. The mango salsa. Doubt crept in.

Five seconds. Vince's fingers counting down.

Two, one. She took a deep breath. Rolling.

"*Bonjour,* and welcome to *Flavors…*"

Veronique breezed through the crabmeat appetizer and whizzed through preparation for the Polynesian pork, trying to shave minutes to allow for the mango salsa. She hurried so much the knife slipped while she was chopping an onion, and bright red blood welled across the tip of her left index finger.

"*Merde!*" She sucked on her finger.

Vince made a slashing motion to stop the cameras. Burton skimmed down the spiral stairs, flinging off the plastic glasses as he strode onto the set. "How's that finger?"

She hid her hand behind her back. "It's okay. We must go on. The time."

"Let's see it." He pulled her arm around, cradling her hand in his. A line of blood seeped out of the cut. He called to someone on the floor. "Band-Aid here for Ms. Dutot."

She tried to tug away. "It won't look good."

"It'll look worse if you're bleeding all over the main course." Someone handed him a Band-Aid. He tore the wrapper off and swiftly taped it in place, his warm, strong fingers moving over hers.

"What happened back there?" he said. "Wasn't there supposed to be a glaze on the pork?"

She froze. Should she speak the truth—that the pineapple glaze had made way for mango salsa? He knew about cameras and schedules, but she was the chef, and for her, it was the food that must be perfect.

Swallowing, she glanced away. "We made a change, remember?"

Silence while he wondered. Doubted. Regained faith. "Okay." He put his glasses back on and waggled his plastic eyebrows at her. "Let's go."

Then he was gone, and Vince was counting down again. "Three, two, one…rolling."

Veronique took a deep breath. She smiled into the camera and held up her bandaged finger. "This step in the recipe, you may omit." Then she wiped down the cutting board with a clean cloth. "*Bon. En suite,* a perfect accompaniment to the succulent Polynesian grilled pork is mango salsa."

If Ernie groaned quietly on the sidelines, she didn't hear. If Burton was tearing the hair on his fright wig, she wasn't going to risk a look. The camera was rolling, and nothing short of Burton yelling "cut" was going to stop her now.

She whipped out the mango and the other ingredients, babbling nervously to the audience as she chopped them into small dice. Maybe if she'd had time to talk to him before the taping, she could have convinced him... Too late, too late.

"Mango salsa is an amazing condiment," she told the elderly man in the front row as she scored the halved mango and its pungent aroma filled her nostrils. "It contains all the tastes—salty, bitter, sweet and sour. Add to that the sensual texture of the mango, the crunch of the cucumber and the juiciness of the tomato—"

"Cut!" She heard Burton's barked command right through Vince's headset. Vince winced at the sound and brought his hand across his throat in a quick slicing motion.

Veronique threw a pleading smile in Bill's direction and kept on going. She threw the chopped ingredients into a bowl and mixed in fresh lime juice, Tabasco and cilantro. *"Voilà!"* she announced proudly to the sound of applause while Burton stormed back down the stairs and onto the set.

"Take five," he called to Vince. "Ernie, amuse the audience with one of your dog-show anecdotes."

He strode into the kitchen, snatched off his wig and flung it on the counter where it landed in a puddle of juice from the chopped tomato. "What the hell do you think you're doing?"

He spoke in an undertone that nobody else could hear, but his voice was harsh. Graham had talked to her like that, and now Burton was doing it. Veronique drew in a deep breath. "I make mango salsa, the perfect side dish for the pork. We omitted it from the menu—a mistake. I simply correct that fact."

How dare he force her to justify a culinary necessity? Couldn't he see she'd done the right thing? How could she help it if he wasn't around to give permission? Didn't he know she only wanted to please him?

Mon Dieu, what was she thinking? Aghast and flustered, she picked up the wig and mopped furiously at the tomato juice.

Burton edged in closer, looming over her. "Everything is planned down to the exact second. To a fifth of a second. You know that."

His voice was controlled, but he didn't need to yell for her to hear his anger. And she didn't need to look at him to know a storm raged in the blue seas of his eyes, like a typhoon stirring the South Pacific.

Across the vast room, she heard a knock at the studio door, not the big double doors the audience had come through, but the smaller door at the back of the set. The crew wouldn't knock.

She didn't have time to wonder who it could be. Up close and in living color, she was face-to-chest with Burton's displeasure. Unchastened and mutinous as a child unfairly accused, she twined a lock of hair with the bandaged finger while her outrage mounted, squeezing her breath into a compressed knot that prevented her from speaking. Burton had no such problem.

"Look, I'd love to let you do whatever you want," he continued. "But we've got a schedule and we've got to stick to it or else it's…it's chaos. You may think it's only a little thing, but little things add up. Sponsors have paid for airtime. If we go over, we can't cut a commercial, so out goes your mango salsa, anyway."

"You said we had plenty of time to tape the first show."

"Plenty of time relative to shows two through thirteen. And that's the taping. The allotted airtime is fixed. We can't play around with that. You can't just take it into your head to change the menu without consulting me. Why did you do that?"

"I wanted… Oh, never mind." She pushed a hand

through her hair, bringing curls flying around her flushed cheeks. *This isn't like me,* she wanted to tell him. *I am orderly and efficient, the way a good cook should be.* Her outrage subsided. She'd wanted to impress, not defy him. Just as he'd tried to ease her discomfort by wearing that ridiculous mask. It didn't seem funny now. She reached up and pulled the glasses down his nose, forgetting till it was too late whom she would see.

His eyes burned into hers. Her heart seemed to stop beating and for once she couldn't look away. *Mon Dieu.*

Burton stared into Veronique's wide green eyes, and his irritation disappeared. Her gaze held apprehension, and if he didn't know better, a pinch of...sexual awareness? Hell, he did know better, but it still looked like desire. The thought dried his mouth and weakened his knees. He was losing it. Mr. Cool-as-a-cuke was in emotional free fall. In front of a live audience.

The whole place had fallen silent. For a second he thought everyone somehow knew what had just happened between him and Veronique. Then behind him, Ernie cleared his throat.

"Excuse me, Burton..."

He spun around. With Ernie were a man and a woman, conservatively dressed, carrying briefcases. They had "faceless government employee" stamped all over them.

Except they weren't faceless. They were right here in his studio, interrupting a live taping and looking at Veronique with grave expressions. In one of those too-vivid visual flashes he was prone to, Burton imagined them escorting her to a waiting black limousine, which would whisk her straight to the airport and back to Tahiti.

"James Jackson," the stony-faced man said, extending his right hand. He had a broad face, black hair precisely cut and a heard-it-all-before tone of voice. "My colleague, Wendy Connery," he said, indicating a forty-something woman with thick chestnut hair that had a swathe of white arising from a pronounced widow's peak. "We're from the Department of Immigration. It is my duty to inform you that Veronique Dutot is illegally employed under Section 27 of the Immigration Act. Ms. Dutot, if you'd like to come with us."

Adrenaline flooded Burton's body. His first instinct was to smash a fist in the bureaucrat's pasty white face. He forced himself under control. The way to deal with this was to be rational, calm, professional. Facing the immigration officials squarely, he crossed his arms over his chest. "Over my dead body."

CHAPTER EIGHT

"BURTON!" VERONIQUE exclaimed. To the Immigration officers, she said, "I am sorry. Of course I will come with you."

"Veronique! Don't just give in like that." Burton took her arm and gestured to Jackson and Connery to follow him away from the set and crew. "I've written to you people twice now on Ms. Dutot's behalf and haven't received an answer."

"Ms. Dutot doesn't fill the criteria for acquiring residency on the basis of work," Jackson said. "Although you claim she's uniquely suited to her position, there are probably several hundred French chefs in this country, if not more."

Burton jammed his hands on his hips and took a deep breath to regain some semblance of calm. "I didn't hire her because she spoke French," he said, enunciating slowly and clearly. "By 'unique,' I meant her personality, the way she comes across on camera. But putting aside her job for the moment, don't you have some kind of leniency clause that allows people to stay on compassionate grounds? She has an elderly female relative who's an invalid and is emotionally dependent upon her."

"We are aware of Mrs. Gerritson's condition and of her relationship with Ms. Dutot," James Jackson replied. "Compassionate stay of deportation is allowed only if the person in question, that is, Ms. Dutot, is medically incapacitated. I'm afraid we have no choice, given her widowed status and expired work visa, but to deny Ms. Dutot further residency. She is required to leave the country without delay.''

Ernie, apparently out of shaggy-dog stories, had returned to stand a few paces away. At this ominous pronouncement, he gave a little gasp. Veronique tugged at her hair.

Burton held up a hand. ''Pause. Rewind. Are you saying she can't stay because she isn't married to a Canadian citizen?''

''That is correct.'' Jackson turned to Veronique. ''You are required to file a deposition at the Immigration office. We can accommodate you immediately.''

Before she could answer, Burton put his arm around her waist and drew her to his side. ''That won't be necessary, will it...darling?'' She glanced up, eyes wide. He held her gaze, hoping she wouldn't flinch.

''Wh-what are you talking about?'' She tried to tug away, but he held her fast.

Smiling through gritted teeth, he replied, ''I'm talking about our forthcoming marriage of course.''

She was speechless, thank God.

Behind him, he heard Ernie's squeak of protest.

Officer Connery spoke for the first time, her smooth face unsmiling. ''I must inform you it is against federal law to marry for the purpose of obtaining residency on Canadian soil.''

Burton laughed, a bit too heartily. ''It would sound fishy to you people, I suppose. But we...we're crazy about each other. We can't wait to get married.'' Good God, had he really just said that?

James Jackson and Wendy Connery exchanged a glance that suggested they didn't believe he had either. ''Naturally we have criteria to determine whether a couple is marrying out of a genuine desire to be husband and wife or out of expediency.''

Burton swallowed. ''Naturally.''

"There will be an investigation, and interviews with both parties," Jackson went on. "So far we've only your word for it, Mr. O'Rourke, that you and Ms. Dutot are getting married."

"Say something," Burton hissed to Veronique, willing her to go along with this. Yes, he was doing it for *Flavors,* and for his documentary on farming, and even for Marion whom he'd never met, because she was important to Veronique. But there was another reason. It had something to do with the effect Veronique had on his central nervous system, and the way her face kept appearing before him at odd times of the day and night. He didn't have time to analyze it now, he just knew he wasn't ready to let her out of his life yet.

"Are you in love with this man?" Officer Connery prompted.

Veronique swallowed, conscious all eyes were upon her. "I...ah, already sometimes I feel like he is my husband." She tugged on Burton's hand, dragging him aside. "Excuse us, please," she said to the woman. "Burton and I need to talk."

"What is it?" He took her other hand and gripped them both tightly. "We're in a tight spot here."

"I know!" she said in a hoarse whisper. For a moment she clung to his hands, then loosened her hold on him. "What you are suggesting is crazy and wrong. You don't need to do this. You can get another chef. One that will not make you so angry."

Burton renewed his hold on her hands, and despite her protest, the firmness and strength of his grip felt reassuring. It took him a moment to speak, as though he was searching for words. "I don't want another chef. I want you."

Her heart did a funny little flip-flop, but he couldn't have meant it the way it sounded. And he didn't.

"I'm not being altruistic or romantic, Veronique," he added. "I want you, because crazy as you make me—and you do make me crazy—you also have charisma in front of the audience. I need this show to be a success or I can kiss goodbye the chance to make my documentary. Now do you understand?''

Of course she understood when he put it so clearly. It was a neat, clean thrust, like a filleting knife between the ribs. ''*Mais oui*. What else could it be?'' she asked with an elaborate shrug. ''It's not as though I thought for a moment you might love me, or that I could love you.'' And she laughed, to prove to them both how ridiculous it was.

A small silence followed. She glanced up to see hurt and confusion in his eyes. ''Is the idea of marrying me really so repugnant?''

''Repug… I don't know that word, but it means something bad, *non?* I think you are a nice man. I only know I don't want to marry anyone. I had enough of that for a while.''

''What about your mother-in-law if you have to leave Canada?''

''She will be all right.'' Marion could exist without her. Of course she could. The hospital, or a social worker, would find her a home help and make sure she had what she needed to survive. But it would be hard for her, and lonely, and she might sink further into that place in her mind where she was afraid to leave the house even to collect the mail at the end of the drive. Would a public-health worker or even a private nurse have the time to prod poor Marion into recovering her joy in life?

''Do you really think it will work?'' she asked doubtfully.

''Long enough for us both to get what we need, I hope.''

The whole idea was monstrous. Why was she even pretending to think about it? She glanced at the Immigration officers. They were watching her and Burton, skepticism evident in their expressions and body language. How would Marion feel if Veronique got married again so soon after Graham died? Yet how much worse would it be for Marion if she had to suddenly leave the country?

"Veronique," Burton murmured urgently, "you've got to make a decision." He raised her hands and kissed her white knuckles.

The touch of his lips on her fingers sent confusion into another dimension. She couldn't be feeling this…this… whatever it was she was feeling. He wasn't Graham. *He wasn't Graham.*

Somehow she got enough breath past her constricted throat and into her lungs to say "Okay." She could do this…for Marion.

He released his death grip on her hands to pull her into his embrace. With his cheek on her temple, his breath warm in her ear, she stiffened, trying not to feel the swirling heat that was filling her veins.

"Do you think you can hug me back?" he whispered. "Make this look real?"

She swallowed a hysterical bark of laughter. She had no idea what was real anymore. She put her arms around his waist, and pressed her head against his chest. The cloth beneath her cheek covered warm flesh and a beating heart. She clung to hope, which was really only the absence of despair, and prayed the government people would interpret the moisture in her eyes as tears of happiness.

Awkwardly they pulled apart, but Burton kept his arm around her waist as they walked back to Officers Jackson and Connery. On the other side of the studio, the crew had gathered in a low buzz of wondering. Ernie stood on his own and appeared to be going into shock.

Burton cleared his throat. "Sorry to keep you waiting," he said to Jackson and Conner. "My, ahem, fiancée and I were just discussing moving up the wedding date to accommodate the, uh, changed circumstances. We'd planned a big church wedding, caterers, live band, the whole shebang, but well, the most important thing is that we're together. Isn't that right, Veronique?''

"Oui, c'est vrai." She spoke quietly, not looking anyone in the eye. It was important they be together. What did it matter what the reason was?

James Jackson handed her his card. ''You must come to the office within the next day or two and complete some forms, then we'll schedule interviews to establish your eligibility for residency. If you plan to marry, I wouldn't waste any time sending out the invitations.''

His dry tone made it obvious that James Jackson and Wendy Connery, no longer faceless bureaucrats but living, breathing enemies, wanted to give Burton and Veronique as little time as possible to cook up a story between them.

Burton left to see them out, and Ernie came up to Veronique, his young face as round and white as a bowl of blancmange. ''Congratulations, Veronique. I had no idea you and Burton were…I mean, that you two—'' He broke off as color flooded his cheeks.

''Pah! Ernie, we are not lovers.'' She spoke in a low voice, so no one else would hear her confession.

Ernie blushed harder. ''I wasn't sure. You must really want to stay in Canada.''

She threw up her hands. ''That is the last thing I want, but my mother-in-law is ill. I must take care of her.''

Ernie scratched the top of his head. ''You mean Mrs. O'Rourke? I didn't know she was sick.''

"Mais non. I have never met Burton's mother.'' She would have to now, she realized with a start. What a box of worms they had opened!

The studio door opened and Burton reappeared. The buzz of talk from the crew faded and died. His gaze swept over them, hardening briefly when it rested on Ernie and Veronique huddled together.

''Where's the audience, Ern?''

"I told them to stretch their legs and asked Brigit in PR to organize coffee for them."

"Good work. Gather round, folks," he said to the milling crew members. "I'd like a quick word with all of you."

Veronique moved forward with the rest. Burton came through the crowd to put his arm around her shoulders. She tried to relax but felt unnatural standing at his side pretending to be his fiancée. How would she manage as his bride?

"I guess you're all wondering what's going on." Heads nodded amid a murmur of assent. "Veronique and I are getting married. It's sudden, I know, but…well, when you know what you want, you've got to grab it with both hands and hang on tight. If anyone from Immigration asks you about our relationship, you can say you don't know anything because I am a very private individual who does not discuss his personal life with his co-workers."

"That's true enough," Vince said. He lifted his cap to smooth back his thinning head of hair. "Just one thing. I'm sure no one wants to screw up whatever you two have got cooking—if you'll pardon the pun—but what if they ask us how you two get along on the set?"

"Hmm…" Burton released Veronique to pace while he thought. "How about, we fell instantly and madly in love, but we're both strong-willed people who strike sparks off each other." He glanced around the faces before him. "Okay?"

"Oka-a-ay." Bill didn't look convinced.

"Maybe you're right. As a story line, it's a bit trite." Burton scratched his jaw, paced some more. And came up with zilch. "Come on, guys. What's the big deal? We're professionals. How do you suppose we'd act? Veronique and I aren't likely to go off in a corner and start making out, are we?"

No, no, their heads shook in agreement.

"If we're a little tense, it's because we're working out the bugs at the start of a new series."

"Aah, you're always tense," someone said from the back of the room.

"Well, thank you very much."

"Excuse me, Burt...on," Ernie piped up. "They might wonder why Veronique doesn't have an engagement ring."

"Good point, Ern. We'll take care of it right away." He spun around to Veronique.

Her face was very white, her green eyes wide and wary. Mutely she nodded her head just a fraction. Burton felt a sinking sensation in his stomach. He rarely experienced self-doubt, but marriage, Veronique, the federal government—it was huge. They were all unknown quantities, and Veronique the biggest unknown of all. Had his ego been so caught up in the challenge that he'd gambled until the stakes exceeded the prize? He wouldn't know till it all shook down, but right now, one thing was certain—he had to brazen it out.

"Okay, let's get back to work. Ernie, get Rita in here to fix Veronique's hair. Vince, round up the audience. Bill, let's set up a mirror over the range top so it'll look like we're shooting from directly above the pan. Veronique..."

He moved over to her as the others dispersed to perform their various tasks. He stood close, but without touching, afraid of touching, now that it could mean so much. "It's going to be all right."

"We cannot fool them, Burton."

"I don't have to pretend an attraction to you, Veronique."

She glanced up, alarm in her eyes. "Attraction is not love. Anyway, I don't want you to be attracted to me."

"I only meant that we can fool them. You don't have to worry about me demanding my conjugal rights. This marriage will be temporary and platonic. In name only.

Even so, we need to get to know each other in a hurry. Are you busy tonight?''

"I am going to help Marion move to the nursing home. She is finished with the rehab center, but her doctor doesn't think she is ready to be on her own. I don't know how I'm going to tell her I'm getting married again.''

He would have to tell his mother, he realized. Which meant her book club friends and the whole aerobics class would know. He groaned. At least it would get her off his back about Melissa.

"Tomorrow then. Don't think about it now. We have to finish the segment.''

He reached up to brush her cheek with his fingers, caught her eye and was about to stop. Then he saw Bill watching them curiously. Might as well play the part if it made it easier for people to believe and back them up. Deliberately he let his fingers slide through her hair to the back of her neck, then bent his head to press a kiss on her temple. Beneath his fingertips and his lips, he could feel her tremble. He pulled away, not wanting to speculate on the whys or wherefores.

She wouldn't meet his gaze, so he handed her over to Rita, armed with brushes and powder, and walked away, his heart beating fast.

BURTON WAS HURRIEDLY going through his in-tray, determined to have an early night for once. The first day of taping hadn't gone too badly, considering, but what with the mango salsa and the feds he was exhausted.

Damn, he thought, when he came across a hand-written memo from Ed Murphy. The old man wanted to see him. Now. The time noted was 5:00 p.m. It was now 6:15.

Murphy must have heard the news. Burton headed for the elevators, going over in his mind various arguments justifying his forthcoming marriage. He could either present it as evidence of supreme company loyalty, or as succumbing to uncontrollable passion. On the whole, he thought Murphy might be more inclined to buy the loyalty defense.

Burton stepped into the elevator and punched the button for the fifth floor. The one thing he must *not* do was mention *Lost Harvest* in connection with this particular escapade. It would only convince Murphy he was becoming unhinged and further jeopardize the chances of his documentary.

Sylvia had left for the day, her computer keys silent, her monitor shrouded in plastic. Burton knocked and was about to walk in when he heard Murphy call ''Wait a minute.''

Something odd about his voice made Burton pause, hand on the knob. ''Murph?''

''That you, Burton?'' Murphy said, coughing. ''Hang on.''

Hearing muffled sounds, Burton unabashedly put his ear to the door. A drawer banged shut, there was a faint hissing sound and then, finally, Murphy bellowed for him to come in.

The odor of fresh cigar smoke combined with pine-scented air-freshener almost choked him on the spot. He swung the door open and shut a few times before stepping into the office. ''When did you take up smoking again, Murph?''

His boss glared him straight in the eye. ''I didn't.''

Burton glanced at the thin curl of smoke seeping out of the desk drawer. Murphy wasn't getting off this easy. He sniffed the air. ''I'm sure I smell something.''

The lines etching either side of Murphy's down-turned mouth sunk deeper. ''Well, you don't.''

Burton strolled over to the desk, affecting an air of unconcern. ''What the hell, eh, Murph? They're probably wrong about smoking being bad for you. Everybody knows statistics can be made to show any damn thing at all. And if it helps you to concentrate—''

"Go to hell, O'Rourke, or you'll drive me to drink, as well. Now, park your butt in that chair and tell me what in God's good name is going on down there. Sylvia came back from coffee this afternoon babbling about how you're getting married to that Frenchwoman.''

Burton pulled up a chair and told Murphy the whole story.

When he was done, Ed just sat there, shaking his head. "You've got yourself in a real mess this time, O'Rourke. What's the matter, can't stand your own cooking anymore?'' He started to chuckle at his own joke, then frowned as the laugh turned into a cough. "You're not going to go through with it, are you?''

Burton got to his feet, spreading his hands helplessly. "I don't have any choice, unless I can get someone else to marry her. Ernie might, but Rita would have my balls for breakfast.''

"Why didn't you check her residency status before you hired her, damn it? And why didn't she have the decency to mention her work visa was running out?''

"She did. She told me about it before she signed the contract,'' he admitted, scraping a hand through his hair. "I knew it was a gamble, but I thought I could sort it out. I didn't count on red tape being so bloody binding.''

"The solution's simple,'' Murphy grunted. "Get another chef.''

Burton shook his head. "Veronique's too perfect. Well, maybe not perfect. In fact, she's a pain in the butt most of the time, but on camera she's fantastic. She's going to make this show.''

Murphy reached for the humidor and extracted a handful of jelly beans. "I thought you didn't even want to do this show.''

"I'm committed now. I want it to be a success.''

Murphy chewed. "Is what you're doing legal?"

"The question is, can they prove it's not?" Burton leaned two hands on the back of the chair and gazed earnestly at Murphy. "What is love all about, anyway? How do you define when it begins? Look at love at first sight. Lots of whirlwind romances culminate in legitimate marriages."

"Which is probably why the divorce rate is so high," Murphy growled.

Burton waved the objection away and took up pacing again. "If circumstances were different—" like if Veronique didn't hate the sight of him "—I'd take her out, get to know her, quite possibly fall in love—" if he wasn't halfway there already "—and, after a suitable time had passed, I might very well ask her to marry me." At least his mother was going to be pleased, he thought. "The same scenario is happening now, except we've bypassed the dinner-and-drinks stage, and gone straight to—"

"The marriage bed?"

It was a pleasant thought, but not to be dwelled on. Not if he wanted to keep a rein on his libido. He'd promised Veronique a platonic relationship, and that was what she was going to get.

"What are you saying to me, Ed?" he said, frustration coming to the fore. "Are you telling me not to marry her? Because if you are, you're doing Channel Seven a big disfavor."

"The hell with the station! I don't want you getting burned. You barely know this woman. For all you know this could be a setup and she could take you for all you've got. Get a prenuptial agreement. Protect yourself."

Burton had always found the idea of prenup agreements abhorrent. He was certain Veronique had no designs on his bank account, but he was touched by the old man's concern. "Thanks, Murph. I'll check into it."

"Aah, it's nothin'. I want *Flavors* to be a success, too.

If it's not, I know you'll never get off my back until you get to do your damn documentary.''

"You're right there," Burton agreed cheerfully as he prepared to leave. "If at first you don't succeed, try, try, again. Right, Murph?''

He saw Murphy glance at his desk drawer. The smoke had stopped, but cigars went out, they didn't burn down. As soon as he was out of the room, he'd lay five to one Murphy would be lighting up again.

"Right, Murph?''

"Yeah, yeah, right.'' With a last regretful glance at the drawer, he pushed on the armrests to heave himself up from his chair. "Hang on. I'll walk out with you.''

IT WAS ALMOST EIGHT by the time Burton chugged up the gravel drive to the farmhouse and parked beside his mother's Volvo. Across the fields to the south, Mount Baker floated above the horizon, a white shark's tooth gleaming in a salmon-pink sky. Since he was off early and Veronique was busy, he'd called Catherine to see if she wanted to finish sorting through Granddad's things together. And if the subject came up, he might just mention that, oh, by the way, he was getting married on Friday. Would she like to come?

The door was open, so he pulled on the screen door and walked in. "Mother?" he called. "Where are you?''

"Hi, Burtie. I'm in your grandfather's room.'' Her voice sounded muffled.

He walked down the hall and paused in the doorway to Grandad's room. "How's it going?''

Catherine was kneeling on the rag rug, her head and shoulders beneath the bed. At the sound of his voice she withdrew, dragging with her a battered cardboard box. She lifted the top copy of what must have been several decades' worth of *Playboy* magazines. "What on earth?''

"Why that dirty old son of a gun," Burton said with a

surprised grin. He took the magazine from Catherine's hand and flipped to the center to study Miss March, 1975. "Now, why couldn't I have found these when I was a teenager?"

Catherine rolled her eyes. "Thank heavens Dad had the sense to hide them." She rose to her feet, a hand on the small of her back. Her navy blue sweatpants and top were laced with dust. She sneezed. "You can put them out for recycling."

"Gee, I don't know, Mother. A collection like this is probably worth a mint. Will you look at that." He tipped the magazine sideways, a mischievous eye out for his mother's certain disapproval.

"Don't be crude, Burton."

Burton tossed the magazine back into the box. "I didn't think to look under the bed when I was here last. You didn't come across the chess set there, did you?"

"No," she said, dusting off her knees. "Do you remember the last time you saw it?" Her voice sounded artificially casual.

The bedsprings were old and sank beneath his weight. Had he just imagined the flicker of guilt in her eyes? "I think it was Easter," he said. "Granddad and I played a game before dinner, but I remember putting it back in its cabinet. You know how he always liked having things in their proper place."

Catherine moved to the dresser, opening and shutting drawers he knew to be empty. "Maybe he took it out later and left it somewhere. He was eighty-one. Getting a little forgetful."

"He would never have forgotten where he put that chess set." He watched his mother twitch the curtains shut against the coming twilight, then glance agitatedly around the room. Was she looking for something else to be sorted out, cleaned up, tidied away forever? "What is it, Mother?"

"I beg your pardon?" She tried for innocence, but within an instant her face crumpled. "Oh, Burtie!" she cried, and came to sit beside him on the bed. "I'm so sorry."

He put his arm around her. "Why? It's not your fault the chess set is missing."

"Maybe it is." She wiped at her wet cheeks with the flat of her hand. "The week before Dad died, I was out here. He…I…we had a fight."

"What about?"

"It was April, and he was doing his income tax. He had all his financial papers spread out on the kitchen table. I happened to see the insurance premiums that were due to be paid against death taxes." She paused, indignant. "Did you know that without insurance, when someone dies, whoever inherits has to pay tax on the property the same as if it had been sold? Do you have any idea how much that would be on a place this size? A quarter of a million, at least."

Burton nodded. "Mr. Bingham explained all that to me the day after the will was read. But don't worry, Granddad had insurance. Well, you must know, you just said you saw the papers. If he hadn't, I would have had to sell the farm just to pay the taxes."

"It's outrageous. The thing is, last year was so wet his crop was practically ruined. He had hardly any income and not enough to cover the insurance premiums. I suggested he get a loan, but the stubborn old fool wouldn't hear of it. Said he didn't want to pass on debts when he died. It was almost as if he knew he was going to go." Tears filled her eyes. "The last time I ever saw him, we fought. Oh, Burtie, if only I could live that day over again."

Burton put his other arm around her and held her, his eyes squeezing shut against the tears. "Shh, Mother, it's okay. It's okay." His voice was thick and he could hardly speak. "He knew you loved him."

Grief and love wrapped them in silence. They held each other, remembering, slowly gaining comfort from shared sorrow.

At last Catherine heaved a deep sigh and drew back. She smiled bravely and blinked away the moisture in her eyes. Sniffing a little, she continued. "I couldn't let the matter drop. I could tell he was really worried and not wanting to admit it. I told him if he wouldn't borrow, he should sell off a few acres to get the money."

Burton snorted. "He'd never agree to that. But what does all this have to do with the chess set?"

Catherine pulled at the handkerchief tucked in the cuff of her sweatshirt sleeve and dabbed at her eyes. "It was sitting on the table, half-covered by papers, one of his games against himself in progress. I picked up one of the pieces and...I don't know, I guess my subconscious was at work because I said, 'This set is an antique. It must be worth a lot of money.'"

A sudden chill prickled the back of Burton's neck. "You think he sold it to pay the insurance premiums?"

"I don't know. But right away he picked up the chess set and started packing it away, saying, 'You're right, it's worth a great deal of money.'" Then he looked me through and through with those fierce blue eyes. I swear, Burtie, I didn't mean for him to sell it. I knew how much it meant to him, and to you."

"Exactly. That's why I can't believe he would sell it." Burton rose from the bed to pace across the room. "But what if he thought *you* might sell it to get him the insurance money."

"I wouldn't do that!"

"I know. But what if he was so afraid of losing it that he didn't want to take any chances? He must have been under a lot of stress, trying to pay his taxes and insurance. What if he hid it somewhere?"

"It's possible, I suppose," Catherine said slowly. "But

if he hid it instead of selling it, how was he able to pay the insurance?''

Burton stared out the window at the barn and the chickens scratching in the dust. And thought about an old man for whom passing on his land intact to future generations had been paramount, even if it meant dying poor.

Catherine got up and put a hand on his shoulder. ''I guess the important thing is, he saved the farm. Have you decided whether to rent this place out or live here yourself?''

Burton wiped a hand down his face and moved away. Selling didn't occur to his mother as an option. He felt like a traitor even thinking of it, and he sure wasn't ready to talk about it. ''No. Let's take these boxes out, then start on the other downstairs bedroom.''

''Okay. First thing tomorrow I'll call around the antique shops just to make sure he didn't sell the chess set.''

''That would be a huge task,'' he protested. ''You'd have to check every antique store and pawnshop from Vancouver to Hope.''

''That's okay. I'll do it.''

Burton took a step back to wrap his arms around his mother, feeling her sorrow and her fear and her determination to make it up to him. He should at least tell her about his meeting with Don Chetwynd, but why add to her worries now? He wasn't going to do anything till that chess set was found.

''We'll get it back, don't worry.'' He placed a smaller box of farming magazines into his mother's arms, then hoisted Granddad's box of secret pleasure onto his shoulder. They walked out to the car and waited until Catherine had placed her load in the trunk of his Tercel for transport to the recycling depot before he said, ''Are you doing anything next Friday?''

''I'm getting my hair done in the afternoon,'' she replied, dusting off her hands. ''Why?''

"I'm getting married at lunchtime."

When her knees started to buckle, he wished he'd told her when they were in the house and there was a chair she could collapse onto. As it was, he had to take her arm and sit her down on a granite boulder by the edge of the driveway, her hand over her heart, while the grass turned dewy in the dusk and the neighboring farm dogs took turns barking the news out over the valley.

"Oh, Burtie, I'm so happy for you!" she said when at last she was able to speak. She got up again to hug him, and her eyes glistened in the fading light. "This is so quick! But Melissa is such a lovely girl. I just knew you'd like her."

He rolled his eyes at his mother's willful optimism. "I never even called Melissa. It's Veronique, the Frenchwoman you saw on tape. The one who's hosting the cooking show."

"Oh. Her." Catherine wiped the corners of her eyes with her fingertips, blinked and smiled. She was already adjusting to the news, starting to like it.

"It's not exactly a love match." He had to get that in before she started naming her grandchildren.

"What is it, then? Should I sit down again?"

"Let's go inside and make some coffee."

"Oh, my goodness, Burton! She's not pregnant, is she?"

Once he'd told Catherine the whole story, it took three cups of coffee before she calmed down. Like Ed Murphy, she was against the match. Unlike Ed, her objection wasn't over what Veronique might do to his unsuspecting bank account, but how she would ruin his chances of finding, and marrying, someone he did love.

"For crying out loud, Mother," he said finally, setting his cup down hard on the pine table in the kitchen. "This isn't till death do us part. It's just temporary, two or three months at the most. When it's time for her to go back to Tahiti, we'll just have it annulled.''

Annulled. The word had a hollow, barren sound. He'd never given marriage a whole lot of thought, but somewhere at the back of his mind he'd expected to be in love, at least. Well, this wasn't the time for sentiment. Entering a temporary marriage wasn't that big a sacrifice. Despite his assurances to Veronique, the only thing that worried him was whether they'd be able to pull it off with Immigration.

VERONIQUE WAS WORRIED, and because she couldn't pin down the exact source of her anxiety, her worry grew. She rolled her assorted problems over in her mind. There was Marion—she was an obvious source of concern. The same went for the threat of deportation and the Immigration people in general. And then there was Burton's crazy idea of forming a marriage of convenience—*oh la la.* All of these were bad, but none of them quite accounted for the nebulous feeling of disquiet that floated around the edges of her mind.

So in spite of the lowering clouds and the blustery wind, she put on her wet suit and carried her sailboard across Cornwall Avenue and through the little park to the beach. Leaving her shoes on the seawall, she hopped barefoot onto the cold, pebbly sand. Briefly, she shut her eyes, recalling the fine-grained beaches of Tahiti, black as the pearls for which the island was famous, and hot as a stovetop. Water so warm it felt like a lover's embrace.

The water of English Bay was choppy and cold, and the salt spray stung her eyes. She waded out, pushing the board before her. Icy water seeped into her suit through the ankles and wrists and trickled down her neck, making her shiver. When she was waist deep, she climbed aboard, kneeling to drag the heavy sail dripping from the water.

Wind caught the sail, and the board gusted forward on

the crest of a wave. Many times during her claustrophobic marriage she'd sought the freedom of the wind and the waves. Or like now, she'd taken to the ocean to empty her mind of the tangled details of her problems, so a solution could work its way into her consciousness.

In Tahiti she used to sail around the island or across to Moorea, wearing only a bikini, sometimes just a *pareau* knotted around her hips, while the frigate birds wheeled overhead. Here, she went back and forth across the bay clothed neck to ankles in a constricting wet suit, sometimes ending up on Wreck Beach where nudists sunbathed among the scattering of salt-bleached logs. There she would peel off her wet suit and lay naked in the sand against a giant Douglas fir. She'd never mentioned this to Graham, of course. Such freedom was just an illusion.

She hadn't told Marion about her upcoming marriage because there seemed little point. The whole thing would be over before they knew it. She was used to protecting her mother-in-law, so it wasn't this minor deception that worried her.

The wind shifted to the north, and Veronique changed tack, the muscles in her arms straining to maintain a firm grip on the crossbar as she crossed the board to the opposite side. Strength, balance, flexibility—a person needed them all.

The marriage might not even take place if Immigration denied her claim. At the moment she would almost welcome a deportation order. It would absolve her of responsibility and send her to where she wanted to go.

A sailboat came toward her, its prow dipping into the troughs of the waves and back up. Seasick, a boy hung over the rail. Veronique turned her sailboard out of the boat's path, lifting on the crest of a wave and surfing down the other side.

Marriage to Burton. He had no claim of love on her, no right to expect…anything. Except, of course, that she fulfill her contract for *Flavors*. She was surprised he'd committed himself in front of everyone, but she supposed that, like Graham, for him work was everything. Or perhaps marriage meant so little that he could treat it as mere words on paper. He, she felt certain, would have no trouble dealing with the platonic nature of their marriage.

Her sailboard cut through a white-capped wave and dashed a spray of icy saltwater in her face. Stung, her eyes shut, and the memory flashed back of that moment on the set when she'd looked into Burton's eyes and felt something inside catch fire. She flicked her head, tossing the water out of her eyes. Her anxiety crystallized. So *that* was what had sent her out here on this miserable day.

She felt something for him. But was it leftover attraction from early days with Graham, or worse—something new?

The more she went over it, the more her perceptions became muddied. She couldn't, after all, separate Burton from her image of Graham. So she blanked her mind, letting the roar of the wind and the cry of the gulls displace her eddying thoughts. At last she turned back to the beach, chilled to the bone, her arms and legs trembling with fatigue.

She had no solution to her problem, except a resolve not to let these feelings, whatever they were, grow. She was going home.

Nothing, and no one, was going to stop her.

CHAPTER NINE

ERNIE WAS WORRIED, TOO—about Rita. His first mistake was not complimenting her on her new haircut when he'd picked her up after work. *Styled,* she called what Lillian's grandniece had done to it during lunch break. He could have done better with his dad's tin snips and a jar of Vaseline. He'd liked her hair the way it was before, a soft, shiny curtain that hung to her shoulders.

Gearing down his trusty old Volkswagen Beetle at the entrance to the subdivision where Rita lived with her mother, he wondered what the big deal was about a haircut. He bet Veronique didn't fuss over her hair.

He sure knew better than to say that, because his second mistake had been to innocently agree that Veronique was chic—whatever the hell *chic* meant. He'd just wanted to make amends for screwing up on the hair thing, but right away Rita had gone all huffy. She'd crossed her arms beneath her breasts and stared silently out the window all the way back to Surrey.

Petunias bloomed in two neat circles of earth cut into Rita's front lawn and were watched over by a pair of garden gnomes in red trousers. Ernie pulled into the driveway of the two-story house and cut the engine. A marmalade tabby jumped onto the hood of his car and eyed him through the windshield. Rita's standard poodle poked her curly black head over the top of the fence separating the side yard from the front and let out a few joyous yips.

"Rita?" he said tentatively. That morning she'd invited

him to stay for dinner, but maybe she'd be in a better mood if she didn't have to cook. She didn't really like cooking, though she was pretty good at it.

Rita made a production out of getting her purse and her shopping bag full of hair-care products together. "Yes?"

"What do you say we go out to eat?" He was going to suggest Stavros, their favorite restaurant, then he remembered Burton saying that Greek food was passé. "There's that new French restaurant over in White Rock—"

"So you want French food now? Is that it?" Her voice had an injured sound, and two spots of red stained her cheeks.

"Huh?"

"You know what I'm talking about, Ernie. I saw the way you looked at her."

"Who?" he squeaked, though he knew darn well who she was talking about. He just hadn't thought he was so obvious.

"Veronique."

"I thought you liked her. You said yourself she was chic."

"Oh, Ernie! Sometimes you just don't have a clue." Rita swiped angrily at a tear that had broken free and threatened to run down her cheek. "Do you have any idea how humiliating it is for me to see you fawning all over her in front of everybody?"

"She's going to marry Burton!"

"You *know* that's just a setup so she can stay in Canada. You spent all day Tuesday shopping with her, but you never want to go shopping with me."

"We had to get things for the show!"

"Oh, sure. How do I know what else you two got up to?"

"Nothing." Then he remembered that afternoon when a mango had been all that stood between Veronique's hand and his thigh. He couldn't help it, he blushed.

Rita's eyes widened and filled with glistening tears. "Oh, Ernie!"

He reached for her, but she twisted away from him and pushed open the door. Her bag dropped and a bottle of shampoo rolled down the driveway. While she bent to retrieve it, Ernie got out and hurried around the car.

"Rita. Honey." When she straightened, he put his arms around her and her bags. She averted her face but didn't move away. "It's you I love. Nothing happened, I swear."

She looked up, her expression a mixture of grief and accusation. "But you wanted something to happen."

Maybe in some parallel universe, but Ernie knew better than to say such a thing. "No, honestly. Please, Rita, don't cry. I love you. Your hair is beautiful. You're beautiful."

She sniffed and glanced up at him beneath wet lashes. "Do you really like my hair?"

Oh, boy. Ernie took off his glasses and began to polish them, partly out of nervous habit, partly so he wouldn't have to look at her in full focus. "I...I like you *any* way you are. I really mean that."

Rita heaved a big sigh and wiped her eyes. "Oh, Ernie. I know you do. I'm sorry I got so silly. It's just...I don't know. Lately you don't seem to even see me when you look at me. I thought maybe if I did something different... That's why I got Sandy to cut my hair. I'm not totally sure I like it myself. I just wanted something different."

Ernie listened to her with a sinking heart. He didn't understand half of what she was saying, but he did hear her say she wanted something different. As in different boyfriend? No, no, no. He leaned over her bags and, ignoring the twitch in the living-room curtains, took her lips in a deep kiss. A French kiss. For a split second, a corner of his mind flashed on Veronique. He moaned, blocking his thoughts and deepening the kiss further.

"Oh, Ernie," Rita breathed when they broke apart. "I've got goose bumps."

It was Rita he wanted. No question. "So, how about dinner?"

She hesitated. "Mother's expecting us to stay in."

"She's a big girl." Then he winced, because Sheila Grafton *was* big—as in very overweight. "Sorry, I mean, why don't we see if she wants to come with us?"

"She doesn't like eating out unless it's Chinese. You wait in the car and I'll sort it out." Rita planted a tiny kiss on his lips and ran up the path to the front door.

Ernie backhanded the perspiration off his forehead as he walked back to the Volkswagen. He'd had no idea Rita was so jealous. He wasn't the type to play around, but he had to admit it was a boost to his ego that she thought Veronique would even look at him.

Rita was back in ten minutes with fresh lipstick and dry eyes. "Mom doesn't mind staying home," she said, fastening the seat belt across her lap. "She's on some new diet, anyway."

"So…have you thought about which restaurant you want to go to?" he said, starting up the engine.

She sighed. "If you really want French, I guess we'll go French."

"We don't have to go French. I like Greek, too. In fact, I like Greek better."

"Do you really?" Her glance was wistful.

"Yes."

"Okay," she said, smiling happily. "Let's go French."

DAMN. DAMN, DAMN, damn, damn.

Burton glanced at his watch as he burst out of the conference room and broke into a lope down the corridor toward his office. Today of all days, his meeting with the writers of *Lovers and Strangers* had run overtime. His mother had called at least a dozen times. And Ernie had driven him crazy by humming the wedding march all morning.

He hated being late, even for his own wedding.

He grabbed his coat and the umbrella he'd bought this morning—dark green with a varnished teak handle and brass fittings—and hurried down to reception.

"Where's Ernie?" he asked Lillian, pulling on his coat.

"Right here, boss." Ernie came puffing around the corner.

"Have you got the ring?" Lillian asked. The figure of calm, she came around her desk to straighten Burton's tie.

Burton jammed a hand into his pants pocket. "Yep."

"And the license?"

"Yep. Let's go, Ern."

"Wait a minute." Lillian picked a white carnation out of her vase, broke off the stem and poked the fresh, peppery-scented flower into Burton's lapel. "You look very handsome."

"Thanks, Lil. You're a doll." He kissed her on the cheek.

She held on to his arms and whispered in his ear, "This could turn out better than you think."

"I sure hope so." He turned to go, then on impulse, pulled the whole dripping mass of flowers from the vase. "You don't mind, do you, Lil? I won't have time to stop at a florist."

"Of course not." She helped him wrap the stems in computer paper and all but pushed him out the door.

They arrived at the courthouse, a modern hanging garden of glass and greenery, a few minutes past noon. Burton groaned when he saw his mother. She wore a dark blue suit, a silk corsage left over from Easter and a resigned smile. There was no sign of Veronique.

"Maybe she changed her mind," Catherine said, looking hopeful.

"No, Mother. She's probably just…" He broke off, having no idea what might be keeping her. Other than her visits to Marion, he knew nothing of her life off the set.

Going back through the revolving door, he scanned the sidewalk in both directions, peering through the lunchtime crowd for his reluctant bride. Why was he so nervous? It was just a piece of paper. A piece of paper that ought to stand for love and cherish till death did them part—not for the length of a television series. He paced the sidewalk, feeling like a character in one of his old sitcoms.

Then he saw her. Hurrying toward him, hair loose and glowing, the black cashmere dress he liked so well clinging to her shoulders and hips. It wouldn't have been his choice for a wedding dress, but what the hell. Maybe, he thought in a burst of optimism, when she got to know him she would like him better. After all, familiarity bred... No, no, that wasn't right. He rubbed his temples, trying to collect his thoughts.

When she got within ten feet, she looked up and their eyes met. It was hard to say if it was alarm or anticipation that widened her eyes, but for him, that instant of eye contact went way beyond platonic.

"Hi," he said, nervously smoothing back his cowlick. He handed her the bunch of flowers, then leaned over to kiss her on the cheek. Her skin was cool and soft, and slightly damp with the moisture in the air. She started to jerk away from his lips, so he whispered, "They might be watching. No, don't look around. Look at me."

She couldn't, of course. She buried her face in his shoulder while pedestrians parted around them. He put his other arm around her and felt her trembling. "It's okay," he said in a low voice. "It's going to be okay. Our kisses will only be in public."

She glanced up, brushing her curls from her forehead, and smiled briefly. "I am sorry I'm late. Thank you for the flowers. I don't think about a bouquet."

Or an appropriate dress, or anything else associated with a real wedding. He felt suddenly foolish and wanted to rip the boutonniere from his lapel. "The others are inside," he said, and guided her through the revolving door.

Ernie turned as they entered the lobby, his expression a tragicomic mixture of eager and wistful at the sight of Veronique. She kissed him on both cheeks, making him bloom with pleasure. "*Bonjour,* Ernie."

"Uh, bon-joor, Veronique."

Burton's hand tightened around hers. She still didn't kiss him in greeting. She kissed Lillian and Ernie and God knew who else, but not him. Stepping back, he said, "Mother, this is Veronique Dutot. Veronique, Catherine O'Rourke."

His mother held out her hand with a too-gracious smile and murmured a cool pleasantry. Then she took his free arm, pulling him aside. Burton glanced back to see Veronique looking at them and twining a finger through her hair.

"She's wearing black to her own wedding?" Catherine said in an undertone. "I hate to say it, Burton, but I'm beginning to think you were right the first time—this woman is trouble."

"It's just a dress," he whispered. "It's not as though this is a church wedding. Or, or…we're in love."

One perfectly shaped eyebrow arched infinitesimally. "I saw the way you looked when she kissed Ernie."

"She can't kiss me—I'm her boss," he said, not having the foggiest notion of French etiquette. He glanced over to see Veronique straightening Ernie's tie and teasing him. His blood pressure soared. She only ever looked at *his* tie to avoid looking at his face.

"So why does it make you so tense? And why doesn't she look you in the eye?" She put a hand on his jacket, imploring him. "Oh, Burtie, I don't want to see you hurt. It's not too late to call it off. You don't owe this woman anything."

"We've been through this," he said grimly. "I'm not

changing my mind." He glanced at his watch. "We'd better get down to the registrar's office. Please, Mother, be nice."

Veronique watched the exchange between Burton and his mother with a sick feeling in her stomach. But she took Burton's arm and together they led the little procession down the stairs to the basement floor where the registrar's office was located.

Two other couples and their witnesses were in the waiting room when they entered. One bride was decked out in ankle-length white muslin and had flowers in her hair, while her husband-to-be wore a tuxedo jacket over blue jeans. They sat nose-to-nose, arms wrapped around each other, giggling. The other couple was about twenty years older and more staid, but the way they held hands and the quiet glances they exchanged left no doubt of their affection.

"I am very hungry," Veronique said suddenly. "Maybe we eat lunch first, *non?*" All morning she'd been too nervous to eat, and now, when the moment was upon them, her stomach did nothing but rumble.

She hadn't meant for Burton's mother to hear, but Catherine O'Rourke slanted her son one of those arched-eyebrow looks. He just uttered a hapless laugh and said nothing.

Oh la la. Veronique shrank back, a hand to her stomach. His mother hated her, and Burton thought it was all a joke.

Still, it was thoughtful of him to bring her flowers. Avoiding their eyes, she buried her nose in the fragrant mass. And saw, half-hidden by stems and leaves, the Channel Seven logo and a few lines from one of Lillian's spreadsheets. Her empty stomach turned over on itself, and her eyes threatened to weep like the sky.

A clerk came out of an inner office and called their names.

The service was mercifully short. When the registrar

pronounced them husband and wife, Veronique lifted her head high. She was a Frenchwoman. She would fulfill her part in this marriage with no weak longings for false sentiment.

Burton touched his lips to hers and she fought to still the inner trembling, vowing if she could ever bear to go through this again in the future, she would marry for nothing less than love.

Then Ernie gave her a peck on the mouth and his eyes were moist, too. Burton glared at him but for once didn't make some snappy remark. Catherine O'Rourke's eyes were cold and dry.

"Be good to him," her new mother-in-law said, embracing her stiffly. "He's all I have."

"I do not harm him." Impulsively Veronique hugged her. Catherine had been cheated out of a proper daughter-in-law and a church wedding. She wanted the real thing for her son. What woman wouldn't?

Catherine responded with a perplexed smile. Veronique wondered if Burton had told her about the resemblance he bore to her first husband. How close was he to his mother? So many things she didn't know about her new husband. It had been the same with Graham. And it filled her with trepidation.

They emerged onto the street, newly wed. This was not the way she and Ghislaine had pictured their weddings as little girls. There was no music, no flowers, no friends and family to wish her love and happiness in her new life. Only gray, drizzling skies and the uncaring faces of strangers hurrying along crowded downtown sidewalks.

"So," Burton said, clapping his hands together with a forced smile, "how about that lunch?"

"I'd better get back to the studio," Ernie said, looking regretfully at Veronique. "Rita's waiting for me."

"See you later, then. Thanks, Ernie." Burton turned up his collar at a gust of wind and, in doing so, knocked the carnation from his lapel. He made a grab for it, but it landed in a puddle and a pedestrian stepped on it, leaving the petals muddy and bruised. Straightening, he said, "Mother?"

"No thank you, darling. I'm having my hair done, remember? Anyway, I'm sure you two will want to be alone." Catherine gave him a peck on the cheek, threw a vague smile in Veronique's direction and hurried down the sidewalk, pushed along by the wind.

Having her hair done? Veronique thought. *After* the wedding? Outrage coursed through her on Burton's behalf. Yet he did not seem concerned. It did not matter, she told herself. It did not matter.

Then they were alone and Burton was pressing something solid into her hand. "This is for you."

She glanced down, surprised. "Thank you, but…an umbrella? I lose them."

"You won't lose this one. We could go to Marietta's. I haven't made a reservation, but I know the head waiter."

This wasn't a wedding feast. "A hamburger will do."

A smile crept onto his face. A real smile. "I didn't know haute chefs ate hamburgers. With ketchup and relish and everything?"

She laughed, her mood lightening. "No, with béarnaise sauce and pickled truffles. Of course, with ketchup and relish. Just no fast-food burger. I refuse to eat off cardboard and plastic."

He tucked her hand into the crook of his arm. "Come on, then, Mrs. O'Rourke, let's go have lunch."

His warmth spread down her arm and chased the chill from her toes. But…Mrs. O'Rourke? That was his mother, not her.

Burton took her to the Jolly Jumbuck, a pub just around the corner. While he went to the bar for drinks, Veronique fingered the shiny gold wedding band he'd placed on her finger. She'd just gotten used to not wearing a ring and here she was with another. When he'd talked about rings a couple of days before, she'd suggested she wear the old wedding band Graham had given her rather than buy a new one. Burton had looked at her strangely and said "No" very firmly, adding a second later that the Immigration officials would be bound to notice the ring wasn't new. She hadn't thought of that, but most likely he was right.

"Champagne!" she exclaimed when he came back with a bottle of Dom Pérignon. Could this mean more to him than she'd thought?

"It occurred to me they might be watching," he said, untwisting the wire around the cork.

Veronique glanced dubiously around the smoky, crowded pub. "Do you really think so?"

"I have no idea, but we don't want to screw up now." He popped the cork and poured out two glasses, then clinked his glass against hers. "To us—for better or for lunch."

She smiled at that and took a sip. The bubbles tickled her nose, and the alcohol went straight to her head. It felt very strange to be Mrs. Burton O'Rourke.

"Now, let's get down to business." He pulled out a notepad and pen and began to jot down notes. "You don't like fast-food restaurants but you do eat hamburgers. Champagne, yes… What's your favorite color?" He glanced up, pen poised expectantly.

She had to laugh. "In what—clothes or flowers? Do you think you can find out all my likes and dislikes over lunch?"

"We've got to start somewhere." He ripped a page out of the notebook and passed it across the table. "You'd better make notes, too. My favorite color is blue—clothes and flowers. I grew up in Vancouver, the only child of an only child."

"Lonely child," she murmured.

"Not at all." He sipped at his champagne. "My best friend lived next door. Mother had lots of friends, many with children about my age."

"What about your father? Where is he?"

"He died five years ago of a heart attack. We weren't very close—he was away on business a lot—but we had a good relationship. Granddad was more of a father to me. Birthday?"

"December 25."

"No kidding. What a bummer." He noted it down. "Where were you born?"

"Bordeaux. My father was *capitaine* in the *gendarmerie*. The French police," she explained. "I have three sisters—I am the youngest. When I was very small we lived in Algérie before we move to Tahiti."

"Ah, Tahiti. I picture a tropical paradise with beautiful bare-breasted women lounging on the banks of coral lagoons."

She laughed. "You have been influenced by Gauguin."

"More like *Mutiny on the Bounty*," he admitted. "So what's it really like?"

Her eyes closed as she transported herself mentally. "It is paradise," she said, her voice dreamy. "You awake to the sound of the cock crowing, and every day is so warm you need put on only a *pareau*—a strip of colorful cotton, like a…sarong. Home was a Tahitian-style wooden house with big windows—no glass, you understand—but sides that prop up to let the breeze flow through and give shade. In the backyard we have an avocado tree and a mango. The beach is close by, black sand. The water is warm like a bath and the coral is many colors. Fish of all shapes and sizes flash like the neon through the clear turquoise water."

Burton had propped his chin in his hand to listen to her. "I can see why you'd want to go back. What about your family? Tell me more."

He sounded as though he was really interested. Unlike Graham, who hated to hear her talk about her life in Tahiti or her family. Or any part of her life he couldn't dominate. But then, Burton was probably interested only to the extent he needed the information for the interview.

"My parents are retired and live in Bordeaux, but they spend the winters in Tahiti. My sister, Ghislaine, lives outside Papeete. She is married and has two children, Coralie and Hugo."

"Go on," he said, writing quickly in his bold, slanted hand.

"Ghislaine is a flight attendant, but she is looking for a job closer to home. Her husband, Donaldo—his mother came from Spain—is captain on a charter sailboat. His cousin, Jean-Paul, owns a marina and is building a floating restaurant. I might get a job there when I go back."

"Oh." He frowned when he heard that, but he noted it down.

"Not everything about Tahiti is paradise," she continued. "There are tropical ulcers that take months to heal, mold that grows everywhere, and the wet season where we snap at one another's throats. And typhoons that can smash your house and scatter the pieces like twigs."

She twirled her champagne glass by its stem, watching the bubbles float to the top. "As time goes on, you learn to accept the bad with the good. My first husband didn't experience Tahiti long enough to really love it. Probably he never would have." She sighed.

There was a silence. Burton put down his pen. "I'm sorry."

Her gaze dropped. She shrugged. "Me, too."

"I think we should stay at the farmhouse," he said.

Her head came up, and her alarmed gaze danced around his shoulders. "We?"

"Our marriage won't look genuine unless we live together. My apartment only has one bedroom, and if you're going back to Tahiti it doesn't make sense for you to keep your apartment. Anyway, I've got to fix the place up before I can sell, and it's easier to do it if I'm staying out there.''

She frowned. ''But it is so far. I must be close to Marion.''

''We'll be coming in every day for work. The nursing home you mentioned isn't far from the studio. I'll drive you or you can use my car.''

''I didn't think about us…living together.''

''Don't worry. The farmhouse has lots of bedrooms, so we won't get in each other's way. I'll pick you up after work. We can take some of your stuff out to the farm and stay for the weekend. Okay?''

Like Graham, he'd taken charge. She glanced around the pub, wondering if one of the gray-suited men sipping their second pint over a long Friday lunch was taking notes for the government.

''Okay.''

''Good.'' Burton checked his watch. ''I have to get back for *Lovers and Strangers.* Give me your address and I'll pick you up around six o'clock.''

She wrote it down on the piece of paper he'd given her—still barren of any details of his life—and passed it back. This marriage was different to her first in at least one respect. She could not get hurt because she didn't love Burton. How could she? She didn't see him as a person in his own right.

MARION NOTICED THE RING right away.

''Some flowers for you, Marion.'' Veronique tucked her bridal bouquet into an empty vase and filled it with water from the bathroom. Only one flower was missing—a gardenia—which she'd pressed between the pages of the book of English sayings she carried in her backpack to read on the bus.

Marion set her crutches aside and lowered herself into a cushioned wicker armchair in the glassed-in porch that overlooked the garden. "What's that on your finger?"

"Pardon?" Veronique instinctively covered the ring, then took her hand away to regard the plain gold band with feigned surprise.

"The ring," Marion said. "It looks like a wedding band."

Veronique swallowed. *"Oui."*

"It's not the one Graham gave you. That had rows of diamonds on it."

Veronique had always hated the ostentatiousness of that ring—something else she'd never been able to say. She took a deep breath, and when she exhaled, the bare facts tumbled out. "I am married again. To my producer, Burton O'Rourke. It was this morning."

Marion gripped the arms of her chair, the bluish veins on her thin hands standing out. "Married! But...it's only been six months since Graham died." Tears filled her eyes. "Married. I wasn't even aware you were seeing anyone."

Of course Marion couldn't possibly understand. Not only did she not know the facts, Marion was a woman who talked to her husband's photo, who still had all his clothes hanging in her closet, who cooked his favorite meals even though he wasn't alive to eat them.

Veronique scooted her chair forward and placed her hands over Marion's. "Please do not distress yourself, *chère* Marion. It is the marriage of convenience only, although you must not say so to anyone."

"I don't understand," Marion said, her voice teary. She cast about for a tissue.

Veronique reached into the side pocket of her backpack and drew out the handkerchief with the letter *B* monogrammed in the corner. She handed it to Marion, wondering if she would comment on that, as well. "My work visa ran out," she explained. "The immigration officials say I must leave the country. The only way to stay was to marry another Canadian.''

"But you said you were going back to Tahiti." Abruptly, she lowered the handkerchief, eyes wide. "Oh! You did it for me. Oh, my dear Veronique. You shouldn't have done that. How do you know what he's even like?"

Veronique made a sudden decision. She handed Marion her crutches and helped her to her feet. "Come, let us kill two birds with one bone. We will get your wheelchair and take you up the street to the studio. You are going to meet him."

"What? But I can't possibly. I don't want to meet the man who's taken you away from Graham."

Veronique held her ex-mother-in-law's arms and looked her directly in the eye. "Marion, Graham was a wond...won...he was your son. And my husband. But he was gone long before I met Burton. They are two separate people with nothing to do with each other, except..."

Oh la la. How could she have forgotten?

"Except what, Ronnie?" Marion struggled to get the crutches under her arms.

Veronique thrust her fingers into the back of her hair, tugging and twining it into knots. "You mustn't be shocked, but Burton, he look just like Graham."

Marion laughed nervously. "My dear, that's impossible."

"DOES MY HAIR LOOK all right?" Marion fretted as Veronique pushed her through the doors into the Channel Seven building.

"You look wonderful." Veronique wheeled her across the lobby, pausing at the front desk to say hello to Lillian.

Lillian looked up from her computer. "Veronique! I didn't expect to see you here today. Congratulations, by the way. You may not realize it, but Burton is considered quite a catch."

Veronique shrugged, too embarrassed to reply directly. "Lillian, this is Marion. Has Burton started taping *Lovers and Strangers* yet?"

"Hello, Marion," Lillian said warmly. "Veronique has told us all about you. I hope your hip is starting to heal."

"It gives me trouble in the damp weather, but it's on the mend, thank you." She reached back to pat Veronique's hand. "Don't know what I'd do without Ronnie."

Lillian smiled and turned to Veronique. "Taping starts in a few minutes, but if you hurry you might catch Burton in his office. I just put a call through to him a minute ago." She turned to Marion. "Are you going to watch the show being taped?"

"Oh, I would love to. It's my favorite show. I've watched it every day for the last twelve years."

"We better hurry, Marion. See you later, Lillian." She pushed on down the corridor.

"Did you see her hair?" Marion asked in an astonished whisper when they were out of earshot of the front desk.

Veronique laughed. Lillian's hair had undergone some amazing transformations in the past couple of weeks. Currently it was a luscious pale caramel color with sugar frosted tips that looked surprisingly good against Lillian's delicate skin. "Maybe we try that shade on you next, eh?"

"Not on your life!"

Ahead of them, an office door opened. Burton's door. Veronique's hands turned clammy and slipped on the plastic handles of the wheelchair. She let go and stepped forward, wishing she could somehow prevent this meeting now that it was actually about to happen.

Burton's expression when he saw her—surprise and warmth in equal parts—did something funny to the pit of her stomach. Her gaze went to the wedding band on his left hand. Somehow she'd half expected him to take it off when she wasn't around.

She glanced back at Marion and was shocked. Far from

being surprised or upset at seeing Graham's double, her mother-in-law merely smiled expectantly. *Zut alors!* Had she dreamed the whole thing?

"*Salut,* Bur-r-rton." Nerves thickened her accent. "Zis ees Marion, my ex-muzzer-in-law. Marion, zis ees Burton O'Rourke, my—" She choked over what to call him. Husband? Producer?

"Pleased to meet you, Marion." Burton bent to take her hand. "I'm sorry about your accident. Although it's thanks to you we have Veronique with us."

"It's wonderful to meet you, Mr. O'Rourke," Marion exclaimed. "I just love your show."

"Marion would like to watch *Lovers and Strangers* being taped," Veronique said. "Okay?"

"No problem." He glanced at his watch. "I'm going to the studio now. Want to come along?" And without appearing to hurry them, he had them moving quickly down the corridor.

"You know, I haven't missed an episode in twelve years," Marion said.

Burton smiled. "I'm glad you enjoy it. I've only been producing it for seven years, but it's always nice to meet a fan."

"I'm a fan, all right. Although lately that Tiffany has made me so cross," Marion complained as Veronique wheeled her along beside Burton. "Ever since she came out of the institute, she's been a different person. And so mean to poor Reilly. I had hopes they were going to get married."

Burton nudged Veronique aside and took over the wheelchair. "Can you keep a secret?" he asked Marion in a low voice.

"Oh, yes!" Marion's reply was breathless with excitement.

"Tiffany is Reilly's mother."

"No!"

"It's true," he replied. "She's keeping Reilly at a distance because she doesn't want him to find out it was she who stabbed his uncle—who is really his father—with a fondue fork."

Marion gasped. "She murdered Jonathon?"

"Don't you dare tell a soul," he warned. "Or my boss will have my head."

"Cross my heart." Marion pursed her lips tight. "I can keep a secret, can't I, Ronnie?"

Biting her lip, Veronique nodded. Then Burton placed his hand in the small of her back and murmured in her ear, "Can you keep a secret, Mrs. O'Rourke?" Her laughter vanished as a rush of pleasure spiraled through her. She drew away, murmuring something, she hardly knew what.

In the studio Burton parked Marion in a level spot and said goodbye before striding down to the set.

Veronique sat in an aisle seat next to Marion. "So, does he not look like Graham?"

Marion's thin gray brows came together as she appeared to give the question some thought. "Not really. Oh, maybe a little around the nose and the mouth."

"And the eyes and the jaw…" Veronique couldn't believe Marion didn't see it.

"No, not so much the eyes. Possibly you see more of a resemblance than I do. You see…" Marion's voice became soft. "I still think of Graham as he was when he was a little boy."

She peered at Veronique through the semidarkness. "You married him because you think he looks like Graham, didn't you?" she said gently. "Oh, my dear, I know how much you must miss him." Her glance strayed to the set where Burton had gathered the talent for a last-minute pep talk. "I hope for Mr. O'Rourke's sake he'll be able to live up to Graham's memory."

CHAPTER TEN

THE HUMIDITY IN VERONIQUE'S apartment hit Burton like a sauna. She answered the door wearing a saronglike wrap of hot pinks and orange, and a short, tight pink T-shirt that hugged her firm breasts and exposed her navel. Wow. This was not the sort of wife he'd once vaguely imagined having, but he could probably learn to live with her.

"Come in." She clutched a large copper watering can to her chest. Silver earrings tinkling, she slipped away into the apartment before he could recover enough to say hello.

Her apartment was like her, warm and bright, and there was more greenery than in the conservatory at Queen Elizabeth Park. Burton half expected to find a parrot squawking in the foliage, or an outrigger beached near the sofa. Ah, there was a sailboard propped in a corner. *Close.* He glanced around, noting the interesting bits of pottery and carved wood lining the mantelpiece and the framed watercolors decorating the walls. Nice. Very nice.

But none of it was packed and ready for the trip out to Langley.

He glanced at his watch. "Have you got any boxes or suitcases ready? I'll take them down to the car. I thought we could grab a hamburger at a drive-through on our way to the farm."

She stopped pouring water into an asparagus fern that reminded him of a Triffid, and her mouth twisted delicately in disgust. "I do not eat fast food, remember? Relax. I will be a moment only."

Relax. Sure. Like her definition of a moment was the same as his. Even though he'd allowed time for it, getting married had thrown his whole schedule out of whack. "Can I help you with the watering?"

"No, thank you. Sit down. You look tired. We are in no hurry." She moved languidly among her plants to the bluesy warble of a French chanteuse as if she had all the time in the world.

He *was* tired. Chronically tired. But he wanted to get going, get all the awkwardness over with. Yes, it was a platonic marriage, but all afternoon he'd been picturing the two of them, alone in his grandfather's house as husband and wife.... With a start he realized he was staring at her bare midriff. That did it. He'd give her fifteen minutes, then he was packing for her.

Man, it was hot in here. He removed his jacket and pulled his sweater off over his head, wondering if she'd object to him stripping down to his boxers. "Must be a helluva heating bill."

She passed him on her way to the kitchen to refill the watering can. "The landlord pays it," she said over the sound of running water. "For the basement suite to get enough heat, the thermostat must be turned way up, and so the top floor gets very hot. He had a hard time renting the place, but for me, it's perfect." She came back out of the kitchen and glanced around with a sigh. "I am going to miss it. I'm also worried about what to do with my plants. Can we take them to the farm?"

"I'm not sure they'd survive the climatic shift. Do you have a friend you can give them to?"

She bobbed her head back and forth sideways in that funny way he'd come to interpret as "I don't want to talk about it." She said, "I will ask the woman who lives downstairs to water them for me until I can find them a home." She paused in front of him, watering can in hand. "Would you like a drink?"

Burton smiled. "I soaked my roots this morning. Perhaps something cold, in a glass?"

"There is beer in the fridge. Would you like to help yourself while I finish?"

"Sure." He entered the kitchen through an arch in the wall. It was long and narrow and looked as if it had once been part of a much larger room that had been partitioned when the house had been broken up into apartments. "I wouldn't have picked you for a beer drinker," he remarked, about to take two bottles from the top shelf of the fridge. "Can I pour you one?"

"*Non, merci.* I don't drink beer."

Had she bought them for him? Or someone else? Burton put one bottle back and set the other on the counter. He pulled out his notebook and pen and flipped to the page headed Veronique. He wrote: "Doesn't drink beer."

She swished past him, as beautiful and delicately scented as any tropical flower, and set the watering can in the sink. At the sight of his notebook her eyebrows lifted. "Are you writing about me again?"

He folded the notebook and tucked it back in his pocket. "I've got a lot on my mind. If I don't write things down, I forget."

"So when Monsieur Jackson asks you a question during the interview, you will say, excuse me one moment, I must consult my Veronique handbook." She made a comical face and mimicked him flipping through a notepad. "Let's see, is it filed under *D* for drink or is it *B* for beer?" She laughed her throaty laugh.

Burton gazed at her, fascinated by the way the sarong-thing shifted on her hips, creating a shadowed crevice where cloth parted from skin over the hollow of her flat belly. He took a step closer to her.

Her laughter faded to a smile as she cast him a quick, shrewd glance and neatly sidestepped him. "Go and sit in the chair by the fireplace while I will finish watering my plants.''

Burton took his beer and did as commanded. He rubbed a hand along the wooden arm, admiring the smooth, glowing grain and even finish. The chair was obviously old, but the dark purple upholstery covering the seat and back looked new. It was similar to his grandfather's chair except that the legs were straight and not on rockers. ''Nice job on the refinishing, whoever did it.''

''I did,'' Veronique said, turning the apartment into an Amazonian rainforest with a mister.

''Very nice. And these other pieces…?'' He waved his beer bottle, indicating a refinished coffee table and a wooden stool with a puffy fabric top. Nothing matched, but the polished wood and the traces of dark purple that ran through fabric and pottery tied everything together.

''I did them all. Graham called it junk, but they have much character. Better than that awful modern stuff.''

Burton thought of his spare teak furniture he was rarely around long enough to sit on. It was comfortable enough but utilitarian rather than inviting. Not like this. He leaned back in the chair and shut his eyes. He drifted. The bluesy music, the steamy heat, the scent of tropical flowers… His mind conjured up a sultry evening in the French Quarter of New Orleans, a doorway, and leaning in it was an exotically beautiful woman with bewitching green eyes. She spoke and her voice was a purr. ''Do you like French music?''

''Love it,'' he murmured. Without opening his eyes, he lifted his beer to let the icy bitter liquid slide down his throat.

He wanted to reach for her, but his arms were too heavy to move. With a throaty laugh the woman drifted away down the street, her curving backside briefly illuminated by a street lamp before she disappeared into swirling mist….

He slumped further into the chair, hovering between consciousness and sleep in a dreamlike trance, vaguely aware of Veronique moving around the room. At some point the bottle was removed from his hand and placed on the stone hearth. The quiet sound of things being shuffled into boxes and the faint clang of clothes hangers skipped off the surface of his deep relaxation.

He had no idea how long he sat like that, neither awake nor asleep. Eventually he surfaced into consciousness to the aroma of butter and garlic and the sound of something sizzling in a pan. Blinking, he sat up and stretched, yawned, and was instantly alert, more rested than he'd felt in weeks.

Veronique peeked in from the kitchen. "Ah, you are awake now."

"Yes. Are you cooking?" He tried not to sound too hopeful, but the rumbling in his stomach threatened to drown him out.

"Just an omelet. Come and eat."

Just an omelet turned out to be a creamy concoction of eggs and wild mushrooms and some savory green bits that made it into one of the most delectable dishes he'd ever eaten.

"Fabulous," he said, tearing off a chunk of crusty baguette and layering on thick, sweet butter. If he had to marry, he could have done worse than to marry a chef. "What is that herb? I know the taste—I just can't remember the name."

"Tarragon. I grow my own herbs. They are coming with me, so I hope you don't mind."

With a nod of her head, she indicated two big cardboard boxes loaded with potted herbs. Beside them was another box containing copper-bottomed pots and a knife block bristling with deadly culinary weapons. Beside that, a huge, soft-sided suitcase that bulged like a pregnant horse.

He swallowed. All this was supposed to fit in his Tercel—a small car already packed with his gear?

"Uh, sure. Whatever we can't take tonight we'll come back for tomorrow."

"Did you ever find your chess set?" she asked, laying knife and fork across her empty plate.

"No. My mother thinks Granddad may have sold it to pay some insurance premiums."

"What do you think?"

"I don't think he would sell it for anything. But I haven't a clue what could have happened to it." He pushed back from the table. "I'll do the dishes."

"Thank you." Veronique stretched, showing a tantalizing length of rib cage. "I like the cooking, but not the cleanup."

Burton made a mental note to install a dishwasher at the farm. He liked to eat, but also not "zee clean-up." If possible, he'd encourage the one without incurring the hassle of the other.

"Tell me," he said, rinsing a soapy plate under a stream of hot water, "how do you eat like that and stay so thin?"

Veronique shrugged. "I work long hours in hot kitchens. I do the furniture. I windsurf. I am never, how you say, 'lazing about.' But mainly I don't eat a lot—just well." She leaned an elbow on the table and propped her chin on her hand. A tiny smile played around the corners of her mouth. "Aren't you going to write that down?"

"Good idea." Burton drained the water from the sink and, quickly wiping his hands, left the dishes to dry in the rack and pulled out his notebook.

"Non, non, non." Veronique was on her feet and grabbing for a dish towel.

Burton stopped writing. *"Non?* What do you mean, *non?"*

She extracted her expensive chef's knife from the drying rack and brandished it at him. "You wash up in my kitchen, you always, but always, dry the knives immediately."

"It's just a knife..." he started to say, then thought better of it. It was her kitchen, her knife, and the French, he seemed to recall, were known for crimes of passion. "I'll make a note of that."

He started to write, then stopped. "Say, do you have any photograph albums? Pictures of your childhood? Your family? I would remember pictures far more clearly than words."

Veronique slid the knife back into the block of wood. "But of course."

Going to the living room, she pulled out a thick and battered photo album from the bookshelf beside the fireplace and sat on the couch. With no other option, if he was to look and she to explain, Burton sat beside her. They were far enough apart that they didn't need to touch, yet close enough for him to be fully aware of her warmth, the bare skin of her arms and her intoxicating scent.

"What's that perfume you're wearing?"

She cast him a shy smile. "It's not really perfume. It's Monoï, pure coconut oil perfumed with petals of the *tiaré* flower, the gardenia of Tahiti."

"May I?" he asked, and gently lifted her wrist to press his nose to her skin, which was pale and soft on the inner surface. "It's very nice," he said, feeling a little faint. Before he knew what he was doing, he brushed his face along her inner arm to the hollow of her elbow, touching his lips to her skin for one shuddering second. It was more than wanting to kiss her—he wanted to inhale her.

"You're tickling me." She laughed, a nervous sound, and took her arm back. Yet when he looked up, she was staring at him, eyes dark green and intent.

She glanced quickly back at the photo album. "This is in Algérie with my sisters," she said, pointing at a faded photograph. "I was four and a half."

He squinted down at the album. "Is that a parrot on your head?"

She laughed. "They are peacock feathers we found on the lawn of the French Embassy. We played dress-up while the grown-ups had a garden party." She turned the page. "Here are my mother and father."

"Your mother looks like she enjoys a laugh, though I couldn't say the same about your father. Is he as forbidding as he looks?"

"He is a good man, but sometimes he wears his *képi*, his policeman's hat, at home, as well as at work. We were scared of him when we were little. Now we tease him and don't let him take himself too seriously."

She turned to the next set of photos, and a look of bittersweet nostalgia that might have been mistaken for physical pain crossed her face. "That was my home in Tahiti. Look at the bougainvillea," she said, pointing to a profusion of scarlet-and-fuchsia-colored flowers massed along a low stone wall. "That is me on my Vespa. I must have been on my way to work at the resort on the other side of the island. And there is Moustache, my little cat. Ghislaine has him now."

"Moustache," he repeated. "Is that…mustache?"

She beamed. "That's right. See his long whiskers? But you must be *exactement* with the pronunciation. Moostash." Her lips pushed outward, making a kiss out of the word, then retreated, causing him to ask her to repeat it. "Moos-tash," she obliged.

"Teach me to speak French," he said, enthralled.

"*Non*. What for?"

"I mean it. I know the basics everyone learns in school, but I've always wanted to be able to converse in French."

"Yes?" She was still skeptical.

"Yes," he said. "Please?"

She gave a little shrug. "Okay."

Burton went back to poring over the photographs. He

actually wanted to speak French, she marveled. She was thrilled by his absorption in her island—and reluctant to believe in it. How much of his interest had to do with getting past Immigration?

"What do you do for entertainment?" he asked. "Are there theaters, nightclubs?"

"Papeete has all sorts of modern entertainment. But mostly we come together with friends and cook a big feast. Maybe one of the guys go to the wharf and buy a fish freshly caught, and we prepare it with some nice sauce. We drink a little, we talk a lot. We have a good time. The night breeze is so soft and warm we sit outside. Someone have a guitar…"

She broke off with a shrug. How could she convey the feeling of life in Tahiti to someone who thought a freezing-cold rain shower was refreshing?

"I went to Bali once for a little R and R after covering the war in East Timor," he said, stretching an arm along the back of the couch. "No telephones, no computers, no hurry, no worry. If Tahiti is even half as nice, you're lucky to be going back there. The French love of food and culture and the island way of life—what a great combination."

He didn't sound like Graham, Veronique thought, aware of the gentle touch of his hand in her hair. He wasn't scornful, skeptical or disparaging of her language and culture. Cautiously she glanced sideways at him. At that moment he hardly even looked like Graham. At least, he did look like Graham on the surface, but she seemed now to be seeing past the familiar features to something deeper. It was so confusing. Confusing, too, were the threads of desire weaving themselves into the erotic tapestry his fingertips made as they lightly stroked the nape of her neck….

"Maybe I'll come for a visit sometime," he continued. "Would you show me around?"

Veronique went very still, remembering. *Maybe you*

could show me around, Graham had said after complimenting her on the *poisson cru.* Now she bobbed her head
sideways. *"Peut-être."* Maybe.

She turned another page, and instinctively flinched.
Burton's fingers tightened on his side of the album. Graham's tanned face gazed up from every photo.

There was a close-up of him smiling at her over lunch
at the resort. Graham coming from the water, snorkel gear
in hand. She and Graham on the beach at Venus Point, his
arms wrapped around her while she gazed adoringly into
his face. It hurt, that one, because they looked so very
much in love. Ten months later she'd cut up her wedding
dress for kitchen rags.

"You can see the resemblance?" she asked. Marion
might not think Burton and Graham looked alike, but Veronique would dare any stranger to tell them apart.

"Yes, it's uncanny. Spooky, even." He stroked back a
lock of hair from her cheek, exposing her face. "Are you
all right?" he asked, so gently she almost wept.

She shrugged, wishing she could go back to that time
when love was simple and desire an emotion she welcomed. Burton's other arm was around her shoulders now,
pulling her toward him.

"I know it hurts," he said, "but don't be sad."

And then his lips were coming closer to hers, his blue
eyes familiar yet newly dazzling…. God help her, she
wanted to kiss him. At the last second, Graham's face su-
perimposed itself over Burton's. She turned away, gasping
for breath. *Oh la la.* Just who had she been about to kiss?

"Veronique?"

She picked at the edges of the plastic sheets holding the
photos in place. "Just because we are married doesn't
mean we are husband and wife."

"I know." Rebuffed, his voice was no longer gentle.

Veronique made a move to replace the album in the
bookshelf.

"Wait. We can use those photos of you and Graham," he said, still in that hard voice she'd never heard before. "It'll look to Immigration as though we've known each other longer than we have."

"Non!" She clung to the album, appalled. It was bad enough marrying a stranger who resembled her hated late husband. It would be quite impossible to look at the past and smile.

He eased it from her grasp. "I know you're not over him," he said, compassion softening his voice. "Maybe you never will be. But think of Marion."

Knuckles clenched in front of her tightened mouth, she watched as he tore back the sticky pages and peeled off photo after photo of her and Graham. Oddly enough, it seemed to pain Burton, too, for two sharp lines had appeared between his eyes.

Burton grimly completed his task, feeling like the biggest jerk who'd ever lived for what this was doing to Veronique. He didn't know why the hell it should hurt him so much. Ego, he guessed. When he was done, he offered Veronique the loose photos for safekeeping, but with a burst of fresh tears, she pushed them away. Frowning, he tucked the photos into his breast pocket and carried his rival's image like a ghostly doppelgänger next to his heart.

VERONIQUE OPENED HER EYES and, for a moment, didn't know where she was. In the center of the white-painted plank ceiling squatted a pearly pink glass light fixture that seemed to double as a fly trap. Ah, the farmhouse.

She put on blue jeans and thick socks, a turtlenecked shirt and Marion's big ivory sweater, and went out to the kitchen. She made herself coffee and toast, and sat down in the upholstered wooden rocker. It would be very nice sanded down and oiled, she thought, chipping at the peeling varnish with her thumbnail.

Burton came in, buttoning the sleeves of his tan corduroy shirt, his coppery hair wet and gleaming. "Good mor—" He stopped short.

"*Bonjour,*" she corrected him, then noticed the odd expression on his face. "What is it?"

He gave his head a little shake and moved toward the counter and the coffeepot. "That was my grandfather's chair."

She sprang out of it. "You don't like me sitting there."

"No, it's okay. It's just…when I saw you there, it reminded me that now we're living here and he's gone."

She went to stand on top of the heating vent beneath the window to warm her feet. "You sit there. It's your chair now."

His chair. His farm. He realized suddenly the source of his ambivalence. He wanted the farm, but he wanted it the way it was when he was a child—worry free. He didn't want the responsibility of hundreds of bushels of seed potatoes waiting to be planted, later to be harvested. If he sat in Granddad's chair, he had to walk in Granddad's shoes and ride Granddad's tractor….

The phone rang.

He walked over to where it hung on the wall and picked up the receiver. "Hello?"

"Burton? Don Chetwynd here. Glad I caught you. Listen, I've got a couple of young fellas in my office right now, brothers they are, who're looking to buy a parcel of land in your area."

"I told you I'm not ready to—"

"Sell. I know, but just hear me out. These boys are just starting out, pooling their resources to buy some land. Their daddy's got a farm over near Chilliwack, but there are four sons and they all want to farm."

"Look, Mr. Chetwynd—"

"I've told them you're not ready to vacate, and they're willing to let you stay in the house till the end of the year, just so long as they can start working the land. Now, do yourself a favor and think about it. I can bring 'em by for a look any time you say. No obligation. I'm not trying to pressure you, but you don't know when you'll get another offer like this.''

''They haven't made an offer.''

''I'm betting my bottom dollar that once they see your property, they're going to make you that offer. Whaddaya say? Shall I bring 'em by?''

It seemed the perfect solution. Granddad's place would remain a farm, and he could go back to doing what he did best with a clear conscience. But in spite of what Chetwynd said, Burton did feel pressured. ''I'll have to think about it and call you back.''

Hanging up, he took a cup from the cupboard and poured himself a coffee. Veronique had returned to the table to sit on a straight-backed chair with her knees tucked up to her chest. Her hands were wrapped around her steaming cup, and her face held a mildly questioning expression.

''That was the real-estate agent,'' he said. ''He's got an interested buyer. Farmers.''

''But you haven't found the chess set.''

''That's why I put him off.'' Burton spread jam on a piece of toast and walked over to the window. The orchard which his grandparents had planted nearly fifty years ago would be spared the ax. Yet even selling to farmers was hard to accept. Was he just hanging on to childhood memories? Was he having trouble letting go of the last link to Granddad? The path toward the future suddenly seemed muddy and indistinct. What if he took a wrong turn and there was no way back? He hated this feeling of weakness and indecision. He needed to do something.

He took his cup to the sink and brushed the crumbs from his hands. ''I'm going to fix the front steps,'' he said. ''Make yourself at home. Do whatever.''

She uncurled her legs and tipped her cup to drain the

last of her coffee. "Would you like me to help? I can use a hammer and a saw."

Frowning, he shook his head and started to leave the room. "This is something I need to do myself."

"Burton?"

He paused at the doorway and looked back.

"Do not be too hard on yourself. You will make the right decision in the end."

He nodded, oddly touched by her confidence. And grateful that although she thought he was wrong, she didn't feel the need to keep telling him so.

Granddad's tool chest was in the barn, along with the ten-foot length of two-by-six lumber with which he'd intended to replace the broken step. Burton had stored it in here after the ambulance had taken Granddad away. Now he hoisted it to his waist. It was awkward and unwieldy, but not that heavy. Not for a man who'd spent his life doing physical labor. Maybe the doctor was right, and Granddad's heart attack was a fluke of timing. It was a consoling thought, even if it didn't help Granddad.

Burton carried it back across the yard and around to the front of the house, visualizing Granddad making the same short journey. Had he staggered the last few steps? Had he felt a stab of pain in his heart as he fell? What were his thoughts in those final seconds? If Burton had turned up half an hour earlier, could he have been saved?

He dropped the length of wood to the ground with a thud, flattening the grass beside the path. Then he set to work prising the nails out of the broken board to lift it off and make way for the new. He'd measured and cut the new piece of wood and was setting it in place when Veronique came out the front door, her backpack slung over her shoulder, the umbrella he'd given her in hand.

"I'm going to walk down to the farmer's market we passed last night to get some things for dinner," she said, pausing at the step above the one he was working on.

Burton pushed the hair off his forehead. "Take the car if you want."

"Thanks, but I like to walk. Guess what? I found five new eggs in the henhouse. And one of the hens is nesting. I wonder who has been feeding them."

"The Vandermeres, our neighbors to the east," he said. "I really should get over there to thank them and let them know we're here."

"I also found a few vegetables out back. Someone had a garden there between the orchard and the house."

He straightened and went to rummage through the toolbox for a level. "My grandmother. She grew everything under the sun. Canned most of it, too."

"The soil is good," Veronique said. "It wouldn't take much work to make again the garden. Tomatoes would grow well by the side fence. And there is room for lettuce and peas...."

Her excitement seemed to check midsentence. "Well, I better not get carried away."

Burton could see what she was thinking—whatever she planted she wouldn't be around to harvest. Nor would he. The seed potatoes weighed on his conscience.

She stepped over the loose board to the bottom step, and down to the ground. "For dinner I am thinking perhaps some asparagus with hollandaise sauce to start, followed by chicken grilled à la diable. Accompanied by the baby potatoes roasted with rosemary and garlic."

Burton squinted at the liquid-enclosed bubble floating dead-center in the level atop the new board. "Sounds great," he said, beginning to salivate. "You know, you don't have to cook...." He broke off at the hurt look on her face.

"I love to cook," she said, "especially in a real country kitchen. But it's no fun cooking for just myself..."

"I guarantee I'll be appreciative."

"You better," she teased, bopping him lightly with the

umbrella as she turned to leave. "Or next time you get tuna casserole."

THE MARKET OFFERED less choice in imported fruits and vegetables than the city, but the produce was as fresh as if it had come out of the field that morning. There was also a small butcher-cum-deli where she picked out a plump chicken. On impulse, she bought some packets of seeds and a tray of marigold seedlings to plant beside the front door.

Her laden backpack was starting to feel heavy by the time she turned into the driveway. Behind her, a horn beeped and a white pickup truck rolled to a stop, its motor idling. A woman of about her own age with an open, friendly face and short dark hair escaping from a ponytail poked her head out the window. "Hop in. I'll take you up to the house."

"Merci." Veronique laid the seedlings on the floor of the truck, hoisted her backpack onto the seat and climbed in. "Are you—"

"Jill Vandermere, from next door. I was coming over to feed the chickens." She put the truck back in gear and started up the hill.

"So it is you we have to thank for taking care of them. I am Veronique. I am…staying here with Burton for a while."

"Great. It'll be nice having another woman my own age close by. We can always use new blood around here."

Veronique's eyebrows rose. "New blood?"

Jill laughed. "It's just an expression."

"New blood. That's good," she said, smiling. "I collect expressions."

Jill's brown gaze strayed to Veronique's wedding ring. "Are you and Burton married?"

"Sort of."

Grinning, Jill shook her head. "I didn't know there was

such a thing as 'sort of' when it came to marriage. You're either in it or you're not. I'm married to Rick, Hank and Mary's son. It's their farm, but we're gradually taking it over. We'd like to expand, but—'' she shrugged ''—it's hard to find land close by.'' She glanced down at the seedlings. ''I see you're planting flowers. You're welcome to come over and take cuttings any time. We've got a huge garden.''

Veronique smiled at her and at the serendipity of their instant rapport, knowing even without further words they would have things in common. There could be details and confidences exchanged…if. Always the *if*. She thought of the seed packets tucked in her backpack and felt unaccountably sad by what could and could not be allowed to grow. ''Thank you,'' she said, ''but I probably won't be here very long.''

When they arrived at the house. Burton was nowhere in sight. But as Veronique got out and set the marigolds beside the newly repaired step, she heard the sound of hammering coming from the barn. More repairs. She admired the fact that he did the jobs around the farm himself. Many men would have disdained dirtying their hands or simply not known how to use the tools. His grandfather had taught him well.

She went back to the truck where Jill waited, the engine running. ''Would you like to come in for coffee?''

''Thanks, I'd love to another time. But if you don't need me, I'd better get back and help Rick and his dad finish planting the potatoes while the weather's clear. They say more rain is on the way. Oh, by the way, tell Burton we'll bring back the…''

She broke off as a pale blue Volvo came up the drive and parked beside the truck.

Another neighbor? Veronique wondered. The real-estate

agent with someone to view the property? The car door opened, and a tall, dark-haired woman holding a brown paper bag emerged.

Zut alors. It was Burton's mother.

CHAPTER ELEVEN

CATHERINE O'ROURKE WORE a cherry red linen dress, the simple lines of which accented the smooth sweep of her shoulder-length dark hair and elegant gold jewelry. She had style, Veronique gave her that. And from the size of her smile, she clearly intended to be a good mother-in-law.

Veronique said *au revoir* to Jill and, as the truck rumbled back down the hill, went to greet Catherine. *"Bonjour,"* she called cheerfully, equally determined that discord not originate with her.

"Hello, Veronique."

Veronique's eyebrows lifted. This mother-in-law actually pronounced her name correctly. She felt Catherine's bright blue gaze, disconcertingly like Burton's, inspecting her. "Burton is in the barn," she said, hoping she'd want to see him right away.

But Catherine proceeded to the steps, pausing to test the new board with one black patent pump before continuing on into the house. "I'll wait for him to finish. I know how he hates to be disturbed when he's working. Here, I brought you a little housewarming gift."

"How thoughtful…" Her voice trailed away. The bag contained something heavy, solid and still warm. She heard the clink of a lid against its base and caught a faint but distinctive aroma.

"Tuna casserole," Catherine said with a bright smile. "Burton's favorite. I know you must be too busy to cook."

"Merci bien," she murmured, forcing a smile in return.

She was never too busy to cook. But she stepped back so Catherine could precede her down the hallway and into the kitchen.

At the counter, she slid the casserole out of the bag onto a hot mat and gave a little gasp of surprise. The dish was not Pyrex but pottery, the glaze a medley of natural greens with dark brown accents. She turned to Catherine, her smile genuine. "It is beautiful."

Catherine waved a hand. "One of the ladies in my book club makes them. After all, you missed out on wedding presents."

Her tone was faintly accusatory, as though Veronique had caused her own misfortune. Who did Catherine imagine would keep the casserole dish when the marriage was over? Veronique wondered. Her son, whose idea of a good dinner was dinner out? Or Veronique, who would soon be shedding belongings in preparation for departure? Still, it was a nice thought. Maybe. She cast a sideways glance at her new mother-in-law. She wasn't quite sure about Catherine.

"You will stay to dinner, of course?" Veronique picked up an oven mitt and lifted the lid by the cluster of acorns that formed the handle. On top of the casserole was a layer of…crushed potato chips? *Mon Dieu.* Quickly, she put the lid back on.

"Oh, I wouldn't like to intrude…." Catherine said, moving toward the sink.

"*Non,* I insist. You will stay for dinner." If for no other reason than to help them eat this…this… Veronique switched on the oven, placed the casserole inside, then turned to Catherine. "Would you like a glass of wine?"

Catherine was filling the kettle. Faint color rose in her cheeks, matching her dress. "Oh, I'm sorry," she said. "I grew up in this house. I guess I haven't adjusted to it not being my home anymore."

Her sigh was just loud enough to be heard, yet not so

loud as to sound complaining. *Formidable*. "But of course it is your home," Veronique said. "It certainly is not mine, though I like it very much." She threw down her oven mitts and faced Catherine squarely. "I know you are worried about Burton, but I am not the problem."

Catherine looked taken aback. "Well, I know he's upset about the chess set and his documentary. But if I may speak frankly, I don't feel this is the best time for him to take on a wife, especially one who's not in love with him."

"He does not love me, either." Surprisingly it hurt a little to say that. "We have the understanding. I do like him, and I wish him well. That is why you must talk to him, convince him that even after he finds the chess set, he should not sell the farm."

Catherine laughed shortly. "Burton would never sell the farm."

"The real-estate man called this morning to say someone is interested in buying. Burton is thinking about letting them come and look."

Catherine's face went pale. She reached for a chair.

"You did not know?" Catherine shook her head. Veronique threw up her hands and burst into an impassioned tirade in French about *les hommes*. While she ranted, she got out a glass tumbler and a bottle of cognac, and poured Catherine a stiff drink.

Catherine took a big sip. Coughed, blinked and gave her head a rapid shake. "That's better, thank you. I agree men can be pigs, but I rather object to being the mother of a swine."

Heat rose in Veronique's cheeks. "You understood?"

"*Oui*." A faint smile appeared on Catherine's face. "I majored in languages at university," she continued in French. "And did a year as an exchange student in Paris. I'm a bit rusty."

Rusty, perhaps, but it was music to Veronique's ears. She pulled up a chair and poured herself a small cognac.

"You speak very well," she said in French. "I can't believe Burton didn't tell you he was thinking of selling the farm."

"He talked about the impracticality of living here, and how he didn't like the idea of renting, but I didn't ever think he'd seriously consider selling. But you say he's had an offer?"

Veronique shook her head. "It hasn't gone that far yet. All he said was some farmers were interested in looking at it."

"If he sells to anyone it will be to a farmer." Catherine's manicured fingernails tapped the table in little clicks of frustration. "I'd hoped he would marry and have children and raise them out here on the farm." She sighed. "I'm not wrong to want that, am I?"

"No," Veronique said slowly, "but perhaps that is not his dream."

Catherine snorted. "Burton dreams in Technicolor, with his finger on the fast-forward button."

Veronique laughed. Her eyes met Catherine's and the other woman gave her a warm smile, the first genuine smile since they'd met.

Catherine reached for her hand and gave her fingers a squeeze. "Slow him down, Veronique," she said, her voice suddenly urgent. "Slow him down long enough for him to find out what his dream really is."

Veronique's smile disappeared. "We are husband and wife on paper only. I cannot influence him."

"I think you can. I've seen the way he looks at you." She paused. "His father died of a heart attack when he was fifty-five. Burton's not like Tom—he doesn't drink much or smoke, and he doesn't overeat—but he pushes himself too hard. Maybe I'm just being a typical mother, but I worry about him."

Veronique tugged at a lock of hair. She and Burton would have to be far more intimate than they were, or were likely to be, for her to affect his future. Such intimacy was impossible for her, and possibly damaging for him, if what Catherine said about the way he regarded her was true.

"You could persuade him better than I—" She broke off, hearing his footsteps outside on the porch. Already she recognized his walk.

"Speak of the devil," Catherine said wryly, reverting to English. "Burton hasn't listened to his mother since he was a teenager."

"I heard that," Burton said, coming down the hall into the kitchen. Two pairs of curious female eyes turned at his entrance. He stopped short at the unlikely sight of his mother and Veronique gossiping over a drink. Suddenly wary, he fought the impulse to hightail it back to the barn.

"You were supposed to. Because it's true, isn't it, Burton?" His mother's voice held an undercurrent he couldn't place.

He laughed the fatalistic laugh of the doomed. "I refuse to answer on the grounds it might incriminate me." He went to the sink and washed his hands. Drying them on the towel, he sniffed the air. "What's that?" he said, glancing at Veronique. "I thought you were making some fancy—"

Her warning glare cut him off. "Your mother very kindly brought your favorite dish."

Funny, it didn't smell like grilled chicken with French mustard, the latest in a string of new favorite dishes, each a product of Veronique's mastery in the kitchen and worth pulling rank over the camera crew for.

No, it smelled like...tuna casserole. His favorite, all right. When he'd been ten years old. "Thank you, Mother. You really didn't have to."

"It was meant as a housewarming gift, but apparently that's not exactly in order." Catherine twisted her nearly empty cognac glass. "Why didn't you tell me you'd taken steps toward selling the farm?"

Burton glanced at Veronique. For once she met his gaze head on, transmitting waves of courage and support. It was only for an instant, and then she disappeared out the back door with a murmured comment about picking something or other.

He got a beer from the fridge and sat in the chair Veronique had vacated. She'd abandoned him to his mother's reproach, but it didn't matter. They'd just exchanged their first ever silent communication.

"I kept hoping I'd come up with another solution," he said, twisting off the cap, "but there are only so many options."

"You could have talked to me about it," Catherine replied, sounding hurt. "You don't have to take the whole burden on yourself."

"I was going to that night we were out here, but I thought you had enough to worry about. Or maybe I just knew you'd be unhappy about it and I didn't want you to try and talk me out of it." Before she could do so now, he went on. "I think I've figured out what Granddad sold to pay the insurance premium on his death taxes."

"Oh?"

"The pick-planter."

Catherine looked taken aback. "The machine he used to plant potatoes? It's gone, too?"

"Yep. I knew something was missing from the barn the first day I came out here after he died, I just couldn't put my finger on it."

"He sold the pick-planter when he had a barn full of seed potatoes and a crop to put in," Catherine said slowly. She slapped her hand down on the table. "That just shows you how much he wanted to hang on to the farm. Don't let him down by selling out."

Guilt propelled Burton to his feet, and his chair scraped backward against the lino. He paced across the room to grip the side of the window frame. Outside, in the remnants of Gram's garden, Veronique was picking something and putting it into her wicker basket. "For God's sake, Mother, I'm not a farmer and I have no intention of becoming one."

"I wasn't suggesting that. But you could still live here."

"It's too far from my work."

"Maybe you work too much." She held up a hand. "Okay, I won't start on that. But you could always rent it out."

"And have to deal with strangers living here? People who might wreck the place?" He rubbed his temples, feeling the beginnings of a tension headache.

"There'll be strangers living here if you sell," she replied sharply.

"Drop it, Mother. We've had this argument before."

"All I can say is, your granddad was lucky he didn't live to see you disappoint him."

He shot her an angry glance and she covered her face with her hands. "I'm sorry, Burtie. That was an awful thing to say."

"I didn't know this place was so important to you," he said stiffly.

"It's not for myself," she replied, wiping her wet eyes with her fingers, "But for you and your children. If you ever have any, that is."

"Definitely don't start on that, Mother. If it makes you feel any better, I'm not selling until I find that chess set. And at my present rate of success that could be well into the next century."

The back door creaked and Veronique came in through the laundry room, her basket filled with delicate green stalks.

"Oh, you found the asparagus bed!" Catherine exclaimed, getting up to look. "I can't believe it's still going. My mother and I planted that together over ten years ago."

"It needs some thinning and some weeding, but it grows

beautifully,'' Veronique said, holding up a stalk and pretending not to see Catherine's red-rimmed eyes. "Asparagus with lemon butter will go nicely with tuna casserole, *non?*''

"Perfect,'' Catherine said.

"Perfect,'' Burton echoed, thinking longingly of hollandaise sauce and poulet à la diable.

DUSK WAS FALLING when they stepped onto the front porch to wave Catherine off. Veronique hung back, but Catherine came up and gave her a hug. "*Bon chance,* my dear,'' she whispered.

Veronique saw her own emotions reflected in Catherine's clouded blue eyes—confusion, worry and hope. "*Merci.* Good luck to you, too.''

Catherine turned to Burton and he gathered her into a hug. "Oh, Burtie,'' she said, "I know it's a dilemma. But please, don't be afraid to talk it over with me.''

"I won't,'' he said gruffly. "As long as you remember it's my decision.'' With one last squeeze, he released her.

Catherine started down the steps. When she reached the one Burton had repaired, she glanced at it, then at Burton. As Veronique watched, an odd look passed between them, a baffling exchange of some deep emotion. She glanced away, unwilling to intrude, but curious to know more about this family she'd married into. The more she learned about Burton, the more she liked and admired him. He'd not only eaten his mother's tuna casserole without a grimace—an action as courageous as it was caring—but even when Catherine had gone out of the room briefly, he hadn't betrayed her by expressing his true feelings. Feelings that were obvious to Veronique after witnessing the gusto with which he devoured her meals.

Veronique and Burton watched in silence as Catherine's car disappeared down the gravel drive.

The clouds had disappeared, leaving the pearly sky

streaked with salmon and aqua. Shadows stretched across the grass, but the air was balmy and softly scented. The perfect summer evening beckoned.

"I guess I'll go look in the cellar for the chess set," Burton said, but he made no move to leave. He turned to Veronique and in the dusky twilight his eyes were a deep blue.

A shivery anticipation raised gooseflesh along her arms. This…attraction she felt for Burton didn't mesh with her plans. She was falling for him when she should be keeping her distance.

Yet she was loathe to part with his company. "What is it about that step?" she asked, gesturing to the bottom plank.

Burton jammed his hands into his back pockets, and his gaze swept past her, across the farmyard and up the green slope behind the barn. His shirt flattened against his chest as he sucked in the soft evening air. At last he said, "My grandfather had a heart attack while repairing it."

"But—"

"I was supposed to be helping him, but I was too busy." His voice was bitter with regret.

She could see it was eating him up inside.

"And you think it is your fault he's dead." She kept her tone flat, used deliberately stark words.

"No! Okay, I did at first," he admitted. "But when you put it like that…well, it's nonsense." He sighed. "I just wish we'd had time to talk about some things."

She placed a hand on his forearm, feeling the texture of the dark hairs laid over his skin and the muscle underneath. It was the first time she'd voluntarily touched him. "It is natural to wish for more time."

"I guess you know what it's like to miss someone." His gaze, responsive, flicked down to her hand before meeting her eyes.

"Don't go into the cold, dark basement on such a beautiful evening,'' she implored. ''Stay. Enjoy the sunset with me.''

Her words brought a warm, glad smile to his lips. He moved closer, till she was sure he was going to take her in his arms. Wanting, yet fearful, she held her breath, a wave of anticipation thrilling through her.

Then, inexplicably, he backed away. His hands dropped to his sides and his fingers curled into his palms. ''Don't tempt me,'' he said with a short laugh. ''It's hard enough—'' He cut it short and abruptly turned on his heel.

The screen door banged shut behind him.

Veronique put a hand to her forehead, feeling the adrenaline subside, cooled by his curt reaction. What was happening to her? When had she started craving his touch? Part of her longed to run after him. She took a step toward the front door, then stopped herself. If he was strong, she could be, too. This temporary marriage, this situation, would only work if they didn't let their attraction grow.

Keeping busy would help.

She found Burton in the laundry room putting new batteries in a flashlight. The door leading down to the basement was open.

Veronique hovered on the kitchen side of the doorway. ''Do you have sandpaper?''

''Sure, what for?'' He didn't look at her, just clicked the battered steel flashlight on and off, testing the light.

''If you don't mind, I would like to refinish your grandfather's chair. I think it is oak underneath.''

''You'd be wasting your time,'' he said shortly. ''Everything will go when I sell the farm.''

''You might be foolish enough to let this farm go,'' she said gently, ''but you will never get rid of your grandfather's chair.''

He smiled and shook his head. ''Okay, you got me there. But you don't have to do this. It's too much.''

She shrugged. "I enjoy the work. It gives me satisfaction to restore something to beauty and usefulness."

"Go ahead, then," he said. "Just don't give me any more lectures about working too hard."

They laughed together, and although she felt a pang of loss for what hadn't happened, Veronique was relieved she and Burton were still friends.

The big hand on the clock over the stove moved slowly around to the next hour while she sanded down the chair arms to a pale, wide-grained wood. Outside the kitchen window, night fell. The house was quiet and peaceful, but for the rasp of sandpaper on wood and the faint sounds of Burton moving around in the basement.

When she'd finished the arms, she rose, stretched and made herself a cup of tea. Sipping it, she studied the chair. To sand the base properly she'd have to take off the seat cover. She had an idea the springs needed replacing, anyway, so hard was the seat. Setting her cup on the table, she grasped the chair at the top of the rockers and turned it over. Oof, it was heavy.

Using a pair of pliers and a hammer, she pulled out the upholstery tacks that held the worn fabric in place. They came away easily, and she noticed curiously that there were sets of tack holes in the wood; apparently the cover had been pulled off and replaced sometime in the past.

The last tack came out and she popped it into a glass jar with the others. Righting the chair, she peeled off the old fabric. Underneath lay a thick layer of foam padding, which she lifted off so she could get at the springs.

Mon Dieu! What was this? She let the square of foam drop to the floor and leaned over to lift a large wooden box from inside the base of the chair. It was heavy and old, with squares of light and dark wood inlaid in an alternating pattern. It rattled when she picked it up. The chess set. Her heart beating fast, she fumbled to undo the metal latch at the side.

Veronique picked up one of the large, elaborately carved chessmen and slowly turned it in her fingers. They were very beautiful, definitely old, and it was quite believable that Burton's grandfather, or anyone, could have sold them for a lot of money. Burton would be so happy to have them back. He would...

She gripped the black knight so hard the tip of his lance bit into her palm. He would sell the farm.

Her first instinct had been to run to the top of the basement stairs and shout out the good news. Now she went very still and thought of a mother's plea for her son. She agreed with Catherine that the farm was good for Burton. If only he lived here a little longer, she was sure he would decide to keep it, whatever the cost.

It wasn't her decision to make, a little voice told her.

In the end, she argued with herself, he would have the chess set *and* the farm.

Not daring to let herself think any further about what she was doing, she placed the knight back in the box and relatched the lid. Silently she tiptoed out of the kitchen, the box clutched to her chest to stop it from rattling.

She was halfway down the hall when she heard his footsteps coming up from the basement.

For a moment she couldn't move. Then with a burst of energy, she ran the rest of the way to her bedroom. Swiftly she opened the cupboard and shoved the chess set into her empty suitcase, then threw some dirty clothes on top. She stood back, breathing hard and telling herself it was for his own good.

She had other reasons, vaguely formulated, that had nothing to do with Burton's needs and everything to do with her own. Perhaps she was projecting on him her own longing for a place to belong. She didn't want to think about it too deeply. She only knew she wasn't ready for Burton to sell the farm.

Burton came into the kitchen and saw Granddad's

disassembled chair spread over the floor. He went through to the hallway, brushing cobwebs off his shoulders. "Veronique?"

She came out of her room, shutting the door behind her. Her face was pale and she licked her lips nervously. *"Oui?"*

"Is something wrong?" he asked.

"Non, what could be wrong?" She walked past him back into the kitchen, took her place in front of the chair and started to sand the base around the tack holes. Without looking up, she said, "You did not find the chess set?" Her voice was curiously flat, making it more a statement than a question.

"I found cobwebs and dust and a lifetime of stored junk, but no chess set." He noticed the worn and discarded upholstery fabric tossed to one side. "My grandmother kept fabric remnants in the cedar chest in the dining room. You could probably find something in there to recover the seat."

She nodded and kept on sanding, scraping away the varnish in large sweeps of the gritty paper.

Burton leaned back in his chair and tried to cast an objective glance around the room. Maybe he should paint the walls and replace the lino with something more modern. On the other hand, whoever bought the place would want to choose their own color scheme and floor coverings. It was the land that was worth something, not the house. Not to anyone but him and his mother, anyway. And, it seemed, curiously enough, to Veronique.

"We should talk some more about the interview with Immigration," he said.

"You want some more facts about me?"

"No, this time I want to know how you think."

She glanced up, almost, but not quite, looking him in the eye. "Do you mean like, what do I think of the Middle

East situation, or do you mean, if I had to come back as another animal, what would I choose?"

He smiled. "I was thinking of something closer to home, such as…oh, why is it you don't like the rain?"

She laughed huskily. "You have to ask? Because it is cold and wet. I get the cold and the sneezing. All the time."

"Viruses cause colds, not the weather. Once you adapt to the different bugs here, you'll get fewer colds."

She tossed away the worn piece of sandpaper and sent him a skeptical sideways glance. "I do not intend to adapt to your bugs. Anyway, it's not just the rain, it is the constant threat of rain."

"It must rain in Tahiti."

"Yes, but it's a warm rain," she said, taking up a new piece of sandpaper. "In Tahiti, everything you touch is warm. The sand, the trees, the buildings."

"It does sound nice. Is there anything you like about Vancouver?"

"Oh, yes. The mountains, the cherry trees that line the streets in spring, so pink and fluffy and sweet-smelling. And the air is very fresh and energy-giving." She started to scrape again. One leg of the chair was bared to the pale gold wood beneath.

"What would you like to come back as?"

"A seabird," she said without hesitation. "One that could fly all the way to the South Pacific."

He had to ask. "I'd come back as a horse."

"Why a horse?"

"Granddad used to keep a couple of Arabian horses. He taught me to ride, and whenever I came to visit I'd take off for hours of cantering along the road or through the fields. It was great."

Veronique turned the chair and started another leg. "And you think the horse shares your enthusiasm for running all day?'' she said humorously. ''What you really want is to relive your boyhood.''

He thought about that for a moment. ''I think,'' he said slowly, ''that what I'd like is to take the best bits of my boyhood and incorporate them into my adult life. Do you think that's possible?''

''I think they are already there, in your memory and in your imagination. It is what you choose to do with them that counts.''

He saw where this was leading, right back to his plans for the farm. Rising, he strode across the room. ''Maybe we should concentrate on our recent history. We'll have to show Immigration it's plausible for us to have fallen in love.''

''How do we do that when we are not always at ease with each other?'' she murmured.

''You're right, we have to deal with that. We need to do something physical together, to be comfortable touching without one of us jumping out of our skin.'' He thought for a moment. ''I've got it.'' Striding back to where she was sitting, he took the sandpaper from her hands and pulled her to her feet.

Alarm leaped to her eyes. ''What are you doing?''

''It's an exercise I learned in a management course.'' He led her to the middle of the living-room floor, then turned her so she was facing away from him. Beneath his hands, her shoulders trembled. With the interview less than a week away, it underscored just how far they had to go.

He stepped back a pace. ''When I count to three, I want you to fall backward, arms at your sides, as though you were falling into a swimming pool or onto a bed. I'll catch you.''

''But—'' Her head swiveled around, eyes wide.

''Marriage is based on trust. I'll catch you.''

''Trust,'' she repeated, sounding agonized. ''I will try.''

She clenched her fists, then unclenched them. Started to fall, then caught herself, tottering a little.

"Come on. You can do it. I'm right behind you."

"That's what I'm afraid of," she muttered.

"One, two, thr—"

"*Attention!*" she cried, and fell backward, straight as a ramrod.

Burton caught her easily, his arms tightening around her waist. Through her silk sweater he could feel the warmth of her body, and the soft fabric slid sensuously beneath his fingers. Her head fell back on his shoulder, sending the scent of her hair into his nostrils and directly to his brain. He'd barely managed to resist kissing her earlier. Now that she was in his arms...

"Let me up!" she cried.

Reluctantly he set her back on her feet. "Are you okay?" he asked, wishing he could remember an exercise for establishing and maintaining eye contact.

"Yes," she said, her cheeks pink. "Do you do this with Ernie?"

"Ernie doesn't have a problem trusting me. He almost hero-worships me."

"Sometimes you are too much making the joke with him," she scolded gently. "He is sensitive."

"He can take it." Burton turned his back to her. "Now, you catch me."

"*Mon Dieu!* You are so tall. But I will try."

"Maybe this isn't such a good idea," he said, starting to have second thoughts. "You are a lot smaller than me."

She braced one foot in back of the other and held out her arms. "You can squash me like the bug, but I will not let you down."

"Okay, here goes." But he couldn't move. Her imagery had set off a vivid motion picture of real damage in his mind.

"Come on," she urged. "Don't be a baby."

"I'll hurt you."

"No, you won't. I am very strong. I lift the big pots, I beat the sauce. *Un, deux, trois...allez!*"

Without allowing himself to think about it another second, Burton put out his arms and fell back.

She let out a soft grunt as the full impact of his height and weight landed on her. Gripping hard to support him, she staggered backward, preventing him from regaining his balance.

"Let go—"

"Oof!

They were both down. Veronique lay motionless beneath his back. He rolled off immediately, but her eyes were wide and staring. He gathered her up in his arms, and then they were on their knees, facing each other. Her mouth opened, her hands clutched at his shirt, but she couldn't speak.

"Are you all right?" he asked urgently. "Breathe out slowly. Now in. Do it again. Okay?"

She nodded. He released his own breath, relieved. He didn't know which had taken the greater act of faith—for her to catch him or for him to fall. But amazingly, she was looking straight at him without flinching. More than that, for the second time tonight there was a light in her eyes and a tremulous smile on her lips. He just had to believe she wanted him to kiss her.

"You're so beautiful," he whispered. And lowered his mouth to hers.

This was no chaste kiss meant for public consumption. He tasted her eagerly and she responded. For weeks he'd hungered for this, and now she was in his arms. Her lips were heaven and earth combined. While his head spun in starry infinity, his blood flowed hot and thick as lava. And when he gathered her closer still, feeling her slight body press against him, passion warred with tenderness, until passion threatened to overwhelm.

She eased away a little, her breath both warm and cool on his moistened lips. He pressed her head onto his shoulder and stroked her hair. They were both trembling. Shock. Nerves. Desire. Suddenly he didn't want to look into her eyes. Afraid he might see that her feelings didn't, after all, match his.

"Burton?"

"Yes?" He loosened his hold and slowly met her gaze.

Her face was alive with wonder; her skin flushed and glowing. "I caught you."

He smiled into his wife's eyes. They were shy, but welcoming. He could hardly believe his good fortune. Wanted to kiss her again. "I knew you would."

She laughed, a rich, throaty sound. "You did not."

"I wanted to believe."

"Maybe that's enough."

Drawn by the way her mouth moved, he leaned closer. "I can do better if you want me to."

They hovered on the brink of another kiss. He was willing; she seemed to be debating. Private kissing hadn't been part of the deal. But things had changed since he'd said that. He'd changed.

"I think…I think I'm falling in love with you." His voice was husky.

Her gaze turned wary and she pulled away a little more. Within the space of seconds, the mood changed abruptly. Then it hit him. Maybe all the time she'd been kissing him she'd been thinking of Graham. The thought made him feel sick.

"I know you miss your husband…." he began, his voice tight.

She swallowed hard.

He was in agony but compelled to continue. "I think it's fine and right that you loved him so much you can't be with another man so soon. But I can wait, because—" with a finger he lifted her face to his and couldn't stop the yearning note from entering his voice ''—when I kiss you I want it to be me you're making love to, not the memory of your dead husband.''

Her eyes widened in horror, reminding him of the night they'd met. "You have it wrong," she said in a choked voice. "The reason I couldn't look at you is not because I miss him. His memory fills me with rage. I didn't love my husband, I hated him."

Burton couldn't breathe. Couldn't comprehend. Janus-like, his image of Veronique turned on itself and showed the opposite face. All this time he'd thought she'd loved her husband and was grieving his loss. Instead—what did this mean? That when she looked at him she saw not the painful memory of someone loved and lost, but...a man she hated?

The thought was staggering, the situation appalling. One look at her stricken expression assured him she hadn't deliberately misled him. Still, he felt horribly tricked. It was all an optical illusion. He'd been looking at the outline of the vase when he should have been seeing the image of opposing faces.

One thing hadn't changed—Graham still stood between them.

Love or hate, Burton thought fiercely, he would overcome her memory of her late husband. He would make her see him for himself, and love or hate him on his own merits.

Veronique couldn't look one more second at the turbulent emotions blowing across Burton's face. He obviously thought she was a monster, but she couldn't explain. She hardly knew what to make of her confused longing for him; she only knew she couldn't allow herself to feel this way. Or for him to know and feel encouraged.

"I'm sorry," she cried, forgetting he had no knowledge of either her feelings or her betrayal. She got to her feet

and ran. And when she'd put the length of the house and
a locked door between them, she fell on the bed and
sobbed. For herself, for Burton and for what might have
been.

CHAPTER TWELVE

ANOTHER MONDAY MORNING. Rita turned at the knock on the makeup room door, half hoping, half afraid it would be Ernie. Lately nothing seemed right between them. But it was Veronique, coming to have her hair and face done in preparation for the taping of the fifth and sixth segments of *Flavors*.

"You have changed your hair!" Veronique said, walking around Rita to see the back. *"C'est fantastique!"*

Rita blushed under Veronique's admiring gaze. "Lillian's grandniece, Sandy, did it." Rita pulled at one newly dyed reddish lock uncertainly. "Do you think it suits me?" Part of her hated asking her rival to bolster her confidence, but it wasn't Veronique's fault Ernie was acting so dumb. Veronique always looked good no matter what she wore, and Rita would have given anything to know how she did it.

"But of course! The color brings out those pretty amber lights in your eyes." Veronique plopped down in the makeup chair and swiveled to the mirror. "Don't you like it?"

Rita got out the plastic cape and tied it around Veronique's neck. "Er… My boyfriend thinks it's awful. He didn't actually say so, but I could tell." It hurt, especially when all she'd wanted was for him to notice her again.

"Poof! What do men know? He will get used to it." Veronique flipped her hair out from under the plastic collar. "We must be quick, please. When I checked the kitchen this morning, the food had not yet been delivered and I forgot I need to prepare the pomegranates *en avance.* Burton is already in a terrible state.''

"I can imagine," Rita said, rolling her eyes. "Oops, sorry," she added, a hand to her mouth. "I forgot you two are married now."

"It's all right. You can talk to me the same as before."

Well, that was hardly true, even though everyone at the station knew the real reason Veronique and Burton had gotten married. But Rita kept her mouth shut and her expression bland as she smoothed on the Pan-Cake makeup. She'd gotten some practice at that when those government people had come snooping around. Like everyone else at Channel Seven, she'd said nothing that could work against Burton and Veronique. "Do you want the Fresh Melon lip gloss or the Succulent Succotash?"

"*Oh la la.* You decide, Rita. You have good color sense. I am used to putting food in my mouth, not smearing it on my lips."

Through the mirror, Veronique saw Ernie go by the open door. "Oh, look, there's Ernie. He will know what to do about the food. *Salut,* Ernie!"

Rita ground her teeth at the warm familiarity in Veronique's voice. Sometimes she wished she and Ernie had made their relationship public. She didn't seriously think Veronique was interested in Ernie, but she could be awfully flirtatious. Okay, she was French, but that didn't make it any easier to bear.

Ernie poked his head around the door. "Morning, Veronique," he said in that deep-voiced unconscious imitation of Burton he only used around Veronique. Then he squeaked back to normal. "Hi, Rita."

Rita felt a flood of misery and jealousy at rating second.

Veronique was oblivious, of course. "Ernie," she said, "do you know if the food has arrived?"

"Yes. It's all laid out in the kitchen."

"You are *très* genial!" She blew him a kiss in the mirror.

"Uh, I gotta go," he said, his cheeks reddening. "One of the mikes is on the blink." He waved and disappeared out the door.

Veronique waved back. "He is sweet, *non?*" she said to Rita.

Ernie didn't have a chance of resisting a woman like Veronique. Rita dug the comb in harder than she meant to. "As sweet as Burton?"

"Ouch!" Veronique cast her a surprised glance in the mirror.

Rita felt ashamed and angry at herself. "Sorry," she muttered, on the verge of tears.

"So tell me about your boyfriend, Rita, the one who does not like your new hair?"

Rita darted her a pained glance in the mirror. "It's Ernie." Her tone said, *Of course you know this.*

"Ernie?" Veronique looked astounded. "Burton's Ernie?"

"My Ernie," Rita asserted. "We're engaged."

"Engaged? How wonderful." Her brilliant smile lit her face. Then she sobered. "You mustn't take any notice of the way I tease him, Rita. As for your question, Ernie is as sweet as apple tart, but for me, Burton is breakfast, lunch and dinner."

A weight seemed to lift from Rita's heart. "Really?" Then her smile faded and she sighed. "Ernie is really special, you know? He's just not very…assertive. He's easily led."

Veronique patted her hand. "Give him time. He will gain confidence."

Rita untied the cape and removed it, careful not to get any dustings of powder on Veronique's dress. "It's not just that. Lately he doesn't seem to appreciate me. I…I was wondering, actually, if you would give me some fashion tips. You always look so great.''

''Moi!'' Veronique exclaimed, laughing. She slipped down off the chair. "I am glad to help if I can. Turn around. Yes, with legs like yours the skirt should be shorter. Tuck in at the waist, like so. You have a wonderful figure, Rita. All you need to do is show it off.''

Rita stood in front of the mirror, feeling quite racy with her skirt hiked up and her sweater cinched in. Could she do it? Yes. To keep Ernie, she could do anything.

Veronique gazed at her, smiling, and her next words seemed to mirror Rita's thoughts. "Don't underestimate Ernie's love for you. I bet if he thought he was losing you, he would do anything to get you back.''

CHAOS. HE WAS SURROUNDED by chaos. Burton ran down the spiral staircase, his headset looped around his neck, his feet barely touching the steps. He took a flying leap off the third to last stair and landed running. With a commanding flick of his hand, he summoned Vince and Ernie.

"What's the holdup?" he demanded. "Is that microphone working yet?''

Vince lifted his baseball cap to run a hand over his scalp. "We pulled one off another set. It's being hooked up.''

"Good. Ernie, what's the status of our chef? Is she ready yet?''

He could see Veronique over in the kitchen, making last-minute preparations. She'd hardly spoken on the drive in this morning, and not knowing where they stood was making him very tense.

Ernie pushed his glasses up his nose. "It's kind of complicated....''

"Just give me the facts," Burton snapped.

"She's ready, but the pomegranates she ordered aren't

ripe enough. She can't start the appetizer till we get some more.''

"Have you got someone onto that?"

"I sent Joe down to Granville Market as soon as I found out."

"Okay, fine." Burton tried to think calmly. "We'll just have to begin with the main course."

Ernie shook his head. "Problem is, boss, she needs pomegranate juice for the main course, too. She's making some Persian lamb thing."

"In that case, we'll start with dessert."

Ernie consulted his clipboard. "Uh, that would be the pomegranate granita."

"What!" It was all a bad dream, and any second he would wake up.

"Granita is a kind of icy, sherbety thing—"

"I know what granita is," Burton said, pinching the bridge of his nose. "What I don't understand is why we have three dishes all using pomegranates! Did I approve this?"

"Yessir. You liked the idea of a theme tying the show together. I think your exact words were 'That's the most sensational—'"

Burton cut him off by starting toward the kitchen at a fast clip. "In the future, Ernie, when I start tossing around superlatives, give me a swift kick and remind me of the time I allowed an entire show to be based on one temperamental fruit."

"Yessir." Ernie hurried along beside him.

"We're doing week six this afternoon, right, Ern?"

"Yes, but—"

"So we'll switch the order and do it this morning."

"I don't think she'll go for that," Ernie said. "Part of week six's menu builds on something she makes in week five."

Burton stopped in his tracks. "She's not constructing a

fourth lane for the Lion's Gate Bridge, for crying out loud.'' He took a deep breath. "I'm almost afraid to ask… Week seven?''

"We don't have the ingredients. I told you it was complicated.''

Burton resumed his long-legged stride toward the kitchen. "No, Ernie. Calculus is complicated. Einstein's theory of relativity is complicated. This is chaos. Chaos, Ernie. To be avoided at all costs.''

"Gee, sorry, Burt.''

Burton had neither the time nor the inclination to take notice of Ernie's slip. The crew dodged him and cameras rolled out of his way. None of it was her fault, he reminded himself. Not the pomegranates, not the farm, not even the fact that he was falling in love with a woman who hated the sight of him.

Veronique watched his long-legged approach, her stomach fluttering nervously. *Oh la la.* All that energy and tension was not good for him. But it made her feel justified for hiding the chess set and delaying the sale of the farm. Then he was stepping around the counter, and the tiny kitchen was filled with his overwhelming aura of urgency.

"I understand the pomegranates haven't arrived.''

Her fingers formed a death grip around a wooden spoon. "Ernie has ordered more.''

"When you auditioned, you said 'A good cook makes do.' Can't you substitute something? Raspberry juice?''

The suggestion brought on a near-hysterical burst of laughter. She'd stayed out of his way yesterday but still slept badly last night, and this morning Burton had hardly spoken to her. They couldn't go on ignoring the kiss. She was frazzled and tired and she had a horrible feeling Rita had applied her makeup unevenly. "Raspberry juice is no substitute for pomegranate juice, which is tart, not sweet. More pomegranates are coming. We can wait a few minutes, *non?*''

"No." He rubbed the back of his neck. "We don't even have time for this discussion. Is there anything we can do?"

She thought for a moment. "We could start the Lamb Faisinjan, I suppose. The pomegranate juice isn't added until about halfway through."

"Now you're talking. I'm going to stay on the floor while we retape the opening sequence. It wasn't bad the first time, but now that you're a little more practiced, I think we can make it even better. Do you still remember it? Good." He adjusted his headset and started to back off the set. "Veronique, can you look at me?"

Something in his voice, some hint of hurt quickly covered up, made her look. For an instant their eyes connected. *Mon Dieu.* He still thought she was seeing her first husband.

She twisted a lock of hair at the back of her head around one finger. "Yes, Burton, I can look at you. But about the other night—"

He glanced at his watch. "Can we talk about this later?"

"All I want to say is, I don't think we should talk about it. I think we should forget it happened."

"Forget we kissed? I don't know if I can." He stepped forward again to tucked a strand of hair behind her ear, barely skimming the lobe with his finger. "What if I said, The appetizer made me ravenous and I'm ready for the next course?"

"Then you better eat somewhere else," she said quietly, her skin still tingling from his touch. "In three months we divorce."

He wasted five whole seconds just looking at her. "We're not going to last even three months if we don't convince Immigration our marriage is genuine. Like it or not, we have to pretend we're in love."

TWO HOURS LATER, the gofer Ernie had sent to the market reported back after making the rounds of Granville Island,

New Westminster and Lonsdale Quay Markets, plus dozens of produce outlets in between. The pomegranates he brought back would be ready tomorrow at the earliest, Veronique declared, and not a minute before.

Burton had nothing else scheduled and was too frustrated by the delay to sit at his desk doing paperwork, so he consigned the half-finished lamb to the fridge and took off with Veronique for the farm.

"Are you still angry?" Veronique asked as they pulled off the freeway and onto the exit ramp for Langley. Burton hadn't said a word since they left the station.

Startled out of his worries about mountains of sprouting potatoes, Burton said, "Angry? No. It wasn't your fault. It's a bad season for pomegranates or something."

"I do not mean the pomegranates." She cast him a sideways glance that slid away even as he turned to look at her.

"Oh, that," he said with a wave calculated to look more casual than he felt. "Don't give it another thought." He didn't see any percentage in further exposing his feelings. His misunderstanding about her husband aside, they'd both made it clear from the beginning that the arrangement was short-term. Today she'd confirmed that; in spite of their kiss, nothing had changed. He was still determined to make her see him for himself, but he wasn't so pathetic he had to beg for it. And he wasn't going to mention the word *love* again. Ever.

"You were so quiet," she persisted, "I couldn't help wonder…"

"I was planning the rest of the day."

And then there was more silence. It was just after noon when he turned the car into the driveway. The sky was overcast but the air temperature warm, and rain looked some way off. After a quick lunch of reheated soup, Burton went out to the back porch and stuck his feet into

Granddad's gum boots. He came back through the kitchen pulling on a pair of worn leather gardening gloves.

"What are you doing?" Veronique asked lazily. She was still seated at the pine table sipping coffee, her feet tucked up under her on the chair.

"The pomegranates defeated me, but the potatoes won't. I can't look at those empty fields another day. If Granddad were still alive he'd have the whole crop planted by now."

"How you going to plant potatoes without the machinery?"

"The old-fashioned way. By hand."

"Are you crazy?"

"Probably."

She put her feet down and drained the last of her cup. "Then I will help you."

In the barn Burton loaded potatoes into a wheelbarrow while Veronique shook the straw out of some buckets she found in a corner and filled those, too. With the barrow bumping over the rough ground and buckets in hand, they walked out to the plowed field that rose in a gentle slope behind the barn and the house.

Veronique scanned the long rows of turned dirt that stretched ahead of them to the horizon and for hundreds of yards to the right and left. "How many acres did you say?"

"Two hundred," Burton replied, "but only one hundred are plowed." They turned and headed for the row of poplars that marked the eastern boundary. "Granddad would likely have put the rest into corn, but I'm not going to worry about that now."

Only one hundred acres, Veronique thought. For two people to plant a field that size by hand would take weeks. But she said nothing. This exercise in futility—and her willingness to help—had nothing to do with growing potatoes. Burton needed to do this one last thing for his grandfather. To make amends, to carry on, to somehow keep the old man alive through working his land. And she had this idiotic desire to spend time with Burton. To be physically close to him. *He was falling in love with her.* She couldn't get his words out of her mind even though she prayed he wouldn't utter them again. Head down, once again avoiding his eyes, she stepped clumsily through the soft hillocky dirt in Burton's grandmother's big rubber boots.

At first they tried planting side by side on parallel rows. Burton showed her how deep to plant, how far apart. It was not so very different from growing potatoes in her kitchen garden. Bend, scoop out a hole, drop the potato in, shovel over the dirt. Bending and straightening, inching along, it was backbreaking work. After twenty minutes she paused to stretch, pushing a hand into the small of her already-aching back.

Burton looked up. "Go back to the house. You don't need to do this."

"Perhaps if we work together," she suggested. "You dig the holes and I put in the potatoes."

"Let's try it."

They worked in short sections, Burton hoeing a trench while Veronique followed, dropping in the potatoes at regular intervals. Then she shoveled the dirt back over them while Burton hoed another trench. The method was a little faster, a little smoother, and as they progressed, they developed a rhythm. Hoe, plant, shovel, hoe, plant, shovel…

"Do they not need fertilizer?" Veronique asked, pausing to separate two potatoes whose sprouts had tangled and grown together.

Burton leaned on his hoe. He brushed a gloved hand across his forehead, leaving a dirty streak in its wake. "Granddad did things the old-fashioned way. He grew peas in this field last year—they add nitrogen to the soil."

"For someone who is not a farmer, you know a lot about it."

He seemed a little surprised himself. "I guess I've spent so much time here over the years some of it rubbed off." He sunk his hoe into the dirt and, with a grunt, dragged it along, furrowing through the dark, rich soil. "Doesn't mean I like it."

Veronique turned away to hide a smile. "No, of course not."

Eventually they had planted one entire row. Standing at the top of the slope, Veronique gazed at their accomplishment with silent pride. A warm hand gripped her shoulder, and she glanced up into Burton's smile. "Pretty good, eh?" Burton said.

"It's very good." She didn't point out the hundreds of rows left to plant. Or the fact that tomorrow they'd have to leave it and go back to the studio. They both knew the magnitude of the job and the impossibility of finishing. Nor did she suggest he rent a picker-plant, or whatever they called it. Maybe later he would get the machine and finish the job properly. But she could see that for now he felt good to have simply made a start. And she felt good for having helped him.

"Tell me about yourself," Veronique said when they'd started back hoeing and planting. "What do you like to do when you're not working?"

He told her he liked listening to blues, but not country and western; when he read, it was science fiction; and he'd seen every Hitchcock film half a dozen times. His friends were scattered over the globe, a legacy of years on the road as a photojournalist. He kept in touch, but visits were sporadic, and although he didn't come right out and say so, Veronique got the impression he would have liked to have a circle of friends closer to home—if he wasn't so busy with his work.

She was pondering the similar gaps in their lives when a gust of wind caught her across the cheek, and a cool, wet drop splashed onto her nose. She glanced up. Dark streaks of heavy rain were slanting across the base of the mountains, and in the middle distance, a bank of black clouds was rolling in across the valley. A storm was heading their way.

"Burton," she called, but he'd already seen it.

"You head in," he said. "I'll just finish this row." They were about a third of the way through the fourth row, heading toward the house. Finishing the row together would take an hour; twice as long if he did it by himself.

"Are you crazy? You'll get soaked." Drops were falling steadily now.

He shrugged and dug a trench with his hoe. Reaching past her for the bucket of spuds, he placed it in the trough between the rows and picked up the shovel. "Go on," he said. "Just because I can't leave a job half-done doesn't mean you should suffer."

She wanted to leave, but she couldn't let him do this alone. She was married to a madman, but he was her husband—for better or worse, for colder and wetter, in sickness and in health....

Wresting the shovel from his hands, she began to mound the dirt around the seed potatoes nestled in their earthy beds. He frowned and started to say something. She lifted her chin, silently defying him to try to make her go back. His brief smile warmed her through despite the chilling drops falling on her neck and hands.

The rain poured down. The soil became wetter, heavier and more and more slippery. Rivulets snaked down the slope between the rows, and Veronique discovered that her boots leaked. It was hard to shovel, hard to see, hard to stay upright. Twice she slipped and fell into the soft, wet dirt and had to struggle back up, aided by a strong hand from Burton. Rain soaked her thin jacket and her jeans, got in her eyes, dripped from her hair. Conversation ceased in their determination to get the row planted.

She sneezed twice, jamming wet, mud-streaked fingers

against her nose so Burton wouldn't hear and tell her to go in. She'd built up a sweat that, added to the chill and wet, made her feel feverish.

Finally, soaking wet, muddy from head to toe, backs aching, they reached the end of the row. This time when Burton told her to go inside while he put everything away, she didn't argue. Sneezing and shivering and aching in her bones, she ran splashing across the yard to the house.

Merde, she thought, another cold.

THE NEXT DAY STARTED badly and got steadily worse.

Veronique awoke with a congested nose and a prickly feeling at the back of her throat. Burton loaded her up with cold remedies she didn't want to take and dropped her off at the nursing home with a terse "If it's raining, call me. I'll come and get you."

She paused at the half-open doorway to Marion's room. Her spirits sank further when she saw Mother-in-Law Number One in her wheelchair staring morosely out the window, her hair uncombed, her face pale and unmadeup. Depressed again.

Suddenly Veronique felt unbearably burdened by the task of coaxing Marion into a happy, functional future. Why had she taken it on? Why had she even thought she was capable of it? Every week seemed to be one step forward and two steps back. Getting Marion to join the home's bridge club, her goal for today, now appeared to be monumentally out of reach.

"*Bonjour,* Marion," she sang out with determined cheerfulness as she gave a knock and entered the room. "How are you today?"

"Oh, hello, Veronica." Marion turned, mustering a feeble smile. Her eyes were bright, as though she'd been crying. "I guess I'm fine. Janice, my roommate at the rehab center, came to visit me. She's back in her apartment, fully recovered." Marion went back to staring out the window.

"She came to visit? But I thought you did not get along."

"Oh, she's quite nice once you get to know her. It's just that she was in such a lot of pain at first."

"I'm glad. It's not right that you sit here by yourself. Hey, you know what? There is a bridge club here, too. They meet this morning. I am going to get your brush and your lipstick and a mirror, and we will get you ready. *D'accord?*"

"Oh, I don't know," she said listlessly. "I won't enjoy it."

Veronique felt like screaming, she was so frustrated. Maybe she was wrong to jolly Marion along. Maybe she should stop pushing and let the woman take responsibility for her own happiness. Then again, maybe if she persisted just a little longer, Marion would make a breakthrough. It was so hard to know what was right.

It wasn't until she'd brought the toiletry bag from the bathroom and handed it to her that she noticed something in Marion's lap, half hidden under her palm. "What is that?"

Marion turned her hand over. Photographs. Graham as a boy. Graham as a teenager. Graham and Veronique on their wedding day. Graham and Stan, smiling widely, all decked out in their fishing gear. Dressed for death.

Marion sifted through the photos, selected those that didn't include Stan and handed the rest to Veronique. "I'd like you to have these."

Veronique didn't know how to refuse, only that she had to. "*Merci,* Marion. But I cannot take them from you. Please, you keep them. I have others." More than she wanted.

"Not of him as a boy. See, he doesn't look like your nice Mr. O'Rourke in this picture, does he?"

Veronique held the photo closer. Perhaps not surprisingly, there was little resemblance between the ten-year-

old and Burton, although it made her wonder what Burton
had looked like as a boy. The longer she knew him the
less he reminded her of her first husband. That was both
a blessing and a danger, she was just beginning to realize.
"No, he doesn't."

"Well, then, you keep it. I know you said you married
Burton to stay in Canada, but I can't help think you chose
him because he looks like Graham. I understand, I really
do, though I worry about you. I'm too old to think about
marrying again, but you shouldn't live in the past."

Veronique pulled up a chair and sat down facing Marion, their knees nearly touching. "Your life is not over.
You must believe that. Also, you must not worry about
me."

"You're grieving over Graham," Marion replied. "It's
natural, but is it fair to Mr. O'Rourke?"

Mon Dieu. She could not let Marion go on thinking this
way. "Marion, there is something I must tell you," she
said gravely. "It is not easy for me to say, and it will not
be easy for you to hear."

"What is it?" Marion's face looked naked and vulnerable.

Veronique took a deep breath and clasped both of Marion's hands in hers. "I married Burton not because he
looks like Graham, but in spite of it."

Marion's brows knit together. "I don't understand.
Didn't you like Graham's looks?"

"Yes, at first. You see…" She hesitated. How little did
Marion need to know to understand? How much could she
say without Marion hating her?

"At first, Graham and I were very much in love," she
began again. Marion smiled. "But we didn't really know
each other. We married too quickly."

Marion nodded wisely. "You did it again."

Veronique made a face in frustration. Marion was still
having trouble with the concept of a temporary marriage.

"Forget about Burton for now. The truth is…" Suddenly she was fed up with pussyfooting around. "The truth is, when Graham and I got to know each other we discovered that our love was not real and lasting."

Marion slipped her hand out and patted Veronique's. "You don't know what you're saying, my dear. You're rationalizing your new marriage. You and Graham would have gone on forever."

"Non!" Veronique jumped to her feet. "I am telling you, I did not love Graham. He did not love me."

"Graham adored you."

"He didn't even *like* me. He was horrible to me. I was going to leave him."

"No!" Marion's denial was firm and swift, but traces of anxiety creased her gentle face.

"He cheated on me."

"Not my son—"

"And he hit me."

"Stop!" Marion burst into tears and covered her face with her hands. "Oh, please stop."

Veronique hugged her arms around herself. She hadn't meant to say so much. Marion was sobbing, and tears streamed from her own eyes, as well.

"I'm sorry, Marion," she said, kneeling to put her arms around the other woman. "I didn't want to hurt you."

"He really…hit you?" Marion's face was wet and pale, her voice trembling.

"Once." Discovering the other woman had made her pack her bags; the blow he'd struck had made her impervious to all pleas, threats and demands. Thank goodness they'd had no children.

Marion was shaking her head, tears streaming. "Not Graham. Not my sweet little boy. He'd never do anything like that. I can't believe it. I won't believe it."

Marion wept as though she'd lost her son all over again. She voiced her disbelief over and over, until Veronique wondered who she was trying to convince, herself or Veronique. Veronique held her, wishing with all her heart she hadn't destroyed Marion's image of her son. Being understood wasn't worth taking away Marion's happy memories when memories were all she had.

"I'm sorry, Marion," she said, stroking her hair back from her damp face. "I should not have told you this. I'm sure Graham was a good man," she lied. "We just weren't right for each other."

Marion's sobs slowed. She took the handkerchief Veronique held out and dried her reddened eyes. "Don't go trying to make it out to be nothing now that you've said it."

The harshness of the reprimand chastened and surprised her. With Marion, she sometimes felt as though she were dealing with a child. Now the tables had turned. Inflicting wounds had taken away Veronique's authority; receiving them had given Marion dignity. The last, at least, was good, but it was so unfair. Veronique had been hurt, too.

"He was a good son," Veronique offered meekly.

Marion clutched the photos of Graham to her breast, and fresh tears filled her eyes. "Of course he was a good son. There was never any question of that."

"Come," Veronique said. "I will help you to the bathroom to wash your face. Maybe the bridge club will take your mind off this."

Marion's face set mulishly. "Don't push me, Veronica. When I'm ready to go to the bridge club, I will, and not a moment sooner."

"Yes, Marion."

There was no answering squeeze when Veronique bent to hug her goodbye. Veronique felt a sneeze coming on and pressed a finger beneath her nose. "My handkerchief," she requested. It was too wet to use, but too important to lose.

When she stepped outside, rain was pouring onto the

city from the dark clouds banked against Grouse Mountain. Half a block away, a bus swooshed in close to the curb. With no time to open her umbrella, Veronique ran for it. She was soaked, but she got aboard. Her change clinked down through the cash receptacle, and she swung into a seat as the bus swayed back into traffic.

The vinyl seat was cold beneath her wet stockinged legs. She hooked the umbrella over the seat back in front. Only then did she remember Burton telling her to call him for a ride. Oh, well, she thought apathetically. She would be there soon enough.

Misery and habit sent her thumb curving repetitively over the monogrammed *B* in the corner of the handkerchief. She'd hurt Marion—maybe even set her recovery back. And in the process, she'd hurt herself.

If a lie had bound them together, the truth had set them adrift. She felt as though she were bobbing lonely on the open sea, with Marion moving away in the distance like a sailboard that had been knocked out from under her. For, like a sailboard, Marion had been both drag and lift—responsibility and support. Veronique wished she could transfer her guilt and Marion's pain into anger at the man who had created this situation, but he'd become a speck on the horizon, too insignificant to attach any emotion to at all. She shut her eyes and tried to pretend she was floating on the warm waters of her homeland. She would give anything to see her sister, to be back in the loving embrace of her family, to let her weary soul make landfall on the warm sands of Tahiti.

CHAPTER THIRTEEN

BURTON STOOD AT HIS DESK, rapidly dividing papers between his out-box, his still-to-do box and the circular file on the floor. He checked his watch. Veronique should have been back by now, but maybe she'd probably gone directly to Makeup. Taping of *Flavors* was due to start in five minutes, and after yesterday's fiasco, the budget couldn't afford another minute wasted.

Ernie poked his head in the door, puffing as though he'd been running. "Hi. The crew's ready to go. Where's Veronique?"

"What! You mean she hasn't shown up yet?" Burton threw down his papers. "She said she'd only be a few minutes at the nursing home. I knew I should have waited and driven her to the studio."

"Maybe she missed her bus," Ernie suggested.

"Maybe she isn't paying attention to the time," Burton countered, scowling. He was annoyed she was late, but he was even more worried something could have happened to her. When had that started? He checked outside the window. Raining. What a summer. At least she had her umbrella.

"Let's get down to the studio. I want everything double-checked," Burton said, coming around the desk. "By the way, everything okay between you and Rita?"

Ernie, about to stride off, stopped so fast he wobbled on his cross-trainers. "Y-yes, why do you ask?"

"Rita came to me yesterday asking if it was really your

job to be running around after Veronique's pomegranates.''

"Isn't it?" His voice came out on a squeak.

"It is. But Rita's a nice girl. You don't want to lose her by making a fool of yourself over an older woman." Burton scowled again. "A married woman."

"Gee, Burton, I thought you and Veronique weren't really...I mean I thought your marriage wasn't r-real...." Ernie's glasses started to fog up.

Burton stepped to the doorway and loomed over him. "As long as she and I are together, the marriage is real. Got that, Ernie?"

Ernie's Adam's apple bobbed up and down. "I g-got it, boss. Nothing's going on between me and Veronique."

"I know that. Maybe you should let Rita know, too."

"Yessir. Right away, sir." Ernie shot off down the corridor.

Burton followed, feeling worse, not better, for having slapped Ernie down. The kid didn't deserve it, and Burton knew his own obsessing over Veronique was not good. She wanted to forget the kiss he couldn't get out of his mind. With that kiss, he'd kissed goodbye any objectivity he'd ever had about her as an employee. With that kiss, he sealed his fate—he was no longer the reluctant bridegroom, but a frustrated lover. He groaned. Why had he gone and said he was falling in love with her? Ernie wasn't the only one in danger of making a fool of himself.

Burton was pacing the set like a trapped wolverine, snarling and snapping when Veronique arrived twenty minutes late. She was dripping wet and sneezing, her hair a bedraggled mess, and her clothes, which ought to have been adequate for June, were drenched through.

He stood back and took deep breaths while Lillian brought her a cup of hot tea with lemon. He paced some more while Rita whipped the hair dryer into action. He ground his teeth while Ernie fussed over her and handed her a tissue every time she sneezed. Thin-lipped and silent, he waited till the others had finished with her, then he shooed them out of earshot.

"What happened?" he said, his voice low and tense. "You told me you'd only be a few minutes. You're late. And you're soaked. Where's your umbrella?"

Veronique's hand went to her mouth. "My umbrella! I must have left it on the bus. Oh, I am so sorry. It was your wedding gift to me."

A wedding gift for a nonwedding. Burton tried to contain his irritation, to keep it separate from the job. So it hadn't been a romantic present or anything she'd wanted, just something she'd badly needed. So what? Why should she take care of it? Just because it had been the nicest-looking, the highest-quality, the absolutely best umbrella he could find.

"Forget it," he said, tight-lipped. "We have more important things to worry about. Like the fact we're now half an hour behind schedule. Do you know what overtime for an entire crew does to a programming budget?"

She bit her lip and looked away. "I am sorry."

Hell, now she was going to cry. "Don't do that. Your eyes are red enough as it is. Did you have to go and get a cold just when we're in the thick of taping?" He remembered too late that she'd caught the cold by helping him carry out his insane notion of planting potatoes by hand.

He was about to apologize when she snapped back, "Yes, I got a cold—just to annoy you. What do you think?"

"I think you're not taking this show seriously. Yesterday was a mistake. But today? Running around in the rain, getting soaked, leaving your umbrella on the bus—" His voice had become more strident with every word. He broke off and shoved a hand through his spiky hair. He was losing it. Really losing it.

"I had to see Marion. You knew when you hired me she was the only reason I am here. And now…and now…" Her eyes filled with tears, but she set her shoulders defiantly. "You are upset over a lost umbrella when she is struggling just to cope. I am struggling to cope.…"

"I am not upset about the umbrella. It's just…it's typical of your ambivalence—toward me, toward the show, toward this whole damn country." He flung an arm wide. And almost clipped Ernie on the nose.

"What is it, Ernie?" he barked, turning on him.

"Don't yell at him!" Veronique shouted. "If I am so ambi—ambilva…" Her hand flew upward in a sharp gesture. "Whatever it is you say—maybe you should find another chef."

"Maybe I should," he snarled.

Outrage flashed in her vivid green eyes. "I will not hold you to our contract. Call Monsieur Mumbling Mustache. Better still, call Madame Emily Up-Herself. She is the one you really wanted, *non?*"

"No!" At his protest, Veronique seemed to have no trouble looking—no, glaring—him in the eye.

"Excuse me, B-B-Burt…on," Ernie cut in again. "We're ready to start."

"Not now, Ernie." Burton took his eyes off Veronique for only a second, but when he looked back, she was striding away, waving her hands, turning the air blue with her French.

He charged after her and caught her by the arm. "Where the hell do you think you're going?"

"I'm quitting," she snapped. "You don't care about me, or the farm, or anything but the show and your career. You think I need you, but I don't."

"Without me and my show, you'll be deported."

Veronique went pale. "Then I will be deported. I am going back to my apartment. *Au revoir.*"

Burton threw his hands in the air. "Fine, go. I don't

need prima donnas around here. I'll find another chef, no problem."

He watched her walk away, their angry words echoing in his ears while a sick feeling formed in the hollow of his stomach.

Au revoir. Finis.

ERNIE THREW A FURIOUS glare at Burton—how could he just let her go?—then took off after her himself. He caught up with her in the corridor, a little way down from Makeup. He glanced nervously at the open door, wondered where Rita was right now, and decided it couldn't be helped. *Flavors,* everything, was at stake.

"Veronique!" He reached out to touch her arm. "Don't go."

"He sent me away. I have no choice." Her shoulders lifted in a careless shrug, but her face was white.

"He didn't mean it. He's like that, sort of abrupt. He does it to me all the time."

"Ah, but he doesn't appreciate you, Ernie." Veronique touched him on the cheek. "He doesn't take you seriously."

Ernie couldn't help himself, he leaned into her palm. "He does. He just doesn't always show it."

Part of him wanted to trash Burton, instead of defend him, but he liked his job, and Burton really was a pretty great guy, and Veronique wouldn't ever go for him, anyway, and it was Rita he wanted to marry, and…oh, hell, it was all so complicated.

"Goodbye, sweet Ernie." She put her hands on his shoulders and kissed him one, twice, thrice, on the cheeks.

"Bye." Ernie watched her go in a kind of swoon.

"Ernie."

Oh, no. He'd never heard quite that mixture of anger and anguish from Rita. Slowly he turned to face her.

THURSDAY AFTERNOON, two days since Veronique's defection. Burton had a lot on his mind—all of it bad. The potatoes were still unplanted and his admittedly sketchy efforts to locate a pick-planter and someone to operate it had so far met with failure. The two young brothers Don Chetwynd kept pestering him about had seen the property and made an offer. Burton was sorely tempted to hand over the farm and be done with it, but the chess set still hadn't turned up.

At work, things weren't much better. He'd gotten a tentative agreement from Emily Harper-Smythe to take over on *Flavors*. All he had to do was pick up the phone and confirm. But if he went that route, it would mean starting over practically from scratch. He'd never complete *Lost Harvest*. At least not this year.

Plaguing his mind through it all was the image of Veronique alone and sick. He told himself he was being ridiculous; she was made of some steely Gallic wonderstuff that was as robust as French roast. But he'd been too harsh. Too caught up in his own problems. She'd been right about that.

And she was his wife. He had an obligation to look after her. After all, who else did she have? Veronique's only friend and relation required full-time care herself.

A knock at the door brought his weary head up. "Oh, hi, Ernie. No, I don't know when we're going to start taping again."

"It's not that. Some of the gang are going to the pub for a drink. I just wondered if you wanted to come."

"Thanks, but no. I've got to haul my sorry ass out of this pit I dug for myself." He leaned back in his chair and with a vague gesture indicated the paperwork on *Flavors*. He could take legal action against Veronique, and she'd have to come back to work, but she'd hate him for it, and what was the point of that? Then there was their interview with Immigration tomorrow, and he couldn't imagine what he was going to say to Officers Jackson and Connery. If they even went through with the charade. Maybe even now she was packing her bags to return to Tahiti. The thought made him groan.

"Why don't you go see her?" Ernie suggested, looking sympathetic. "Ask her to come back?"

"I don't beg."

"Nobody's asking you to beg. Just talk to her."

Burton hated having anyone suggest what he'd already decided to do on his own. "Is talk working with Rita?"

Ernie looked away. "She gave me back my engagement ring."

Burton sighed. "Sorry, Ern. I didn't mean to rub it in. Go drown your sorrows. I'll..." He didn't want to say what he was planning to do in case he failed. "I'll figure out something. See you tomorrow."

"Why don't you come? Just for a while."

Burton looked at Ernie more closely. His round face seemed gaunt and haunted. Sort of the way he himself had felt these past few days. "What the hell," he said, pushing back his chair. "I guess one won't hurt."

"ANOTHER ROUND, ERNIE?" Burton raised his hand and caught the eye of the waiter circling the crowd with his drinks tray. They sat on high wooden stools, their elbows resting on a narrow shelf overlooking the sunken central floor of the bar. Great view, if there'd been anyone he wanted to see.

"My turn, Burt," Ernie said, digging his hand in his pocket. "Whoops, sorry, Bur-ton."

Under the influence of two and a half beers, Burton waved a benevolent hand. "Just call me Burt. It must be some natural phenomenon too powerful to fight." Someone caught his eye in the far corner. "Is that Rita? She looks different. She looks great!"

Ernie glanced over to where Rita was laughing with the

guys from research. "You mean this is the first time you've seen her today?"

"Yes. What happened?"

Ernie frowned into his beer. "Apparently the hairstyle wasn't enough. Veronique gave her some fashion tips, and she's gone hog-wild buying new clothes. Rita's changed, Burt. Says she doesn't need me."

Burton used the bottom of his beer glass to make soggy circles on his paper coaster. "Veronique said she didn't need me, either. Love is a mug's game, Ernie. You have to be crazy to get involved, and insane not to be grateful when it's over."

"So it's really over between you and Veronique?"

"Veronique is not only finished with the show, she's finished with our marriage." He pulled on his beer. "It may have been a phony arrangement, but I can't get her out of my skull. Do you know what I do at night? I watch tapes of the show. I pause the tape in the middle of one of her fabulous smiles and just stare at her. Or I replay over and over that cute way she has of tossing her head from side to side."

"She's so great," Ernie mumbled morosely into his beer.

Burton put down his glass and turned to look at his companion in misery. He could almost forgive the guy for his crush on Veronique. "Listen, I…" Damn, this was hard to say. "I realize you're missing Veronique, too."

Ernie glanced up at him. "Oh, hey, no. I've gotten over missing Veronique. It was Rita I was missing just then." His head dropped again. "It's Rita I'm always missing."

A sweet-looking girl with long, blond hair walked slowly past their table cradling a half-pint mug to her pink angora sweater. As she glanced around for a place to sit, she cast them a shy smile and continued on.

Sensing a diversion, Burton nudged Ernie in the ribs. "Ernie, you devil. That little fox had her eye on you."

Ernie's gaze strayed, wavered, then snapped back to the far corner. "Forget it. I love Rita."

"Listen, pal, if you want Rita, you've got to go out there and win her back."

"Yeah, how?"

Burton scratched his jaw, thinking. "You say she's changed? Show her that you can change, too. You have been a tad neglectful lately, right?"

Ernie squirmed uncomfortably on his bar stool. "Maybe a little."

"Okay then, listen up. I'm going to let you in on the Secret."

"The Secret?"

"Yes. Not many men know about it, but the ones who do have no trouble at all in the love department."

Ernie's face scrunched in confusion. "But you say *you* know it…?"

"Yeah, well, maybe I've been a little slow in applying it," Burton said, testily. "You want to hear this or not?"

"Go on," Ernie said, looking attentive.

"Okay. The Secret is really very simple. You've got to give your woman, not a little, but a lot of tender loving care. Show her she means something to you. Show her she's the one in a million made just for you."

Ernie's shoulders slumped. "Rita would walk all over me."

Burton jabbed a finger at him. "Now that's just what you can't let her do. You've got to go in strong, like you deserve to be with her. Self-confidence is a major turn-on with women. Not arrogance, they don't like that. Just know your own worth."

Ernie lifted his head and eyed him skeptically. "That's it? That's the Secret?"

"Its beauty lies in its simplicity. Treat her like a million bucks. Then act like she's lucky to have you. Which she is, goddamn it."

Ernie took a sip of beer, looking thoughtful as he licked away a trace of foam mustache. "You might have something there."

"Now, here's the most important part," Burton said, and leaned in closer. "The secret to the Secret is not to use it as a pickup scam to get women into bed. You've got to live it, for that one special woman in your life."

"Live it," Ernie repeated.

"That's right. Actions speak louder than words."

"You really think it'll work?"

"I know it'll work," Burton said, crossing his fingers under the table.

Ernie straightened his spine to sit taller. "I could request her favorite song."

"That's the idea."

"I could buy her a rose from that flower girl who's making the rounds...."

"Yeah, go on." Burton was busy thinking about what he could do to win Veronique back.

"Then I'll go over there and ask her to dance as if we'd never met." Ernie's cheeks grew flushed with excitement. "I could join her table— No, wait. I'll ask her to come to me."

"Now you're talking." Burton clapped a hand on his shoulder.

Ernie stiffened. He drew back and looked Burton straight in the eye. "You know, Burton, I really hate it when you do that."

Three things flashed through Burton's mind simultaneously. One, Ernie had called him Burton for the first time without being prompted. Two, his assistant was displaying uncharacteristic, but not unwelcome, assertiveness. Three, it was far too easy to slap a short man on the back.

"Sure, pal," he said, a little dazed by all the revelations. He held out his hand. "I gotta go. See you Monday."

Ernie blinked, smiled and shook hands, man-to-man.

On the way over to Veronique's, Burton stopped off at his apartment to change his shirt and pick up a package from the freezer. Then, because it wasn't raining and he wanted time to think, he set off on foot over the Burrard Street bridge. At a brisk pace it would take him no more than forty minutes to reach her apartment on the other side of English Bay.

Fluttering red-and-black banners announcing the annual Salmon Festival lined both sides of the bridge. High in the night sky, stars peeked out between towering clouds of luminous gray-white. On the far shore of Burrard Inlet, the Planetarium squatted like a UFO about to take off.

At the crest of the bridge, Burton leaned on the rail and gazed beyond the bay into the blackness of Georgia Strait. What the hell was he going to say to Veronique? Stay a month and finish the series? Stay a year and give our relationship a real shot? Stay a lifetime because I already know I want you forever?

He sucked in a lungful of the moist night air and moved on. What had happened to old "love 'em and leave 'em" O'Rourke? When had his emotions gotten involved and made it all so tangled and complicated?

Twenty minutes later he leaned his forehead against Veronique's door and imagined he could feel the warmth of her home right through the wood. He could hear the indistinct murmur of her voice, made lower and huskier by her cold, speaking to someone in French. A visitor? A stab of possessiveness made him feel like a real husband.

He knocked.

A moment later she stood before him, wearing a beige cashmere shawl over her pink T-shirt and colorful *pareau.* "Come in," she said, her gaze wary, her mouth unsmiling.

Entering the relaxing warmth and humidity of her apartment, Burton had to force himself to remember that once again he was a man on a mission. Bring Veronique back to the studio. To the farmhouse. He knew better than to think she'd come to his bed, but he couldn't help thinking about that, too. In fact, he thought about it almost all the time.

He laid the back of his hand on her forehead. "Shouldn't you be in bed?"

"I am much better. This cold was a mild one. You have been out drinking?"

"I had a couple of beers at the pub with Ernie."

"How is Ernie?"

"The worm has turned."

She raised her eyebrows, said "Ahh" and smiled mysteriously, as though she knew all about it. Damn. Just when he thought he had women figured out.

She turned and walked back to the living area. "Have you eaten?"

"I brought you some soup. My mother made it, but it's good." He handed her the paper bag with total confidence in Catherine's chicken soup—both for its restorative powers and its acceptability. There were no shortcuts here, no canned cream soup or crushed potato chips.

She pulled the frozen Tupperware container out of the bag. "I'll heat it up."

He followed her into the kitchen, pausing to take off his jacket and drape it over the back of the sofa.

The microwave hummed. Veronique stretched to reach into a top cupboard for bowls. Turned to say something and broke off in surprised laughter at the sight of his colorful Hawaiian shirt. *"Oh la la!"* she exclaimed. "You want a *pareau?"*

"I don't think I'm quite ready for that, but thanks, anyway." If he could still make her smile, hope was not lost. He came a little closer. "I'm sorry about the other day."

Her shoulders went up in a full body shrug. "You had some right to be angry. But it does not change anything. We make a big mistake—"

Burton touched her arm and felt the warmth, the softness

of her skin. "Let's not talk about it just yet. Rejection doesn't sit well on an empty stomach." He sat on one of the mismatched kitchen chairs, and that reminded him of Granddad's rocker. Would she come back and finish what she'd started to refinish?

"I had an offer on the farm."

She went still, her hand in the cutlery drawer. "Oh?"

"Those brothers from Chilliwack. Chetwynd called again, so I let them have a look."

She pulled out a couple of spoons. "What did you say?"

"I told him I needed more time." Her face went suddenly pale under the fluorescent light. "Maybe you shouldn't be doing this. Sit down. I'll get it."

"I'm fine, really." She set the spoons on the table and went back for water glasses.

Burton shook his head and got up to guide her to a chair. "Sit. How is Marion?"

"Not so good. I told her the truth about Graham. About why I was going to leave him."

Burton felt an irrational tug of sympathy for the luckless Graham. "Why exactly did you hate him so much?"

Veronique's shawl slipped over one shoulder as she reached up to tug on a curl, and her mouth pursed in remembered pain. "You don't want to know."

"Yes, I do," Burton said, taking her hand in his. "I want to know all about you. What makes you laugh. And what makes you cry. And then, if I can, I want to stop the tears."

At that, moisture welled in her eyes and a smile spread across her face. Laughing, she brushed the tears away. "There, now you have both. You make me feel so…"

Burton brought her hand to his mouth and pressed his lips against her knuckles. "What? How do I make you feel?"

She glanced shyly up at him. "Opposite to what I felt for Graham."

Warmth rose like a flame in Burton, sending heat pulsing between them. Then he said, "Exactly why did you hate Graham?" and it was as though he'd dashed cold water over her.

Veronique's smile faded. Frown lines appeared between her brows and she pulled her hand away to tuck it in her lap. "A few months after Graham and I were married I discovered he went back to an old girlfriend."

"The man must have been insane."

Veronique threw Burton a grateful smile. "I told Graham he must give her up. He just laughed and said the French have an easy attitude to that. It may be true for some, but not for me. I said I would leave him. He couldn't stand that—not to have control over me. He said my family wouldn't want me back after I ran away from them. I didn't care what he said anymore. I went to pack my bags…he followed me into the bedroom…" Her eyes became bright with tears, and she blinked angrily. "And then…and then…"

"What?" Burton was full of foreboding.

"He told me to put my things back in the closet, and when I wouldn't—" she took a deep breath "—he hit me."

Burton felt the impact of her statement like a hard right to his gut. Adrenaline poured through his veins. He clenched his hands into fists and got to his feet, wanting to smash a dead man into pulp. Instead, he pulled Veronique, his beautiful, precious Veronique, into a protective embrace. "Oh, God, Veronique. That bastard."

He held her tightly, and gradually her arms slipped around his waist and she was holding him tightly, too. She was very still. Then he felt her breathe a deep sigh, and when she drew back there was moisture in her eyes—and a greater closeness between them.

"Were you badly hurt?" He hated even talking about it, but he needed to know.

"No. A bruise here," she said, touching her left cheek-bone. "It healed faster than my heart or my pride." She looked down. "I've never told anybody all of it. It was hard to tell you."

"I know."

"He tried to make me feel like I deserved it—"

"No!" He pulled her close again.

"Maybe I was weak to allow it to happen and—"

He put his fingers against her lips. "The man was a Neanderthal. Evolution should have weeded him out at birth."

She giggled. "Don't tell Marion that." Then her smile faded and her chin came up. "I am not a victim."

He pulled her into another hug. "I wouldn't think that in a million years."

She laid her head on his chest and sighed again. "Thank you for understanding." Her arms tightened around him. "You are a good man. I...I like you very much."

Then she eased away. Burton watched her move across the kitchen to get a jug of water from the fridge. No wonder she'd hated Graham. But wasn't love the opposite of hate?

"It must have been hard for Marion to hear that about her son."

"I should never have told her," Veronique said. "She refused to believe me, and so she pushed me away, her closest friend. But I think deep down she must believe me. She never say a word against her husband, but once I came into their house—the door was open and they didn't hear me knock—and I saw Stan holding her arm so tight she had tears in her eyes. I was shocked. I didn't know what to do. I tiptoed out and knocked loudly before coming in again."

"Did you ever ask her about it?"

"Yes, but she made some excuse to cover up for Stan. Now she covers up for her son. She doesn't want to admit the truth because if she does, it will destroy one of her few comforts, her fond memories of Graham."

Burton took the jug from her and set it on the table. "She's deluding herself. The truth will make her stronger."

"I thought it would break the barrier between us, but it seems to have created a bigger one. And I have lost a good friend. I should go see her again, but I dread it."

The microwave beeped. She took the container out and stirred it. While she ladled soup into two bowls, Burton thought about Veronique and himself, and how this Graham character had more than one barrier to answer for.

"I don't want to talk about Graham anymore," she said. "Did you get another chef?" A tiny crease formed between her eyes.

"Nothing has been finalized," he said cautiously. "Do you—"

She placed a bowl of fragrant, steaming soup before him. "Eat first. Then we talk turnip."

He laughed. "Turkey. We talk turkey."

"Whatever." She tasted a spoonful of soup. "This is good. Was it still raining when you came?"

"No, it stopped. You know, Veronique, I hate to think you're getting such a bad impression of Vancouver. This is an unusually wet year."

She laughed. "Everyone I meet tell me the same thing. Then I ask Tom—"

"The station's weatherman?"

"Yes. He show me graphs of rainfall. This year is not so very different from last year. Or the year before. Which reminds me." She jumped up, went into the other room and returned brandishing her umbrella. "Look," she said, pushing it open. "It was in the Lost and Found at the bus station."

She did care, Burton thought as a smile started in his heart and worked its way to his lips. The Lost and Found was in the main bus terminal over on Cambie, several miles and at least two bus changes away. A trip she must have made in the pouring rain and sick with a cold. He ought to scold her for going out in the weather, but instead, he said warmly, "I'm glad you got it back. Now furl that thing or you'll bring us bad luck."

"Can it get any worse?" she said with a grin. "What else has happened while I am away?"

He pushed his empty bowl to one side. "Well—"

"Wait." She rose and took his hand. "Come and sit where it's more comfortable."

Burton leaned against the cushions in one corner of the sofa. Veronique put on some quiet piano music, then tucked her legs beneath her *pareau* and rested against the other arm, facing him.

He told her all the gossip at the station: Sylvia had a new boyfriend, Murphy had turned into a rabid antismoker, and Lillian's grandniece, Sandy, was coming in at lunchtime to do female staff members' hair in the makeup room. They chatted and laughed, and Burton silently admired the gleam of lamplight in Veronique's hair and on the ridge of her collarbone, and wished he could trace his tongue down that smooth path to dip into the shadowed hollow....

"Come back, Veronique," he said, leaning forward to clasp her hands and pull her closer. Breathing in her scent, he pressed his mouth to her inner wrist, to the hollow of her elbow. This time she didn't pull away.

Her eyes closed. "To the studio...or the farm?"

"Both." He felt her quickened pulse beneath his lips. "I need you."

Her eyes, still half closed, lifted to meet his. "You, the producer, or—" her voice dropped to a purr "—you, the man?"

"Again, both. But the man takes precedence."

He bent his head, and she lifted her mouth to meet his. Sensation focused, then diffused, till he was enveloped by warmth. Desire grew and expanded, like a living thing.

"Who do you...?" His voice cracked.

She knew what he meant. "I see you, Burton. Only you."

They moved closer on the sofa. The scent of *tiaré* was gradually replaced by the musky aroma of two bodies entwined, the quiet strains of Debussy overcome by breathless sighs and gentle moans. Her *pareau* parted just where he knew it would, a tantalizing revelation of slim brown thighs. His hand slid up that satiny skin to the source of her warmth, and wonder of heavenly wonders, encountered soft, moist curls, instead of panties. Here at least, there were no barriers.

His fingers found her breasts beneath her shirt, and they, too, were bare. And full and firm and... He drew back, breathing deep. "Is this what you want, too?"

Wordlessly she nodded. With one hand, she pressed his fingers against her hardened nipple; with the other she palmed his aching groin. She pressed and half rose to her knees, swaying toward him. Her *pareau* fell further open. Then, her open mouth hot and wet on his, she slowly slid his zipper down.

VERONIQUE AWOKE AS DAWN filtered through the chinks in the curtains. The previous night came back to her in a rush of aching limbs and remembered pleasure. She turned over to gaze across her pillow at Burton. His dark copper hair clashed with her hot pink comforter, and stuck up in spikes and cowlicks, but this was the most peaceful she'd ever seen him. Having him in her bed flooded her with warmth and made her smile. Such a sweet, silly grin he wore. Must be a nice dream.

Mon Dieu, but he was adorable. He might do everything else in a speedy fashion, but when it came to making love he took his time—and was very thorough. Thinking about it made her wriggle closer. She contemplated waking him up, but the poor man needed his rest.

Close up, he looked nothing like Graham. He had a different body—strong, but sleek rather than thick-set. What a pity that hatred of Graham had kept her from really seeing Burton for so long. Now, when they had just a short time left, she wanted to look her fill.

She thought of the chess set suddenly. She should tell him. She must tell him. But she hated the thought of anything disturbing this newfound closeness between them, even though their relationship would only last until the cooking series was over. Then she would go back to Tahiti. He would keep the farm or he would sell it. Either way, he would finish his documentary and move on to something else. They would sign divorce papers sent through the mail. Someday he would meet someone else, fall in love and start a family....

No, she couldn't bear to envisage such a future for Burton. All she wanted to see was the present, with her in it. The immediate present, to be exact. His nose twitched, and he scratched it in his sleep. There was that grin again. It made her want to touch his lips. Perhaps she would allow herself just a little stroke across his full lower lip....

Burton's eyes opened. Their direct blueness stopped her breath. *"Bonjour,"* she whispered.

"Bonjour," Burton replied, and laughed. "My accent is terrible."

"No, that was pretty good. Now say, *Tu es une femme formidable,* Veronique." She couldn't resist teasing him.

"You are a formidable woman, Veronique," he agreed in English. He shifted closer and nuzzled behind her ear, while his fingers slid up her rib cage to cup her breast.

"I thought you wanted to learn French," she reproached him.

"Let's start with the language of lovemaking," he murmured, his warm breath bathing her ear.

Suddenly she was afraid of how badly she wanted him, and how soon she would lose him. She rolled onto her back and stared up at the ceiling. "Our marriage is only temporary. I don't want either of us to get hurt."

"We won't, as long as we keep doing these wonderful things to each other." he stroked a hand up the inside of her thigh to illustrate.

"You're not taking this seriously," she said, even as her eyes closed and warm tendrils of desire curled through her. "Last night was *fantastique,* but—"

He kissed her nose. "No 'buts.'"

She grasped his hand to still it and opened her eyes so he could see she was serious. "Before you arrived last night, I had a call from Ghislaine."

"What did she have to say?" he asked, paying more attention to the movement of her lips than her words.

"Do you remember I told you about the floating restaurant in Papeete? Jean-Paul has offered me the position of head chef."

His smile faded. "Are you going to take it?"

"Such opportunities do not come often in Tahiti. I always said I would leave at the end of the summer." She bit her lip, glancing away. The pain was already starting.

"So you did." His voice sounded strained. "What about *Flavors?*"

"I will finish the series," she whispered, on the verge of tears. "I cannot promise more."

He ran the back of his finger down her cheek, his eyes sad. "In that case, we'd better make the most of the time we've got."

With a sigh, she shifted closer to rest her head on his chest. She breathed in his scent and smoothed her palm across the ridges of muscle and bone beneath his skin.

Already she missed what she was losing. "Let's just hold each other."

He slid an arm around her back and rolled to face her. "I'd like that."

Their bodies touched all down the front. Some places touched more than others. "Can't help it," he murmured as he grew hard against her.

Neither could she help the melting heat softening her womb, spreading through all her secret places. With a moan, she wriggled closer, pressing her breasts and hips against him.

"One of us has got to have some willpower," he complained even as he spread his hands over her hips to pull her in more snugly. "Our appointment with Immigration is in an hour."

"You're the man. You're supposed to be strong." She stroked a hand down his buttock to the back of his thigh.

"Not when it comes to you." His kisses began with her lips and drifted downward, lingering in the hollow of her hip before searing a path to the moist cleft between her legs. "How do you say in French 'I want to make love to you'?"

She whispered the words and more besides, crooning the soft, musical syllables of her passion while his lips and tongue spoke directly to her heated flesh.

"Don't stop," he murmured when his intimate kisses had reduced her to speechless desire.

"Don't stop," she begged in turn, and urged him on with a throaty description of the way he was making her feel, and the pleasure she would give in return. For the moment, at least, there was no more talk of the future and their diverging paths.

CHAPTER FOURTEEN

WENDY CONNERY SLIPPED the pair of glasses that dangled from a black plastic chain around her neck onto her rather pointed nose. With silent deliberation, she read through the contents of the manila folder she'd brought with her to this small bare box of an interview room. Veronique sat opposite her in one of the two hard plastic chairs and studied her bent head from across the table, noting where the thick streak of white hair fanned out and blended by degrees with the dark.

Somewhere down the corridor, in another room such as this, Burton was undergoing a similar ordeal at the hands of James Jackson. Her heart and mind called out to him, recalling the encouraging lift of his mouth and warm wink before he was led away. Just before they'd left her apartment Burton had taken the photos of her and Graham from his pocket and laid them facedown on the mantelpiece, saying, "I don't want to ever pretend to be him."

Wendy Connery cleared her throat and raised two sharp gray eyes to peer at Veronique over the top of her reading glasses. "You married Burton William O'Rourke on June 4. Is that correct?"

"*Oui*. That is correct." Veronique tugged on a curl of hair.

"Where and when did you and Mr. O'Rourke first meet?" Mrs. Connery went on in her spare, clipped voice.

Veronique and Burton had decided in the end to stick to the truth and not to worry if they didn't know every detail about each other. Their lovemaking seemed to lend legitimacy to their relationship—regardless of how long it was destined to last.

"May 3," Veronique replied. "Burton was dining in the restaurant where I worked and asked to compliment the chef. That was me." It was, strictly speaking, the truth, if not quite the whole truth.

Connery checked her file again. "You remarried six months after losing your first husband and only four weeks after meeting Mr. O'Rourke." Short black lashes narrowed over slashes of eyes. "Would you say you are impulsive by nature, Ms. Dutot?"

"It's Mrs. O'Rourke." Wendy Connery was probably a nice woman, just doing her job, but Veronique didn't care for her attitude. "I knew my first husband only two weeks before I agreed to marry him." She smiled. "When it comes to love, it would seem that, yes, I am impulsive."

"Or very determined to stay in Canada."

Veronique shivered. "*Non,* absolutely not. I wanted to go back to my home in Tahiti, but…love happens."

Wendy Connery had undoubtedly had a lot of practice perfecting that skeptical noise she made in the back of her throat. "Do you and Mr. O'Rourke reside at the same address?"

"Yes. Burton's grandfather died just over a month ago and left him a farm in Langley. We've moved out there until it can be sold."

"Yet I understand you've kept your apartment on Cornwall Avenue." Her severe, dark eyebrows slanted with suspicion.

Veronique shrugged. "I have many tropical plants that would not take well to a move. I wait until Burton sell his farm and we decide which of our apartments to live in before I give up mine."

"I see." Connery made a note on the form. "Do you share a bedroom?"

Since last night. "Yes."

"And the marriage has been consummated?" The question was clipped and impersonal, as though she was inquiring into Veronique's choice of laundry detergent.

Veronique felt her cheeks grow warm, not with embarrassment, but remembered desire. *"Oui."*

Something in her voice must have penetrated Mrs. Connery's bureaucratic consciousness. She glanced up and took stock of Veronique. "Are you in love with him?"

Asked point-blank, Veronique was astonished to find she could lie with ease. In fact, she liked Burton so much it didn't even feel like lying. "Yes," she replied warmly, "I love him very much."

"And is your marriage based on this love?"

Down the hall, Burton was presumably undergoing a similar interrogation. "Not entirely."

"Oh?" Wendy Connery's features sharpened.

"I also respect and admire him. He is a good friend, not just to me, but to the people he works with. He is funny and kind. He has his faults—like being too much in a hurry sometimes, and he is also a little stubborn. But I would trust him with anything. He is an honorable man and an honest one."

"I see." The Immigration officer's face softened thoughtfully. "And Mr. O'Rourke shares these feelings?"

"Yes, he does," Veronique replied without hesitation. Burton might pretend the marriage was only one of expediency, and there might have been a time when it was true. But she knew another side of him now. No man could be such a tender and passionate lover and be indifferent. Besides, he'd said... She pushed the thought away, annoyed with herself for yearning after what she couldn't have. He'd had plenty of opportunity to say he loved her again last night, or even this morning, yet he hadn't.

Wendy Connery scribbled something at the bottom of

the page. "Thank you, Mrs. O'Rourke. That's all for now. We'll be in touch if we need further information."

Burton was waiting for her outside. He opened his arms and she practically leaped into them. He kissed her on the mouth, on her cheeks and on the tip of her nose till she was laughing and giddy.

"How did it go?" he demanded.

Gleefully, she danced him around in a circle. "I think we're going to make it."

"I do, too. It was easier than I thought. They didn't even ask me what color of lipstick you wear."

"I don't wear lipstick, silly, except on the show." She stopped laughing and stood still. "I guess we'd better go to the studio. We've missed two days of taping."

He shook his head. "You're sick."

"I am not. I feel fantastic."

"Your voice is still husky. You should rest it over the weekend. I'll call Ernie from the farm and get him to organize the crew to resume taping on Monday. Come on," he said, tucking her hand in the crook of his arm. "Let's go home."

HOME. IT WAS NATURAL for Burton to call it that, but Veronique hadn't expected the strong sense of homecoming she felt as they bumped up the long gravel driveway to the farmhouse. She wanted to run to the orchard and see if the blush was on the plums, to stroll by the henhouse and see if the chicks had hatched. To dig in the rich earth of the garden, to feel the soft grass between her bare toes. To come out on the porch at dawn and see Mount Baker drift like a mystical white sail on a rose sunrise. Only a week and already she'd ceased to view it as Burton's grandfather's home. It was Burton's home...and hers.

Ridiculous, she tried to tell herself. Her home was thousands of miles away, and the sooner she got there the better. Once she'd honored her commitments and tied up the loose threads of her life in Canada, she would be on the plane to Tahiti. For now, she followed Burton up the steps to the porch.

He opened the squeaky screen door and put the key in the lock. "First thing I'm going to do is put some oil on that hinge."

"No, it isn't," she said, tugging on his wrist to pull him back outside. "First thing you're going to do is…"

His arms swept around her. "Make love in the long grass?"

The murmured suggestion made her heart beat faster. The threads that bound her to him were not so loose as she might have liked. "No, silly. Go for a walk and show me around the farm."

"You've already seen most of it." His eyes narrowed as though he suspected a plot.

She smiled innocently back at him. *Of course it is a plot, you big, foolish, beautiful man.* A plot to remind him how much he loved this place. So that when he got his chess set back he would take down the For Sale sign from the fence by the road, and keep the farm—for himself, for his children and his children's children.

"I want to see it all. Every acre, every tree, every special spot you knew as a child. I want to see it through your eyes."

Burton gazed at her and realized suddenly that he wanted her to see his farm. Relating to James Jackson the story of how she'd worked by his side in the mud and the rain had made him understand for the first time how marriage could be a partnership. But that hadn't expressed everything he felt, so he'd tried to put into words the sunshine she'd brought into his life, the warmth and companionship, the excitement and anticipation of each new day together. He'd been surprised by his eagerness to talk about her, just saying her name gave him pleasure. He wanted to know all about her, not just for Immigration, but for himself. And he wanted to share with her the things that were special to him.

"Why not?" he said with a smile. "Hang on—I'll get my camera."

Burton was in his grandfather's room, slinging the camera strap around his neck, when he heard the sound of a diesel engine coming up the driveway. He walked quickly back down the hall and pushed through the screen door. Veronique was on her knees in the flower bed, inspecting her marigold seedlings. She got to her feet as he came down the steps, and together they watched a big green tractor come over the rise. In the driver's seat was a burly man in his fifties, wearing a jeans jacket and a red Mack hat. Behind the tractor, he was towing another piece of farm machinery.

"Hank!" Burton called, recognizing his neighbor.

Hank Vandermere brought the tractor to a halt outside the barn. Switching off the ignition, he climbed down and came forward to clasp Burton's hand in an iron grip. "Sorry to hear about your granddad. He was a real fine man. We'll miss him around here."

Burton nodded. "Thanks. I miss him, too. So how've you been? How's Mary? This is Veronique. Veronique, Hank Vandermere."

"Bonjour," Veronique said. "I met your daughter-in-law, Jill."

"She mentioned that," Hank replied with a friendly grin as he shook her hand. "Said she was glad to see another young woman close by. Kinda misses her city friends. Mary's fine," he added, getting around to Burton's question. "She said to say hello and ask if there's anything she could do to help."

"Tell her thanks, we appreciate the help with the chickens, but everything else is pretty much under control. Everything except the potato crop, that is. You don't know where I could beg, borrow or steal a pick-planter, do you?'' He glanced hopefully at the one Hank was towing.

Hank scratched his head under his cap. ''Well, now, I feel real bad for keeping your granddad's machine this long. Been meaning to get over here for some time, but this damn rain's slowed everything down. I did come by once or twice just to say hello, but you weren't around.''

Burton's head jerked in surprise. ''Wait a minute. Did you say 'Granddad's machine'?''

''Yeah, didn't he tell you he rented it to me? Sure was a help. Rick and I were able to get the job done a lot faster…. Say, are you all right, son?''

Burton was walking openmouthed toward the machine attached to Hank's tractor. ''This is Granddad's pick-planter?''

''Yep. My south-facing slope is drier'n his field here, so I rented it off him to use first. Didn't figure on keeping it this long. Hope I haven't held you up.''

Burton dragged a hand through his hair. He glanced at Veronique and they burst out laughing.

Hank rubbed his weathered jaw. ''Is there some joke I'm missing?''

''It's a long story,'' Burton replied, still chuckling. ''I'll tell you sometime, but I've got to warn you, it's not really funny. Rented, you said.''

''Yeah. I paid him up front. Said he needed the money for something.''

Insurance premiums, Burton thought as another piece of the mystery fell into place.

Hank went around to the back of the trailer and started to unhitch the pick-planter. ''We're all done over there. You want some help getting your spuds in the ground?''

''You bet I would,'' Burton said. ''Just let me know what it's worth to you.'' Together they pushed the pick-planter toward the barn while Vernonique ran ahead to open the big double doors.

As they came back out into the sunlight, Burton said, "Say, Hank, you've been farming a long time...."

Hank rubbed a hand over a neck reddened and roughened by years of exposure to all kinds of weather. "All my life. Just like my father before me. In a few years, Rick'll take over."

Burton grinned. "How'd you like to be on TV?"

Hank let out a snort of disbelieving laughter, but when Burton explained about his documentary, he readily agreed to participate if it would mean raising the profile of farming in the valley.

"That's great," Burton said, shaking his hand to seal the deal. "Thanks again."

Hank climbed back on the tractor and turned the key in the ignition. "No problem," he said over the noise of the engine. "Rick'n I'll be over first thing Monday to start on your fields."

Burton and Veronique waved him out of sight, then, hand in hand, they walked along the fence line bordering the potato field. Veronique gazed over the endless rows of plowed land and gave a half laugh, half shudder. "I can't believe we thought we could plant the whole thing by hand."

"I knew better," Burton said. "I was just...possessed, or something. I'm sorry I dragged you into it. It was a stupid idea—"

"No, don't say that. It was important at the time." She paused. "You know, Burton, you are looking for another farmer to replace your granddad in the documentary, and I guess that's a good idea, but—" she squinted up at him "—it makes sense to interview yourself, no? You are part of the new generation that is moving off the land for one reason or another."

The sting of truth made him turn from her gentle questioning gaze. How could he presume to lecture others? What would Granddad think of him right now? "You're right. I keep telling myself I'm helping work toward a solution when really I'm part of the problem.''

She squeezed his hand. ''Nothing's black and white, and I do not judge you. I just think you would regret letting the farm go.''

''I already regret it,'' he said quietly, and walked on.

In silence they continued their climb to the top of the ridge, their footsteps falling in the uneven ruts left by the tractor. ''At least this year's crop is taken care of,'' Burton said. ''Now if only I could find out where Granddad hid the chess set. I've searched practically everywhere. Where is it?''

It was a rhetorical question, and he'd been speaking half to himself, but Veronique made no response at all, quite unlike her. He tugged on her hand, needing to feel her presence. ''Hey, you with me?''

She gave him a weak smile and changed the subject. ''If Hank and his son plant the potatoes, will they also harvest?''

Burton shrugged. ''I guess so, if I ask them to. Or maybe I'll sell the crop in the field to those guys from Chilliwack along with the farm. When I was a boy, Granddad always said, A man with land is a rich man.'' He chuckled. ''I thought he meant rich as in money and imagined granaries heaped with coins, like Scrooge McDuck's money vault.'' His laughter faded. What Granddad had left him was more valuable than mere money. Did he have the courage and the vision to take it on?

Walking the land on this balmy summer day brought back memories of childhood, of days when he'd been intimately aware of his natural surroundings: the heavy drone of bees among the clover, the slither of a garter snake in the thick grass beside the ditch, the earthy scent of sun-warmed dirt in the plowed field, and the sight of sun-haloed dandelion seeds drifting on the light breeze. Burton walked his land with a slow pace, breathing deeply, taking in every nuance of light and color, every sight and smell. Veronique's delighted reaction to his special spots put a gloss on the day.

He showed her the creek that dwindled to a trickle in August, and the banks of clay that could be molded by small hands. The stand of quick-growing alder that hadn't existed when he was a boy, and the giant maple that had split in two when the tail end of Hurricane Frieda lashed Vancouver the year he was born. They stopped at the fallen trunk for a rest, and Veronique sat cross-legged on the log, braiding a daisy chain. He told her stories of making forts among the fallen branches, of hurling chestnuts and brandishing fern swords at imaginary invaders. Later, as a teenager, he'd sat up here out of sight of the farmhouse and coughed over his first, and last, cigarette.

Now, as a man, he raised his camera and looked through the lens at the woman who for some unfathomable reason seemed to belong to this place almost as much as he.

Engrossed in weaving starry white flowers into a circle, Veronique wasn't aware he'd taken her photo until the shutter clicked. Then she glanced up, startled, and the second shot he got was of a comical face with a tongue sticking out. He clicked again, and she became demure, hiding behind a strand of curling hair that glinted like gold in the sun. He moved to a different angle and she posed outrageously, one elbow crooked behind her head like an old-fashioned movie star, with a smirk that said she wasn't taking any of this seriously.

Then her arms dropped, and she looked straight into the camera, her mobile face composed in an expression both winsome and grave, and so light it might change with the breeze. Yet laughter lurked in eyes the color of the grass at her feet. And—dare he believe it was for him?—a loving tenderness that made him feel ten feet tall, ready to slay the advancing hordes with his fern swords and horse chestnuts.

He slowly lowered the camera, still gazing at her. His mental VCR fast-forwarded, and with a catch of his heart, he saw their child, tousled blond head and grubby, tanned limbs, playing at her feet. For an instant, time compressed and light expanded; the past, present and future composed a picture of love so tangible he wanted to reach out and touch it. Family. His family. His future.

"Burton? Are you okay?"

He lowered the camera to the ground. "Yeah, I'm fine. Just fine."

Still in a dream, he walked over to the log. He took the completed circle of daisies and placed it on her head. Then he pulled her down to the grass to lie by his side, and memorized the shape and color of her face the way he'd memorized the topography of the land that had been passed to him for safekeeping. He loved them both. Unbelievably, he was going to let them go.

"Make love to me," she murmured, touching his cheek with the tip of one finger.

Slowly, tenderly, with smiles and whispers, they joined together there in the grass, warmed by the summer sun, buoyed by the solid, patient land. It was a marriage of body and soul, more real than any piece of paper, more binding than any legal document He touched her with the exquisite care he'd use if she were made of fine china. When she came, he came, too, trembling and in awe.

"Heaven on earth," he murmured, gazing into her eyes.

Afterward Burton slept, his head resting on her breast, while she lightly stroked his temple. The soft, throaty sound of a French lullaby mingled in his consciousness with the whisper of the wind in the trees and the distant thrum of a tractor turning over sun-warmed earth. When he awoke to long shadows and the imprint of grass stems on his skin, he was rested soul-deep.

"I had the most fantastic dream," he told her excitedly as they walked back to the house. "I was a young teenager again, living here at the farm. One night a spaceship landed in the potato field. Don't laugh, I'm serious. It was like a movie, and even in my dream, I remember thinking, this would make a great teen drama series...."

COCOONED IN THEIR farmhouse, tending to garden and chickens, Burton and Veronique spent an idyllic weekend, choosing by mutual consent not to speak of the future. By Monday morning, Veronique had an abundance of ripe pomegranates, and taping of week five proceeded without a hitch. The rest of the week passed in a blissful haze, as the series progressed through to week eleven.

Veronique knew she ought to go see Marion, but the pain of their last meeting was still too raw, and she kept putting it off. She was hurt, too, that Marion had made no attempt to call her. Finally, around midweek, she rang the nursing home only to be told Marion was napping. Marion never returned her call.

She tried not to mind, to concentrate, instead, on life at the studio and at the farm. In the long golden evenings after work, Burton would film Hank and Rick planting potatoes, afterward capturing their thoughts and fears and dreams for the future of farming on video and audiotape. Murphy hadn't officially given him the okay, but he was doing it, anyway, getting in the footage while the sun shone and the tractors were running. Whenever he had a spare minute, he searched the house and even the barn for the chess set.

During those times, Veronique always found something else important to do. Every day that passed without her returning the chess set made the act harder and harder to initiate. Their happiness was so short-lived, and so fragile. She knew the moment she gave it back would mark the beginning of the end. So she puttered around the farm-house, fixing up a holder for her many spice jars, finishing Granddad's chair...and thinking about her own hopes and fears for the future. Nights were sweet. Burton never again said he was falling in love with her, but his gentle touch and passionate response conveyed the message that he was already there. She cherished the time with him, knowing it would be all too short.

As the days passed and they approached the end of their third week of married life, Veronique knew if anyone was living in a dream world, it was her. The series was almost over. Marion didn't seem to need her anymore. She and Burton couldn't ignore the realities of their lives for much longer. Soon it would be time for her to go home.

That Sunday night, she prepared one of Burton's favorite dinners. All through the rainy summer afternoon he'd been plotting a pilot episode for his sci-fi series. Now he rocked back in Granddad's chair, sipping cold beer and munching prawn crackers while she ground aromatic spices together with fresh garlic and chili in a mortar and pestle.

"Your idea sounds good," she said when she had a chance to get a word in. "You have the perfect place to film, right here."

His smile faded. "The farm won't belong to me by the time this series is produced."

He hadn't mentioned selling for so long she'd begun to think he'd given up the idea. "Even now you want to sell? After this wonderful time we've spent here?" She tossed the spice paste into a heated wok and stirred rapidly, speaking above the hiss of oil and pungent steam. "How can you sell your past, Burton? How can you sell your children's future?"

His beer glass came down hard on the table. "How can I make the farm a viable part of my present? Tell me that."

She tossed fresh prawns into the wok, flicking him a disappointed glance. The prawns turned pink as she stirred them into the spice mixture, and she dumped in cold, cooked basmati rice and a generous slurp of *ketjap*—Indonesian soy sauce. "I don't understand you," she exclaimed, giving the mixture a vigorous stir. "You said you wouldn't sell until you found the chess set."

His shoulders hunched over the table. "I didn't know it would take so long. Maybe the set isn't even here. I've decided to give myself till the end of July to find it. That way I'll have a month or two to put the farm on the market before the autumn rains come."

Veronique lifted fragrant, steaming spoonfuls of Indonesian fried rice into wide, shallow bowls and topped them with fried eggs and chopped cilantro. Burton pulled in his legs as she placed the bowls on the table and sat down catercorner from him.

"It's like I always say, you are in too much of a hurry." She picked up a fork and poked at her rice. "I thought about you living here and I thought, just thought, that if I stayed in Canada, this is the sort of place I could live— with land, and animals, and real neighbors. A place with…community."

Burton sat up straighter. "Do you mean…?"

Her sharp glance was curiously painful. "I said, *if* I stayed."

He stabbed a forkful of rice and vegetables and poked it into his mouth. When the autumn rains came, Veronique would be gone. The thought hung in the air between them like low-lying cloud. He would move back to his lonely apartment and concentrate on his career. His mother would go back to matchmaking. Veronique would prepare delicious meals for strangers.

Burton toyed with the idea of himself in Tahiti, lazing in the tropical sun by day, making love to Veronique by night. It sounded like the perfect vacation. But that was all it could be. She wouldn't stay here, and for him to go live on a tiny island in the middle of nowhere would be professional suicide.

He took another bite of the rice, but the taste had gone

out of it. If he told her again he loved her, would she stay? Or would she run that much faster?

"Tomorrow we tape the last two segments." He spoke impersonally, as he would to a mere colleague, not the woman he'd made love to dozens of times. "You'll need to stick around for another week until editing is complete in case something has to be redone. After that you'll be...free to go. Have you made plans yet?"

"It will depend on Marion." Veronique, too, sounded stiff. "I will see her tomorrow, make a decision."

For a moment he thought of playing on her sympathy, trying to convince her that Marion shouldn't be left, but it wouldn't be fair and would only delay the inevitable. "You've done all you could. Far more than you had any obligation to do."

She stared at her untouched plate, making no pretense at eating. "I have done wrong things. I have tried to play God, thinking I know best for people. Instead, I have messed everything up."

"You did what you thought best at the time. That's all anyone can do. But I agree you should talk to her again. Don't let her drive you away. That will only make her feel worse in the long run."

"I am so ashamed." Without warning she burst into tears.

"You didn't do anything wrong," Burton said, at a loss to understand the outburst. "Marion will be all right."

"You don't know." She snatched up the gingham napkin from beside her plate and wiped her eyes, struggling to regain control.

Pushing his plate away, he held out a hand, thinking to comfort her the best way he knew how. "Come to bed?"

She let him pull her to her feet, then let go his hand without meeting his eyes. "Tomorrow is the last day, and we must be up early for work. I'll stay in the other bedroom tonight."

"Stay with me," he urged softly. "I'll let you sleep."

"You know it's not a good idea." Her wet-lashed glance conveyed love and desire, sorrow and regret, all at the same time.

His heart thudded dully, heavy as stone in his chest. Was it over so suddenly? The sense of loss was achingly powerful. "This time together has been...wonderful and—" He stopped. Words were so damned inadequate.

"Shh, Burton." Her fingers, light and cool, touched his lips. "You are wonderful. It is I who... Tomorrow I will go to my apartment. It is time I made arrangements for my plants. Thank you, and...forgive me." She turned and disappeared down the darkened hallway.

Forgive her? he thought, gazing after her. For what? For making him love her? For leaving him? For showing him he would be nothing without the farm, and her, to fill his life with meaning? The honeymoon was over. She was easing herself out of his life, and there was not a damn thing he could do about it.

Early the next morning, before Burton was awake, Veronique took the chess set out of the bottom of her cupboard where she'd hidden it and put it on the kitchen table. Then she called Ernie, who answered the phone sleepily and thought at first he was still dreaming when he realized who it was. She asked him for a ride to work, as soon as he could possibly get there.

Veronique hoisted her suitcase and walked down the long, gravel driveway, away from the farmhouse and everything that mattered. The fresh summer morning was breathtakingly beautiful, but she barely noticed the pink blush of dawn or the riotous chorus of birdsong coming from the broadleaf maples lining the road.

She could delude herself no longer. For Burton, putting his inner visions on film was top priority. If he wouldn't compromise his career for the sake of the farm, there was no way he would give it up to come to Tahiti with her.

Nor would she ask him to. He was not her husband, not really. His home was not her home, after all. Hollow and dejected, she sat down on her bag to wait.

Before too long, she saw Ernie's rusty beige Volkswagen put-putting down the narrow country road, watching for the driveway. He had been courting Rita all week, but as far as Veronique knew, Rita, although encouraging, had yet to commit herself. Veronique suspected she was enjoying the attention and didn't blame her a bit.

Veronique stood up and stepped onto the road to wave at him. He slowed to a stop and got out, leaving the engine popping and spitting in the still morning air, to help her with her bag.

"*Salut,* Ernie," she said, kissing him on both cheeks. "I am sorry to get you up so early. You look tired."

"I don't mind, honestly." He yawned and tried to cover it.

"You should," she said severely, then smiled.

He opened the door for her, then went around to the driver's seat. "Are you okay, Veronique?"

She knew her eyes were red, but she just shrugged and made a production of rolling the window up and down to clear it of condensation. "I am okay."

Ernie put the car into gear, checked the rearview mirror and putted back onto the road. "Did you and Burton have a fight?"

"No. Yes. I don't know. We haven't had the fight yet, but it's coming." She glanced at him. "How are you and Rita doing?"

"Good." In spite of the circles under his eyes, he looked very happy. "We were up till two last night, hashing things out."

"And...?"

A smile split his round face. "She took my ring back. We've set a date for next April. Rita wants to be married in spring."

"Oh, Ernie, I am so happy for you!"

He heaved a sigh. "Oh, boy, me, too. You wouldn't believe what a rough couple of weeks it's been."

"True love is not easy, Ernie."

"You're telling me." He stared straight ahead. "You know there was a time when—"

"*Non.*" She cut him off firmly. "Some things it is better not to say. Part of growing older is learning the difference between the puppy-dog love and the real thing."

He sighed. "Maybe you're right. Anyway, I've got Burton to thank for setting me on the right path." He glanced over at her. "Do you think you two will, you know, stay together?"

She sighed. "Who knows, Ernie. Who knows."

BURTON OPENED HIS bedroom door and a note fluttered to the hardwood floor. He picked it up.

"Dear Burton, I've gone in early with Ernie...." Burton almost crumpled the paper then and there, but there was more. "You are right, I cannot wait any longer to talk to Marion, but I will be on time today, I promise! Look on the kitchen table. Sorry, sorry, sorry. Love, Veronique."

Sorry for what? he wondered, but he appreciated that she'd made him breakfast. He was probably being incredibly chauvinistic to want a woman who was a fabulous cook, but as long as he didn't say it aloud, maybe he'd get away with it. Humming, he strolled down the hall to the kitchen.

"SHE CAN'T BE GONE," Veronique insisted. "She doesn't go anywhere by herself."

The nurse on duty at the home just shook her head and repeated what she'd already said three times. "She went out with Mrs. Webster after an early breakfast."

Janice Webster. Marion had said that her old roommate came by to visit, but if she, Veronique, couldn't entice

Marion out on an outing, how could anyone else? There had to be something wrong.

She glanced at the clock on the wall behind the reception desk. Taping of *Flavors* would start in just thirty minutes, and first there was makeup.... "When are they coming back?"

"She didn't say. Our residents are free to come and go—in fact, we encourage independence. They need to learn to cope on their own before they leave here. Why don't you check back, say, at lunchtime?"

"I'll do that." Veronique started toward the front door, then stopped. "But could you ask her to call me at Channel Seven if she comes in before then?"

"I wouldn't worry so much, Mrs. O'Rourke. A sixty-one-year-old woman on crutches can't get far."

"She could fall again and hurt herself."

The nurse's face was patient. "There comes a time when you've got to let go. Let her stand on her own two feet."

Veronique blinked. Wasn't that just what she'd been trying to do all this time? She was glad Marion had taken her first steps toward self-sufficiency.

She hurried down to the station and through the revolving door. Lillian's latest hairdo was a soft, white-blond version of the latest fashion. It made her look ten years younger.

"Oh la la!" Veronique exclaimed. "Your niece is a genius. Perhaps I get her to do my hair before I go ba—" She broke off, unwilling to destroy the fiction of her marriage and her life in Canada quite yet.

Lillian's eyebrows rose slightly, but she merely opened her drawer and handed Veronique one of her grandniece's business cards. "Burton is in his office. He'd like to see you before the taping."

Veronique walked slowly down the corridor. She was not looking forward to this encounter. When he found out how long she'd had the chess set he was going to be very angry.

She knocked lightly at his door and poked her head around the corner.

"Come in."

His voice sounded distracted, but when he saw her, he leaped up and came around his desk to spin her around in his arms. "You wonderful, wonderful woman," he said, interspersing his words with kisses. "Where on earth did you find Granddad's chess set?"

Veronique couldn't reply, partly because he was still kissing her and partly because she was trying to think of a reasonable excuse for not telling him about the chess set sooner. But after a bit she needed to take a breath, and so did he. He drew back, still holding her hands, and gazed at her expectantly.

"It was in your grandfather's chair. When I took out the bottom to change the fabric on the seat cover, there it was."

"In the chair! I would never have thought of looking there."

"It was a good hiding place." She waited for him to realize the significance of the timing of her discovery.

Too excited for that, Burton snapped his fingers and paced across his office. "So I was right. He must have been afraid Mother would sell it to raise money for his insurance premiums, so he hid it in the bottom of the chair."

"Your mother wouldn't have taken it, would she? Not without telling him."

"No, of course not. But aside from Mother and me, the farm and the chess set were the only things that mattered to him. He wouldn't have taken chances on losing them. I guess we'll never know exactly what went through his mind. But it doesn't matter now that we've got it back." He strode quickly back to where she stood, kissed her hard again, then pushed her toward the door. "Quick now, you've got to get down to Makeup."

"But—"

"Go on. We'll talk some more after the show."

Oh la la. His pleasure and excitement would make her betrayal seem so much worse when he finally realized the truth.

As she entered the makeup room, she put aside her worries. "Congratulations, Rita, on your reengagement. You've made Ernie a very happy man."

"I'm just so excited," Rita said, bubbling over with happiness and a new self-assurance. "Ernie's changed. I'd just about given up on him until that night he went to the pub with Burton. Ever since then he's been so romantic. Thoughtful and considerate, too, and…oh, I don't know, strong, without being domineering."

"That's wonderful, Rita. I'm thrilled for you."

"You've got to come to the wedding," Rita said, getting out the Pan-Cake makeup. "I told Ernie I wanted to be a spring bride. It's my favorite season, but also it gives us a little more time. I mean, I'm sure about him, but I don't think it hurts to be absolutely sure."

"I think you're very wise, Rita." Veronique played with the hem of the plastic cape and decided this wasn't the time to mention she wouldn't be around in the spring. If she thought about leaving Burton, she'd burst into tears, and Rita would have to do her face all over again.

Rita babbled on about her and Ernie's plans, fortunately not noticing that Veronique hardly said a word. When she finally stepped down from the chair, Veronique gave Rita a hug. "You will make a beautiful bride."

"Thanks, Veronique. It might not have happened if not for you and Burton. Apparently Burton told Ernie the 'Secret,' or something mysterious like that. He wouldn't tell me what it was. Do you know what he's talking about?"

Veronique shook her head, mystified. "Never heard of it."

Rita shrugged. "Must be a guy thing. See you later."

When Veronique opened the door to the studio, the crew was already hyped at wrapping up the series. The buzz of conversation was louder than usual, and the atmosphere was charged with excitement. Burton had his headset slung around his neck, and his long legs carried him from group to group with purpose and energy. He was scanning his clipboard and was laughing at something Vince said when Veronique stepped inside, but with his uncanny instinct, he turned to her at that exact moment.

Burton's smile died on his face, and his eyes turned cold. She knew then he'd figured it out. The light seemed to go out of the room. Her heart seemed to shrivel, like an apple left out to dry. Deliberately Burton turned his back on her and began issuing directions to the crew. People began to move into place.

Mon Dieu. She hadn't realized till now how much she'd come to depend on his good nature and caring. How much she'd taken his affection for her for granted. How much she...loved him. The shattering realization flooded her with the bittersweet agony that came from knowing she herself had destroyed her chance at happiness.

She loved Burton. And now he hated her.

Ernie waved her over to the set. Chin up, smiling and chatting on her way to the kitchen, she didn't dare glance at Burton again. These past two weeks, all the joy and laughter they'd shared, the tender moments, the whispered confidences in the dark of night, the plans hatched at dawn—all that was over. *Finis.*

Burton stood to one side as Bill moved around her, checking the settings on his light meter. The sound man handed her the tiny microphone to clip to the front of her blouse.

Then Burton came up to her, his impersonal gaze sweeping over her for stray hairs or a shiny nose. "You started working on that chair almost three weeks ago," he said in an undertone, his voice colder than winter rain. "I remember because that was the day Don Chetwynd called to say he had a potential buyer. Why didn't you tell me you'd found the chess set? You knew how much it meant to me. All this time you knew where it was."

She wanted to reach out and touch him, to feel his warmth, to stroke his cowlick back from his forehead. All she could do was listen to a litany of her sins and try not to cry. She'd been so naive, thinking he would forgive her anything.

"And that night I came to your apartment—" he continued, still in that cold, horrible voice.

The night they'd first made love.

"I told you I had a definite offer. Yet still you didn't tell me. Why, Veronique? I could have sold the farm if it hadn't been for you."

Enough. She slammed a pot onto the stove, grateful for the anger that superseded pain. It was anger directed at herself, but that didn't matter. "That's exactly why I didn't tell you. Okay, I was wrong. I'm sorry. But I couldn't let you sell your farm when it means so much to you." And to her, she thought, but she couldn't say it. She had no right.

"How dare you make that decision for me?" As well as anger in his voice, there was now hurt. "You knew I didn't *want* to sell. You knew why I thought I had to. Why did you keep that chess set from me? Why?"

She put her hand on his where it rested on the granite countertop, conscious of the crew standing by, conscious of the urgency and inappropriateness of this time and place for the end of a love affair. Conscious of her desperation. "Because I love you."

Pain flashed through his eyes and tightened the muscles along his jaw. "Lousy timing, Veronique."

"This isn't a TV show!" she cried, furious with herself and with him. And petrified because with every word she spoke, his expression just got harder and colder.

Deliberately he removed his hand from beneath hers. "If you loved me, you would have given me the chess set."

"I should have. I see that now. Please, Burton..." Too choked up to continue speaking, she gazed at him, silently pleading for the light of love to come back to his eyes. Her heart beat hard and fast in a chest tight with pain. She longed for a wink or a smile, something to let her know she still had a place in his heart. Nothing.

"Can we talk about it later?" she begged.

"There's nothing left to say." He gave a sharp nod to Vince, and the floor manager motioned the camera operators back into place. Without a backward glance, Burton strode across to the spiral staircase and went up to the control booth.

Taping went smoothly, considering. Gradually Veronique relaxed enough to smile and joke with the audience while she cooked. She'd done this enough times to be able to call upon a certain detachment between her inner self and the woman being filmed. Her glance went repeatedly to the control booth, hoping for a sign of forgiveness and receiving none. On the back burner of her consciousness, thoughts of Marion simmered.

She wrapped up the last dish for that segment, the audience applauded, and the banks of floodlights went out with a series of heavy thuds. Lunch break. Veronique hurried to the dressing room to call the nursing home.

After a few words with the nurse receptionist, Veronique put the phone down and tugged on a curl. Marion had come in twenty minutes earlier, gotten her message and gone straight out again. What could she be doing? All the walking will tire her out, and make her hip sore. Why hadn't she called her? Veronique couldn't take back what she'd said about Graham, nor, now that she'd said it, did she want to. But she wanted Marion safe and sound. And she wanted her friend back.

Lunch hadn't improved Burton's disposition, and she suspected he hadn't even eaten. He used to be first in line to sample her food with the rest of the crew. Now he didn't even show up.

She stopped at Makeup for a touch-up, then went back to the studio. Ernie was talking to the audience, making jokes and telling stories till the crew was ready to shoot again. Veronique took her place behind the counter and checked that the ingredients were arranged the way she wanted them. Burton seemed to be everywhere but where she was, and she half feared, half hoped he'd forget to do his usual check of her before they started taping.

And then, still talking to Kate, the audio technician, via his headset, Burton came onto the set. His mind clearly elsewhere, he straightened Veronique's collar, then paused, his fingers lightly resting on her shoulder while he listened intently to whatever it was Kate was saying. Barely breathing, Veronique trembled on the verge of tears. He had no idea what he was doing to her. Indeed, he seemed hardly aware of her, so intense was his concentration.

He nodded to his unseen discussion partner, then his full attention focused on her. "Murphy's on his way down. There's someone in the audience cheering for you. This is our last show. Let's make it good."

She nodded and smiled tightly, fighting the urge to reach for him. He smiled back, but it was the smile of someone who had lost faith, who'd found to his cost that there was no such thing as eternity when it came to heaven on earth.

She watched him run up the stairs to the control booth and turned away to dab at her eyes with a tea towel. Then she took three deep breaths to calm herself and smiled out at the rows of seats. What had he meant, "Someone in the audience"?

She scanned the rows, and just before the banks of lights

snapped on, she saw Marion in the front row, beaming up at her. Astonished, Veronique smiled and blew her a kiss. But how? She glanced up at the control booth and directed a questioning lift of her eyebrows at Burton. He gave a two-fingered salute, then stepped out of sight before she could blow him a kiss, too.

His generosity gave her strength. Knowing Marion was in the audience gave her hope. She put all her energy into her performance, cutting off worries about the future to make the most of the present. This was the last show; she would go out with a bang, not a whimper.

Afterward, amid the applause, Murphy stepped forward from the sidelines to congratulate her. Burton came down to the set, and everybody crowded around, shaking hands and hugging and clapping one another on the back. Murphy predicted the ratings would top the charts. He declared to all present that Veronique would be the next Julia Child, and that anything Burton set his heart on was his for the asking.

The audience was filing out of the studio. Veronique saw Marion making her way slowly through the seats to the central aisle. Veronique glanced at Burton. He jerked his head, indicating she should go after Marion. But she wanted to talk to him, too. She tugged on her hair. Which way? Marion paused at the end of the row of seats and looked expectantly at her.

Veronique waved to her, then ran back to Burton. Silently, her heart breaking at his stony expression, she kissed him farewell, once, twice, thrice, on the cheeks. His eyes pressed shut, and she thought she saw a line of moisture beneath his lashes. But he didn't reach for her, and Marion was waiting.

CHAPTER FIFTEEN

MARION LEANED ON HER crutches with a welcoming smile. "The show was wonderful, Ronnie, dear. I'm so glad Mr. O'Rourke invited me to come and see it."

"I'm glad, too," Veronique said, kissing her on both cheeks.

"You remember Janice, my roommate at the rehab center?" Marion nodded to a thin, dark-haired woman standing to one side.

"How do you do?" Veronique said. Janice Webster didn't look nearly so grouchy without those tubes stuck in her. In fact, she had quite a nice smile.

"I'm fine, thank you," Janice said. "And please thank your husband for our tickets. It was a wonderful treat." She glanced at Marion. "I'll wait outside."

"Okay. I won't be long."

"I'm so glad you're all right," Veronique said when Janice had left. "I was worried when I didn't know where you were."

"I'm so sorry you were worried. I called the studio this morning. You weren't here yet, but Burton suggested I come down for your last show." Marion glanced around. "Could we sit down? My hip is a little sore."

"Of course." She helped Marion into a seat on the aisle, then slid into the one directly in front and twisted to face her. Lines of fatigue were etched around Marion's eyes and mouth, but Veronique noticed the new lipstick, gold earrings and matching necklace. "You look well."

"Thank you, my dear. I'm feeling much better." Marion put a hand over Veronique's where it lay on the seat back. "I want to apologize for the way I treated you last time. You took me by surprise. I'm so sorry, Ronnie."

Veronique looked down. "I should be the one to apologize. I should never have burdened you with Graham's wrongdoings."

"I thought so, too, at first. I was so angry at you for saying those things about my son. But gradually I cooled down, and then I just felt badly that he hurt you. You see—" Marion's voice wavered "—your accusations shocked me, but they didn't really surprise me. I know you must think Stan and I had the perfect marriage, but it wasn't. He could get very impatient with me...." Her words trailed off as tears filled her eyes.

"Marion," Veronique said urgently, "Stan's temper, his need to always be the big boss, was not your fault." Veronique had to make her believe this, if nothing else.

Marion stared at her, astonishment overtaking her anguish. "How did you know what he was like?"

She shrugged. "Graham must have gotten it from somewhere, and it certainly wasn't from you. I'm truly sorry if that hurts you."

Marion sighed heavily. "It's all right, Ronnie. In spite of everything, I did love Stan. But I'm grateful you brought things out in the open. It's made me think. In a way, it's freed me to be me. If Stan wasn't always right, then it means I wasn't always wrong—if you know what I mean."

"I know exactly what you mean. I am so glad we're friends again," Veronique said, clasping Marion's hand.

"You're more like a daughter to me," Marion said, smiling through her tears. She took a tissue from her cuff and dabbed at her eyes. "There's something else I've been meaning to tell you. Janice is going to move in with me when I get out of the nursing home."

"Oh, Marion, are you sure?"

"Yes. She lost her husband last year, too. She'll help me out in the house in exchange for reduced rent. We've become good friends. We're even going to join a bridge club together."

"I…I'm pleased for you." Veronique smiled hard to hide her hurt. What she'd been trying to get Marion to do for months, Janice had accomplished in a few weeks. "You have become independent."

"If it hadn't been for you, I probably would have curled up and stayed in a corner when Stan died," Marion replied. "I was too reliant on him. Your patience and good humor taught me it's easier to get through the hard times when you've got someone to talk to. That's why I was able to help Janice. I recognized loneliness and fear underneath her bad temper, so whenever she started acting unpleasant, I'd say, 'Tell me what's really bothering you.' And we just went on from there. You know that saying, 'What goes around, comes around'? If I've learned to cope, it's only because you made me believe I could. Janice and I went shopping this morning for something special to wear here today. Do you like my new earrings? I wanted you to be proud of me."

"I am," Veronique said, tears filling her eyes. "I am so very proud of you."

Marion patted her hand. "And now that you're married again, and to such a nice man, I can stop worrying about you."

Veronique started to laugh. "You were worried about *me?*"

Marion's gaze was tender. "You seemed so lost and alone."

Veronique glanced back at the set. The crowd was breaking up. Burton and Murphy were going off together, arms around each other's shoulders. Burton didn't look back. He had performed his final act of kindness. He was free. Free to finish his documentary. Free to begin work on another of the ideas spinning in his fertile brain. Free to find himself a real bride.

"Our marriage is over," Veronique said, turning back to Marion. "I'm going home."

She tried to smile, but her heart was breaking, and Marion seemed to know it at a glance. Her hand, so cool to the touch, pressed against Veronique's hot cheek.

"Oh, my dear, I'm going to miss you. I think you're making a big mistake."

Veronique blinked back her tears. The only mistake she'd made was in coming to this country in the first place. The sooner she was out of it, the sooner she could forget.

"So now will you take back Graham's money?" she said, changing the subject. "Now that you know why I don't want it?"

Marion's mouth set in a firm line. "No. As I've said many times, Stan left me well-provided for. Whatever Graham's faults, he married you and that's a commitment he'd never made before. The money he left rightfully belongs to you." Her voice softened. "He loved you, in his own way."

It was pointless arguing that if Graham had really loved her he wouldn't have hurt her. Marion had achieved a shaky truce between reality and happiness, having arranged her memories and beliefs in such a way that she could acknowledge the truth and still live with it.

"Well, if you won't take it back, what do you think of this idea?" she said, and explained an alternative use for Graham's money.

Marion smiled. "I think it's wonderful! Be sure and let me know how it turns out." She reached for her crutches.

Veronique rose to help her up. She hugged Marion goodbye. "Come and visit me in Tahiti."

Marion kissed her on both cheeks. "Next year, if you're in Tahiti, I just might take a cruise down that way."

Veronique got her things from the dressing room and left the building. The sky had been overcast when she'd entered the studio that morning; it was still overcast when she came out. The streak of aqua and gold along the western horizon might presage a coming high pressure system, or it might be the last glimpse of fine weather before another storm. Whatever. It didn't matter. Nothing mattered anymore.

Back at her apartment, she tried to take comfort in her plants and her familiar surroundings, but it didn't feel like home any longer. When she watered her gardenia, teardrops mingled with the shower from the big copper can. And when she called her travel agent to book her flight to Tahiti, she felt no joy, only pain. She wasn't going home, she was going into exile.

Veronique hung up the phone. She leaned back on the sofa where she and Burton had first made love and brought her knees up, wrapping her arms tightly around them. She ached with missing him.

She missed his crooked smile, his bright blue eyes, even his cowlick. She missed his energy and intensity, the way he leaped to his feet in his eagerness to start something new. She missed his long, lean body and his gentle, exciting touch. She missed his generosity and his kindness, the way he could make her smile with a flicker of his eyebrows and laugh with just a word or two. She missed seeing his face grow animated as an inner vision took hold of his imagination. She missed seeing the fondness in his eyes when he looked at his mother, and the passion in his gaze when he looked at her. She missed the tender way he held her close after making love. She missed talking, laughing, walking, making plans and seeing them through with him.

In short, she missed everything about him. From her living-room window she saw the lights of Vancouver wink on as dusk fell and knew she would not stop missing him even in Tahiti. Surrounded by her family and friends, speaking her own language, basking in the heat of the southern sun and swimming in the warmth of the South Pacific—she could have all this and still miss him. She would miss him for as long as she lived.

So it was really, really stupid to even *think* of leaving him.

THAT NIGHT, BURTON wandered through the farmhouse, trying to pinpoint exactly why the place he'd known for thirty-odd years without Veronique should feel so empty just because she'd gone. How could she have made such an impact on his life in such a short time?

Everything had turned out great in the end, he told himself. He had Granddad's chess set. He had his documentary in the bag. And on his way home from work, he'd stopped by Chetwynd's office in Langley to say he was ready to accept the offer on the farm. Within two hours Don had delivered the deposit to his door.

Lonely footsteps took him to the kitchen. Granddad's chair gleamed softly with wood oil and a dark blue brocade cover he recognized as the old living-room curtains. Taking refuge in the chair's familiar embrace, he rocked back and forth, seeing all around him the ways in which Veronique had made her mark. The kitchen was as clean as it had been in Gram's time. On the counter was the old wooden bread box Veronique had rescued from the basement and turned into a spice rack. Through the open front door he could hear the tinkle of the tropical shell mobile she'd hung on the porch. From the kitchen window he could see a corner of the garden in which she'd planted vegetables and herbs she would never see to fruition.

Suddenly he couldn't bear to stay a minute longer. Not if he had to stay there without her. He called Mary Vandermere and asked if they'd mind looking after the chickens again. Then he packed his bags and headed back to town. To his real life.

But if the farmhouse was lonely, then his apartment was as bleak as a monk's cell. Not another living thing inhabited these three small rooms, he noticed—no plants, no pets—and you could hardly call what he was doing "living." He could see now how little effort he'd put into creating a home for himself. Maybe it was from living on the road for so long. Maybe it was because he had too much on his mind and not enough in his heart.

A vague rumbling in his stomach suggested hunger, so he scavenged the nearly bare cupboards. The can opener scraping around the tin of beans was surely the loneliest sound in the universe. There was a time when he'd considered baked beans adequate sustenance. Now he pushed away the unappetizing plate of food. This was not what he hungered for.

He lay on his bed and leafed through the photos of Veronique he'd developed and printed in the studio dark room the previous week. The sunlight reflected in her expressive eyes made him yearn to live that day on the hill over again. The mobile mouth he loved to watch while she talked was still, but the impression of laughter had been captured. They'd had nearly three perfect weeks together. He'd rediscovered his childhood and begun to think about the future—with her.

It didn't matter a damn about the chess set. In fact, he realized now that he'd used it as an excuse to distance himself before she left him. The real problem was that they belonged to two different worlds. A fact not even love could change.

He fell asleep still clutching her photo.

The next morning, Burton did something he'd never done before—he called in sick when he wasn't ill. He knew he was just lovesick, but he seemed to have developed a physical pain in his chest that he suspected might lead to serious illness if left untreated. Unfortunately he was constitutionally incapable of lying about. He tried rolling the TV into the bedroom but was bored within minutes. By midmorning, he got out of bed, disgusted at wallowing in his own misery. He had to get out and move—walk, run, anywhere, it didn't matter. He had to burn off this energy before it burned him up.

Snatching up his camera, he headed out the door. He walked down to Denman Street with its traffic and cafés, then turned north, his restless footsteps pulling him toward the water and the seawall that circumnavigated Stanley Park.

He felt a little better just being out in the fresh air. Summer in Vancouver could be unpredictable, but nothing beat the days like today when the air was clear and warm, the sky an infinite blue, and the mountains seemed to rise straight from the chuckling blue-green sea.

Near the yacht harbor he came upon a bent old man tossing French fries to a trio of honking Canada geese. He raised his camera and snapped a few rapid frames, then caught the old man's eye and exchanged a smile over the beautiful day.

Moving on, he lengthened his stride. Tourists dawdled and pointed to the sights; they didn't bother him. He made a game of weaving between them, outrunning his thoughts. Under the Lion's Gate Bridge, he paused to watch an Alaskan cruise liner move majestically past on its way to dock. Burton raised his camera and caught the gleaming white prow just as the ship turned toward the soaring white sails of Canada Place. Above the liner a snowy jetstream of a 747 bound across the Pacific streaked across the brilliant blue sky.

Burton lowered the camera as an image of Veronique boarding a plane to Tahiti darkened his mood. Scenery was all very beautiful, but it didn't warm your bed at night.

What the hell was he going to do without her?

Driven by the ferocity of his thoughts, he rounded Prospect Point to face the open water of Georgia Strait. There, he put the telephoto lens on his camera and shot off half a roll of film on the California sea lions basking on the rocks offshore.

Out of nowhere a bald eagle swooped for a fish in the surge at the edge of the rocky intertidal. He crouched low to get the underside of the wings as the magnificent bird lifted off into the sun. *Click, click, click.* He'd almost forgotten what it was like taking pictures, the intense concentration and the burst of exhilaration when he got a really great shot. He could easily do this for a living again.

Burton's finger froze on the button. He could easily do this for a living. Straightening, he put the lens cap back on. It wasn't like he was married to Channel Seven. However, he *was* married to Veronique. More important, he wanted to stay married to her. He wanted to marry her all over again, for that matter.

Burton pictured himself leaving the studio and striking out on his own. The thought put his feet in gear, and he headed off again along the seawall. He didn't have to wait till he was fifty to pick and choose what he wanted to do. He could do that right now. He could choose to leave. And later he could choose to come back. And if there wasn't a spot for him right away, he'd make do.

The wind gusted around his face, and he sucked back strong salt air and the invigorating tang of ozone. Excitement lengthened his stride. An image came of himself under a beach umbrella in Tahiti, clacking away on a laptop, writing the script for his teenage sci-fi drama series. Next spring he'd slap it on Murphy's desk and say, "How about it, chief?"

Next spring. Would Veronique return with him? He could only ask. Well, he could beg, too, and though he hoped it wouldn't come to that, he knew he would do it if he had to.

He suspected getting Veronique to agree to marriage a second time would not be an easy task, but it was a goal worth striving for. He glanced at his watch. If he hurried, he could catch Murphy and square things away before the old man went to lunch. With a clear head, and a heart full of life and energy and the will to be happy, Burton headed for the studio.

"*MERCI,* Lillian. *Merci,* Sandy. I love my hair," Veronique called to Lillian and her grandniece as she went out the door of Channel Seven. Catherine's Volvo waited at the curb, its motor idling. "*Bonjour,* Catherine," she said, ducking into the car. "*Ça va?*"

"*Bien, merci.* Your hair looks wonderful," Catherine said, pulling into traffic. "I might get your friend to do mine next time I need a cut."

"She's getting a lot of experience." Veronique pulled down the visor and peered into the mirror. She ran her fingers through her newly trimmed locks, and watched the thick, honey-dark curls bounce back around her nape and ears. The blond bits were gone, but they seemed unimportant now. Why tie herself to the past when the future had so much to offer?

"Thank you for giving me a ride out to Langley," she said, glancing at Mother-in-law Number Two a little shyly. "I hope I'm not keeping you from anything important."

"Not at all. I'm glad you called me, and that Lillian had my home phone number. If you can stop the farm from going out of the family like you say you can, why, I'd drive to Hope and back if I thought it would help. But now that Burton has the chess set back, I'm afraid he won't waste any time putting the farm on the market."

"I know." Veronique reached up to twine her fingers into the hair at the back of her head and found there was not enough to catch hold of. She felt more nervous than ever. Was she doing the right thing?

"I'm not even sure Burton will be at the farm," Catherine continued. "He moved back to his apartment on the weekend."

Veronique frowned. "Lillian said he phoned in sick this morning, but when I called his apartment he wasn't there. The only other place I can think he would be is the farm. Anyway, it's not necessary for him to be there for my plan to work."

"And you're not going to tell me what that is, are you."

She glanced apologetically at Catherine. "I'd like Burton to be the first to know. Everything depends on whether we stay married."

Catherine slowed for a stoplight and turned to look at her. "Do you want to stay married to him?"

"Yes. More than anything. I love Burton very much."

Catherine smiled, and her eyes became bright. Then the light changed and she hit the gas. "Burtie told me your home was very important to you. Are you still going back to Tahiti?"

Veronique shrugged. "That's one of the things we need to work out between us."

Traffic was light and they swept through the city and onto the freeway in record time. Gradually Veronique began to relax a little. Her gaze swept from the mountains, across the spreading farmland, to Mount Baker in the south. What a magnificent day! There was not a cloud in sight to dim the sun. The ice-capped peaks were sharply etched against a deep blue sky. Every leaf, every blade of lush, green grass seemed to sparkle. She had never seen the Fraser Valley quite like this. She rolled down the passenger-side window and inhaled the freshest, sweetest air she'd ever smelled. She could see why Burton loved this place.

"Beautiful, isn't it?" Catherine said. "When the sun comes out, you forget all about the rainy days."

"Like love," Veronique said, throwing her head back and smiling. The weather had changed, and so had she.

And if, at the end of it all, Burton didn't want her, he would still have the farm. She would like to do that for him, and it would wash clean Graham's money. Certainly she didn't want it for herself. Marion knew of her plans and approved. *Chère* Marion. At last they were truly friends.

She folded the leather strap on her backpack into a little concertina. Inside, next to her checkbook, was her ticket to Papeete. If only Burton would wait for her, just a little while, till she had some time with Ghislaine and the others, she would come back. It would be easier if she had the farm to come back to, but if she didn't?

She would still come back.

She would take that leap of faith because things were different this time. She was in love with Burton, whereas she'd only been infatuated with Graham. How could you love someone with whom you couldn't communicate? If she and Graham had been able to talk to each other, they probably wouldn't have married so impulsively.

Burton's resemblance to Graham had blinded her to the fact that, right from the start, it was his character that had attracted her, not his looks. In so many ways, large and small, Burton had shown her that he cared about the person she was, not the person he wanted her to be. He'd gone out of his way to make her feel special. Like giving her a hankie after she'd pushed him away. Marrying her so she could stay in the country. Bringing her chicken soup when she was sick. Even that silly wig—she laughed just to think of it.

And the fact that he wanted to learn French! What further evidence of a noble soul did anyone need? He could never *be* French, of course; one had to be born to such an honor. But he could belong. Just as she'd found she could belong out there on the farm. And best of all, they belonged to each other.

ERNIE WAS WALKING SLOWLY toward Burton's office, his nose buried in the want ads, when Burton came striding around a corner and barreled into him.

"Hey, Ernie. Watch where you're going, ol' buddy."

"I was just on my way to see you," Ernie said.

Burton helped smoothed the crumpled newspaper. "You're not looking for another job, I hope. Murphy's going to need a man of your experience around here."

Ernie glanced up to see if he was joking, but Burton's smile was genuine and encouraging. His boss's attitude toward him had changed. Nowadays he treated him, well, not exactly like an equal, but at least as though he was playing in the same league. "I was looking for a place to live," Ernie said. "Now that Rita and I are so solid, it's time I moved out of my parents' home."

Burton gave him a little punch in the shoulder. "Way to go, Ern. You want to walk as far as the lobby with me? I was just on my way up to see Murphy."

"Sure."

"So what area are you looking in?" Burton asked, striding along. "The West End is handy to just about everything."

Ernie still had to hurry to keep up, but he didn't mind so much now. "I can't move to the city. I've got a dog, remember?"

Burton shrugged. "Stanley Park is just a hop, skip and a jump away."

"Oh, no. Edward needs room to run all day, not just when I can take him for a walk."

"Your dog is named Edward? Ernie and Edward?" At his amused tone, Ernie started to frown, and Burton brought his grin to heel. "So," Burton went on, "Edward likes to live in the country...."

Ernie had been around Burton long enough to know when his mental camera had switched on, but what the boss could possibly be picturing with regard to Edward boggled the mind. "Yeah, but places with acreage are usually too expensive for one person."

"Not necessarily. Sometimes people just want a reliable house-sitter for a certain time period. Would you be interested if something like that came up? Say, on a farm?"

"Of course, if it was for at least six months. Do you know of someplace near your grandfather's farm?"

"Could be, Ernie." They reached the elevators, and Burton pushed the button. "What was it you wanted to see me about?"

"A reference, in case I need one for a prospective landlord."

Burton chuckled. "No problem." The elevator arrived and the doors opened. Instead of getting in, Burton leaned a hand against the wall and asked, "Did I ever tell you the joke about the penguin and the pogo stick?"

The elevator doors closed again, and with a quiet hum, the empty cage responded to a summons from above. Ernie glanced at his watch. "Is Mr. Murphy expecting you?"

With a careless shrug, Burton jabbed the button again. "No rush, Ern. Plenty of time." He laughed. "Not for you, of course. Once the new season starts there'll be no rest for the wicked. Or the gainfully employed." He was still laughing when the elevator returned, and he stepped inside.

Ernie stared at the closing doors. The boss had finally cracked. He was out of his ever-lovin' tree.

Poor Ern, Burton thought as he rode up to the fifth floor. He'd clarify the situation as soon as he could, but first he had to sort out a few things with Murphy. And with Veronique.

The elevator made its way slowly upward, past Research, past the cafeteria, past whole floors of offices. Burton stuck his hands in his pockets and idly studied the notices taped to the wall. They were of little interest; he wasn't going to be around here much longer.

The doors opened and Burton stepped onto the fifth floor. He hardly recognized Sylvia with her new hairstyle. She waggled dark blue nails at him as he strolled past. He smiled and nodded. "Nice 'do, Sylvia." Lillian's grand-niece was getting good.

The door was ajar and Murphy was expecting him, so he knocked once and pushed it open. The big man was standing at the window, flipping worry beads and staring out. There was not a whiff of smoke in the air. Burton cleared his throat. "Hiya, boss."

Murphy turned. "Burton, m'boy. How's it going?" He walked back to his desk and motioned Burton to have a seat.

"Not bad. So was the board happy with *Flavors* when you showed them the tapes?"

"Ecstatic. I'm giving you the official green light."

Burton's smile lingered. "For what?"

Murphy spread his arms wide. "Anything you want. Hell, the station bosses are so pleased you could write your own ticket for the next twelve months."

Burton leaned forward in his chair, elbows on knees. "Funny you should say that, Murph. I do have a certain ticket in mind."

The creases around Murphy's mouth deepened in a frown. "What do you mean?"

"My wife is going back to Tahiti soon, and once I finish my current projects, I intend to join her. I expect we'll be there for the winter at least."

Murphy snorted. "And you'll do what for a living? Nice place, don't get me wrong, but you can't even speak the lingo."

"I'm learning. As far as making a living goes, I'll free-lance for a while. I've had seven fat years—and they've been great years, Murph, don't get me wrong—but I'm ready for some lean times. Chance to take stock, explore new directions.''

Murphy rolled his eyes. "Here I thought you were turning into a beach bum when all you're looking for is another challenge. Goddamn it, O'Rourke, you're approaching the peak of your career. Don't you get enough of a challenge around here?"

"It's not like that." Burton frowned. Was it? Was he going to have to consciously not look for something to do in order to slow down? "I'll have to talk to Veronique about this," he muttered.

"Now, there's your problem right there," Murphy said with a jab of his stubby forefinger. "You've gone and let marriage change you. You used to be my best producer— hell, you're still the best producer, you're just not mine anymore."

"If you mean, I'm not married to my job anymore, you're right. But don't worry, I'll be back. I'll be back with a pilot script for a series that'll knock your socks off—*90210* meets *X-Files*. What do you think? Interested?"

"Hmm." Murphy rocked back in his swivel chair. "You say you've got a script?"

"Not yet. I'll probably be the only beach bum in Tahiti with a laptop."

"You are going to write it? A documentary is one thing, but…" Murphy's eyebrows lifted in unflattering surprise.

"I'm going to take a stab at it." Just thinking about it made Burton get to his feet and pace across the room.

"You can't sit still long enough to write a treatment, let alone a whole script," Murphy rumbled.

Burton ignored the sarcasm. "I'm thinking a rural community…a farm lad, fourteen or fifteen…bored with school…too old for 4-H, too young to drive. A hostile alien spacecraft lands in his field. Toss in an intergalactic teen romance and a ticking clock, and you've got one helluva story.''

"Sounds promising, O'Rourke. You come up with a script and I'll fast-track the proposal—if you'll stay put.''

Burton stopped short and planted his hands on the back of the chair. "Sorry, Murph. I'm changing my life-style for a while. It might not happen overnight, but I'm going to try."

"Nothing happens overnight, O'Rourke. It's taken me two months to go a whole week without cigars."

"Doesn't matter, as long as you get there in the end. I'm only just starting to feel married. It's opened up a whole new world for me. *Liberating,* I guess, is the word to describe it."

"That's not the word most men use."

"They don't have wives like Veronique."

"When you have kids, you'll feel differently," Murphy said. "You won't be swanning off to the South Pacific whenever the urge hits. You'll be stuck in one place, ferrying the ankle-biters around to soccer games and pep rallys."

Burton shrugged. "I never said I wouldn't have to make sacrifices."

"You're going into this very blithely for a condemned man.''

"Everything will be okay when it happens," Burton said serenely. He noticed the empty humidor. "Have you given up jelly beans, as well, Murph?"

"Unfortunately, no. I've got a hundred-a-day habit." He took a big bag out of the drawer and emptied them in a steady tinkle into the jar. "When are you leaving?"

Burton got up and peered into the jar, searching for the licorice ones. He popped a couple in his mouth. "Now that *Flavors* is over, I should be able to wrap up *Lost Harvest* in three or four weeks. Trudy has been itching to get her hands on *Lovers and Strangers* for ages. My current contract is almost up, so as long as I'm not leaving you in the lurch, I'll be cleaning out my office before September.''

"Goddamn short-term contracts," Murphy muttered. "I knew I should have talked the board into putting you on permanent staff."

"It would have only delayed the inevitable."

Murphy pushed back his chair and got to his feet, his hand reaching for Burton's. Burton gripped his friend's hand, realizing for the first time how much he was going to miss Murphy, and Ernie and Lillian and, oh, hell, everyone in the whole damn place. "Thanks for everything, Murph," he said.

"See you around O'Rourke," Murphy said gruffly. "Give my love to Veronique."

"Will do." He started to back out of the room. "Ernie's a good kid. He's ready to take on more."

"I'll look after him. He's a baseball fan, you know."

"Thanks. Give my regards to Mrs. Murph."

"No, NOT TO THE FARM YET, Catherine," Veronique said as they approached the turnoff to the secondary road. "Do you know the way to Don Chetwynd's real-estate office?"

Catherine laughed and obediently continued along the main road into Langley. "Of course I know the way. I used to go to high school with Don. What are you up to?"

VERONIQUE WASN'T AT HER apartment when Burton called. Nor was she at Marion's nursing home. On his way out of town, he stopped by her apartment just in case, and when he didn't find her, carried on out of the city on a stream of commuter traffic. While he had a spare moment, he'd return the deposit those young Chilliwack farmers had made on Granddad's property before the cooling-off period was over. It wasn't just that he thought he'd have a better chance of convincing Veronique to stay if he kept the farm.

He wanted it for himself, as well. And for his and Veronique's children. Surely one of their future progeny would take after their grandfather and want to till the soil.

He took the turnoff to the town of Langley, and instead of making a right onto the secondary road, he continued on into town and parked outside Chetwynd Real Estate.

"I'M SORRY, MRS. O'ROURKE," Don Chetwynd said. "It's been sold. The buyers put a deposit on the farm yesterday."

"I will offer more," she said desperately.

The bell over the doorway tinkled as someone entered the office, but no one turned to look.

"This is highly unusual," Chetwynd continued. "I think you'd better discuss the matter with Mr. O'Rourke—"

"Is someone taking my name in vain?"

They all turned.

"Burton!" Veronique cried with joy.

"Burton!" his mother exclaimed in surprise.

"O'Rourke!" Chetwynd said with relief.

"Don, here's the check back from the deposit on the farm," Burton said, his gaze fixed on Veronique.

Don wagged his head back and forth. "Those Chilliwack boys are going to be awfully disappointed. Hadn't you better think on it awhile?"

"I'm not selling."

The agent reluctantly accepted the check dangling from Burton's outstretched fingers.

"Come on, Don," Catherine said, taking her old friend by the arm. "Let's go get a coffee and let these two work things out by themselves. Call me when the dust settles," she whispered in Veronique's ear. As they went out, Don flipped over the sign on the door reading Back in Fifteen Minutes.

Veronique and Burton just stood there, gazing at each

other. There was so much to be said, so many questions to be answered, neither knew where to begin.

"You're not selling?" Veronique said at last.

"You're trying to buy my farm?" Burton asked at the same time. "I thought you wanted me to hang on to my heritage."

"I wanted to make sure the farm stays in the family. I am not going to divorce you. Sorry."

"I guess I'll get over it," he said, smiling a little. "The question is, will you?"

Her eyes were huge, and dark with uncertainty. "That's just it," she said. "I'm not going to get over you."

He shut his eyes and breathed in deeply, afraid of taking a false step. Afraid that what he thought she was saying might be just a miscommunication resulting from their different languages. Then he opened his eyes and took the leap. "I love you."

Her eyes became bright. "I love you, also."

He exhaled a relieved burst of laughter. "What are we going to do about it?"

Smiling, she said, "I don't know, but I think we must do something."

"Well, for a start..." He opened his arms.

Veronique stepped forward, and Burton stepped forward, and the distance between them was closed. He shut his eyes again, and he held her as tightly as if he'd pulled her back from a precipice. God, she felt good.

He drew back a little. "You can't buy the farm if you already own it. What's mine is yours."

She smiled. "I didn't want you to do our children out of their inheritance."

And then he knew he hadn't misunderstood. Slowly he lowered his mouth to hers. Thought became feeling, then feeling blazed into sensation, and within seconds, he not only couldn't think straight, he couldn't think at all.

"Whoa," Veronique said, pulling back, breathless.

"We cannot start with the hormones yet. We have much to discuss. I have some ideas."

"Start talking," he murmured, nuzzling her ear.

"I have it all figured out. Stop it— Oh, mmm... Are you listening?"

"Yes." Sort of.

"We will live in the farmhouse and build a French country restaurant on the property. I will be haute chef, naturally." She spoke quickly so he couldn't interrupt. "There is a helipad at the top of the Channel Seven building. To save time, you can go to and from work by helicopter—"

"Hold on a minute!" Burton said, finally waking up to what she was saying. "What's all this about restaurants and helipads, and general nesting-syndrome behavior? I've quit my job, I've psyched myself up to go freelance, and I'm frothing at the mouth to get on a plane and go to Tahiti. I haven't felt so free in years."

She drew back, her gaze uncertain. "You maybe want to be totally free?"

"Not free of you. Never that." He brushed his fingers through her short hair. "What about you? Are you pulling a Rita on me?"

She feigned indignation. "You wanted me to cut my hair."

"Yeah, and as usual, you're late." He stopped her protests with another kiss.

"Okay, what do you think we should do?" she asked a few minutes later.

"You've got to agree," he warned.

"But, of course—if I can change the parts I don't like."

"Mmm. Okay, the plan is this—we go to Tahiti, give it a year and then see what we feel like doing."

"That is a plan?" She gazed at him dubiously.

"You want something more definite? Okay, I think your idea of a restaurant at the farm is great. We could also do a second series of *Flavors*. Everything will fall into place, you'll see."

She smiled a little. "You're not the man I married."

"Lucky you," he said, and grinned back. "Murphy says he'll listen if I want to pitch my teen sci-fi series next year."

"Do you really want to stop your career for a whole year? Right now you have so much that is certain."

"I'd like to take credit for being noble, but the more I think about it, the more I feel like I'm gaining something rather than giving something up. I'll work on a script. I'll recharge my batteries. It's exciting not knowing what I'm going to be doing."

"I think it's better we stay here. What about your mother?"

"It's only for a year. And if I know her, she'll be on the next plane to Papeete, nagging us about grandchildren. If not, Ernie will love her chicken soup."

"And what about the farm while we are away?"

"Ernie's more or less already said he'll house-sit. The land, we'll lease to the boys from Chilliwack. Or the Vandermeres. How were you planning on purchasing the farm, by the way?"

"I have an inheritance, too. From Graham. But I want to give it away."

Burton laid one hand across her mouth and the other across his chest. "Never talk about giving away large sums of money so casually. You could always finance the restaurant with it. Graham owes you. But if you really don't want it, you could make a donation to the women's shelter."

"I like that idea. And maybe just a little in a trust fund for the children."

He gazed at her with admiration. "That's what I like about you. You're so practical. Veronique, will you marry me? Again?"

She tilted her head to one side and pretended to think about it. "Only if we do it in Tahiti so my sister can be matron of honor."

"I knew you'd come around to my way of thinking." His smile returned, irrepressible.

"We'll be all right wherever we live," she said complacently. "But when we're here, we must have a big, big heater."

"And plenty of umbrellas. What do I need for Tahiti?" She whispered in his ear.

"Veronique, you're making me crazy. I want you—right here, right now."

"You *are* crazy. Those vinyl seats look very uncomfortable."

"Then let's go back to the farm." He nuzzled behind her ear.

"We have no time for this," she murmured.

But he could tell by the way she slipped her hands under his shirt that she was weakening. "We have all the time in the world," he said, and hand in hand they went out of the office and into the sunlight.

MOTIVE FOR MARRIAGE

Linda Markowiak

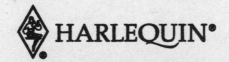

TORONTO • NEW YORK • LONDON
AMSTERDAM • PARIS • SYDNEY • HAMBURG
STOCKHOLM • ATHENS • TOKYO • MILAN • MADRID
PRAGUE • WARSAW • BUDAPEST • AUCKLAND

I'd like to thank Ann and Dick Hamilton, Kent and
Sandy Gordam and Andy Phillips for answering
my questions about sailing and for 'giving' Nate
their fantasy racing boat, a Quest 30.

I knew I was dealing with a hardy bunch of sailors
when I asked Dick how easy it would be for an
experienced sailor to get caught in a storm
on the lake. 'Very easy,' he replied.
'Ann and I were in a bad one once. It was fun.'

Again, thanks, everyone. May the wind be
steady and true and the beer cold as
you sail your Quests into the sunset.

CHAPTER ONE

NATHAN PERRY shouldered his way to the front of the line at the airport, too impatient to wait his turn for a cab. He yanked open the door of the only taxi in sight and threw his overnight bag into the back seat. "Hey," a fellow passenger from the Chicago flight protested. "Get in line."

"Sorry," Nate mumbled. He hadn't really paid attention to the queue of people, except as obstacles in his path. He'd been shell-shocked, not really *there* for hours, ever since he'd got the telegram from Chet.

For the last eight years, the annual telegram had said the same thing. "Package Safe. Chet." And for eight years, Nate had fallen into a chair, weak with relief, flooded with memories.

This year had been different. He'd got home from work at 9:00 p.m. last night, and found his telegram there a day early, on top of a pile of mail his housekeeper had left on the table. He'd snatched it up. *Please, God. Let Melissa be safe.*

This year, the telegram had been longer. "Package Safe, but moved to another warehouse."

Melissa was safe. For a moment, that had been all of the message that had registered.

Then he studied the rest of the telegram. Moved to another warehouse. What the hell did that mean?

Maybe the government had been forced to give Eve and Lloyd and Melissa another identity, move them to yet another place. As the years had passed, he'd told himself over and over that he'd done the right thing, letting his daughter enter the federal witness protection program. The proof was always in these telegrams. Package Safe. But now...

"Where to, mon?" The cabdriver had a Jamaican accent and a friendly smile as he looked back at Nate.

"The Justice Department."

"I know where that is, no problem. Hey, are you with the FBI?"

"No," Nate said shortly.

"You look like an agent, with that haircut and good-lookin' suit. I know those guys over in Justice, too. My daughter dated a federal marshal." He pushed the button to show the fare for the proper zone. "He was a guy who knew how to crack computer codes. You got big business with the feds?"

"No." Nate leaned forward. "Listen, can't you cut the chat and hurry?"

The cabdriver's smile faded. His face disappeared from the rearview mirror. He wrenched the steering wheel left and the cab bounced out of place and shot into a narrow opening in the traffic. "How the hell was that for a hurry, mon?"

Nate didn't answer, staring out the window without really seeing anything. It was his first trip to Washington, but the city made no impression on him.

Instead, he was remembering his two-and-a-half-year-old daughter. The last time he'd seen her, Melissa had been on a weekend visit. He'd had to meet a client on Saturday, but Sunday had been all theirs.

Their last day together. He could remember it with perfect clarity. The temperature had been near freezing. He'd bundled Melissa in snowsuit, hat, hood and mittens, until she'd resembled a fat red hen, and carried her on his shoulders when her legs got tired at the zoo. At dinner she'd eaten nothing but french fries—out of her bag, then his.

Then, as he was buckling Melissa into her car seat, she said out of the blue, "Daddy, kittens say meow, meow."

"Hey." He smiled down at her. "You just said your first sentence! No more mama and dada and 'Melissa want.' This one had a noun, a verb. Kiddo, you're *great*." He'd planted a kiss on her forehead.

Reluctantly, he took Melissa back to Eve's. But Eve wasn't waiting on the porch with her new husband, Lloyd. So Nate walked Melissa to the door and rang the bell. At the time, he'd been too fixed on telling Eve about their daughter's first sentence to realize how strange it was that nobody was there to meet them.

Now Nate squeezed his eyes shut against the memories that came after.

The dark man who'd been there with Eve and Lloyd introduced himself as a federal marshal. Then had come the brief, terse explanation that Lloyd had seen too much, learned too much, in his job with the insurance company. The insurance company hadn't been legit, merely a money-laundering scheme for a big crime family. The Kallons. Surely Nate had heard of them?

Nate hadn't. But Lloyd Lapulski was going to testify against the Kallons, and then he and his family were going to disappear into the witness protection program. Surely Nate had heard of that.

Nate had. But he didn't really believe it. At first, he'd thought this was another attempt by Eve to discourage his visitation. Because—perversely—the harder he tried to be a father to Melissa, the more resentful Eve became. So it had taken a while for it to sink in that his ex-wife and daughter were actually going to be part of a program that up to now had just been an item on the television news. It took even longer to realize that Melissa was going to disappear from his life forever.

"You can't do this!" he had roared, first at Eve, then at Lloyd, then at the federal marshal who tried to explain that for Melissa's safety there was no other choice.

"Nate, see reason for once." Eve laid a hand on his arm. "For God's sake, we can't stay here. They might kill her."

Eve was dramatizing the situation again. She had to be. Nate waited for the marshal to say it wasn't *that* serious. Soon things would calm down, get back to normal. But the man was nodding in agreement.

Nate's hands fisted. "I'll take her home with me. You two can do what you want."

Eve laughed scornfully, but with a nervous high note. "How will you take care of her? When were you ever home from the office early enough to do squat for Melissa? *You'll* take care of her? What a joke."

He knew he hadn't been much of a family man, and Eve never hesitated to remind him of his limitations. But these visitations with Melissa, well, he'd got to know his daughter. He didn't want another fight with Eve. He just wanted Melissa. "Damn it, Eve—"

"Eve has custody under your divorce order. You agreed to that," Lloyd cut in.

"Well, I never agreed to let her take my kid and walk out of my life! I'm Melissa's father. I have visitation rights. From that same court order." Nate started to reach for Melissa. The little girl looked from one parent to the other and her mouth wobbled. "I'll call my lawyer. You can't do this. Please." Fiercely, he willed down his pride, pleading with Eve, with the two men.

"Believe me, Mr. Perry, it's the only way." The marshal stepped forward. "If you really love your daughter, you'll let her go and never try to see her again."

"I'm calling my lawyer, then Chet McMasters." Nate had gone to the other room. His attorney assured him it was perfectly legal for the government and his ex-wife to take his baby away and give her another name. Thoroughly rattled, he'd called Chet at home. Chet, an old friend of Nate's, was a lawyer at the Justice Department. His friend made a couple of calls then phoned back to assure Nate everything was on the level.

Nate had listened while his whole world came crashing down. Chet had managed to convince him of the urgency of the situation, told him Melissa's life could be at stake.

Then, as if sensing that Nate was still reluctant to let Melissa go, he'd made a promise. Once a year, he'd let Nate know his daughter was safe. No, he couldn't let Nate know more often than that. To bring up information on the computer too frequently could compromise the operation. But once a year, that would be all right. If everything was okay, he'd only say, "Package Safe."

Nate hung up the telephone. It was as if Melissa had died. As if *he'd* died. He thought fleetingly of all the hours he'd been working, how all along, everything he'd worked for was only for his daughter. For Melissa.

Once back in the living room, he talked Eve into letting him hold Melissa one more time. Under the watchful gaze of Eve, Lloyd and the federal marshal, he'd scooped his daughter into his arms. "Hey, kiddo," he'd whispered. Her dark curls were so soft against his cheek, like springy flannel. "Be safe, baby. And remember…" He swallowed. She would not remember. She would not be allowed to remember. "Remember what kittens say." He'd set her down gently and walked out the door.

And for eight years, no matter how complicated his real-estate development business became, how hard he worked or how successful he was, his whole life seemed geared to

February 15th, the day he'd hear about Melissa. Nathan Perry had played the game the government's way.

Now he wasn't as naive as he'd been the day they took away his daughter. Over the years, he'd found out a lot more about the Witness Protection Program. Most of what he'd learned wasn't favorable. The program was riddled with leaks. He'd worried about how safe Melissa really was, but he'd been too afraid of hurting her by delving deeper. But he was going to talk to Chet McMasters today, and he wasn't leaving Washington until he found out where his daughter was living.

"Package Safe, but..." Now Nathan Perry was going to do only one thing.

Pick up his "package" from the "warehouse," and take it home.

LIBBY JAMIESON'S hand shook as she set down the telephone receiver. Her attorney, Cameron Holling, was out of town for the day, so she couldn't ask him if there was a problem with the adoption, or why Judge Wyatt wanted a meeting with them. They were to be in court at 9:00 a.m. tomorrow, and Libby wasn't supposed to mention anything to Sara.

Automatically, Libby picked up a blue-tinted carnation and wopped off the stem at a forty-five-degree angle before sticking it in the foam base. Up to now, her plan to adopt Sara had been going perfectly. Libby had hardly seen her lawyer since she'd finished her duties as executor of her friend's estate and taken up her duties as Sara's guardian.

Now she was scared. A judge wanting to see you was something like getting stopped by the cops. You automatically assumed you'd done something wrong. And there'd always been those hints Julia, Sara's mother, had dropped. Secrets... Then those puzzling last words of hers, at the hospital before her death. But Julia had always liked attention, drama.

Of course, the reason for this meeting could just be to iron out a technicality. Still…

Get a grip, she told herself. *If you're late with the Smithson wedding flowers, you won't have the money to pay your lawyer, and that will create more complications than Judge Wyatt could dream up.*

Another bill. That was all she needed. It was always tough to wait out this time, to husband the funds she earned in the summer, when Harborside, Ohio, was clogged with both wedding dates and tourists. Holding her lower lip between her teeth in concentration, Libby broke stems of baby's breath. Placing some into the greenery, she took a step back and eyed the arrangement. Triangular. Competent and stiff, the fake gentian-blue of the carnations was an insult to the flower.

The doorbell jangled and Libby looked up, her heart going soft at the sight of Sara.

"Hey, Lib, guess what happened!" Sara blew a couple of black curls out of her eyes and flung her book bag on a tabletop covered with dried-flower bouquets. Her cheeks were red from the chilly late-winter air

"Careful of my stuff," Libby warned automatically. But she was smiling. "Now. What happened?"

"Kathleen invited me to her birthday party. We're going *horseback riding.*" Her eyes danced as she took off her coat, scarf and mittens, leaving a trail through the shop. Her gold heart, with its tiny chip of blue topaz, glinted against the neck of her navy blue sweater. "I can't *wait.*"

Sara had never been on a horse in her life.

"If I have a good time, can I have lessons?"

Sara had been wanting horseback-riding lessons since before Julia's death. Neither her mother nor Libby could afford them, or the rental and stabling for a horse. Now the meeting tomorrow and the possible complications in the pending adoption flashed through Libby's mind. "I wish we could swing it." How terrific it would be to walk into Judge Wyatt's courtroom and say that Sara had everything she'd ever wanted.

She looked down at her hands. The nails were bluntly filed, more functional than beautiful. Like herself, Libby thought ruefully, thinking of her unruly, copper-red hair. The skin of her hands was chapped, cut in places from the hard stems of the flowers and misses with the clippers. Suddenly she felt the hot sting of tears behind her eyelids.

"Hey, Lib." A small, very cold hand stole over hers. "It's okay about the lessons. I was just asking."

Libby looked into eyes as blue as Lake Erie on a cloudless day. "I know, sweetheart."

Sara's skin was fair and freckled, with the high-contrast coloring of the Black Irish. But Libby, who loved beautiful things, loved Sara more for her irrepressible personality, her sense of humor, her maturity. Sometimes Sara seemed older than ten. But the girl had had a lot to deal with. Her father drank, and last year had killed both himself and her mother in a collision on the causeway.

"Wow, that's ugly," Sara exclaimed, her gaze on the arrangement Libby had just finished. She grinned. "What'd you do, dunk those flowers in toilet-bowl cleaner?"

Despite her anxiety about tomorrow, Libby chuckled. "Disgusting, huh?"

"Worse. Gross."

They looked at each other and giggled. Finally, Libby sobered a bit. "They're for Karen Smithson, and she wanted everything to match. The dresses, the flowers, the—"

"Cake," Sara finished, and she burst into laughter again. "Tidybowl cake."

"She's the customer."

"Right," Sara said in quick agreement. Libby always tried to be honest though reassuring about their financial situation. Sara understood it was important to please a customer of the shop.

Sara picked up a frond of Christmas fern. "So, can I help?"

Libby sighed. Sara had been "helping" around the shop since she could walk. Her mother used to bring her here so that the women could rehearse their lines for the community theater group they both belonged to. Tina Samms, a third friend, would often join them. "I don't suppose the help you have in mind is sweeping up this mess."

"I could make something. You know, for the wedding."

Libby made one last try. "Have you got homework?"

"Naw." She paused and looked away. "Well, a little. But I can help here a while."

Libby pointed with the clippers she held in one hand. "To the desk with you, fair maiden." She waved the clippers in mock threat. "Or off with your head."

"But Your Majesty, I wanna play with the flowers." Sara's blue gaze turned pleading. "I don't have *that* much homework."

Libby relented. It was hard to deny the kid when she turned on that preadolescent charm. But Sara's experiments cut into the slim profit margin of Country Tastes. "Well, okay. You can make a couple of small arrangements for the reception."

"Do they have to be blue?"

"Well, they didn't specify. Use a carnation or two, and see if you can use up some of this stuff instead of hitting the cooler for more."

"Cool!" Sara eyed the pile with delight.

For a few minutes they worked together, while Sara talked about everything from a food fight in the school cafeteria to how she wanted her own wedding to look. Libby glued foam bases for bigger arrangements. The tall gladioli the customer had specified looked stiff, so she tucked in a few daisies at a rakish angle. Daisies the customer hadn't paid for. But what the heck. She might get a referral or two out of this job. The high society of Harborside, such as it was, would be in attendance. She headed to the cooler for more material.

When she came back, Sara was admiring her handiwork. Libby looked at the arrangements and couldn't help a rush of pride. Karen Smithson might not appreciate these arrangements because Sara had broken the Rule of the Triangle, but if you appreciated art and flowers, you couldn't miss the rough talent the girl brought to the work. Libby smiled. "You, fair maiden, are good," she said softly.

"I like flowers." Sara hesitated. "I like living with you, Lib, and I feel really bad about bringing up those riding lessons again. I know Mom and Dad didn't leave too much—"

"Stop right there." Libby waited until Sara was looking at her. "I'd want you no matter what your parents left. We aren't using any of your parents' money until it's time for you to go to college. We agreed, remember?" She brushed the thick bangs out of Sara's eyes. Libby's voice softened to a whisper. "I always wanted a daughter. And I love you as if you were mine."

Sara blushed and averted her eyes. "I like it here," she repeated.

THE NEXT DAY, Libby put a damp herbal tea bag over each eye, willing herself to relax. Her eyelids were puffy, they always swelled when she hadn't slept well. She'd spent several hours before bed last night poring over the adoption paperwork, speculating on her mysterious meeting with Judge Wyatt. She'd called her friend Tina, who'd helped her rationalize.

Today she wanted to look her best, so she'd braided her hair into a chignon that felt ready to burst each time she turned her head, and now she was screwing around with these tea bags.

Two minutes later she was up and checking the mirror. Nope. They were still there, tiny swellings under each eye.

Deciding there wasn't any point in lingering, she put on her coat and walked to the courthouse. She was a half hour early, and some of the courthouse personnel were just arriving. She'd lived in Harborside all her life, and knew most of them. With a wave, she greeted the janitor, then headed for the clerk's office where Barbara Fielding was working. Barb and she had gone to school together, and were now both members of the garden club.

"Hey, Lib, just the person I wanted to see." Barb leaned forward over the counter. "Can we have a casserole for the meeting next week? Some of that brown-rice-and-herb medley?"

"Sure," Libby said quietly.

"What's up?" Barb asked immediately. "You seem sort of…subdued."

Libby quickly explained. Barb might just know what *i* Libby or her attorney had failed to dot in the adoption papers.

"I swear I don't know anything." The woman's expression was serious. "But you have my support…this *town's* support. Everybody's seen how Sara's become so talkative and bubbly this past year."

"Thanks." Libby felt comforted by the brisk, kind words.

"But, Lib?" Her voice lowered. "There's someone in the waiting room who's here on Sara's case, too."

Quickly, Libby craned her neck, but she could see no one.

"He was waiting on the steps when I got to work. I think he's a lawyer, an out-of-town guy. A way-out-of-town guy."

Barb leaned forward and lowered her voice once more. "I mean, the man's gorgeous, and I don't think he bought that suit of his off the rack."

Libby frowned, ignoring the invitation to gossip. "I've got Cam Holling. What would another lawyer want with Sara's case?"

"I don't know, but you'll be okay. This is Harborside, and Judge Wyatt won't take kindly to some outsider in a thousand-dollar suit telling him what to do."

That was true. And standing here worrying wasn't Libby's style. She'd done far too much of it these past sixteen hours. She made a quick decision. It was time to see what Mr. Gorgeous wanted with Sara's case. Plunking her tote bag on the floor, and slinging her jacket over a chair, she headed through the double doors into the waiting room.

She spotted the man in question immediately. Barb wasn't kidding. The man did look as if he was from somewhere urban and rich. And he was gorgeous. Libby's heart gave a tiny lurch, of nerves and something else entirely.

She hadn't been really attracted to a man in years, not since Brian, a slick charmer from out of town who'd shown his true colors eventually. The lesson had hurt. And the single men in Harborside were her buddies. Or maybe it was that she had never, ever been attracted like this. She certainly couldn't remember when the sight of a man had made her heart thump erratically and her mouth go suddenly dry.

He was tall. With hands in the pockets of his perfectly draped trench coat, he stood, half facing her, in front of a row of windows and stared out intently. The dim light of early morning streaming in brought out the shine in his wavy black hair. It was as black as Sara's. In profile, his features were almost aristocratic.

Damned if he didn't look like a lawyer. Somehow, this man was part of the trouble that brought her to the courthouse this morning. Libby took a deep breath and strode forward.

He turned to face her fully as she approached.

"Are you ready for me?" he asked. "My lawyer isn't here yet, but I don't mind getting started."

"You're not a lawyer?"

His mouth thinned with impatience. "Of course not. I'm the litigant." Then, as if just remembering his manners, he smiled and extended his hand. "Sorry. I've got a lot on my mind. I'm Nathan Perry. Are you the judge's bailiff?" A tilt of his head indicated the employees-only area Libby had come from.

She shook his hand. So he was a "litigant." She wasn't sure exactly what that meant. And she was irritated with herself, because she was sure that smile was designed precisely to charm, and she *was* charmed.

Without being blatant about it, he seemed to look more closely at her face and figure. Then his smile deepened, reached his eyes, became genuine...and devastating.

She was all mixed up—nervous, anxious about Sara's case, attracted to this handsome stranger—and as usual, overly conscious of her appearance. "I had to wear these tights," she blurted out. "I forgot to buy nylons again." *Oh, God, had she really said that?*

He chuckled, a sound as rich as a cup of espresso. Was there nothing about this man that wasn't perfect? "You look fine."

"Sure," she said lightly, hoping her cheeks weren't as red as they felt. "I'm Libby—Elizabeth—Jamieson, by the way."

He was still looking down into her eyes, so she could tell the precise moment that recognition crossed his face. Then his mouth tightened into a white line and his eyes narrowed. "You!"

"Excuse me?"

"*You're* Elizabeth Jamieson? The one who has Melissa?"

Melissa? Melissa...

All of a sudden, some things fell into place. Julia and secrets, her oft-repeated statement that things weren't what they seemed. And those last words of Julia's, just before she died: *Her name is Melissa. Tell Nate I'm sorry.*

OhmyGod. Sara must be, had to be...Melissa. And Nathan Perry was a litigant. *Nate* Perry. *Tell Nate I'm sorry.*

But what could all this mean? Libby wet her lips. "Just what is your interest in Sara?"

"Melissa," he corrected.

"Nate!" another voice called. They both turned as a tall, well-groomed woman approached, clutching a briefcase and wearing a trench coat that looked practically identical to the one Nathan Perry wore. "I knew I should have driven out from Toledo last night. These country roads—" She cut herself off as she reached them. "Sorry. You know I don't make a habit of being late."

Nate frowned. "But this was not the day to start, Marta. For chrissake, you know how important—"

"Sorry," she repeated briskly. "Has the judge called us yet?"

"No."

She shrugged. "Well, with judges it's hurry up and wait." She laid a light hand on his arm for a second. "Relax. You'll have Melissa soon enough."

Libby was confused, but one thing was clear. This Marta, whoever she was, was wrong. Nathan Perry would not have Melissa anytime soon.

Nathan shook his head slightly at Marta, indicating Libby. "This is Elizabeth Jamieson. And we have not talked," he added in a tone that suggested he and Libby had plenty to talk about.

"Oh. Really." An initial start gave way to a smooth introduction as Marta reached out a hand to Libby. "I'm Marta Wainwright, of Severn and Coxton, Chicago. We represent Mr. Perry in the matter of his daughter, Melissa."

His *daughter?* But Sara…Melissa's father had been Heywood Clark. Libby's mind searched frantically for any smidgen of information she had, any indication from Sara herself that Heywood Clark had been a stepfather. She could come up with nothing. But it was hard to think with her heart pounding against her ribs and her stomach feeling so tight.

Now Nate was looking at her, a strange, intent expression on his face. For a moment the courthouse walls and the other woman seemed to fade, as Libby was caught in his compelling blue gaze. "Yes. Melissa is my daughter," Nate said in a husky voice. "Tell me. Did you know?"

Know what? Libby thought half-hysterically. Know her name is somehow Melissa? Know you're somehow her father?

His gaze sharpened. "I asked, *did you know?*"

She could not look away. "No," she said softly.

He stared at her as if he was searching for something

beyond her denial. Finally he looked away, his shoulders slumping slightly.

The spell was broken, but the whole situation was unreal. In a numb fog, Libby heard their names called, went into the judge's chambers ahead of Marta Wainwright and Nathan Perry, explained to the judge that Cameron Holling was late and barely heard the judge growl, "Again!"

They all took seats around the conference table. The small conference area was paneled, intimidating, clearly a place where serious decisions were made. The judge sat at the head of the table, just underneath a huge plaque of the Great Seal of the state of Ohio.

Marta opened her briefcase and made a great show of arranging a stack of papers. Libby caught sight of the top one. Motion to Intervene in the Matter of the Adoption of Sara Clark.

Nate Perry sat still, straight. His hands were open, resting palm down on the polished oak table. She had a feeling that what he really wanted to do was fist them.

Nate Perry wanted his daughter. That much had penetrated her shell-shocked brain. But the situation still made no sense. Julia had been sort of dizzy at times, dramatic, but essentially a timid woman. Her husband had been a jerk, and Libby had always suspected Julia was afraid of him. At times, she had seemed anxious and sad.

But maybe Julia had been more than anxious. Maybe she'd had a good reason to be scared. Maybe her friend had kidnapped Sara—Melissa—from her father. Those kinds of things happened, she knew. But Libby had known Sara since the child had been about three years old. Didn't the FBI or someone track down missing kids? Would that kind of thing take seven years? And Libby truly couldn't imagine Julia as a kidnapper.

But one thing was certain. Libby loved Sara. She thought

of the nervous, quiet kid Sara had been a year ago, and knew that Barb Fielding was right. Libby *was* good for Sara; they were a real family. They belonged together.

The judge settled in at the head of the table and silence descended over the group. Marta had arranged every paper four times and had finally quit. Nate Perry looked as if he was beginning a slow boil he wouldn't be able to contain for long.

Where in God's name was Cameron? Libby hoped he was a good lawyer. The people in town used him, but she wondered if he would be intimidated by the formidable-looking Marta Wainwright of Severn and Coxton, Chicago. Cam was perpetually rumpled, and his idea of dressing up was to put on a corduroy blazer.

But appearances didn't mean a thing. Like Libby, Cam had chosen to come home to Harborside when he could have taken a job in the city. As far as she knew, Cam was competent. Looking at the single-minded determination on Nate Perry's face, Libby had a feeling that she would need more than just competent.

CHAPTER TWO

FINALLY, Cameron Holling arrived. As he settled into his seat, he whispered an apology in Libby's ear. She whispered back, "That's okay," but it wasn't. She felt as if she were going to explode with her unanswered questions.

At the head of the table, the judge pulled a set of papers toward him. "I've asked you all together because of an extraordinary situation. Yesterday I received a Motion to Intervene in Sara Clark's adoption, which is Mr. Perry's legal way of challenging Ms. Jamieson's right to keep Sara. I tried to reach you yesterday, Mr. Holling, but you were out of town."

There it was, out in the open. Nathan Perry wanted Sara. Libby realized that until that moment, she'd hoped she'd misread the situation. She looked up, across the table toward Nate. He was looking straight at her, too, and for a second, their gazes meshed. It was as if there had never been that brief moment of shared warmth in the waiting room. This man now had eyes as cold as ice, and as determined. There wasn't even the barest hint of a smile. *I want to win,* she read in his eyes. And it was obvious he was a man who was used to winning.

The judge cleared his throat. "Mr. Perry's story is extraordinary, but his attorney has provided all the documentation to assure me he's the natural father of Sara Clark, and that he hasn't been allowed to see his daughter, or even know where she was living. Eight years ago, while in the custody of her mother, the child entered the federal government's witness protection program.''

Beside her, Cam made a sound of disbelief, at the same time reaching for the documentation Judge Wyatt handed him. The judge explained the mechanics of the program and how Nate had had no choice in the matter.

Libby clenched her hands in her lap and waited as Cam looked over the paperwork. Across the table, she could feel Marta Wainwright's self-assurance. Finally, Cam gave an almost imperceptible nod.

It was true. Nate Perry *was* Sara's father. Studying him, she saw what she should have recognized instantly. He had black hair and sky-blue eyes that tilted at the corners slightly, giving him a look of intelligent curiosity. His cheekbones were a touch more prominent than most. No wonder Libby had found Nate Perry a handsome, appealing man. She was looking at a grown-up, masculine version of Sara.

According to the judge, Nate had lost his daughter eight years ago through no fault of his own. Sara would have been two or three at the time. For a second, Libby pictured what life must have been like for this man, and couldn't hold back the compassion that flowed through her.

Cam handed her a copy of Nate's motion, and Libby read it rapidly. It stated that Nathan Perry was the natural father of Melissa Perry, also known as Sara Clark, and that "simple biology" gave him a "preeminent right" as opposed to "adoption by a legal stranger, Elizabeth Jamieson." He wanted his child returned to him immediately. As she read, Libby grew angrier and angrier.

"Simple biology" be damned. If anybody was a stranger to Sara, Nate Perry was. Libby remembered all the things she and Sara had shared, this past year and in years gone by—the birthdays, the school plays, the community theater,

the flowers, the square-dancing lessons that Sara loathed—
the ones where the girls had to dance with the boys.

"You don't even know her." Libby looked to Nate, who
remained still and impassive. Waiting. "You have no idea
what she likes or dislikes."

He leaned forward. "Of course I don't. You heard the
judge. Eight years ago my ex-wife and the government of
the United States robbed me of my daughter. How could I
possibly know? All I ever got was a telegram telling me
she was safe. I didn't even know until last week that her
mother had died almost a year ago." For a second, his
husky voice went a note or two lower. It was the first sign
that he was feeling anything but impatience at the legal
formalities.

Libby took a deep breath. "You don't know that she
loves celery sticks with peanut butter but won't eat brussels
sprouts. You don't know that she likes cherry icing but
won't touch chocolate."

Cam put his hand on her forearm, said, "Lib—"

But Libby went right on. "Do you know she hates carnations but is crazy about orange tiger lilies? Do you know
her favorite play is *Once Upon a Mattress* and that when
she was a toddler I had to read Beatrix Potter to her over
and over, and you don't know anything about any of
that…"

"Mr. Holling," the judge warned.

"Lib, be quiet," Cam whispered, more urgently.

Libby fell silent immediately, but she had so much more
to say. Surely, if Nate Perry understood how much she
loved Sara, he'd…

His hands on the tabletop fisted. "You don't get it, do
you? I *want* to find out all those things about her. I want—"
his mouth twisted *"—I want my daughter."*

His mask slipped. The Nate Perry who obviously knew

how to charm, who could afford to hire Marta Wainwright of Severn and Coxton, Chicago, was gone. All of a sudden, he looked unsophisticated. Vulnerable.

Judge Wyatt cleared his throat again. "This is a very difficult situation. I'm sure that now you can see why I called you into chambers on an emergency basis. We'll have a hearing eventually, once Mr. Holling has an opportunity to prepare his case. But it would be better if we could decide some things informally now."

Marta Wainwright spoke up. "Of course. As long as Your Honor understands that the only discussion Mr. Perry will engage in is the one wherein we decide how soon he has custody of his daughter."

At the head of the table, the judge visibly tensed. Marta had been polite and formal, but the challenge was unmistakable. "Ah, Ms. Wainwright. We have much more to discuss." He gave her a small smile. "Frankly, as the judge presiding in this courthouse, I set my own agenda and choose the topics for discussion."

"Certainly, Judge." Not looking at all repentant, Marta fell silent.

"Good," the judge said after a moment. "I'm assuming that, due to this extraordinary situation, Sara has no idea that her father wants her back." He looked at Libby.

"No," she said slowly. "I'm sure she doesn't even know she *has* a father. If she knew anything about being in the witness protection program, I think she would have told me." Libby avoided Nate's gaze. "To Sara, her father was Heywood Clark, who was killed a year ago."

She took a deep breath. "Actually, Your Honor, I'm kind of worried about how she'll take the news. Mr. Clark wasn't, well, always nice to Sara."

"What does that mean?" Nate asked sharply.

Libby had been facing the judge, but now she looked briefly to Nate. "He drank."

Nate's features seemed to turn to stone. Marta whispered something in his ear.

The judge leaned back in his chair. "Mr. Perry, I want you to know some of the facts. First, this is a small town, and I am acquainted with Ms. Jamieson's family. I knew her father before he passed away. But we've never been close friends or socialized with each other. Actually, I know almost everyone in town, so I've gotten used to putting personal issues aside. I can be impartial in this matter. Anyone have a problem with me continuing to be the judge here?"

For a moment, Marta Wainwright looked as though she might well have a problem with it. Then apparently thinking better of crossing the judge again, she shook her head.

"Fine. Now, Mr. Perry also needs to know that Sara's home life was far from perfect, and Ms. Jamieson has been kind to her since the child lost her parents almost a year ago. After all, without Ms. Jamieson's intervention, Sara would be in foster care right now. You ought to thank her for that, at least."

Thank her? Libby felt bitter laughter rise within her. They were trying to take Sara!

"But Mr. Perry is her father," Marta said.

The words hung in the air. Libby turned toward Cam. Why was Marta doing all the talking?

The judge wiped a weary hand across his forehead. "I'm a father myself, and I respect the connection you have with your daughter, Mr. Perry. In the law, your rights are protected. But I've got to think about Sara's best interest. Ms. Jamieson has confirmed what I suspected—that Sara has no idea that you exist. And I can't let you simply uproot her and move her to Chicago. After I received your motion yesterday, I was up all night, researching, talking to other judges.''

Marta Wainwright smiled. ''I brought case law, Your Honor, that I'd be happy to share with the court.''

Cam whispered in her ear. ''I'm not quite sure what the law is here, Libby. I'll have to do some research, too.''

Libby nodded. Chalk one up for Marta Wainwright, she thought. The woman had obviously come armed with cases supporting the rights of fathers. But neither she nor Cam had known what was happening, so there'd been no way to prepare for their side yet.

A shiver of fear went through Libby.

The judge made a note in the margin of his paper, then spoke. ''Sara needs to be told, and as soon as possible. But gently, for her sake. And we need to arrange for Mr. Perry to see her.''

''When?'' Nate asked. There was no mistaking the eagerness in his voice, and Libby felt again that unwelcome pang of compassion.

She swallowed. ''I could talk to her.''

''If this is for her best interest,'' Cam said, ''we should let Sara say what she wants.''

The judge smiled for the first time. ''Oh, I don't think we'll let a ten-year-old girl call the shots.'' He picked up the motion Marta had filed. ''This motion is rather combative, Ms. Wainwright. We do things a little differently in Harborside, but I'll give you some time to get used to my courtroom. What I'd like to see, from both the attorneys, is a suggestion to their clients to cooperate with each other. Maybe Ms. Jamieson and Mr. Perry could break the news to Sara together, and we could schedule some visitations for Mr. Perry.''

Marta Wainwright bristled. ''Mr. Perry needs to return to Chicago. He has a property-development business. Right now he's in the middle of building the Iris Complex, a multimillion-dollar resort on Lake Michigan—''

"Marta," Nate interrupted, his voice a clear warning. He turned to the judge. "I'll work with Ms. Jamieson on a visitation plan, and I can stay in town as long as necessary." He glanced toward Libby, his mouth grim with purpose, before turning to the judge. "Apparently I need to pass some sort of test. Of fatherhood, I guess. So be it. I've been passing tests all my adult life. And I'll do anything you ask in order to have my daughter back."

The judge smiled, a man-to-man smile. The knot in Libby's stomach tightened. Nate Perry had obviously said what the judge wanted to hear. Marta might lack the instinct for dealing with Wyatt, but Nate had it.

What would Sara think about all this? Libby had no idea. For the first time since she'd met him, Libby tried very hard to judge Nate objectively. There was no doubt that the man was prepared to go to great lengths to get his daughter back. Even his apparently big-business dealings in Chicago would be put on hold. What other steps would he take? Libby wondered.

Would Sara like him? He was rich. From a big city. With a lurch, Libby remembered the horseback-riding lessons Sara wanted so badly. If Nate ever heard about his daughter's wish, Sara would be learning the feel of the English saddle within a day. How could any ten-year-old girl resist?

"I need to talk to you," she said to Cam in a low voice. "Might we have a moment, Judge?"

"Of course. This is a shock to your client. A year ago, there was nobody for this girl. Without Libby, Sara would have been in the foster-care system. And now we learn she has a father." The judge shook his head. "I'll leave you to talk. Try to come up with a visitation plan. If you can't,

I'll order one when I come back.'' The judge rose and left the room, shutting the old oak door behind him.

''What do I have to do?'' Libby whispered as soon as Wyatt had left.

''I don't know,'' Cam admitted. ''You know how much the judge hates to be crossed. He's already decided Marta's a pain, so if we're cooperative about visitation, I think we'd have a better chance at the final custody hearing. It'll buy us some time. I'll look into this guy. We might uncover shady business practices. Or maybe he's a womanizer...keeps bad company...not a good influence for Sara.''

Libby glanced across the table, feeling sick to her stomach. She didn't know about business practices, but Nate didn't look like the kind of man who lacked female companionship. After all, in the waiting room she'd been charmed by the guy. And she'd thought herself immune to charmers.

She looked more closely at him, trying to see under the surface of the polished businessman. He was sitting there, waiting. Not in conference with his attorney, not looking over his papers, just waiting.

Nate caught her glance. ''Well?''

Cam looked up. ''Do you want to propose something with regard to visitation?''

Marta started to speak, but Nate cut her off. ''No. Whatever Ms. Jamieson decides is fine.'' He hesitated. ''The thing is, a child belongs with her real parent, and I've got plans—'' He stopped, started again. ''Ms. Jamieson, you know her better than I do. I'll defer to your judgment. I don't want to hurt Melissa.''

At his words, Libby was suddenly ashamed. Nate *was* Sara's father, and even if he hadn't seen his daughter in eight years, he'd have strong feelings for her, wouldn't he? After all, she considered Sara her daughter, and Nate's legal challenge had brought out every mother-bear, protective instinct she had.

And didn't Sara deserve to know her father?

"I'll never relent on the custody case," she said. "I love Sara, and I'm convinced she's better off with someone she knows, in a town she's familiar with."

"But visitation?" Nate said.

"Yes."

At the one word, Nate Perry smiled—a slow smile that lit his blue eyes and took Libby's already twisted insides and tied them in knots so tight she was afraid they'd never unravel.

NATE NEEDED a place to live in Harborside, and he figured he might as well be right on the water. He parked at one of the state parks at the edge of the lake, and checked over the small list of houses for rent the real-estate agent had given him. Looking out past the dock, he watched the water. Lake Erie was shallow, and its waters were rougher than Lake Michigan's. And the islands in the distance appeared more numerous. Erie was legendary for its fast-forming storms. Nate had already picked up a chart in town. He intended to learn the waters as soon as possible. Sailing was his passion, so if he was going to stay in Harborside for a while, he was going to sail.

He chewed over his list. There were cottages on the fringes of Harborside, but most were used only seasonally, and were therefore not adequately heated. Besides, few would have electrical systems that could handle his computer, copier and fax machine. There was a restored Victorian mansion for rent in town. Nate had considered it, thinking the place might impress Judge Wyatt. But he really wanted something on the water.

He loved the water. When he was a kid, he'd walk down

by Lake Michigan, hands in his pockets, the wind blowing off the lake buffeting his body. He'd watch the sailboats— white sails, rainbow sails—and he'd think about the people who lived in the glittering towers overlooking the water. And he'd dreamed. Oh, how he'd dreamed.

Now he had his own condo at one of Chicago's prestigious addresses—a complex he'd developed—and he had his own sailboat at the yacht club. On the water he felt free and loose.

If he had a home on the water, he could teach Melissa to sail.

There was one more place to consider. From the car window, Nate saw it in the distance—a condominium, a white sugar cube that stood very close to the water's edge. Bittersweet Point, the developer had called it. The place must have been bitter, because after building only one two-unit structure, the developer had gone bankrupt.

It was a familiar scenario. Real-estate development was a risky game and the stakes were high. Huge amounts of money were made and lost. Bankruptcy happened frequently, and unexpectedly. A number of Nate's colleagues who, one month would be attending every party, supporting the ballet, providing scholarships for ghetto kids, would suddenly lose everything. And when they lost their money, their wives and girlfriends left, too. Nate had seen that situation many times. Nothing survived.

Nate put the rental car in drive. The joke among the high rollers of Chicago real estate was that on every deal you "bet the farm."

Nate no longer bet the farm. As soon as he could stop taking such big risks, he had. But those first years had been scary as hell. No wonder he'd been such a lousy husband and father. He'd worked around the clock, scared to death that he'd lose everything, including his family. He'd been even more terrified that he found the game too enjoyable, that somehow he craved the excitement of being in a business where everything was on the line. That he'd be like his father.

Hell. He'd been so preoccupied with his thoughts that he'd passed the overgrown access road to Bittersweet Point. He pulled over and swung the car into a U-turn.

The gravel access road twisted among the trees. The trees here were smaller than those a few miles inland, deprived of nourishment in the sandy soil, bent into sinewy submission by the wind. Their bark was wet from a recent rain, branches glistening black against a sharp blue sky. Twining through the undergrowth were the bittersweet vines. The bittersweet had been picked at by birds. But here and there were flashes of brilliant orange.

Automatically, almost without realizing that he was doing it, Nate began to weigh the site's attributes. He broke through the trees onto a wide, rough beach. Getting out of the car, he walked to the water's edge.

The beach faced a tiny cove, and on the opposite shoreline were shabby, comfortable homes. Melissa lived in one of them with Elizabeth Jamieson. Marta had obtained the address from the judge's office. It was the third house. You couldn't miss it. Who would put that shade of blue trim with that butter-yellow house? Libby Jamieson didn't follow the ivory/taupe/slate color scheme that his decorators were all slaves to. There was a clothesline out in her backyard, and it was hung with towels and sheets, in a brilliant rush of color that reminded him of the twenty-thousand-dollar antique Amish quilt that hung in the lobby of his condo in Chicago.

In contrast, the sugar cube at his back was stark and ugly, a blight on the unpretentious beach. If he rented this horror, he could sit behind the windows of his living room and look across the cove and wonder what his daughter was doing every minute of every day.

And wonder about her caretaker, Elizabeth Jamieson. Libby, they all called her.

When he'd first met her, Nate had been instantly attracted. He'd always been partial to redheads, and Libby's coppery hair had been a flyaway halo around her face. She wasn't beautiful. Pretty, but definitely not beautiful. These days, he had his pick of beautiful women, and every time he had a beautiful woman on his arm, it proclaimed to the world that he was somebody. And her clothes! What a contrast to the sophisticated, very expensive up-to-the-minute fashions his Chicago women friends wore. He smiled, remembering Libby's too-bright skirt.

Then he remembered her confession about forgetting to buy stockings, and he chuckled aloud. At her comment, he'd had to physically restrain himself from a detailed perusal of her legs.

Nate picked up a stone and whipped it out over the water, trying to make it skip. But it sank like a…stone. God, now he was reduced to dwelling on clichés and smiling over a frizzy-haired, small-town woman.

Okay, so he was attracted. He wasn't about to act on the attraction. Libby Jamieson was the enemy, whether or not he imagined that she looked at him with sympathy, whether or not she had agreed to allow him visitation with Melissa.

Just before she left the courthouse, she'd given him a school picture of Melissa, and Nate had felt his throat tighten painfully. They'd been arranging the next month of his life, careful not to look too directly at each other. She'd hesitated, then asked him to wait a minute. Blushing, she'd chattered inanely while she rummaged in the funny-looking satchel she carried.

Finally, she'd found her wallet and extracted something.

"Here, this is for you," she'd said softly as she'd handed the small snapshot to him. "I thought you might like to have Sara's picture."

He'd taken the photograph, so overcome at the unexpected gesture that he hadn't even managed a thank-you. It was the first likeness he'd seen of his daughter since she was two and a half years old.

He'd been stunned at the changes eight years had brought. Of course, he'd known Melissa wasn't two and a half anymore, but... And his daughter was so beautiful, she took his breath away. Her face was less round than he remembered, her hair straighter. But she still had those blue eyes. "Sara Clark" was embossed in gold script under the photo.

Brought abruptly to the present, his mouth twisted. Sara. He whispered the name, wondering if Eve had picked it or if some anonymous government bureaucrat had chosen his daughter's new name. Well, Sara didn't know she'd ever been Melissa, so Nate had best get used to the idea that she probably would want to be called Sara.

There was plenty to get used to.

This cold white condo, which he'd rent. This town, so small and out-of-the-way that he hadn't been sure if his cellular telephone would work. The fact that, contrary to his dreams, he wasn't going to be able to just sweep Melissa—Sara—up into his arms and take her back to Chicago.

And he'd have to get used to dealing with Libby Jamieson, because, like it or not, she was important in Sara's life.

The real-estate agent had said she'd leave a key under the mat on the deck. The two units were side by side, with matching decks that touched each other and were separated only by a wooden privacy fence. Nate headed toward the building.

"Hello!"

Nate stopped, startled, and turned toward the sound.

A blond boy, maybe fifteen or sixteen, sat on the deck of the second condo. Nate peercd up at him, over the solid wood railing. The kid was smiling.

"Hello," Nate said politely, unhappy at being disturbed. He hadn't thought to ask if the place next door was rented.

"Are you renting this place?" the kid asked.

"Maybe."

"Cool!" The boy smiled. "You'll really like it here. The guy who was building these things was going to build like a hundred more, but he never did. I heard you drive in, and I almost said something to you, but you went right down to the beach. You didn't come up here, like anybody else would. So I watched you. You've got a good arm." He stopped. "With the stone," he explained.

Nate headed for "his" deck. "The stone sank."

"Whatever," the kid said cheerfully.

"Whatever," Nate repeated, not wanting to encourage the boy's chatter.

"Why don't you come over? My mom would make you coffee."

"Thanks, but—"

"She's nice-looking."

Nate gave a mental groan. Just what he needed. A talk-ative, matchmaking kid next door with a nice-looking mother. Now that he was on a level with the teenager, he glanced toward him and froze in shock. The boy was in a wheelchair. A blanket was over his knees, and a few pages from a sketch pad in his lap fluttered in the wind.

The kid grinned at him. "Didn't notice at first that I'm in this chair, did you?"

"No," Nate said honestly, startled at how easily the boy spoke of his disability.

"Man, that is so cool. Whenever you meet someone, you

have to deal with it. They look at you, but not *at* you. But we were talking before you noticed, so you couldn't think anything about it. You sure were chewing over something deep.'' He paused. ''So, you were going to blow me off and go inside, weren't you? But now that you see I'm in a wheelchair, you'll feel like you have to stay and talk.'' He looked very pleased with himself.

Nate felt a flush light his cheekbones. He shoved his hands into his pockets. The kid was perceptive, that was for sure. He settled for introducing himself. ''I'm Nate Perry.''

''Trevor Samms. You got a wife?''

Back to that already! But the damn thing of it was, Nate actually felt himself smiling. ''No wife.''

Trevor waved a hand in the air. ''Terrific. Sure you don't want that coffee?''

''Trevor, you and I might be neighbors. We'll get along a lot better if you understand I'm not interested in marriage.''

''Who said you were? And even if you *were* married, you could still look. I hear a guy never stops looking unless he's dead.''

Nate's mind immediately conjured an image of Libby. Sure, he looked, but he'd never marry again. His four-year marriage had been hell enough that he hadn't been tempted to marry again. Not once in the nine years since his divorce. He lifted the mat, but the key wasn't there. Damn. Before he knew it, he'd be stuck having coffee with the good-looking Mom Next Door. Not that Nate didn't feel sorry for the kid. Trevor probably was lonely. But Nate had his own problems, and plans to make.

He straightened, conscious of Trevor watching him. ''No key,'' he said, though he questioned why he was offering any explanation.

Trevor shrugged. "Mrs. McCurdy forgets things. Not exactly God's gift in real-estate agents." He gave Nate another one of his two-hundred-watt smiles. "To continue the inquisition, you've got no wife, but have you got kids?"

Until Nate had told his story to his attorney and the judge, only a handful of people knew he was a father. And then he'd had to fill out all the personal and financial information the court had required. He felt his mouth harden. "Look, Trevor—"

"Call me Trev. Now, have you got kids? A cute daughter you'd like to keep out of my evil clutches?"

"I have a daughter. Her name's Sara," Nate said shortly.

"Does she live with you or your ex-wife?"

Nate pulled out his car keys. He'd skip the tour. He already had a good idea of what the place was like inside, anyway. "If I'm going to live here, we've got plenty of time for all these questions, don't you think?"

The kid's nose wrinkled. "Sure. Hey, that's right. You and me, man. I just know we're going to be friends."

Not likely, Nate thought. Was everybody in Harborside so nosy? Well, it didn't make any difference. He'd be back in Chicago before he had a chance to get to know anybody except Sara. And that was just as well. Nate had always done best when he'd kept his eye squarely on the task at hand.

And he always, always went it alone.

CHAPTER THREE

THE THREE OF THEM gathered in Libby's living room. Sara had picked up on the tension in the air, and sat very close to Libby on the sofa. Across from her, Nate sat in a high-backed wicker chair. His broad shoulders covered all the curlicues on the back. The chair itself had groaned alarmingly when he'd settled himself into it.

Nate's gaze was intent. It had seldom left his daughter's face, as if he wanted to memorize every line of nose and chin.

Libby said nothing. She had wanted to be here when he told Sara that he was her father. She had no idea how Sara would react. Heywood hadn't been much of a father, and maybe Sara would welcome this handsome stranger with the intense blue eyes, a man who looked so much like her. But Libby was damned if she'd make it easier for Nate to tell his story. After all, this man had the power to change her and Sara's lives forever.

Now Nate sat forward, his knees apart, his hands clasped between them, his eyes on his daughter.

He cleared his throat. "I don't know what Ms. Jamieson—Libby—has told you about me, but…"

"Nothing," Libby said quietly.

"Nothing?" His gaze slid to hers momentarily.

"Just before you came, I explained that you're interested in Sara's adoption, and you want to tell her about that interest and what it might mean for all of us.'' She tried to keep the censure out of her voice.

''Well.'' Nate cleared his throat again. He looked down at his hands. But when he began, his voice was stronger, surer, than Libby had expected. ''You see, Sara, ten years ago, I had a daughter. Her name was Melissa. Her mother and I didn't get along, and we divorced. But I saw my daughter as often as I could because I loved her very much.'' He looked into Sara's eyes, as if willing her to believe that fact.

''So?'' Sara asked rudely. Libby forgave her lack of manners. The girl's back was rigid. Libby took her hand.

''You're that little girl, Sara. Your name used to be Melissa Perry. You're my daughter.''

For a moment the silence was unbearable. Sara did nothing. Then she whirled in her seat to face Libby. ''That's not true.'' She looked terrified as her gaze flicked from Nate to Libby. ''My father is…my father was Heywood Clark.''

Libby put her arm around Sara and held her close. The child felt small and fragile and her shoulders quivered. ''It's true, Sara. Your mom was Julia Clark, but Heywood was your stepfather.''

Sara pulled back to look at her. Her face was so pale that every freckle stood out. A kind of strangled giggle came out of her throat.

Nate spoke again. ''It's a long story. God, that sounds dumb, but—I rehearsed what I would say, but I just couldn't quite imagine telling you, so…'' His voice lowered, softened. ''You're my daughter,'' he repeated, and there was a kind of desperation in his voice.

Libby felt a twinge in her heart.

Sara frowned. ''You can't be my father. How can you? You never even lived with us.'' She turned to Libby. ''My mother never told me anything about this, and she would have said something, wouldn't she?''

Libby took Sara's other hand, so that she held them both. ''I know this is hard to understand, but Cam and Judge Wyatt have checked out what Nate says, and it's true. Nate is your father.''

''And I love you,'' Nate added. He started to stand, as if to move toward her.

''No!'' Sara cried, shrinking into the back of the sofa.

''Okay,'' he agreed immediately, sinking into his chair again with an absurd little squeak of wicker. His mouth settled into a grim line.

For a moment, nobody said anything. The three of them sat in a frozen tableau, Libby and Sara together, Nate across the room. Then Nate explained about the witness protection program, about how he'd thought all these years that he had been keeping Sara safe by staying away.

His story still felt unreal to Libby. And if it felt that way to her, how must it feel to Sara? And how frightened she must be. She'd had so little stability until this past year. Libby had had no idea, before Sara had started telling her things a few months ago, just how rough life had been for the little girl.

Nate finally finished. ''I know you'll have questions for me, and I'll answer every one.'' He smiled a little, more a nervous gesture than an expression of warmth. ''I promise to tell you the truth.''

''I don't have any questions,'' Sara said, her chin coming up.

''Okay,'' Nate said again, carefully.

''Wait.'' Sara took one quick look at Libby. ''I do have a question. Why are you here?'' Her tone made it clear that she could think of no good reason.

"Because I want you back, to live with me. I want for us to be a family again."

There was a breathless pause as the full import of what he was saying settled over Sara. Then she stood. "I don't want to live with you. No way. *No way.*" Her wide eyes sought Libby's. "I don't have to, do I?"

Libby didn't know how to answer, to be both reassuring and truthful. "I want you to stay with me, and I've told the judge that. He's the one who'll decide. But for now, everybody thinks you ought to get to know your father." She had a harder time saying her next words. "For you to give him a chance."

"Is that what you want?"

No, Sara. What I want is for Nate Perry to go away and leave us here, together in Harborside, with my house, my shop and my friends, where nobody's ever given a thought to the witness protection program and fathers don't come out of nowhere demanding their daughters. "What I want," she said instead, "is to make the best of a difficult situation. I want you to stay with me, and Nate wants you, too. You see, baby, everybody wants you, so no matter what happens, someone will be there for you."

Across the room, Nate cleared his throat. "I wanted you to come back to Chicago with me right away, but the judge had other ideas. Now I can definitely see he was right. We should take some time, get to know each other. I have a plan—"

"Forget it," Sara cut in. A red spot had appeared on each cheek. "The judge will decide, and *you* have plans, and Libby says it's okay that you want me, and I thought *she* wanted me, and you're nobody, *nobody*..." Her mouth wobbled as she stared at Nate. "And I wish you would go back where you came from and..." She stopped, obviously searching for the worst word she could think of. "Or you can go to…to hell."

Libby was on her feet, reaching out. "Sara—"

"Leave me alone!" Sara stormed from the room, and Libby could hear her pounding feet on the wooden stairs, and the crash of her bedroom door slamming.

A long silence settled over the two adults. Finally, Libby rose. "You'll have to excuse me. I need to try to talk to her."

He rose, too, but didn't respond. Instead he turned to look out the window. His profile was perfect, but it might have been carved from stone. His shoulders were high, held almost too high, as if he was braced for another blow.

Libby left him to go upstairs, her heart heavy. Just a few days ago, life had seemed so good. Standing in the hallway outside Sara's room, she knocked, and when there was no answer, tried the door. It didn't give. Sara had never locked the door before.

"Go away," Sara said from behind the closed door.

"Can I come in? We need to talk, sweetheart."

"We already talked. And *he* wants to take me away and you don't care if I go."

"That's not true." Tears pricked the back of her eyelids. "I was trying to be fair, that's all, and I didn't mean for you to think for a second that I don't care. I want you very, very much. I love you. Do you remember when I told you that you were like my very own daughter?" She had said that last when she'd given Sara the little blue topaz heart for her birthday that the girl always wore around her neck.

The old lock grated, and Sara wrenched the door open. "Is that true?"

"Oh, yes."

Sara threw herself into Libby's arms and sobbed. And Libby, though she was sure it wasn't a good idea to cry in front of Sara, couldn't stop the tears that coursed down her own cheeks.

Suddenly, Libby thought of Nate. She hadn't heard him leave the house, and now she imagined him downstairs, waiting. What was he still doing in her living room? Hadn't he realized that his plan had failed and it was clear that his daughter wanted nothing to do with him?

Maybe he was relieved that he didn't have to deal with this messy scene upstairs. After all, he was the man who'd hired Marta Wainwright of Severn and Coxton to breeze into Harborside and turn her and his daughter's life upside down.

After a few minutes, Sara's sobs turned to sniffles. Libby smoothed a lock of Sara's hair and gave the top of her head a quick kiss. "Listen, sweetheart, we'll talk some more. Let you get used to things. Maybe have Cam tell us what to expect when this finally goes to court. Would you like that?"

Her features solemn, her cheeks tear-stained, Sara pulled back a notch and nodded. "It's just…I'm in the play at school and in *Fiddler on the Roof* this summer. And you said I could stay forever." She swallowed. "I'm…scared. My dad…he got drunk und stuff. I mean my old dad Oh, Lib—" Her voice caught. "I don't even know what to call that man who says he's my father."

"I know," Libby said softly. "You've got a lot to get used to, but you'll have plenty of time. The judge has given us all lots of time. And for now, why don't you call him Nate?"

For some reason, knowing what to call her father seemed to calm Sara.

Libby added, "Nate might not be anything like your old dad, if you give him a chance. But right now, we have to decide some things about your…Nate. He's still downstairs. Do you want to talk to him, or should I tell him to come back some other time?''

''Some other time.'' The words were whispered.

''Well, I guess I'd better go tell him that. Will you be okay up here?''

When Sara nodded, Libby sighed and headed for the stairs. For a man who loved his daughter, Nate had managed to make her miserable. Maybe if he realized how miserable she was, he'd go. Maybe all the way back to Chicago.

He was waiting for her at the bottom of the stairs. ''Is she all right?'' he asked immediately.

Libby nodded. ''I think so. Your coming here was a shock, but she'll be fine. I'll talk to her some more. After you leave.''

''I planned exactly what to say to her. But somehow, I never expected her to hate me.''

Libby hesitated. She had no reason to offer this man any comfort. Or any hope. ''Right now, she's just confused and scared. You'll have to show her you're different from Heywood.''

He raked a hand through his hair. ''You blame me for upsetting her.'' The words were weary.

Libby was silent. Who else was to blame?

''There was no way to tell her gently,'' he said. ''I knew my news would shock her, but what choice did I have? She has a father. Would it be better if that knowledge were kept from her?''

''I don't know.''

He nodded. He was standing so close to her in the little entryway. Libby would have liked to step back, but she couldn't do that because the stairs were right at her heels. Nate was just so...large. Her house had been built with

enough nooks and crannies to satisfy her love of shapes
and forms. Now every part of the space seemed too small.

"You must hate me," he said abruptly.

"No," she said, and it was the truth. She ought to hate
him. But in truth, she wasn't sure what she felt. She was
afraid of his legal power. He was Sara's father and he had
money. He also made her uneasy with his intensity and
determination. He was obviously stubborn, and she, as a
determined and rather stubborn woman herself, understood
just how single-minded the type could be.

But she didn't hate him. She couldn't hate someone who
cared about his daughter that much, even if what he was
doing was selfish and unfair.

She swallowed. "I think in time Sara will be willing to
see you."

"You think?"

Hope sprang into his eyes. The last thing she should do
was make things easy for him. But she said, "Why don't
you come for dinner tomorrow night? We could rent a
video or something."

"I don't want you to go to any trouble." His body was
taut, as though he was physically restraining himself from
showing his gratitude. His eyes were so very blue, she
thought suddenly, as blue as the line where the sky met the
lake.

"Ah, no trouble. You don't have to have meat, do you?"

"Meat?" He looked startled at the question.

"For dinner, I mean. Do you have to have meat? I'm a
vegetarian and I like to make more unusual things, you
know, like couscous. Of course, you can't get couscous at
the Three Nets Grocery here in Harborside, you have to
drive to Toledo, but I have some in the cupboard..." God,
she was going on and on again. The man always managed

to make her nervous, even when they weren't talking about Sara. *Especially* when they weren't talking about Sara.

"Sure, fine."

"Okay. Well, I guess I'd better check on Sara."

He was standing in her front hall, so only two steps brought him to the front door. Nobody used the front door; everyone came around to the kitchen. But Nate wouldn't know that. Libby reached over to pull open the door. Her hand and his touched the knob at the same time. Both jerked away.

Then Nate opened the door. A sharp, lake-scented breeze rolled into the hallway.

Nate's eyes searched her face. He hesitated for a second, then said, "Look. I just want to know something. Why are you doing this, making things easier for me?"

"The judge wants us to do that. He said we should co-operate for Sara's sake." Libby ignored the voice in her head that said cooking dinner for Nate might be going beyond even Judge Wyatt's expectations.

His face closed immediately, and he nodded slightly to himself. "Of course. You make a meal, and that little fact creeps into your testimony when we go for the hearing. Marta wants a fight. But you, for Sara's sake, invite me over so that my daughter and I can get to know each other, while I'm so unyielding I look like a jerk to the judge—"

"Stop right there." Libby held up her hand. "Let's get one thing straight. I'm making my offer for Sara's sake. The judge is right. She needs to get to know her father, regardless of which one of us she lives with. And I won't have her hurt by you." Now he looked as angry as she was. Fine. Her voice lowered. "And someday, when you do get to know her, maybe you'll explain to your daughter just what makes you so cynical. It's not the world's most attractive fatherly trait."

He yanked at the zipper of his jacket. "Thanks to a woman, I really wouldn't know much about fatherly traits, would I?" None too gently, he pulled the door shut behind him as he stepped out onto the porch.

He didn't trust her. He didn't dare. The more you wanted something, the tougher you had to be. And the only person you could count on was yourself.

THE NEXT MORNING, Nate sat on a red vinyl seat in the Shoreline Diner and poked his fork into one of his sunny-side up eggs. The eggs were delicious, the yolks a dark orange. But there was no small-town friendliness in the Shoreline this morning. The waitress had been sullen when she'd taken his order.

"Mr. Perry?"

Nate set down his coffee cup and looked up at the young man in the suit and topcoat who stood next to the booth. "I'm Nate Perry," he replied.

The young man held out his hand deferentially. "I'm Kevin Smithson, vice president of Harborside Savings and Loan. I heard you were in town."

Of course he'd heard, Nate thought as he stood slightly and shook hands. In the week he'd been in Harborside, Nate had discovered that practically everybody he met had heard he was in town and what he was doing there. Nate knew exactly why the waitress had refilled every coffee cup in the Shoreline except his.

And it didn't matter, he assured himself. He didn't make friends easily. Success attracted admirers, but not friends.

"Can I sit with you a minute?" Smithson asked.

"Sure."

The young man slid into the booth opposite and gestured for the waitress. She slapped a jelly ball on a plate for another patron with much more force than necessary. "Got a bee in your bonnet, Phyllis?'' Kevin asked when she finally approached with her coffeepot and order pad.

"Never you mind," she sniffed, her glance pointedly directed at Nate, so he couldn't mistake who she was snubbing. "The usual, Kevin?"

"Naw, make 'em blueberry today."

She finally offered a smile. "Branching out, are we?"

"Karen's after me to eat more fruits and vegetables." Both of them laughed. Kevin gestured to Nate's cup. "Think you forgot to top off that one, Phyl." Phyllis had the good grace to blush as she filled the cup Nate pushed toward her.

"Thanks," Nate said after Phyllis left. "I figured one cup would be my limit today."

The young man smiled in return. "Rough on you, are they?"

Nate felt his mouth tighten. "I can handle it."

"Sure you can." Kevin picked up his cup. "From what I'm hearing, you can handle just about anything."

Suddenly, the man across from Nate didn't look quite so young. There was an intelligence about him, a serious purpose, that made him appear more mature.

Nate took another bite of egg. "So, what's on your mind?"

Kevin sighed. "Bittersweet Point."

"Ah." Nate chewed thoughtfully.

"Maybe you'd like to do a little business while you're here."

As soon as Kevin had mentioned Bittersweet Point, Nate knew what the other man wanted. The bankrupt developer of Bittersweet Point must owe this small-town bank a lot of money. To Harborside Savings and Loan, Nate must look like a savior.

"Not interested," Nate said flatly.

"You don't even know what I'm proposing," Kevin protested.

"I'm here for one thing, and when I get it I'm heading back to Chicago. I don't have the time or inclination to take on a project here, and once I'm in Chicago, I don't want to have to return to Harborside to supervise a development."

Kevin's eyes narrowed slightly. "You might be here longer than you planned, according to what I heard."

"I've already been here longer than I planned." The younger man flushed, and Nate felt unexpectedly sorry he'd snapped at the guy. It wasn't Kevin's fault that Nate was forced to hang around Harborside. He'd already acknowledged that the judge was right. He could hardly drag Sara back to Chicago with him. Especially since she'd made it clear that she wanted nothing to do with him. Suddenly, Nate pushed his plate away. The eggs didn't taste so good, after all.

As always when his emotions threatened, Nate focused on what he was good at. "Look," Nate said. "The site has environmental problems. You'll need an expensive waste-handling system to avoid polluting the lake. And if that damned white cube I'm living in is any indication, you've got aesthetic problems as well. You've got a fabulous, pristine beach in an area of Cape Cod–style homes. Those cubes won't appeal to upscale buyers; that type of client knows when something isn't well integrated to its site."

Kevin's short stack of blueberry pancakes arrived, but he ignored them. Instead, he simply sat back and listened as Nate continued.

"However, as I've driven along the shore, I've noticed how much of the water's edge is taken up with marinas and older homes. Bittersweet Point is one of the last large undeveloped stretches of beach."

Kevin nodded. "Right. Harborside hasn't exactly been on the beaten path of new development—that's gone more toward Catawba Island."

"Of course, you need to look at the demographics of the major urban areas. The Toledo market might be saturated, and you'd need to determine if Bittersweet Point is too far out—" Abruptly, Nate stopped.

"Thought you weren't interested," Kevin finally said, leaning forward. "You could turn this place around, you know. There are environmental problems. Okay. Who better than you to solve those problems? Didn't you win an environmental award?"

Actually, Nate had two of those awards. He'd got them because he'd put money and thought into making his resorts tread as lightly as possible on the vulnerable shoreline of Lake Michigan. And no matter how much he'd told himself that spending the extra money was really good for business, he knew that hadn't been his only reason. Nate needed no reminders that he had a soft spot for the beaches and the water. He couldn't afford a soft spot.

He also couldn't afford the time and energy to undo the mess at Bittersweet Point. He was already trying to run his business by long distance. In Chicago, the Iris Complex was entering a critical phase. And of course, his first priority must be Sara—finding time to get to know the daughter he'd lost so long ago.

"Sorry. I'll pass this time," he said to Kevin.

There was a small silence while the younger man dunked a forkful of pancakes into a puddle of syrup. Finally, Kevin spoke in a thoughtful tone.

"This is an interesting town." He chewed a bite of pancakes. "Harborside's small, and some of our people have to commute to Toledo for a job. Bittersweet Point, done right, could bring a lot of jobs to town."

"Maybe you'll find the right developer closer to home."

"Anyway," Kevin went on as if Nate hadn't spoken, "the townsfolk are very loyal. They'd take kindly to somebody who brought jobs to this community. I'm not saying they'd be more loyal to an outsider than to one of their own, but it wouldn't hurt, if a person wanted something, to have made a few friends, you know?"

Of course, Nate thought. How slow he'd been to catch on to what the other man was offering—a chance to shore up Nate's case with Sara. Surely that was worth some risk. "If you ever need a job and you want to live in Chicago, look me up," he said.

"I take it that's a yes to taking over Bittersweet Point."

"Yes," Nate said.

"Just like that?"

"Just like that." The project *might* make money; Nate hadn't done enough study to be able to tell, yet. But if Bittersweet Point couldn't be built profitably, if they had cost overruns… Nate took a long swig of coffee. Thanks to the Iris Complex in Chicago, he was leveraged more than he liked to be. Nate was no gambler. He wasn't in any trouble, just a little beyond his comfort level regarding short-term cash flow. But Nate knew he had to accept the other man's offer. Sara was the most important thing in his life. And he needed all the help he could get.

"You know," Kevin said abruptly, "everyone around here's worried about Libby. She was born here, and after her mother died, the ladies in town kind of pitched in to help her father raise her. But me, I'm from Toledo, and I've been married before. My daughter lives there with my ex-wife." He paused. "You think I came to see you because of the money the old developer owed the bank. But you're only partly right. I've been thinking, if my ex-wife pulled something, so that I couldn't see my little girl, I just..."

Nate looked into the other man's eyes. He always knew when he was being flattered or built up in a negotiation. This wasn't one of those times. Kevin Smithson actually had a smidgen of understanding about what he was going through. He smiled in gratitude, even though he usually didn't like to show his feelings. But somehow, sitting in a diner in a place he'd never thought to be, it felt all right. He was hungry again.

Nate picked up a slice of cold toast. "Do you have any idea how Libby Jamieson feels about the development?" Why was he asking, anyway? He didn't care what Libby felt about anything.

At the other man's puzzled expression, he added, "Well, I know the back of her house faces Bittersweet Point."

"Well, I'd guess Lib would feel the same as most, glad something's going to be done with that mess."

Nate nodded, relieved. Somehow, to his surprise, he wanted, well, approval from Libby. She was unusual and pretty, and he felt the stir of desire every time he thought about her. If circumstances were different, and if she were willing, they might have acted on that desire. But to seek her approval of himself, of what he did for a living...

That didn't sit right, because Nate Perry needed approval from no one.

CHAPTER FOUR

HE BROUGHT FLOWERS to dinner. Libby blushed as she caught sight of the bundle in his hand. She recognized the distinctive paper wrap. The peach tulips were from her own shop.

Nate held the bouquet against his chest. "I thought Sara might like tulips."

"Oh." Libby blushed more furiously at her mistaken impression that the bouquet was for her. "Sure she would." She gave a light laugh. "And of course I appreciate the business."

"Yours *is* the only flower shop in town." Then he hesitated. "I guess it wasn't too imaginative, to bring her flowers when she probably sees them pretty often. But I didn't know what else she'd like."

Sara didn't see flowers "pretty often." She saw them every day, when she helped out at the shop. But Nate obviously didn't know that. "Well," Libby said, "she doesn't get flowers from her father every day. She'll like them, Nate."

He cleared his throat and held out his other hand. There was a bottle in a paper bag. "And I brought a bottle of wine. You *do* drink wine, don't you?"

"Well, yes." She was puzzled at his tone.

"You don't eat meat," he said by way of explanation. "I thought maybe you were a...a health nut or something, and you wouldn't approve of alcohol."

"I'm not a real health nut. Just a nut, as everyone in town will tell you." She tried a smile on for size. All of a sudden, she was uncomfortable again. And there was no reason to be uncomfortable.

Unexpectedly, he smiled, too. The warmth of it felt as if someone had suddenly turned on a light in the room. With a start, she remembered that moment at the courthouse, when they'd first met and he'd had no idea she was the one trying to adopt Sara. He had charmed her that day. Heck, he'd bowled her over for a moment. But there was no way she could allow that to happen again.

So she said the one thing she knew would kill that incipient warmth. "I'll see if Sara's ready."

He nodded, the smile fading immediately.

Libby ushered him into the living room and headed upstairs. Usually Sara would be downstairs, complaining if dinner was late. But since coming home from the shop today, she'd been holed up in her room.

Sara met her on the landing. "I'm scared," she whispered. She smoothed down her denim skirt. "What'll I say to him?"

"You'll be fine." Libby gave her a quick hug. "We've talked about this. It's just dinner. You were scared when you came to live with me, and sad because of your mom, and everything worked out."

"It worked out okay."

"You'll have to give him a chance." Any animosity Libby felt toward Nate must remain hidden from Sara. If—*when*—she won the custody suit, Nate would still be a part of Sara's life. Libby owed it to Sara to make getting to know her father as easy as possible.

So she herded a reluctant Sara downstairs. In the living room, Nate had forgone the squeaky rocker to sit on the edge of the sofa. When Sara came into the room, he rose.

"Hello, Sara. You look very pretty." Like an actor in a bad play, he held out the flowers.

Sara came close enough to take them, then backed up a step or two. "Thank you," she said stiffly.

"Tulips," Nate said then, a kind of eagerness in his voice as he nodded toward the flowers.

"Yes. I see that."

"Libby told me you didn't like carnations."

Libby had told him that at the courthouse but given the tension that day, she was surprised he remembered.

Sara said nothing.

"Actually, she said you liked orange tiger lilies, but she didn't have any. I got the tulips at the shop."

"I know. I unpacked them last Saturday and put them in the cooler. It's one of my chores." Sara shrugged.

Nate winced.

It was excruciating to watch Nate's awkward efforts and Sara's refusal to give an inch. Libby knew she needed to do something. "But they're pretty."

Sara tossed her head.

There was a pause. *Do something,* Libby thought. In a moment, Sara would be running for the stairs again.

Before she could think of something to say, Nate moved toward his daughter. Sara flinched. He swallowed, and for a moment Libby thought he was going to touch the girl. But he didn't. "Libby's right. The flowers are pretty. Like you, Sara. You were always pretty. Smart, too."

Sara stared up into his eyes.

Nate's voice dropped. "You said your first words very early. You were an early developer, your mother used to say."

Libby felt her throat swell. So Nate had some memories of his daughter. Certainly not as many memories as Libby had, and not as recent, but... She wondered suddenly if he had been there for his child's birth, if he had held his red, wrinkled baby daughter in his arms and hoped for so much for her.

It took her a moment to realize that the other two weren't speaking. Sara looked as though she might bolt. Nate's mouth was tight; having gone this far, he was obviously out of his depth.

No way were these two ready to be left alone to get to know each other. "Sara, I could use your help with dinner."

"Oh, sure," she agreed with an alacrity that at any other time would be comical in a ten-year-old.

Disappointment flashed across Nate's features.

"You, too, Nate," she invited with a lightness she didn't feel. "How are you with a salad?"

"I don't think there's much to mess up in making a salad. I can handle it."

In the kitchen, she gave him the lettuce while she checked the dish in the oven. She asked Sara to set the table. But the silence was grating. "How about some music," she suggested, poking a disk containing rock oldies into the player on the counter. The bouncy music helped fill the uncomfortable silence.

Sara seemed determined not to talk. Libby asked Nate about his work, then his home in Chicago. When he described his condominium, Libby noted that, although she was pretending not to, Sara was listening.

"Anyway," Nate continued as he washed lettuce under the tap, "I have space at the yacht club for my sailboat."

Libby slid the pan out of the oven. The top looked crusty, although she'd followed her mother's recipe. She set it onto a trivet. "So what kind of boat do you have?" she asked, knowing she sounded falsely bright.

"A beauty." Nate paused for a moment and his voice

unexpectedly softened. A tiny smile touched his lips. "A Quest 30."

Sara stopped, fork in hand, to stare at Nate. Her eyes were round. Harborside was more a power-boating town than a sailing town, but both Sara and Libby knew a thirty-foot Quest was a colossally expensive racing yacht. A couple of kids at Sara's school had fathers who sailed, and in Harborside everybody talked boats. Boats were the true status symbols in town. Libby saw the slowly dawning knowledge on Sara's face that her father was rich. She felt a deep twinge of foreboding.

"That's quite a boat," Libby said, nervously taking note of the obvious. She slipped on her oven mitts again and took the rice medley out of the oven. "Has it got a name?"

There was a pause. In the background, a sixties group sang of falling in love.

"It's got a name," Nate said finally.

Something in his tone seemed strained again. Libby set the casserole down on the counter. Her face was flushed from the oven.

Nate was facing his daughter. The chorus faded out. "I call it the *Melissa*."

"Oh," Sara's breath whooshed out with the one word. "But that...that was my name, wasn't it?"

"Yes."

"Oh," she said again, faintly. Her hand gripped a fork.

Nate gave Libby a questioning glance, a sort of *what now?* Libby shook her head. *Give Sara some time,* she tried to say with her eyes. But she herself was shaken.

She put the food on the table. Sara sat down quickly in a chair across from Nate. That meant the two adults sat together, facing Sara. Libby's kitchen table was a large, scrubbed pine rectangle, so she was sitting at what should be a comfortable distance from Nate. But it wasn't comfortable. In profile, she could see those aristocratic features of his. There was no doubt about it. The man was a work of art.

"Have some rice medley," she said abruptly, pushing the casserole dish his way. A flyaway lock of her hair fluffed up. Impatiently, she tucked it behind her ear.

"Thanks." He eyed the dish doubtfully before spooning a tiny amount onto his plate.

"What's this?" Sara asked, poking her fork into a slice of meat loaf.

"Meat loaf."

"I *know* that. I mean, why'd you make meat loaf?" Sara turned to Nate. "We always have salad and honey-bran rolls when we have rice medley. Libby doesn't make meat." Those were her first voluntary words to her father.

Nate didn't seem to miss the significance of the small exchange. He smiled at his daughter.

The flash of warmth for Sara still lingered in his eyes when he looked at Libby. She blushed to the roots of her hair. Why had she made meat loaf, anyway? She figured Nate probably liked meat for dinner, and he was a guest, that was all. "I thought you might not like rice medley, that was all," she said.

"I'm sure I'll like rice medley. And I like meat, as well. Steak, roast beef..." He looked at Libby. "Meat loaf..."

"McDonald's?" Sara asked hopefully.

"Well, okay, McDonald's."

Sara smiled. Libby might have smiled, too, at the tentative pleasure on Sara's face, but again she had that little flash of foreboding. "Well, the meat loaf's my mom's old recipe. She died when I was a baby, so I like to make things of hers, just to remember her. Only, they don't always turn out. I don't know if she was a bad cook, or if I am." She knew she was chattering, feeling awkward at sharing personal information with Nate.

But as they ate, Sara seemed to thaw noticeably, a couple of times volunteering information to Nate about *Oklahoma!*, her school play. Nate seemed completely focused on his daughter.

But Libby couldn't concentrate. She kept thinking about Nate, wondering what kind of man he was inside and chiding herself for caring.

She started when she realized both Nate and Sara were looking at her. "Sorry, I didn't hear you."

"I said, Sara seems to like the shop," Nate said.

"Yes, she's always been there. She used to come in with her mom, when Julia and I rehearsed our lines for the plays we were in. Then, when the store closed and we had to go to the theater, her father would pick her up."

Oh, Lord, Libby thought with an inner groan as she saw Nate's mouth harden again.

Sara seemed oblivious to the slip. "Now that I'm grown-up I have to do chores."

Nate frowned in earnest now. "Chores? You mean work in the shop?"

"Oh, yes. Every day after school. I have to sweep, and refill the cooler, and dust sometimes, and once Libby made me wash the windows. When I get home, I have to clean my room and everything..." Her voice trailed off dramatically.

"Libby makes you do all this?" Nate sounded stunned. And disapproving.

"Oh, for Heaven's sake." Libby's nerves finally snapped. Now Sara liked her father enough to complain. "Yes, she has a few chores. She's too young to stay alone after school. Besides, I like her with me. And Sara didn't tell you she makes flower arrangements, which she loves to do. And she didn't tell you that when we washed the windows, we had fun—'' Libby fell abruptly silent.

Nate stared at them both. "Fun. Washing windows."

Sara shot Libby a look that might have been a belated apology. "Sure. I mean, I guess it was fun."

Nate looked completely mystified. Libby focused on her plate. "Yeah. We were standing on the sidewalk, and it was a warm day and we kind of had a, well, I guess you'd call it a wet-mop fight. We must have looked a real sight. Our clothes wet and clinging…''

Slowly, Libby raised her head, dreading Nate's response. After all, grown women didn't chase kids down the sidewalk brandishing a soapy squeegee. Sara had ducked, laughing, into the doorway of the sporting goods store, her fingers still curled around the handle of a bucket. It was one of Libby's most precious memories, but Nate would never understand. Steeling herself for disapproval, she looked straight into his eyes.

And was flooded with warmth. He wasn't smiling. But his eyes shone with a pure blue flame, bone-deep and primal. The warmth of that gaze spread along her limbs to her toes, to shoot back and settle, low in her belly, in the very heart of her. She started to tremble. And was the first to look away.

Beside her, Libby felt Nate shift. She could sense his surprise, then his discomfort as he turned to his daughter.

Swiftly, he was in control, giving Sara his full attention. Watching them, Libby decided she must have imagined that look of his. There were facts about life that were inviolate. One of them was that men like Nate did not look at women like Libby with, well, sexual desire. Yes, she was imagining things because she'd had fantasies lately about sexy blue eyes and a perfect mouth, and a man who was all wrong for her, in every way possible.

She stood. The meal was over.

Sara stood also, and Libby had to remind her to take her plate and glass to the sink. Nate got up with his. "You don't have to do that," she protested. "I was reminding Sara."

He didn't reply, just helped her clean the table in silence. Sara went upstairs to get a few rocks and shells to show her father. Plate in hand, Nate surveyed the kitchen. "Where's your dishwasher?"

"I don't have one."

"All the antiques and vases and things arranged everywhere and you don't have a dish—"

"Look, enough said. We don't live your kind of life. And it's not as if I'm trying to save these hands or anything." With defiance, she held her hands up for inspection. "They get ruined working with the flowers, anyway. What's a little dishwater?"

With hardly a glance, he went to the table again. Libby automatically turned on the warm water. Nate wasn't interested in her hands, and why should he be? She was sensitive about how they looked, but there was no choice in her line of work. She'd held them up, almost daring him to criticize. He probably had his own nails buffed regularly. But she already knew how different his life was from hers.

"Here." Sara came into the kitchen with a heavy, overflowing box. "Do you like rocks?" She put the box on the table with a thump.

Nate hesitated. "Sure. I like rocks."

"Cool. What's your favorite?"

Again the hesitation. Nate probably couldn't name a single one. Libby couldn't help a mean little smile. "Surely you have favorites, Nate. Which is your favorite igneous rock, which your favorite sedimentary?"

"Which is *your* favorite, Sara?" Nate hadn't missed a beat.

"This iron pyrite. Fool's gold," she said promptly, holding out a glittering stone for his inspection.

"Is there a rock shop in town?" Nate asked.

Sara shook her head. "No, you have to go to Toledo."

"Why don't we do that? Go to Toledo?" Nate's voice was eager. Too eager, but Sara didn't seem to notice. Libby looked across the room, to where the light from her old globe chandelier brought out the blue highlights on two heads of glossy black hair.

Sara put down the fool's gold. "Yes, let's. But could we go to the mall or something? I *love* the mall."

"Sure. The mall. Next Saturday?" He looked to Libby for confirmation. "After chores, of course."

There was no reason to refuse. "Yes," she said, and he smiled again. It wasn't his cool, practiced smile, but a real one. Almost more powerful for its rarity.

Later, as soon as Sara had gone to bed, Nate rose to leave. If Libby had needed any reminder that Sara was the reason he was here, she had it in his eagerness to leave. Well, it was for the best. She knew she was susceptible to sophisticated charmers. And her best friend, Tina Samms, had married one, and the jerk had left her high and dry years ago. So Libby should be glad that Nate was giving her a reality check. She ought to be grateful; instead she felt a twinge of disappointment.

"Thank you," he said, shrugging into a leather jacket. "Your dinner was delicious." In his tone, she heard the studied charm of the Chicago millionaire, and suddenly, she couldn't stand it.

"Come on. You hated the rice medley and I know the meat loaf was ghastly."

There was a long pause. "But your table was...pretty,

with all those little colored bottles. You're making this so easy for me—for Sara—when you could be..." He shoved his hands in his pockets. His voice had deepened, and she had no doubt of his sincerity now. "Thank you for that."

She swallowed and nodded.

"Look. Why don't you come with us Saturday? Let me buy you a pizza. No pepperoni." He smiled that damn devastating smile. He added quickly, "I want to buy some things for Sara. I never have, you know. And I don't know her sizes, what she likes."

Of course, she thought. He wanted her there for Sara, and to make things easier for him.

"Okay."

"Good."

At the door, Nate lingered. "Would you mind if I came over tomorrow? I'd like to see Sara after school. I know the plan was Wednesdays and Saturdays, but..."

Libby hesitated, wondering what would be best for Sara. But this evening had gone so well—better than she'd hoped— "Okay. Come whenever you can."

He nodded. There was another pause. Then, "Look, I just want to know," he said, "why you're doing this for me. If Sara gets to know me..." His voice trailed off, but she knew what he was going to say. If Sara got to know him, his claim for custody would be all the stronger.

"For Sara." It was for Sara, and only for Sara, she reminded herself.

"Really? Well, I just..." His voice trailed off again. In the dim light he looked oddly vulnerable. That vulnerability touched her, because while she armored herself against the Chicago millionaire, she couldn't seem to armor herself against the father, or the man.

"People don't do things for such selfless reasons." At the bleakness in his tone, Libby's heart ached. In Nate's world, that must be true. Libby pressed the tips of her fingers into her own palm, against the calluses there. She had her flowers, she had Sara, she had so many memories. She had a *life*.

She swallowcd. "Harborside isn't like that. I'm not like that. I love Sara too much to be selfish. And I think you love Sara too much to be selfish, too."

He gave a harsh chuckle. "Most people would hardly describe me as selfless."

She hesitated. "Don't get me wrong. I'll take you to court over Sara, because she's become my daughter, and I'm convinced she's better off in Harborside. After all, what do you have to offer her in Chicago?"

"Ballet, singing, all the lessons she wants. The arts. The best schools."

"Everything money can buy."

He didn't seem to notice her sarcasm. "Right."

"Will you have time for her, Nate? You've got your business, and you'll be a single parent. When you're in Chicago, can you make time?"

He looked confused, and that shocked her. Surely he realized that his life-style would change dramatically if he had Sara. She'd given him food for thought. But now something in that rare less-than-sure expression made her add, "I know you love her. I do, too. Whatever happens, I'll do what's best for her."

He swallowed. "I appreciate that. I do appreciate what you've done for her."

She nodded. The tension between them was thick. She looked up, into his eyes, into a face that was all shadows and angles.

Unexpectedly, his hand came up, stilled, then hovered in the air. He leaned forward slightly.

Dear Lord, he was going to kiss her! Of its own volition,

Libby felt her body sway slightly, hungering for Nate's touch.

He didn't kiss her. Instead, he dropped his hand to his side, opened the door and went through it into the night. Libby shut the door and leaned against it. She was light-headed and dry-mouthed, and scared to death at her own response to nothing more than a look and a gesture that meant…nothing. *Fool's gold,* she said to herself. The man was fool's gold—glitter on the outside, hard as iron within.

TREVOR SAMMS SCOOTED his wheelchair around and pulled open the refrigerator door, then reached into its specially made shallow recesses for a can of soda. The light from the refrigerator dimly illuminated the room, so he left the door open to light his way as he searched through the cupboards for some chips or pretzels or packaged cupcakes or maybe all three. He was starving.

"Trevor? Is that you?"

His mother was silhouetted above him, in her nightgown, leaning on the balcony railing that overlooked the kitchen below.

Trevor smiled. Who else would it be, with the fridge door open? "It's a madman, come for onion dip," he said in a stagey whisper. "Then he'll hold us at gunpoint, till we break and tell him where we've stashed the gold…"

"Cut it out." Tina Samms tried to sound stern, but Trevor knew she liked his sense of humor. Most of the time. He decided to press his luck, and changed his tone, making it deep. "No, I'm the guy next door. Nate Perry. Handsome, rich, come calling…"

"Trevor." Now her voice contained a clear warning.

Trevor stopped. It was fun to bait his mom sometimes, but she didn't like the guy next door. She spoke to Mr. Perry, but only when she had to. It embarrassed Trevor,

how his mom snubbed their neighbor, because he could tell
Mr. Perry was aware of it. 'Course, he could see why his
mom didn't like him. Mr. Perry was going to develop the
Point, and then they wouldn't be able to afford to live here.
And Mr. Perry was trying to take Sara away from Libby,
who was his mother's best friend.

Libby didn't like Nate Perry either. He'd heard her say
that to his mom, when they thought he was in his room
with his headphones on. Libby had got mad about the condos too, said Nate was being self-centered. Trevor had
listened, because for some reason he wanted to know everything about Nate Perry.

Libby had shown his mother all the stuff Mr. Perry had
filed with the court, and his mom had kind of choked and
said he gives about four times as much to charity as she
earned.

"Do you want some company?" His mom was starting
down the stairs.

"Naw. You've got a lot to do in the morning." His mom
was making all the costumes for the community-theater
production of *Fiddler on the Roof.* She made her living
doing alterations mostly, but Libby made sure she always
got the orders for the costumes at the theater. And she
covered Country Tastes on Saturdays so Libby could take
the day off.

"You've got school in the morning," she returned.

"I won't be up long. Honest." Lots of times he had
trouble sleeping. But, though he suspected his mom was
aware of it, he didn't feel like talking about it.

"Well…" She hesitated.

"Go to bed, Mom. Really."

She hesitated a second longer, then turned away. From
her bedroom doorway, she yelled, "Close that refrigerator
door!"

Trevor slammed the door real hard so she'd hear it from upstairs. Then he piled his lap with chips, a container of dip, Oreos and cupcakes, not bothering with a plate or bowl. He could reach the dishes, though, if he wanted to. Unlike their last house, he could reach everything in the kitchen, because originally the place had been built for this super-rich old guy in a wheelchair.

Handicapped accessible, the For Rent advertisement had said. And the condo was a great place. He and his mom had known going in that when the right developer came along, they would have to move. Their unit would become part of a large complex and would eventually be sold. Now Nate Perry was that developer. In a town like Harborside, everybody knew who he was, and they all knew things would change at Bittersweet Point. Only really wealthy people would be able to afford to live here.

His mom was mad about that, and blamed Nate Perry, although she'd admitted Mr. Perry wasn't personally responsible. He was just a businessman.

Trevor knew who was really to blame. Jonathan Samms. His father had left them six months after Trevor's accident, and he hadn't seen his son since, or paid a dime of child support. So he was the one ultimately responsible for the fact they'd had to rent the place before this, so small, with such tight turns and doorways that his mom had had to help him get on the toilet.

Most of the time Trevor didn't mind being stuck in the wheelchair. He'd had four years to adjust as the counselors called it. And everybody, including him, thought he'd adjusted just fine. But he'd silently hated the chair, really and truly hated the chair, when his mom had had to help him in the john. He made jokes about her strength, when she was grunting with the effort of helping him move, but he hated that part when she saw him...bare. He knew who was really responsible for *that,* too.

Trevor would sure like to tell his dad... What? Maybe he'd ask him stuff, instead. Stuff like why wasn't Mom good enough for you, and why didn't you wait around to see how good I can handle the chair, and why...? Sighing, he pulled on his sweatshirt. Then he stuck his pop can between his thighs and opened the sliding glass doors to the deck. He wouldn't get a chance to tell his father anything anytime soon. Nobody knew where Jonathan Samms lived.

The deck was warmer due to an early-spring heat spell. For a few moments Trevor sat at the edge of the deck, watching the dark water.

"So. Can't sleep?"

Startled, Trevor glanced next door. Sitting on the steps of his own deck, with his feet on the sand below, was Nate Perry. Mr. Perry had both hands wrapped around a bottle of beer.

"You startled me," Trevor said.

"Like you did me, that first time."

Trevor felt himself begin to grin. "You figured you owed me."

"Something like that."

Trevor was kind of in awe of Nate Perry, because he was a rich guy from out of town who had cool high-tech stuff. But he liked the guy, too. He'd started conversations with Nate Perry a time or two. Mr. Perry didn't talk much, but he didn't blow Trevor off either.

And the way he'd come back for his kid after all those years... Well, Trevor had got a big lump in his throat when he'd heard that story, and had to blink his eyes real hard. His mom might be upset because of Libby, but all Trevor could think was one sentence, over and over. *He came back. He came back.*

"I just came out to look at the way the moon makes the waves all silvery," Trevor said, and then he felt dumb because he thought that wasn't something he should admit. He should talk about cars or something, not sound like a Hallmark card.

"Me too."

"Oh." That made Trevor feel good somehow. "I just like looking at the water."

"Yeah," Mr. Perry said. "I know."

The way Mr. Perry said that, Trevor just knew this big-time rich guy liked the way the moon went in and out among the clouds and glowed on the waves. Trevor was feeling better and better. He didn't know any other grown-up guys well except Mr. Murphy who always whined if he didn't get the leads in the community plays, and Mr. Carlyle, who used to mow his mom's lawn.

"I don't suppose," he ventured boldly, "you've got another beer on you."

"Oh, I don't think so, Trevor." Trevor thought he heard the hint of a smile in Mr. Perry's voice.

"Just seeing how far I could push you." Trevor popped the top on his soda can. "Mom won't let me have one, either. Want to come over for some chips? Dip? Cupcakes? There're two cupcakes in the package." It would be so cool if Mr. Perry came over.

"Thanks. I'm okay right here."

"Oh." Some of the magic went out of the night. But Mr. Perry didn't go inside after that, as Trevor had half suspected he might.

For a few moments they were quiet, each on his own deck. Trevor figured they were hanging out, the way he'd seen grown-up guys do, clustered around one pickup truck or another on Raft Street, just standing around, a foot on the bumper, beer cans on the hood.

Trevor wondered what a guy like Nate Perry thought about on nights he couldn't sleep. Maybe he thought about Sara. Or maybe he only thought about his business in Chicago, or developing Bittersweet Point. Suddenly, he burned with curiosity. "When you can't sleep, do you think about her?" he asked out of the blue.

"What?" He saw the beer bottle in Mr. Perry's hand hit the sandy beach without a sound.

His reaction puzzled Trevor. "Well, I know Sara's your daughter."

"Oh. Sara."

"Who did you think I meant?"

"Nobody in particular."

His mom used that tone of voice when she wasn't going to tell him something no matter how he pestered. Trevor frowned and drained the last of his soda. "Sara's okay. I mean, for a little girl." Sara talked too much, but she wasn't bad. And Trevor tried very hard not to be jealous of her because she had a father who wanted her so bad he was going to court to get her. Heck, he'd have to be jealous of just about every kid he knew, if he wanted to be jealous of kids with dads.

Nate Perry couldn't be his dad. And he didn't want a dad. One had been more than enough. But Mr. Perry could be kind of a…friend. Trevor frowned as he used his teeth to open the package of cupcakes. That wasn't the word he wanted. Well, maybe it could just be more like a big brother. What did they call it on TV? Male bonding. Yeah, that was it.

"You could call me Trev." He'd made the offer when he'd first met Mr. Perry, but Mr. Perry still called him Trevor, like everyone else. But Trev sounded more masculine somehow.

"Okay. Trev it is."

Cool, Trevor thought. Awesome.

CHAPTER FIVE

NATE'S EUPHORIA about Sara's agreement to go shopping lasted only until he was in the entrance of Libby's house. When he arrived, Sara's greeting was subdued. Libby told her rather sharply to change her jacket for something warmer, so he guessed they'd had a few words about the trip already this morning. Had Sara changed her mind about going? He'd thought things were going so well, at dinner this past Wednesday. He'd been looking forward to the outing more than he had anticipated anything in a long time.

He wished things were as easy with Sara as he'd imagined they'd be, when he had been in Chicago, making plans. His daughter with him, living in the bedroom he was having redecorated for her. No more feeling empty, and the end of his ever-present fears for his daughter's safety. He'd planned the very best for Sara—the best schools, trips to Europe, dancing lessons, all those things he couldn't afford before.

"Ready?" he asked as she finally came into view for the second time, in a hooded jacket.

"Ready," she said, her gaze not quite meeting his. Damn. She was his daughter. If he only knew what to *say* to make things perfect.

She marched ahead of him down the walk.

He raised his eyebrows at Libby, and moved aside so that she could go down the walk in front of him. He was glad she was coming. There was safety in numbers. She could put things right if he said or did something stupid. Today Libby was clad in faded jeans that hugged shapely legs, and a soft peach-colored sweater. Nothing outlandish. The color was great with her red hair, and the turtleneck collar hugged the long, slim line of her neck. He was definitely attracted to her, but she showed no attraction to him. There didn't seem to be a flirtatious bone in her body; he found himself respecting that about her.

As she passed him, he saw that one dangling silver earring had become caught in a strand of her hair, and he could have sworn he caught the scent of her, of spice and greens...

He willed down his reaction. "So Sara's upset with me?" he asked in a low tone.

"Not really." A light frown crossed her features. "Her friend Kathleen asked her to go horseback riding today. Sara wanted to go, but she'd made a promise to you."

Oh. Sara hadn't wanted to go with him. He'd thought all week about this outing, and Sara hadn't wanted to go. Libby must have made her, and he hated the thought of that.

Libby smiled. That smile was so real, so genuine, and again he felt that funny little kick in the gut. "I thought she should keep her promise. And anyway, ten-year-old girls are flaky sometimes, you know."

He didn't know, but it was obviously one of the things he was finding out.

At the mall, Sara perked right up, and he began to see what Libby had meant. Were all kids this moody?

"So, where to?" he asked, pleased that his daughter was finally showing some enthusiasm for the outing.

"The Pumpkin Coach?" she asked hopefully.

Walking beside him, Nate thought he felt Libby hesitate.

But he couldn't be sure. Since he'd never felt so conscious of a woman before, maybe he was misreading her.

"Okay," he agreed.

At the store, Sara went right over to a navy and red rugby shirt and matching slacks. The set was cute. "What's your size?" Nate asked, pulling one off the rack that even he could see was way too small.

Sara rolled her eyes and giggled.

But Libby looked at the price tag and frowned in earnest. "Nate—"

"Here's one that looks like it might fit," Nate interrupted, holding the outfit out to Sara.

Sara took it. She shot Libby a look. "Um, how about some sneakers?" she asked, a little shy, a little bold.

"Sneakers it is," Nate replied. Sara grinned at him. It wasn't one of her shy smiles, it was a grin, wide-open and genuine, and it felt so incredibly good. He felt a smile of his own forming, and for some unearthly reason, he looked to Libby, as if to share it.

She pushed a flyaway lock of hair behind her ear, and she didn't return his smile. "Nate, Sara really doesn't need new shoes, but if you want to buy them, there's a discount place—"

"Aw, Lib, I wanted those silver ones with the glittery laces." Sara gave Nate a pleading look.

That decided it for Nate. "Pick any you want. No, wait, take a pair of each color." He grabbed a pair of hot-pink shoes, a pair of yellow. Piling them up to her chin, he added a pair of neon blue ones for good measure.

"Wow! Thanks! Marie has some like the pink ones. I can't *wait* to wear these." At Nate's direction, Sara picked out some other things—jeans, a purple leather purse—just the thing, he guessed, to go with silver sneakers—and other stuff besides. Girl stuff. Daughter stuff. In Chicago, he'd imagined giving Sara lessons and a fine education. He'd never quite imagined himself out with her, buying her things so...directly. Sara disappeared into the fitting room.

Nate felt on top of the world.

"Nate, listen," Libby said urgently as Sara departed.

He liked how she made his name sound, all low and husky. Then he shook his head, as if to clear it. He had some dangerous notions about this woman. Like that urge to tell her about himself that had hit him as he was leaving her place Wednesday, to say things he'd never shared with anyone. It was a siren call that seemed to come from her, that whispered, *you can tell me anything*.

He'd told Eve a few things about himself, about how scared he felt about the business, about his father's gambling, how it was so hard, sometimes, even to touch her, his wife, with any spontaneity. The next time they'd fought, she'd thrown that admission in his face.

Sure, he thought. Tell Libby things. *Tell her your deepest, darkest secrets so she can use them in court to keep your daughter away from you.* His euphoric mood disappeared.

He shot her a quick, covert glance. She was fiddling with the laces of one of a pair of sneakers on a shelf. He'd been in business long enough to know when someone was working up to something, and Libby was definitely working up to something. Well, he was buying Sara things that made the girl's eyes sparkle. And he was damned if he was going to let anything spoil the occasion.

"So, what's the problem?" he asked a trifle impatiently.

"This place is kind of expensive." She laughed a little, nervously. "I mean, I know you haven't shopped for a girl before, and there are a lot of other shops that offer better values—"

"This was Sara's choice."

"Well, but—"

"I can afford it." All this fuss about a kid's clothes, he thought with rising irritation.

She flared a little, tossing her head, two pink spots on her cheekbones. "Sure. Rub it in."

He put a hand on her forearm. The peachy angora was even softer than it looked, and he had a hint of the warmth of the skin beneath. He pulled away immediately. "I'm not trying to show you up," he insisted.

"Well, it wouldn't be too hard, would it?" She looked at him with a mixture of defiance and defensiveness.

"Just what's that supposed to mean?" She wasn't going to try to spoil this for him, was she? She had so much. She had Sara.

She pressed her lips together, then gave a quick shake of her head. "You know what I earn. More to the point, you know what I don't earn, to the penny. I assume you read the financial and personal-information papers I had to file with the court, just as I read yours."

Nate had, and he'd been appalled at how little his daughter had been living on. Eve and Lloyd had left Sara a small inheritance, but Libby hadn't touched it. He felt a spurt of reluctant admiration. She certainly needed the money, and as Sara's guardian, she could have spent it on his daughter's care. But she was saving it for Sara's education, Marta had told him. Sara wouldn't need Eve's money now. But he smiled at Libby, softening in spite of himself at how much she cared about his daughter.

"Look," he said. "I'm not trying to buy her, I'm trying to buy things *for* her. This is about my daughter, not about court."

She flushed and gave him a half-formed return smile. There was nothing flirtatious about it, but her expression was so unexpectedly sexy that he had to look away. She had the most artless way about her. It set him to hatching never-to-be-executed plots for coaxing her into bed.

He shook his head. He hadn't been celibate in the years since his divorce. But he picked women carefully, women who were interested in the things he was—decent conversation, a handy date for charity functions, an honest, mutually satisfying sexual relationship—and never, never any discussion about the future. It had been a while since he'd been involved with a woman. So perhaps abstinence was responsible for his reaction to Libby.

"Libby?" Sara had reappeared, in a nautical-looking dress, her gaze focused on Libby. "What do you think?"

"It's cute." Libby glanced at the price tag. "But not *that* cute, sweetheart." She sighed. "Though I expect your father will be happy to buy it for you."

Sara's gaze flickered uncertainly from Libby to Nate.

"It's only money," Nate said.

"I think that's my line." Libby's tone was dry as she took a pair of silver lamé sneakers from Sara up to the sales counter.

Nate felt his mouth tighten. Okay, so money was important to him. Didn't Libby understand that with money you could buy anything, even peace of mind? A couple of minutes later he stood before the stack of clothing piled on the sales counter and pulled out his credit card. The sales clerk was smiling. Sara was smiling. That was all that mattered. He was going to leave the boutique, and then they were going to go to shop after shop, anywhere Sara wanted, and buy whatever she wanted, and Libby's disapproval be damned. After all, how could you spoil a kid you hadn't seen in eight years?

In the toy store, he coaxed Sara over to the display of dolls. She murmured something about not playing with dolls much anymore. But he stood beside her at the glass case and watched her carefully, and could see her take in a breath over a porcelain-faced Victorian lady, with a red velvet gown and a tiny, real-fur muff. "We'll take that one," he said to the salesperson.

"Oh," Sara breathed. She hesitated. "I don't need that doll. I wouldn't dare play with something so fancy anyway."

"But you like it?" He heard the eagerness in his voice.

"Yes. Oh, yes."

"Good." He pulled out his credit card again and went up to pay.

It was while the clerk was ringing up the sale that he remembered the train, his Lionel toy train. God, he hadn't thought about that train in years. He'd been about Sara's age when he'd owned it, just young enough to imagine that the train would be spared when everything his family owned was auctioned off…for the second time, thanks to his father's gambling debts. The train had had coal cars, boxcars and cattle cars…oh, and two tiny mountains, a switchback and some fuzzy trees made out of green-colored moss, a bridge…

His mother had understood. She'd wanted his father to keep the train set out of the auction. His parents had fought over the issue, and Nate had hated that part the most, holding his hands over his ears in bed one night as they yelled about that train, hurling wild accusations at one another.

Of course, the train had been sold along with everything else they owned, and of course his father had said next time he'd buy his boy *two* trains, and of course, three years later his father had hit it big again with the numbers, and offered to replace the whole setup, even bigger than before. Nate had refused. He was too old, he'd said, and his father had clapped him on the back and said he was a man and didn't need any old toy train.

He shook off the memory. He had money now, and rock-solid investments, and major holdings in real estate. Land. Solid and real—as long as a man worked hard and kept his wits about him. He'd learned to depend on himself for the things that were important. Sara would know nothing but stability. He forced a smile. "Thirsty?" he asked Sara.

"Real thirsty." Her gaze included Libby. "And I'm kind of hungry too…?" The last was drawn into a question, and he realized that Sara was still uncertain around him, looking to Libby for security. The thought hurt.

"Great. We passed a McDonald's at the food court."

Libby was quiet as they headed that way. Nate and Sara got in line for hamburgers and french fries while she went to the wok place for stir-fry. Nate was buying Sara way too much. Perhaps he really didn't mean just to impress the court, play up for Judge Wyatt the contrasts between what he could provide and what Libby could give Sara. But that's the spin Marta Wainwright would put on things. And regardless, if this buying spree continued, it couldn't be good for Sara. She needed to get to know her father, what kind of person he was inside. She still knew so little about him. Nate seemed to be drawing Sara out but sharing so very little of himself.

Cam had had a fit when he'd found out that Libby had let Nate come over every day after school. He urged her to do no more than comply with the schedule. Her friend Tina had done the same, cautioning Libby more than once not to let Nate get the upper hand.

But Sara needed this time with her father. Libby shook her head, telling herself that, no matter how extravagant, today was their first shopping trip. Nate would learn to slow down. It had been an intense week. Maybe what they all needed was some breathing space.

She looked toward the table in the middle of the food

court, where Nate and Sara were now sitting. Two black heads were leaning toward one another, so close they almost blended. The girl was so beautiful, a delight to be around. The man was so perfectly proportioned that in contrast, she felt plain and...ordinary. She'd always liked life in Harborside, *liked* being ordinary. Now all of a sudden, life just didn't seem fair.

Balancing the foam plate in one hand and holding a too-hot cup of tea in the other, she sighed and headed over to them.

"Libby! Guess what?" Sara jumped up from her seat just as Libby was preparing to set her plate on the table. Libby moved, but not quickly enough. Sara bumped her arm hard. The flimsy plastic plate buckled, sending pea pods flying. The rest of her lunch tumbled down the front of her sweater.

As tea sloshed on her hand, she jerked back with a cry of pain, which promptly sent the contents of the cup arcing through the air.

Nate leaped to his feet, his handkerchief outstretched. "Did you burn yourself?" His voice was deep with concern as he used the handkerchief to make a firm swipe down the front of her sweater.

Libby felt herself blush. What a mess she'd made! "I'm fine," she managed to say. All of a sudden—midswipe—Nate froze. Then, through her mortification, she realized it, too. Nate Perry had a hand on her breast.

Heat raced from her cheeks to her toes in an embarrassing, thrilling combination of sensation that finally settled low in her belly. Through layers of wet sweater and bra and a corner of handkerchief, she could still feel his hand *there,* his palm cupped, the pads of his fingers pressed against her nipple. She started to tremble.

Nate still hadn't moved. Slowly, Libby brought her face

up to look up at him; he looked down. His eyes were brilliant, locked on hers.

Sara said, "Geez, I'm sorry!" and Nate jerked his hand away and shoved it, handkerchief and all, into his pocket. He looked away.

Sara was rattling on. "Gosh, that's *soy sauce* on your sweater, Lib. I don't think soy sauce comes out, does it? I mean, if you take off your top and soak it in cold water when we get home…"

"It's okay." With more of an effort than she should have required, Libby pulled herself together. Nate's touch was accidental. He'd been trying to be a gentleman. He didn't ever need to know how he'd affected her, how she'd had that hungry, tingly two-second flash of utter…lust when she'd felt his touch.

"Now," she said, forcing a smile and sitting down again with Sara. "Donate a french fry to the cause of my lost lunch and tell me what got you so excited in the first place." She resisted an urge to swipe futilely at the stain on her sweater. Nate, she noticed out of the corner of her eye, had retaken his seat next to Sara and now appeared fascinated with his Big Mac.

"Well, Nate's going to get me horseback-riding lessons!" Sara turned a dazzling smile on Nate. "Isn't that just s-o-o neat?" She sighed dramatically. "I've wanted those lessons for s-o-o long." When she looked at Libby, there was no uncertainty, no waiting for Libby's approval, only an expectation that Libby share her joy.

Sara *had* wanted the lessons for the entire year she'd been with Libby. "That's great, sweetheart." Libby almost meant it. Heck, she *did* mean it. She reached over and squeezed the girl's hand. "Thank you," she said softly to Nate.

He nodded but didn't look directly at her. He wasn't still embarrassed, was he?

All right. So things had seemed a tad weird in that moment when they'd looked into each other's eyes. So for a second she'd thought he'd felt something too. Well, even if there *had* been something sexual between them, to a man like Nate it couldn't be anything special. Cam had told her what he'd found out about Nate's personal life. He was seen regularly at society functions, and each time, it seemed, he had a different woman with him. Glamorous, beautiful women. Nate had probably had his hands, his lips, on the bare flesh of many a woman... *Oh, God.*

"And," Sara added, popping a french fry into her mouth, "Nate's getting me a horse."

"Renting you a horse, sweetheart," Libby corrected automatically, blessing her ward's chatty nature.

"Buying me a horse," Sara insisted, her eyes very bright. "We're going to a horse farm and I get to pick out my horse. What he's going to rent is the stable space. Right, Nate?" She waved her cheeseburger at him for confirmation.

The hard planes of Nate's face softened. "Right. And we're going to make sure you get a new saddle, the safest equipment—"

"Right. A saddle maybe better than Kathleen's. Oh, I don't mean a lot better, just kind of better because sometimes she's mean to me because she's got a horse and I don't." Sara paused, her forehead creased. "Well, maybe not better than Kathleen's. She did invite me to her birthday party. And I don't want her to get her feelings hurt. Just a saddle and bridle and stuff that's only as good as Kathleen's. Okay, Nate?"

Nate. Nate. Nate. Suddenly, it was hard to remember that less than a week ago, Sara had been wondering what to call the man who'd appeared in her life wanting to be her father. Things were moving too fast. Sara's cheeks were flushed, her eyes too bright, her tongue going at too frenetic a pace even for her.

Sara was being seduced.

Libby paused, the end of a french fry still poised mid-dunk in a puddle of ketchup. She understood. What woman, young or old, could resist the fantasy of a sinfully handsome stranger who came to town with big, big presents and an urge to be a daddy? Lord, even she herself sometimes— her mind turned abruptly from the thought.

Maybe Cam and Tina were right. Libby looked over at Sara. The girl continued to talk to Nate, cajoling him into buying her what fast-food places called apple pie. Neither father nor daughter seemed to notice that Libby wasn't saying much at all. Neither of them would like what she was thinking now. But Libby knew that when you loved a child and were responsible for raising her, you had to do what you thought was right.

She made a decision. It was almost guaranteed to be met with opposition from both Nate and Sara, but Libby had made up her mind. She looked over at Nate. He was listening to Sara's chatter, telling her nothing at all about himself. Nate Perry was definitely not going to like what she had to say.

WHEN NATE DROPPED them off a couple of hours later, Libby stayed behind as Sara got out of the back seat. "See you next Saturday!" Sara sang out.

Libby rolled down the window. "Here's my key." She handed it to Sara. "It's late. Can you go in and get ready for bed, please? I'll be in soon, but I want to talk to Nate for a minute."

"What about?" Sara asked. Immediately, her smile

faded, and her gaze flickered from Libby to Nate and back again.

"Nothing special. Don't worry, sweetheart," Libby reassured her. After a slight hesitation, Sara smiled a little uncertainly and headed up the walk.

They sat for a moment in the dark. Libby had left the window down. The sound of tree frogs was a constant, underlying noise. Nate waited for Libby to begin.

Finally, she spoke quietly. "Nate, you're buying Sara too much."

That again! Nate never got truly angry, not out-of-control angry. He hated that. But this woman had a way of pushing his buttons. "My choice," he said shortly.

She stared straight ahead. "I think you should do other things with her, things that don't cost money. Ride bikes, take walks. Tell her what kind of man you are, what your own family was like. She has grandparents, for example, and I've never heard you mention…"

"My parents are dead." Nate heard the flatness in his tone, as if he didn't care that Sara wouldn't know her grandparents.

"She's going to have questions—"

"And I said I'd answer them, the very first time I saw her," he cut in, his temper rising in spite of his best efforts to control it.

"But you didn't act as if you meant it, and today you didn't give her time to think about anything but the next item on her wish list. You don't start conversations. You just buy her things."

There was a small silence. It was true; he'd known Sara wanted the doll, and he could relate to her wanting it the way he'd wanted the train. But the thought of telling his daughter tales of his own childhood caused his gut to clench. He preferred to keep some things to himself. What was the point of sharing all that…that pain, anyway? The most difficult truth of all was that he felt a lot more uncomfortable around Sara than he'd ever expected to. He didn't dare admit it to Libby. Her attorney would have a field day with his cross-examination.

"Anyway," Libby finally went on quietly, "I'm thinking that I made a mistake, making visitation so open-ended. Until the court makes some other decision, you'll need to come at your designated times." She took a breath. "Wednesdays after school and Saturdays until noon. And please, slow things down. We don't even know if horseback riding will hold Sara's interest, so maybe you could just rent the horse for now."

Nate made a grab for self-control. Eve had done this. After their divorce, when she'd figured out that Nate genuinely wanted to be a father, she played games with his visits. She threatened him with court action. Sometimes when Nate went to pick up his daughter, neither mother nor daughter had been home. But Libby was not Eve. He had to remember that.

"If I want to buy her a horse, I'll buy her a horse," he said between clenched teeth. "You want to play games? All right. I'll ask the court to give me more visitation." He was tired of negotiation. Negotiation was part of business, but this was his *daughter* they were talking about.

Libby rapped a fist on her thigh. "You're seducing her!"

Seducing. The word conjured images. Strong images. Emotions. Touching Libby's breast. That surge of sexual desire that had been like a flash fire. Seducing, she said. "So this is really about my feeling you up at the mall?" His voice was harsh with disbelief, anger, his choice of word deliberately crude.

She turned toward him swiftly. "How dare you! How

dare you suggest that I'm using Sara because I'm angry at you.''

For a second, they just stared at each other. She was breathing hard; her eyes were wide and shiny in the dark. He could see her breasts rising and falling.

And suddenly, he believed her. She wouldn't use Sara, not deliberately anyway. She had nurtured his daughter, protected her. She had given him Sara's picture, his first image of his growing daughter. It was easier to see Libby as an enemy; he was sure he'd have to fight her for Sara. But she'd play fair.

She'd play fair.

And at that realization, in the space of one heartbeat, anger turned to desire.

He put his hands on her shoulders and drew her toward him. Libby sensed his intent; he didn't move with lightning speed, but with sure purpose. As if by their own volition, her feet came off the floor, her thighs shifted, she turned toward him more fully.

The gearshift pressed into her legs. In the dark, she saw little, felt a lot. Warm breath fanned her face. And then his lips made contact. She heard his sharp intake of breath.

He was good; she'd known he would be. Practiced. She hated that, even as she felt herself responding. He settled his mouth over hers with a heat that made her tremble. She was shy; it had been years since she had kissed a man. She didn't want this. She was dying for this.

Almost tentatively, she opened her mouth, and the stroke of his tongue was like a whole body caress. His hands held her cheeks as he took the kiss deeper.

Then he groaned, and suddenly he wasn't practiced at all. His hands gripped her head more firmly. As he tipped her face closer to his, his lips asked...demanded...then took, and there was a kind of desperation that she didn't understand. It was that desperation that undid her, that sent a surge of longing through her that was more powerful than anything she'd ever known. The noise of the tree frogs outside got louder until she dimly recognized the roaring sound as her own blood in her own ears.

But, oh, God, she shouldn't be kissing Nate. With an effort, Libby raised both hands and shoved at his shoulders. "Damn you," she whispered.

Immediately, he let her go, but stayed close, resting his forehead against hers, his breathing harsh. His hair was a brush of thick silk against her skin, his eyes an inch from hers in the dark. She closed her eyes, overwhelmed by his nearness. He said absolutely nothing, and then with a long, charged sigh, he straightened.

She had no idea what he was thinking. As usual. And she was embarrassed, knowing he had to have felt her response, her yielding to the demand of his mouth. Embarrassment turned to anger. She wanted him and she didn't even know him, and what she did know about him told her to shield her heart. "This doesn't change anything," she said softly. "I won't change my mind about Sara."

He leaned his head back against the seat. "I know. We need a plan."

"A plan?" She was incredulous. How could he kiss her like, well, like that, all heat and sizzle, and then talk about plans? The tips of her fingers and toes still tingled, and he wanted to make *plans?*

"A plan. Look, maybe—" he cleared his throat "—we should start with honesty."

She made fists of her hands. "As in…?"

"I think you wanted that kiss, for instance."

Libby nearly choked. "You arrogant…" Words failed her.

"Male?" he prompted quietly.

"I suppose they all want it," she said bitterly.

"They?"

"Your...women. All the women you sleep with."

He slapped his hand on the steering wheel. "You make it sound like I have a damn harem."

But he hadn't exactly denied that there were other women in his life. Bitter laughter welled in her and threatened to break through. What did she want from him? For him to say, *There won't be any other women now that I've met you?* Come on, she knew the type; she'd had experience with the type. And she didn't love him, didn't care what he did, as long as it didn't hurt Sara.

She reached for the door handle, pulled it open. Her lips felt tender, her legs weak. But her will was strong, she told herself. "We'll never come up with a plan," she said.

"Then it looks like I'll see you in court."

CHAPTER SIX

THREE WEEKS LATER, Nate sat in his Chicago office and gave his assistant, Jeffrey Rand, his full attention. There were problems with the Iris Complex. Iris was a Chicago lakeside development of boutiques and trendy dockside cafes that also featured an indoor sports complex and sky-high, revolving lounge. From the beginning, the resort had had complications—legal problems with the city code, labor trouble. Projects this big always were major management headaches, and this was the biggest project Nate had ever undertaken.

Jeff was writing something on the pad on his lap. A young man in an expensive suit, Jeff was ambitious, a kid on the make. Because Nate needed to be in Harborside, he'd been forced to give Jeff too much responsibility. Jeff had made a few minor decisions so far, and done well. But Nate was still worried. For one thing, ambitious kids tended to gamble too much, risk too much.

"Anyway, the upshot of all this is that the bricklayers are unhappy about the overtime situation," Jeff was saying. He glanced at his memo. He was about halfway down a long list of problems.

"I'll talk to them," Nate said wearily. He was so tired these days, and so torn. He needed to be in Chicago. But Judge Wyatt required him to be in Harborside, so he was commuting constantly, a real hassle because of Harborside's isolation. And the groundbreaking for Bittersweet

Point would begin soon, and he'd have tons of work there, too. Well, there wasn't a choice.

"I already talked to them." For the first time, Jeff smiled a little.

"What happened?" Nate tensed. The guys on the job site were tough, mistrustful of management. Only twenty-six, and with a baby face, Jeff took a lot of ribbing.

"I gave them more money."

Nate groaned.

"A quarter of a percent more." The kid's tentative smile turned positively brilliant.

Nate hid his surprise. He couldn't have done better himself. Jeff had been a good pick as an assistant, though Nate's associates hadn't been sure at the time. He was too raw, they said. He'd come from a tough part of town, he had no polish. But Nate had seen something of himself in Jeff. A burning desire to get ahead. So, despite certain misgivings, he'd hired the kid.

"That's fine, Jeff," he said.

Jeff's smile faded a little. "Sure."

Nate wasn't certain exactly what he'd done wrong. "Look," he said finally, when the silence got too long, "Marta's waiting, and Marta's fees don't stop just because she's in my waiting room reading *Cosmopolitan*. Why don't you use your head on the rest of that stuff, see what you can do on your own and give me a call in Harborside early in the week."

Jeff jumped up, obviously pleased now. "Terrific." He opened the door for Marta Wainwright on his way out.

"Nate. Still afloat financially?" Marta grinned as she breezed into the room, elegant in a blue silk suit and pearls. Putting an enormous leather briefcase on a low table, she sat down in one of his wing chairs. When her skirt hiked up a fraction, she ignored it, giving him a good look at her legs. Marta had never made it a secret that she was interested in him. Nate too had been thinking about a relationship off and on for nearly as long as he'd known her.

But his reaction to her now was rather puzzling. He hadn't been involved with a woman in quite a while. He was available, and so was she. Yet the view of her legs, the fairly obvious invitation, didn't interest him at all.

"I've got the motion to increase visitation you wanted me to draft." Marta rummaged in the briefcase, producing a yellow legal pad and a sheaf of paper.

"Right." Instead of taking the papers from Marta, Nate got up from behind his desk and walked over to the window. He couldn't see Lake Michigan from here, and today the city skyline looked gray and smudged and huge, tower after tower, all the way to the horizon.

Two days ago, he'd been sitting on the steps of his Harborside condo in the dark, talking with Trev Samms—the boy always assumed Nate wanted company. The contrasts of his real life and those days in Harborside were starting to get to Nate, confusing his thoughts, making him lose focus.

From behind him, he heard Marta snap her briefcase closed. "We're asking for some visitation in Chicago, for Sara to come for a whole weekend or two, more when school's out, if the court action is still dragging on come summer."

Nate felt his gut clench. How would he make conversation with Sara, all alone for days at a time? He'd tried to beat Libby at her own game by taking her suggestion that he spend his time with Sara doing simple things. But Libby must have said something to Sara about his more limited visitation, or maybe somehow Sara blamed him, because she'd been much more subdued on the six visits he'd had with her since their shopping trip.

The last time, he'd taken her for a sail on his rented sailboat. He'd tried to show her how to tack at one point, and Sara had held the lines in a death grip and finally asked him to take them back. He'd been disappointed, sure that sailing was something they could share. Sara had been nearly silent on the trip back to dock and then the ride to Libby's.

He turned to Marta. "I had to cancel this Wednesday's visit so I could make the trip here." It was merely coincidence, Nate told himself, that he'd decided he had to come to Chicago right after the sailing incident. And coming here hadn't had anything to do with Libby, with that kiss he'd shared with the enemy, that soft, sweet-smelling enemy who had aroused him so much with one kiss that his hands were still shaking on the steering wheel as he'd driven home. That had never happened before. "What will canceling one time do to my chances of getting visitation increased?"

Marta stood and poured a cup of coffee from the pot on the coffee cart his secretary had just brought in. "Well, it's rather ironic that you're asking for more when you didn't take advantage of what you had. But the judge just needs to understand that you're a hell of a lot more important guy than anyone in Harborside. I'll explain. I'll handle it."

Nate moved from the window and sat down. "This isn't working, Marta. When Sara talks to me at all, she keeps mentioning this play she's in at her school, and all her friends. And the fact that she's in *Fiddler on the Roof* this summer. She doesn't seem interested in my business or anything in Chicago. She seems to have a lot going on in Harborside. I feel like some kind of heel around my own daughter for wanting to uproot her."

"Crap," Marta said sharply. "That's crap, Nate. Keep

talking like that, and you'll never get custody of her. You've got to talk like a winner.''

His father had said that, too. Act like a winner and you'll be a winner. And sometimes, it had worked for his old man. When he was a kid, Nate had actually believed the wild promises his father made, had actually believed that this time, *this time,* his father would make a fortune and then he'd quit playing the numbers, betting at the track, all of it. Nate had actually believed, over and over again, that his mom would be happy, and there'd be money so that he could stay at the prep school with all his friends... Nate's hands fisted on the desk. "I've got to figure out something. If only Sara were older."

"If she were older, her custody would be pretty much up to her. Her choice," Marta said.

Nate knew Marta was right. If Sara were old enough to decide for herself, she'd undoubtedly choose Libby as her guardian. But maybe if she were older, she'd be able to see how much Nate wanted to be a good father to her. Well, he might be a long way from winning the heart of his daughter, but he was working on it. It would be so much easier if he didn't have to deal with her guardian.

A guardian who had that shy, almost wondering way of kissing, who'd smelled like a garden, whose curves had set him on fire.

Nate knew how to behave in business. To his father's advice—act like a winner—he added: work hard, figure out a can't-lose strategy. Winning had become a habit. Nate was used to having it all.

But there was no way to have it all, not in this situation. Unless...

Yes. A plan. And it was so damn simple, after all, that Nate couldn't believe he hadn't thought of it before. His mind said *yes.* But for a moment, his gut clenched. He felt as if he was standing on the edge of something, afraid he'd fall... No. He'd keep his head. This was a plan, a strategy.

"File the motion, Marta," he said decisively. "I'm going to need some leverage for a little negotiation in Harborside."

"I DIDN'T THINK he'd really do it." Libby slapped the copy of Nate's motion onto her kitchen table among the piles of fringe and satin, sending a few glittering sequins flying.

Tina Samms had read the document through twice already. Libby sat down across from Tina and automatically picked up a red satin Western-style shirt in one hand and poked her middle finger into a thimble. She was used to having her hands busy.

"Nate Perry's a jerk," Tina agreed sympathetically as she tacked a length of fringe on a denim skirt.

"He's not a jerk." Sometimes she wished he was. It might make the upcoming court hearings easier to take.

Tina looked up from her work. "No? Then tell me what to call a man who wants to take Sara away, even though she doesn't want to leave you."

Libby started to attach a line of fringe to the yoke of the shirt. Her stitches were big, uneven, but that didn't matter. This was unpaid labor for the school play, and the audience would be seated too far away to see what an unsettled woman could do to a line of hand stitching.

"The thing is, I don't think Sara's nearly as unhappy about her...Nate as she lets on." Her thread tangled, and she yanked. "She really looks up to him. I went out to see her ride the horse he's rented for her, and Nate stopped by to pick her up from the stable for his visit. You should have seen the smile she gave him. Wide-open. For a second there, she was really glad to see him." She sighed. "But then she wanted to show him some trick she learned, a tight double turn, and the horse, Penny, wouldn't cooperate. I got a little scared, afraid she couldn't hang on to that horse, but Sara just kept trying, until Nate told her she should let it go.''

Libby frowned, remembering. Just as she'd been about to say something to Sara, Nate had intervened. When Sara had dismounted, and come with drooping shoulders and slow steps through the gate, Libby had given her a hug and told her she could try again another day. Sara had looked to Nate for reassurance, too, but Nate was rummaging in his pocket for his keys and didn't say a word. Well, maybe because he hadn't been looking into his daughter's eyes, he hadn't noticed how much Sara wanted his approval.

Tina was sorting through the sequins. ''But she still wants to live with you.'' When Libby didn't answer for a moment, she looked up. ''She *does,* doesn't she?''

''Well,'' Libby said slowly, ''she wants to be in her school play, but that's only two weeks away. She'll be in *Fiddler on the Roof* with me this fall. But last night when we were doing the dishes, she said that Nate has a house-keeper. That Nate builds shopping complexes. Sometimes, she's just…overwhelmed, and I can't blame her. Remember when we were kids, Harborside didn't seem exciting at all?''

Tina played with a sequin. ''How could I forget?''

Twenty-five years of friendship meant that many things didn't need to be said. They had both lost mothers when they were young and the loss had been an instant bond between them. Neighbor ladies and teachers had tried to fill the gap in feminine wisdom, but mostly it was Libby and Tina, going it alone.

Bored at first, because both of them were interested in art and drama and Harborside offered nothing in either category. Then scared of boys and growing to womanhood without a mother to talk things over with. When she was fifteen, Libby had been so frightened of a boy who'd coaxed her into a tree house for a kiss and a grope that she'd punched the kid in the nose and pushed him out of the tree. He'd been furious, told her nobody wanted to kiss a girl with hair the color of a copper-pot scrubber anyway. His friends had taunted her in the school hallways for days afterward. Tina had stuck to her like glue.

And Libby had stuck by Tina when, at age seventeen, Tina met Jonathan. Jonathan was older, new in town. He was just out of the service, with a glamorous flyboy image. Tina hadn't had a chance.

Impulsively, Libby put down the shirt and covered Tina's hand with her own. For a second, Tina tried to keep sewing, tiny stitches that were her trademark. Then she stopped. "Oh, Lib, it was all a long time ago."

"But still…" Libby kept her hand where it was, over her friend's.

"Yeah." Tina's bottom lip trembled. Jonathan Samms had left four years ago, shortly after Trevor's accident. Since he'd left, Tina had had a struggle financially. Married too young to pursue an education, she'd also needed to work at home to be with Trevor. A couple of years ago, she'd finally given up on tracking down her husband to collect overdue child support. Her heart wasn't really in the task, anyway. Tina had stubborn pride.

But she was a good friend. She'd tried to warn Libby about Brian Karsten, who'd come to town a few years after Jonathan. He was studying lake pollutants. Libby had just finished art school and had come home to bury her father. Brian was worldly, good-looking, intense. One afternoon, he'd held her for hours as she'd talked about her dad, and that night he'd made love to her. Her first time. She'd waited for the right man.

But at the end of that summer, that summer she'd grieved for her father and come to love Brian Karsten, he'd sat her down for a talk. It had been fun, he said. But surely she knew he wouldn't be in Harborside forever. Surely she'd heard of summer romance. It was good, it was intense, and in September it was over.

Tina turned her hand in Libby's until they were palm to palm, then squeezed and let go. "Well," she said finally, "some people don't think I got much out of twelve years with Jonathan. But we had Trevor, and I'll bless Jonathan for that until the day I die."

"And I guess in a way Nate gave me Sara." Sara of the effervescent chatter. Sara, who'd inherited the most spectacular set of genes. Sara, the reason she couldn't really call Nate Perry a jerk. But just how long would she have Sara? Sure, Sara was anxious around her father, as anxious as she'd been a year ago for Libby's approval. But that only meant she cared about him, didn't it?

Even more unsettled, Libby got to her feet. "How about a cup of tea?" she suggested. She lit the burner under the kettle and got out the tea canister. "And how about some chocolate? I think I need it." But after Tina agreed, Libby realized she didn't have any sweets in the house. Then she remembered the chocolate chips she stored in the freezer, for those times she baked for one town function or another. Pouring some into a small bowl, she brought them back to the table with the tea.

"Look at us," Tina said after they had both had a few icy chocolate chips. "Two thirty-somethings still drowning our sorrows in chocolate."

Libby couldn't help smiling, her heart a little lighter. "And when Harborside didn't have what we needed, we remade Harborside. Who'd ever have thought this town would have so much live theater?"

"Who'd ever have thought we'd come to love it here?" Tina added.

Home. Friends and a good life and Sara—at least for now. A waxy chocolate chip finally melted on Libby's tongue, almost more bitter than sweet. Bittersweet.

"Your Nate Perry *is* a charmer, though." Tina took three chocolate chips and popped them in her mouth before picking up her needle again. "Trevor's really shot with him. Even calls him by his first name. It's Nate this, Nate that."

"Really? Nate buddies it up with Trevor?" Libby was surprised. For Nate to befriend a fifteen-year-old boy seemed out of character.

Tina frowned. "Not exactly. But if Nate's out on his deck and Trevor spots him, he's gone, right out there to talk." She paused. "The thing is, you know how Trevor can't sleep sometimes."

Libby nodded. Trevor didn't get as much exercise as many boys his age. It made him restless. That was Tina's theory, anyway. What remained unspoken between them was a conviction that, despite Trevor's unrelenting cheerfulness, something was on the boy's mind. But every time his mom pressed, he always teased her until she gave up trying to find out what it was.

Tina made a small knot. "Well, he goes out to sit on the deck in the middle of the night. And sometimes, Nate's there."

"Really?" Libby didn't want to examine why any conversation about Nate seemed so important. These days she was hungry to hear his name.

"I've eavesdropped a time or two. I don't mean I listen in. But I've looked down on the deck from my bedroom window, and it's the weirdest thing. Trevor sits on our deck and Nate sits on the other one."

"But they talk."

"Well, I guess so. I've never known Trevor not to talk. Trevor can't go next door. There's no ramp. But Nate never comes over, either."

"Well," Libby said slowly, "I think Trevor maybe needs to talk to an older man. He has no father at home, and so far, no one has seemed to fill the gap for him."

"I know. I used to wish so hard for somebody. But a guy like Perry? A guy who's going to make this place into a resort so expensive, Trevor and I will have to move out. How could they have anything in common? Beyond all the glitz, what is there to the man?"

Libby had the most absurd urge to rise to Nate's defense. He was intelligent, he went to work every day, worked incredibly long hours, from what Cam had been able to find out. But she knew what her friend meant. Both she and Tina had a healthy disrespect for glamour boys. She just couldn't picture Nate befriending a kid, even one as outgoing as Trevor.

"He's rich and successful," Tina continued, picking up a rhinestone. "But you'd think Trevor could see beyond that. I've taught him values, you and the folks in town have pushed those values, and I can't see what there is about this shallow guy from—"

"I kissed him," Libby said abruptly, and immediately felt the heat rush to her cheeks. Oh, God, she'd promised herself to forget that kiss, never to mention it to a living soul, not even to Tina.

Tina's mouth formed a little O of surprise, and the rhinestone in her fingers dropped, bounced, landed in the bowl of chocolate chips. "You *kissed* Nate Perry?"

Libby swallowed and nodded. "Actually, he kissed me. But I kissed him back."

Tina stared. "But you didn't sleep—"

"No!"

"Thank God. Libby, think. This guy's going to take Sara if he can. He's brought in a powerhouse of an attorney, set himself up in town like he's never going to leave you alone and now he's filing this motion for more visits. So far, the judge hasn't gone for anything Nate's proposed. Hasn't it occurred to you that Nate is using you, kissing you, hoping maybe you'll get confused about what you really want?"

"Of course it has." Libby plucked the rhinestone out of the bowl. "Believe me, it's never going to happen again."

"Good." Tina seemed relieved. She even smiled a little. "Don't worry about it, kid. It's just physical, right? Just hormones."

Just sex. Libby couldn't look at her friend. She hadn't been with a man for ages. Of course she had fantasies. A nameless, faceless, oh-so-gentle-but-demanding man who undressed her with exquisite care, who put a mouth to her breast in a sweet caress, who whispered his own need against the hot skin of her neck. A man who, these days, seemed to have shining black hair and sky-blue eyes.

TWO WEEKS LATER the man with the shining black hair and sky-blue eyes stood in one of the attorney conference rooms at the courthouse. He'd dismissed his lawyer, asking to speak to Libby in private. Libby, too, had asked Cam to wait outside. The two attorneys had grumbled together, their shared outrage at being shut out by their clients making them congenial for once.

Sara was out in the waiting room with Cam. The judge had asked her to come down for the hearing, and he planned to see the girl in chambers later. Sara was tense, although both Libby and Cam had tried to reassure her.

Last night, Sara and Libby had had a long talk. Sara was upset about the court hearing. She had come to kind of like Nate, she told Libby with eyes averted. But she was kind of scared, too. After all, Heywood—which was the name Sara used now in referring to her stepfather—had been mean, especially when he drank.

Sara now had mixed feelings about Nate. Sometimes she was effervescent, thrilled to see him. Sometimes she was wary, sizing him up. And even on the days when Sara was glad to see Nate, she was careful to keep some physical space between them. Libby wondered if Nate had noticed.

Now Libby stood, too, across the oak table from Nate. The table was a broad expanse of golden wood that held nothing but Nate's motion. He'd said they could settle the motion, if she'd hear him out.

"Well?" she said finally, as the silence lingered. He was studying her with nerve-racking intensity.

Then, "Has it occurred to you that we could take care of all our problems if we got married?"

Whoa. Libby wasn't sure she'd heard right. "Married? Married?" She sounded shrill.

Nate smiled for the first time, a cool smile. "Believe me, I never thought I'd be doing this, either. But marriage would mean we could both have Sara. And Sara would have both of us."

"Yes, but…married?" She couldn't seem to stop repeating the word. Why couldn't she be cool about this the way Nate was? Just say, "Of course I can't accept, but thank you for offering to share your life with me," as though she received proposals of marriage all the time. Heck, it wasn't even a proposal, not really. Nate's words were a far cry from some guy on bended knee with a velvet box.

He was still studying her. "Sara needs time to get used to me. Things in Chicago are heating up, and I need to spend time there without worrying about the spin some lawyer's going to put on my every move. Sooner or later Judge

Wyatt will make a decision.'' He paused. ''I'm sure Cam Holling has told you that you might lose. I'm her father. You're not even a blood relative. And Sara seems to be coming around slowly, getting to trust me.''

Libby bit her lip. He was right. ''But Sara wants to live with me, and I'm the one who's been caring for her. And I have more time to spend with her. Marta Wainwright shouldn't be too confident, either.'' *So there, Nate. You might just lose.*

Nate knocked a fist lightly on the table and then leaned forward. ''I won't deny it. We need to be honest. In this case, I've gone against every negotiating instinct I have. But I know now how I should have handled things from the beginning.''

Honesty. That was what he'd talked about after the kiss they'd shared. She'd wondered if he'd been in the least affected by that kiss. Well, now she knew—she couldn't forget it, but he didn't even mention it. ''We should have got married when you first tried to interfere in Sara's—in my—life,'' she agreed sarcastically.

''Right.''

''Wrong.''

''Why not?''

For a million reasons, she thought. Nate had to be able to name at least ten of them. For a moment, she was nonplussed. Nate was a master negotiator. This must be a strategy—put your opponent off balance. She *was* off balance, but she gave him a reason. A big one. ''For one thing, I don't love you, and you don't love me.''

Still with that huge table between them, he looked her right in the eye. ''True.''

She felt the oddest pang of disappointment. Of course he didn't love her. She didn't love him, so she didn't want him to have feelings for her. It just hurt to have him say he didn't care, so…blatantly.

Nate spoke again. "You don't have to worry about anything. Marta will draw up a prenuptial agreement. Your shop will be protected."

"*You'll* be protected, you mean. I doubt you want my little shop and its big debt load."

"We'll both be protected."

Sure, she thought. She'd been talking about love, he'd been concerned about his business. *Protect your things, Nate, those things that mean so much to you.* As if she wanted resorts and restaurants and shopping complexes.

Well, he wanted honesty. She could be honest, too. "I don't want anything you have. You might not believe that, but it's true. I'm more concerned about…other issues. For example, I don't believe in marriage without love." She braced herself for a cynical comment. "I suppose to a man like you, that seems hopelessly old-fashioned and naive."

Unexpectedly, he shook his head. "I loved my wife for a long time." Nate stopped, swallowed. "But I've learned. You can't trust love, it doesn't last. And believe me, love alone doesn't get you very far in a marriage. You need shared goals, mutual respect, commitment. We've got those things. We both love Sara. I admire the job you've done raising her, and while I think you could do a hell of a lot more with that shop of yours, you've got talent I recognize and respect. And this might not be a love match, but I take promises seriously."

She'd been shaking her head, daring him to deny the power of love, but his words stopped her for a second. Nate wanted to provide a home for her. She shook off a nagging thought that they had different ideas about what home meant, and Nate wanted big things for Sara, while she only

wanted the child's happiness. But there was no denying that
they both loved Sara.

And he *was* the kind of man who kept his promises. That
much she was certain of. If his reputation in business
wasn't enough to convince her, his quest to reconnect with
his daughter did. Nate might be a loner, and he might be a
glamorous charmer, but he kept his promises. It wasn't
love, but it meant a great deal.

He was studying her. "My idea makes a hell of a lot of
sense."

In the weirdest way, it did make sense if she used her
head. If she ignored her heart and the voice there that said,
It's not supposed to be this way.

She'd long ago given up on romance. She'd come back
to Harborside after art school in New York, glad to have
the chance to pursue her business. For years she'd done the
flower arrangements for weddings, tried hard to make the
occasions lovely. For other women.

She was happy. And if, long ago, she'd dreamed of a
man who liked to walk in the rain and fix the car, who
knew what was really important in life, who'd shyly give
her a chip of a diamond, well, it was a nice fantasy. But
nobody could run a shop like hers and make it pay in a
small, out-of-the-way town like Harborside unless she was
practical. And Libby was nothing if not practical.

Nate was waiting for her to agree. She shivered. Her
fantasies about him were darker, more urgent, more...sexy.
He'd been very outspoken about love, but he hadn't mentioned sex. If she were going to seriously consider his idea
they had to discuss sex. She opened her mouth to speak.
"I don't want to live in Chicago," she said instead of what
she'd planned. But she blushed as though he could read her
thoughts.

"I understand, and actually, I think it's best if I commute, stay in Chicago during the week, come to Harborside on weekends.''

''What kind of marriage is that?''

He smiled again, as though he sensed her weakening. ''The kind for people who aren't pretending to be madly in love. Sara can come with me sometimes when school's out, but basically she'll get to be at home with her friends. It's a great solution.''

''We'll have to talk this over with Sara. I won't marry you unless she's comfortable with the idea,'' she warned. But it *was* a good solution. Surely it would be a relief to Sara if there was no pressure about the pending court hearings.

''We'll talk to her together.'' He paused. ''Let me anticipate some of your other objections.'' He raised a finger as if ticking off imaginary items. ''One. You don't want my money. Fine. But I'll pay my way, and I can afford to be generous.'' He raised another finger. ''Two. We can live in your house. It's not my idea of how to live, but it's, well, kind of surprisingly comfortable. Did I miss anything?''

Sex. You missed sex, Nate. He was going to make her be the one to say it, damn him. Maybe he assumed she was dying to hop into bed with him. Or maybe he wasn't interested in sex…with *her*. For a moment she wondered with a kind of mad, welling humor which would be worse—him wanting her, or not wanting her. She turned and paced, until she realized she was acting like Nate, pacing and analyzing. This was ridiculous. She might be a bit naive, but she wasn't a shy virgin, either.

''And sex?'' The boldness in her tone didn't match the warmth in her cheeks, but she held his gaze.

''It will be good.''

It will be good…good. The word echoed along her nerve endings, starting tiny fires.

His dark, espresso voice dropped another note. "You felt it when I kissed you. I wanted you. I still want you. I'm tired of denying it."

Oh, God. For a moment, thoughts of love, thoughts of their differences went right out of her head. A man like Nate Perry wanted a woman like her, a not-so-pretty woman with two broken fingernails and frizzy red hair. And suddenly, she wanted him, too, with a hunger that was real, fierce and demanding, a desire too long denied. She took one step, two, her gaze on his.

His eyes lit with triumph.

Libby froze. She knew better. Every defense she had sprang to life. This man would hurt her if she let him. "No," she said before she had a chance to change her mind.

"Libby." His voice was low, seductive.

It scared her, how much she wanted him. How on earth could she even think of sleeping with him, a man who didn't believe in love? "I said no!" Her voice shook.

A few swift strides took him around the table. Now he was close. "Come on. Marry me," he said urgently.

Sara needed Libby. Sara needed Nate, too. But how to protect her own vulnerable heart? She took a deep breath. "All right, if Sara agrees and if you want a loveless, *sexless* marriage, I'll say yes."

He looked at her for a long moment, with that compelling gaze. She'd just accepted a proposal of marriage from Nate Perry!

He reached into the trouser pocket of his suit, produced a jewelry box and handed it to her without a word. Her own hands not quite steady, she took it and opened it.

Inside, a ring lay on a bed of white satin. Libby reached out and lightly touched the stone. It was an aquamarine, set in an antique setting of twining vines and cunning golden flowers.

So there was a velvet box, after all. Libby felt the hot prick of tears behind her eyelids. Somehow the ring seemed to symbolize something, if only Nate's promise to take care of her and Sara. For a man like Nate, used to being alone, marriage—any kind of marriage—must be a real leap of faith. She wondered if he really had any idea what a leap it was. For the first time, she felt a faint hope that Nate's crazy scheme might work, that they might be able to work out some way to live together in harmony. "Is this a family piece?" she asked, trying to mask how the gesture touched her.

He gave a harsh chuckle. "Hardly. I bought it in Chicago."

"Rather certain I'd say yes, weren't you?"

He shrugged. "When all's said and done, you're a sensible woman. And when I have a plan, I believe in being prepared. So I thought I'd buy something that suited you."

"Oh." The ring was pretty. No, beautiful. When the full implication of what he'd said dawned on her, her breath caught. He couldn't mean—

"I wanted something unique."

"Oh," she said again.

He took her hand, touched her callused palm, slipped the ring on her finger. "Believe me, Libby, you are nothing if not unique."

Later, she would have cause for regrets, she was certain. But for just a moment, her hand tightened around his.

CHAPTER SEVEN

A FEW DAYS LATER, Nate was driving with his new bride, following a winding route that hugged Lake Erie. Tina was watching Sara for a few days so that he and Libby could honeymoon. Nate had wanted to go somewhere tropical—the Caymans perhaps. He might not believe in love, but it was natural to want his wife. And he was sure if he just got her alone, the tropical moon and nature would take their course. After all, their one kiss had been incredible, a rush of sensation that had been nothing like he'd ever felt before. And he'd known from the way she'd clutched at him and met his mouth with hers, that she felt it too. But Libby had refused the Caymans.

Finally, she'd agreed to a ride along the coast, a stop at a motel. "Two rooms," she'd said firmly. "And only because if we don't go somewhere, we'll be gossiped about at the Shoreline Diner."

Nate had tried to mask his annoyance. God, she was stubborn. Waiting for declarations of undying love, no doubt. Didn't she understand that he'd given her everything he had—his daughter, his protection, anything she wanted?

It had seemed so simple, hatching his plan for marriage from his office perched over Chicago. But in Harborside, he was learning things didn't always go according to his expectations.

Take Sara, for instance. He'd thought it would be hard to convince *Libby,* but that *Sara* would be all for their marriage. After all, they were marrying for her, so why would she object? They'd all sat down on a bench in the courthouse park, right after they'd left the courthouse on the day he'd proposed to Libby. Sara had listened carefully as Nate had told her that he and Libby would be getting married as soon as possible.

"But where will we live?" she'd asked him, her brow wrinkling. He'd explained about his plan to stay in Chicago during the week, come to Harborside to be with them on weekends.

"That's really weird," Sara had said, frowning in earnest. "I mean, you'd be married and everything, but you'd be in Chicago? How is that being married?"

Libby had shot him a helpless look, then talked about how much she and Nate loved Sara.

"But..." She'd turned right back to him. "You two never even went anywhere, like on a date to the movies or anything. My friend Cynthia's mom is divorced, and she goes on lots of dates, but Libby and you never did. And you never even kissed or anything." She paused. "I mean, I've never even seen you kiss. So, *have* you ever even kissed each other?"

What was he supposed to say? He kept forgetting that Sara was half grown-up. Of course she'd have questions. But there was no way to begin to explain all the complications of his relationship with Libby. So he said nothing. After a long, uncomfortable silence, Libby had stepped in.

"Sweetheart, there are all kinds of ways people show that they respect and think about one another, and your dad and I do respect each other. Nate and I have talked things over, and we think we can be a family, just not the kind of family Kathleen has or your other friends have."

"But a real family?" At the hope in his daughter's voice, he'd vowed then and there to make this marriage work.

Libby had hugged Sara, quick and hard. "A real family. A family made for the best reason of all—because we both love you."

Sara had sat still for a moment, obviously thinking things over. Then she had shrugged. "Well, I guess that sounds okay. Definitely weird but okay."

The rush of relief that went through Nate was totally unexpected, and scary in its intensity. He welled down the feeling, telling himself that his plan was good and sound and rational. After all, it was just a wedding—a marriage—for Sara.

The wedding itself had been simple. A civil ceremony. Libby's friends in attendance, Tina Samms looking worried and on edge, then snubbing him afterward. Trevor, shaking his hand. Flowers everywhere, exquisite arrangements, Libby with blooms in her hair like a forest maiden. Sara in delphinium blue, smiling. His daughter always kept that tiny heartbeat of space between them, but after the ceremony, she'd given him a smile that had lit her features. That smile alone told Nate he'd done the right thing.

Now he had to keep things running smoothly. He'd never give a woman power over him again. So he'd keep his condo in Chicago, concentrate on Sara and business like before. He was married, but nothing much had to change.

So why was his mouth suddenly dry, his stomach tight?

"You're quiet," Nate observed.

"So are you," Libby said back, in some ways feeling as awkward as any bride. But she knew so much less than most brides about her husband. For example, did Nate even have any friends, among the developers he partied with, the guys at the yacht club? If so, he'd never said.

Unexpectedly, Nate's hand on the wheel relaxed. "I don't talk that much. But you usually do."

"Okay, rub it in."

"Talk to me." He turned and gave her a lopsided smile. "You're making me nervous."

"I make you nervous?"

He nodded, growing serious immediately. "Let's just say I don't acquire a wife every day. I could use a bit of a distraction."

Wife. She was a wife before she and her new husband had had a courtship. Heck, they'd never even been on a date. "Well, I could talk about Sara. *Oklahoma!* is opening at the elementary school in two weeks, and I know Sara wants you there. She has a big part, you know."

"I'll be there."

"Right. Let's see...I'm doing a garden party for the Smithsons. Karen Smithson read about Vita Sackville-West's white garden in England and wants me to mimic it. So I've got a big order in with my Toledo wholesaler. Whites are challenging to work with. You need form and foliage contrast, because you don't have color to help you." She sighed. "I'm not complaining. She's a good customer. You have no idea how difficult it is to keep the cash flow evened out in a business that—" She cut herself off, thoroughly embarrassed. "I guess you do know, don't you?"

"Yes."

"Yes. Well."

He took a curve smoothly. "You were saying?"

She peered at him. "You can't be interested."

"I asked," he said.

He had. And they needed to find something in common besides Sara if they were to live together. So, she talked, first because she was nervous, then because he was listening. Her nervousness ebbed a little. She'd never realized what a good listener a quiet man could be. He had the funniest little quirk in the corner of his mouth. Not a smile, exactly. Just a...quirk. A sexy quirk.

Staring at that quirk rattled her again. "So this September the community theater's doing *Fiddler on the Roof.* Family entertainment. You should have heard the furor when some of the younger people wanted to do *Cats.* Tina was wild to do the costumes, but Mr. Murphy said he wasn't playing a tomcat, not in this stage of his so-called career. Anyway, I'm in the chorus this year, mostly because this is Sara's first time in an adult role and she could use moral support." Suddenly, she remembered all that financial information Nate had filled out for the court that first day, and her heart sank. He made huge charitable contributions to the arts. *Fiddler on the Roof?* He couldn't possibly be interested in either the play or the machinations of the committee members, all vying to be the biggest fish in a very small pond.

"Hey, look at that," Nate said then, and he made a quick, smooth brake and swung onto an access road that led to the water.

At the water's edge, there was a public boat launch and a long wooden dock, but today the place was deserted. Nate shut off the engine, got out. "Come on. Can you believe this?" His hand swept the lake.

Libby had lived in the area all her life, around the lake that was always changing, around the locals who never seemed to change, among the condominium resorts that were starting to sprinkle their way westward along the shoreline. So she didn't immediately see what Nate was referring to.

Then she looked out over the water and her breath caught. In the distance was a large island. The late-afternoon sun turned its distant line of beach to pure gold. Above it, in a still-blue sky, hung a full moon. She'd always thought there was something, well, magical about a moon that shone in the bright afternoon sky.

Nate walked to the water's edge, Libby beside him. "Will you look at that…" His voice drifted away, his gaze fixed on the horizon. He looked suddenly very young, almost vulnerable.

In that moment, Libby thought, *I could love him someday.* She knew Nate was a cynic. She never would have believed that he could love this, the simple gold of the sun…and the moon, shining in the afternoon.

He gathered her close, and she laid her head on his shoulder, her heart beating fast. He raised his left hand, his other went around her waist. "Dance with me," he whispered softly.

"We d-don't have any music." Her protest was shaky.

He started to move her to nothing but the breeze. "Sing for me." His voice was low, seductive.

"I couldn't do that."

There was a pause. Then, "Just sing something from *Oklahoma!*"

In that moment, she could refuse him nothing. So she sang in a whisper a rollicking song about western skies and cowboys. Nate moved her, turned her, rocked her to some other music entirely. She closed her eyes, and the golden light played against her eyelids. She laid her head on his warm chest, felt his arousal pressing into her belly, and knew that if he led her to the private, lee side of a dune and settled her in the rough grass, she would go.

Her song died away. Helplessly, she brought a palm up to his heart. "You do have one," she said, laying her cheek against her own hand.

He stopped. "Have one what?" He sounded gently amused.

"A heart." Against her, he went rigid, but she persisted, wanting him to acknowledge what she was sure he was feeling. "You love this, this quiet, out-of-the-way place."

"I've always liked the water," he said gruffly.

"But this place." Her voice rose in an effort to be understood. "If you like a place like this, then you must—"

"Don't read too much into it," he said harshly. "I also like Lake Michigan, especially the million-dollar coast, and electric lights that shine over the water whether or not there's a moon." He stepped back from her, but kept his hands on her shoulders. He looked her right in the eye.

"I'm no more than what you see on the surface. A millionaire from Chicago who wants his daughter because she's his." He paused, and slowly his grip relaxed.

She could not speak, so crushing was her disappointment.

He looked away, across the water. "I already destroyed one family, hurt one woman. I don't have what it takes to make a woman happy, Libby. I don't want to hurt you. I thought you understood, or I would never have proposed this, regardless of Sara. Our marriage will work if we just don't get too…involved."

"We're married, Nate. We're *involved*."

"You know what I mean."

"And the dancing? The nuzzling? What's that? Just sex, I suppose," she said bitterly. "I'm not as good as you are at compartmentalizing. My life in Chicago. My life in the hick town. My visits with my daughter. My honeymoon with my wife, where I hold her and dance with her till she gets sand in her shoes and stars in her eyes, and then I remind her we don't get *involved*."

He averted his eyes. "Chalk it up to the champagne in the punch at the reception." There hadn't been a whole bottle of champagne in the punch. In the depths of his eyes, there was genuine confusion. "The lure of the day, I guess. But it's just one day, Libby. Don't make too much of it."

She shook her head, tears blurring her eyes. What in hell had she gotten herself into today?

"I don't want you to get hurt," he repeated.

"Too late," she snapped. "But I'll get over it."

The ride to a simple lakeside motel was made in silence. Nate got two rooms. The next day they returned to Harborside, and the day after that, Nate went to Chicago for pressing business.

A WEEK LATER, Libby awoke to the sound of voices downstairs, a husky, familiar male sound and Sara's higher tone.

Nate was home. Her stomach gave a lurch. When she'd gone to bed last night, she'd half expected him, half not. And she didn't want to think about how long she'd lain awake, listening for his car. He'd said he'd be in late on Friday nights, taking the last commercial flight into Toledo.

The day before their wedding, she'd given him a key and shown him the bedroom down the hall. But after their harsh words out on the beach, she hadn't known what to expect.

All week she'd been on pins and needles, sure she had made a mistake, telling herself she'd be glad if the next weekend brought divorce papers instead of a husband. By Wednesday, she'd convinced herself he wasn't coming, so she'd made only a halfhearted attempt to clean out the craft supplies and Sara's clutter from "his" bedroom.

She'd be damned, though, if she'd ask his plans. The strain of the week had shown. Sara had inadvertently added to that strain, with a question or two about why Nate wasn't going to sleep in Libby's room. At the time, she'd been able to answer casually, explain that Nate would be coming in late on Friday nights and didn't want to disturb her. Sara had accepted her explanation. But a couple of days later, she had been sharp with Sara for no good reason, and Libby

had also broken the stems of some very expensive hydran-
geas when she'd been making an arrangement at the shop.

He'd called. Exactly twice, to talk to Sara.

But apparently their harsh words out by the lake hadn't
changed his plans to be a weekend husband and father. She
had underestimated his determination and commitment to
Sara. That was good; Sara didn't need any more stress.

She was committed, too, she realized. For as long as their
marriage lasted, she was a wife. She was committed for
Sara's sake, but also for herself, because whatever her reasons, she'd married the man of her own free will.

Unable to lie in bed on that thought, she got up and put
on a pair of shorts and a baggy T-shirt. Usually, she padded
downstairs in a nightgown and slippers, not changing until
the breakfast dishes were washed. Well, her nightgown was
modest but its implication was not. She and Nate might be
married, but there would be no such thing as casual intimacy.

Her T-shirt had dahlias on it, purple blooms the size of
dinner plates. It was her biggest fashion mistake in a long
series of them, but the T-shirt was perfect for the impression she wanted to convey this morning. Baggy and sexless.
There would be no mixed messages from her.

She headed to the bathroom. In spite of her resolve not
to primp, she couldn't resist spending a few moments trying
to ease the tangles from her flyaway hair.

On the counter, she found Nate's shaving kit. A basket
of potpourri had been pushed aside to accommodate his
things. She picked up his still-wet razor. A man's razor, in
her bathroom!

His towel was damp, but neatly folded on the towel rack.
Her palm brushed it, and she felt the oddest tingle imagining him in her shower, wiping his bare body with a towel
that had never known a man's skin. A very *neat* man, and

she couldn't help a rueful, nervous-feeling smile as she cast a glance over the clutter of her skin creams and Sara's pale pink nail polish and puffy sponges.

This marriage was definitely going to take some getting used to, in the little things as well as the big. She and Nate had so many differences—big, basic differences. But it was the little things that felt so unsettling this morning. The shaving kit was a travel size, as though Harborside, her house—*their* house now—was a stopping-off place. Libby meant to give this marriage her best shot, but how in God's name could a person be a token weekend wife?

Her thoughts in turmoil, she headed down the stairs. She could hear Sara going on and on as though this were a normal Saturday morning. It was a deceptive normalcy, but strangely compelling. And, she told herself, she was glad that Sara was adjusting already.

"So, then Kathleen didn't turn stage *left* and she ran right into Samantha and knocked down those cardboard trees and Mr. Gerrard yelled, 'Stick with the script, go *on*.' So everybody cracked up because he got so red in the face and Kathleen was sitting on the tops of those trees."

"Must've been funny." Nate's back was turned to Libby, and for a second she watched him. In his too-new designer jeans and oversize Yale Rowing Team T-shirt, he looked good, lean and even more strikingly male than in his tailored suits.

In contrast to the bathroom, the kitchen was a wreck. Flour and sugar were drifts of white on the counter, and a streak of flour also whitened one cupboard door. Dishes were piled both in and next to the sink. A stray shell of an orange dripped juice onto the floor. Libby's mind's eye flashed to that neat shaving kit upstairs and couldn't believe what she was seeing.

Sara stood a careful few steps away from Nate and held

a bowl out him. "Think you should put these in yet?" She craned her neck to look around him. "Those look sort of done."

"Oh, shi—rats," Nate said. "I forgot."

"Hi," Libby said from the doorway.

Both of them, man and daughter, turned. There was a pause. "Hi," Nate finally said softly.

"When did you get in?"

"This morning." He paused. "I showered in your bathroom. I hope you don't mind."

Oh, so he hadn't spent the night. "Of course not. There's only one bathroom. One shower." She was blushing, she realized, and there was no reason to blush. Sara was watching them carefully; this was her first day living in the same household with her father. So Libby added briskly, "After all, this is your home." Of course it wasn't his home; the condo in Chicago was his home.

But he looked at her, then, really looked at her. And she was shocked to see longing sweep across his features at her words. The unexpected, utter yearning in his expression stunned her.

But it was over so fast she wondered if she'd imagined it. Even as she stood there, her heart squeezing painfully, he turned and busied himself at the stove.

There was an awkward pause. Finally Libby asked, "What are you making?"

Sara answered. "Blueberry pancakes. Only Nate forgot the blueberries."

"Here, I can handle this," Nate said firmly, taking the bowl of blueberries from his daughter. He proceeded to push them into each pancake one by one.

"That's not the way," Sara said.

"It'll work." Nate's tone was very grim.

Sara giggled. Libby's own mouth twitched as a few

minutes later Nate gave her a plate with some very brown, very pitted pancakes. Well, you had to give points for effort. "These look worse than my meat loaf," she couldn't help observing as she took them to the table.

"Well, you won't eat meat," Nate grumbled.

"You could maybe do a better job with bacon?" she retorted.

"You can do it in the microwave."

"Don't you cook?" Sara asked as they took their places around the table.

"Well, in Chicago I eat out a lot at my restaurants, or my housekeeper leaves me something to reheat later in the microwave."

"Oh." Sara managed to look both mystified and intrigued.

Nate smiled at his daughter.

"Well, no housekeeper does the dishes here," Libby warned, but she was smiling, too. She had imagined that powerful flash of feeling a few minutes earlier, she decided. But she genuinely liked this side of Nate, when he was trying so hard to be a father. This side of him was the reason she'd married him, this side was her only hope.

Nate worked his fork doggedly against the tough pancakes. "Delicious," he lied.

"Gross," Sara said, her mouth full.

A careful, tentative contentment started to steal over Libby. There was something very appealing about a messy, imperfect Nate.

"I thought we could go somewhere together today. A family kind of thing," Nate suggested.

The sense of contentment threatened to grow. "What did you have in mind?"

"A sail," Nate said immediately.

"Oh," Sara said. She had been chewing a mouthful of

pancakes very hard. Now she swallowed. She didn't take another bite, but instead looked at Libby, her eyes apprehensive.

Ah, Libby thought. For some reason, Sara didn't like sailing. Or she didn't like sailing with Nate. Sara had been quiet when Nate had brought her home from their one previous sailing outing. But Libby hadn't been able to get Sara to talk to her about it. Sara could swim, and Libby knew the water didn't frighten her. But although they'd both been out on powerboats, Sara had never sailed before.

"A nice, long sail to one of the islands." Nate downed his glass of orange juice in one long swallow.

Sara looked again at Libby, and her expression grew pleading.

"Well, Sara and I were going to..." Libby's voice trailed off. With a run-on mouth like hers, she ought to be able to think of something.

Nate, too, had stopped eating. "What were you going to do?"

"Well, Sara and I were going to scrub out the cooler at the shop," Libby improvised. "You know, tackle that mold with scrub brushes and bleach. With Tina holding down the fort, we won't have interruptions. And—" she was getting the hang of this now "—Tina and Trevor are coming for dinner tonight, and I have to cook." She made a mental note to actually call Tina and invite them.

"The *cooler?*" Sara's eyes now were accusing.

Well, I did the best I could, Libby thought.

"Oh, come on," Nate said, rising from the table. "Can't you clean the cooler some other time? We'll pick up something from the deli for later. I don't know about Tina, but I'll bet Trev won't mind skipping the couscous." He took his plate to the sink and started cleaning up, his back to

Libby and Sara. He mumbled something about her lack of a dishwasher, which Libby decided to ignore.

"That cooler's really dirty," Libby said lamely.

"I could hire somebody—"

"So could I, if I could afford to." Libby hoped her tone conveyed finality.

Nate turned on the water. "Sara, work some of that ten-year-old charm on Libby. It'll be fun. I'll give you another lesson."

He was really trying, Libby thought. Considering the way things had been left between them a week ago, could she do less? "Do you want to go, Sara?" she asked gently.

Sara bit her lip, then said, "Sure."

"Great." But Nate hadn't turned from the sink, and he couldn't see how unenthusiastic his daughter was.

They picked up cheese and fruit and headed over to Bittersweet Point, where Nate still docked his boat. The rented Catalina 34 had crisp white sails and an intricate web of roping. The boat itself was huge, but the cockpit had a tidy, miniature feel like a playhouse. Libby put down the bag of groceries and went out on deck, where Nate was using the inboard motor to clear the shallows.

Nate hoisted sail once they were out on the lake. Taking the wheel, he caught a decent westerly and they skimmed over the water. Wind whipped Libby's hair.

Saturday morning with her husband. Her millionaire, yachting husband. *Husband.* Maybe if she repeated that word, she could shake the sense of unreality she felt.

"Want to help me hoist more sail?" Nate gestured for Sara.

Sara had been sitting still and silent next to Libby but she stood at Nate's invitation.

"I don't think Sara wants to sail." Libby had to raise her voice to be heard.

"What?" Nate asked at the same time Sara stuck out her chin and said, "Sure I do."

Nate stood behind her, holding the line. "Now," Nate said to Sara, "you watch the sail till it luffs." He waited until the edge of the sail was flapping in the breeze. "Then you trim until the rippling stops." He pulled on a line. "Got it?"

Sara bit her lip and studied the sail.

"Now it's a steady wind," he said encouragingly. He waited a few moments, then let go and sat down on the seat beside Libby. Sara stood at attention, both hands still on the rope.

"We've got to talk," he said in a low voice only Libby could hear.

She nodded. "I know. We have to get some things straight." No more dances on the beach, she thought. No more singing. They'd just concentrate on what they came into this marriage for. Sara. Saturday mornings with Sara.

Maybe someday they could be friends. She'd never expected her and Nate to be friends, but heck, she'd never expected him to be her husband, either. Friends didn't sound too bad, she thought. She could handle friends.

"Later, on the island, we'll talk." He smiled faintly. "Neutral territory. With Sara around there's no hope of seduction."

She swallowed. "Sounds about right."

He nodded decisively, and glanced toward his daughter. "Sara's getting the hang of this. Before she knows it, she'll be crewing with me. There's a cup race on Lake Michigan I'm going to win with the *Melissa,* and it would be so great if she sailed with me." He paused. "Why did you think she didn't want to sail?"

"I thought something about it scared her."

"Sara wouldn't be scared." Nate looked mystified. "I'm here, and I know what I'm doing."

The man's confidence in his ability was reassuring to Libby, but she wasn't a ten-year-old girl. Since Nate had come into her life, Sara hadn't been sharing as much of her feelings with Libby. It was as though her time with Nate were something removed, something she held close to her heart.

Though Libby felt a sadness at being excluded, she understood Sara was growing up. Now that Libby and Nate were married and there was no immediate threat of losing Sara, Libby could allow herself to be pleased that Sara was coming to have feelings for Nate. Funny, though, they never touched each other. And Sara had yet to call him anything but Nate.

Looking at Sara now, Libby wondered if Sara wasn't getting the hang of sailing, after all. Sara wasn't smiling, hadn't relaxed her wide-legged stance, but she'd readily agreed to handle the sail. Sara was outspoken. If she was afraid, she'd tell Libby, wouldn't she?

"Is sailing dangerous?" Libby asked.

Nate looked up at the rigging. "Sure, it can be. But I minimize all the risks. For example, you wear your life jacket. You don't do stupid, daredevil things. If somebody goes overboard, you can't just stop dead in the water to pick them up."

"Did you tell Sara these things? About not being able to easily pick up someone who falls out?"

"Sure. I'm teaching her to sail. She needs to know the risks. The best way to minimize those risks is not to go overboard in the first place."

"But when you explained all this, did you reassure her that you're here and will help her anytime she needs it?"

He frowned. "Yes, I did." He paused. "Well, I thought I did."

Libby sighed. "Maybe you did. But when you reassured her, did you hug her or anything?" Libby already knew the answer. If Sara was still shy around her father, Nate was downright reticent. Maybe still scared of making a mistake. She could understand that. But it was a shame things had to be so hard for them both. How much easier it would be for Sara if Nate could make the first move—a quick hug, a pat on the back, a tug of a lock of hair. The spontaneous gestures of a caring father.

Nate had all the right moves when it came to grown women, she thought with a flash of bitterness. But he lacked the most basic instinct when it came to his daughter. How very ironic that was.

He flushed. "She doesn't want me to touch her." Swallowing, his eyes went to his daughter. "I tried once. She…flinched. Don't you remember how she was?"

"But that was early on. Before she had a chance to know you."

He acted as though he hadn't heard her. "I hated that she shrank from me."

Her heart went out to him. It was so easy to tell herself that he was an unfeeling man, but he kept giving her glimpses of a different person. A man she could come to care for.

"Try again," she urged softly.

He shook his head.

"Nate, you're the one who has to try again. Make the first move."

He glanced at Sara. "It didn't feel natural to touch her, and that's maybe what she was reacting to. No." He shook his head again, more decisively this time. "It's better this way. Give her time."

She swallowed down disappointment, then felt a surge of hope. Maybe with time… Maybe she could work with Nate, break down his barriers… For what? she thought, suddenly impatient with herself. So that she could spin fantasies of forever-after with a guy she hadn't even been certain would be home this morning?

No. But she did want this marriage to succeed because Sara, the child she loved, needed her father.

"She wants to please you with the sailing," Libby said softly.

"You think?" His eyes lit with a rare pleasure. "Well, she's doing very well."

"Tell her so."

"She must know."

Libby sighed. "Maybe she does, but it never hurts to praise someone."

"Right." Nate cast a more speculative glance at his daughter.

For the first time, Sara was smiling a little. The wind had picked up slightly, and her ponytail rode the wind like a jaunty banner.

Beside her, Nate seemed to relax infinitesimally.

"Do you mind that I asked Tina and Trevor over tonight?" Libby asked. She hadn't consulted him about her last-minute plans, and now it occurred to her that she probably ought to be checking with him, now that she was sure he'd be home for weekends.

"Do what you want." He gave her a half-formed, rather crooked smile. "After all, I think I've disrupted your life enough." When she didn't reply right away, he added, "Actually, I wouldn't mind seeing Trev."

"Really?"

"Of course, things could be awkward with Tina. Does she know I'm here?"

"I told her." Tina had nearly refused to come over, but Libby had heard Trevor in the background, urging his mom to accept.

"Well, wonder of wonders, after the way she turned up her nose at the wedding."

"Tina worries a lot." Suddenly, she wanted them to get along. She wanted her husband and her best friend to like each other. "Her husband hurt her, and she's afraid you'll hurt me."

As soon as the words were out of her mouth, she was sorry she'd said them. A person who wasn't involved couldn't be hurt. She needed to be as cool about this relationship as Nate.

His eyes were intent, his body still. A sudden gust of wind ruffled the hair across his forehead. Then he shook his head. "Libby, whatever you may believe, I don't intend to hurt you."

No danger of that. She had no intention of *letting* him hurt her.

Next to her, Nate was quiet. Then, as they came closer to the nearest in a tiny necklace of islands, he stood and shaded his eyes with his hand. "Let me maneuver this baby in close," he told Sara as he took the lines.

"Didn't I do okay?" Sara asked. She bit her lip.

He looked surprised. "Sure you did. I just want to finish up with the sails so I can take the wheel."

Sara flopped down next to Libby. "Nate said I did okay," she repeated earnestly.

"Of course you did. What did you expect?"

Her eyes clouded. "He wants me to be the best."

"But you don't get to be the best without practice. And besides, sweetheart, there are other things besides being the best."

"Like what?"

"Come on, like this perfect day." She was impatient, but not with Sara. With Nate, for not doing his job of reassuring his daughter, for leaving this part to her. "Did Nate tell you you should be the best?"

Sara nodded, looking down at her knees.

Libby looped her arm around Sara's shoulders and gave her a quick, tight squeeze. "Now listen to me," she said slowly and deliberately. "All I want from you is for you to be you. And whatever Nate said, don't take it too seriously. Nate talks a kind of way, but he doesn't exactly mean it. Besides, he wouldn't have tried so hard to find you if he didn't already think you were the best." She hoped so hard that it was true, that Nate really didn't expect his daughter to be the best at everything she tried.

"He wants me to win a sailing race with him that his yacht club puts on. It's really important." Sara sat with her knees pulled up to her chest, her arms folded over them.

Libby decided then and there that she would add another subject to her forthcoming talk with Nate. Her righteous indignation at the pressure Nate was putting on his daughter felt good.

And Sara was a safe topic.

CHAPTER EIGHT

WHEN THEY PULLED INTO the dock, there was only one other boat tied up. A family Libby didn't know was picnicking near the boat launch. Sara looked over the remaining picnic tables and asked if they could go somewhere and sit on the sand. So with Nate holding the bag of food, and Libby a tattered blanket, they walked behind Sara, uphill and down, in deep sand that tugged at their sneakers.

Libby was puffing from effort but she was having a good time. The breeze was warm, and chicory dotted the meadows with lavender blue. Finally they broke out onto a pretty stretch of beach. Libby shifted the blanket to her other hand and wiped her damp brow.

Sara gestured to them. "Let's go farther. There might be a better beach up ahead. More shells. Cooler rocks." She wasn't even breathing hard.

"No," Libby and Nate said at the same time, and she caught his eye and laughed. Mr. Perfect was winded, as damp and bedraggled-looking as she felt. "Kid, I'm too old to go any farther." When Sara took a couple more steps, Libby reached out, grabbed the end of her ponytail and held on.

"Hey, no fair," Sara said, reaching behind her and trying without success to dislodge Libby's hand. But she finally stopped.

"I'm going to die," Libby pronounced, flopping down

on the sand and using her forearm to take another swipe at her moist forehead.

"Come on," Sara said again, a whine creeping into her voice. "We've never been out here before. Don't you want to see what's up ahead?"

"How could it be better than this?" Libby smiled and shaded her eyes. The dunes rose steeply on one side, protecting the beach from the wind. The sand was hot under her thighs. It wasn't much different from a hundred beaches on what the tourists called the North Coast, but it had a stark, simple beauty.

Nate took the blanket from Libby and spread it on the sand.

"Well, I'm going ahead," Sara said stubbornly. When neither one of them spoke, she turned to Libby. "I can, can't I?"

"Just be careful, and check in." There was nothing to hurt Sara on the island, if she took a few simple precautions.

Sara took off at a near run and in seconds had disappeared around to the windward side of the dune. Nate walked on, more slowly, down to the edge of the water. Bending, he picked up a handful of pebbles and stood silhouetted against the sun, casting them over the water. The day had started out cloudless, but now, here and there was a feathery cloud that raced across the sky. The humidity was building; Libby's skin felt sticky. She scooted over to sit on the blanket and watched Nate.

He'd brought them out here, and one of the reasons was that he wanted to talk to her. She had a pretty good idea what he was going to say. She was his wife. He wanted her. Sex was pleasurable. She remembered sex that way, but she'd been in love with Brian when they'd slept together, had been certain he loved her. Over the years, she'd been occasionally attracted to various men. But she had never had sex with a man just because she wanted to.

And sex with Nate would be…

Judging from their kiss, he'd be an expert lover. Part of her hated that Nate was so good at…that. She wondered if his lack of tender feelings would mean he could be less involved, more distant, more able to judge her performance. She knew instinctively that his touch would burn her, drive her to lose herself in her feelings, and she hated the idea that he'd be assessing her.

She bit her lip. She'd waited so long to feel the touch of a man again. Maybe too long. Maybe her stubborn insistence on love was more than outdated.

And there were…variations. Heck, there were pretty tame positions she'd never even tried. With a husband, she might feel adventurous, but with Nate…

God. He *was* her husband.

"Nate!" she yelled, unable to bear her thoughts a second more.

He jerked, then turned and came toward her.

"You said we had to talk."

He sat down on the sand next to her, holding a little rose-colored pebble. "Right now?"

"Sure. Why not right now?"

"Oh, I don't know. Maybe because we just got here, we're not arguing, and maybe you'd like fifteen minutes to enjoy the day?"

She peered at him. He wasn't smiling. This was a new side of him. She hadn't expected sarcasm. "Sara could come back anytime, you know. And I suspect what you have to say wouldn't be suitable for your ten-year-old daughter to hear." Her cheeks felt warm and she reminded herself that he'd been photographed for the Chicago society pages with any number of women.

He rolled the pebble in his palm. "No, I don't suppose it would." He paused. "Okay. Just what exactly do you want out of this marriage?"

The question surprised her. She'd expected an intense effort to persuade her that, as a married woman, she had no reason not to sleep with her husband, a husband she clearly desired. "I don't know," she admitted slowly. "All I wanted was Sara. I had to take you as part of the package." She tried to smile to soften her words.

"Most women probably wouldn't find it that much of a sacrifice."

She stared at him, struck by his monumental ego.

He looked right back. "After all, I've got lots of money. And you know what? I've still got every one of my teeth."

To her utter surprise, she saw humor glinting in the depths of his eyes. Suddenly, things did seem a tad funny. "I'm pickier than that." But she was smiling. "Okay," she said after a minute. "I guess what I want is for us to be whatever kind of family we can for the time you're here. I don't want you to disappoint Sara or constantly push her, either."

"But what do *you* want?"

A husband who mows the grass. A husband who thinks I'm more than a convenient bed partner, a means to settle a legal dispute. A husband who gets up early and makes breakfast. Whoa. She started again.

I want a baby someday, fathered by a man who loves me. At that thought, she almost went from smiles to tears in one heartbeat. If their marriage failed, it would hurt Sara. If their marriage succeeded, Libby was shackled to this man for life. It was one thing to realize you would never have children because the right man hadn't come along. It was quite another to have a husband who didn't love you and was so focused on another woman's child that he'd never even mentioned the possibility of having a child with you.

"You were saying?" He had no way of reading her mind so he was still smiling teasingly.

He would never understand her. She took a deep, determined breath. She didn't remember her mother. Her father's parenting had been loving, but gruff and haphazard. Once, when she was a kid railing at the unfairness of life, he'd sat her down to a poker game. Then afterward he'd told her, "When things happen to you that aren't fair, you have to play the hand you're dealt." Other times, he'd told her of her mother's saying: When life hands you lemons, you make lemonade.

Simple homilies from simple people. "What I want," she said just as simply, "is for you to respect me and my feelings."

"Done." Now he wasn't smiling, but was staring down at her with sincerity.

"And that means?"

"We're doing it again, you know." His eyes never left her face. "Tiptoeing around our attraction. We're talking about sex. And I admit I want you. But I've never forced my attentions on a woman and I'm sure as hell not about to start forcing my own wife. You have a right to expect respect from your husband, and you'll get it."

She couldn't believe it. "You won't push me to have sex?"

"It's up to you. If. When. Where."

She couldn't believe it. It was more power than she'd ever expected Nate to give her. Tenderness welled in her. "But what will you do when you need—" She stopped, closing her eyes for a second. She didn't want to know.

Nate flipped the stone from one hand to another, his eyes on the shore.

There was a strained silence. Finally, she asked, "What do *you* want, Nate?" Such a simple question. One, she suspected, most married couples covered *before* the ceremony.

"It's not important."

"It is to me."

"Well, I haven't thought about it, I guess. I assume you mean besides sex." He gave her a flash of his charming smile. Libby was beginning to understand him, to realize that at times he used charm to cover his real feelings.

"Besides sex," she agreed.

"Well." Idly, he fingered the little stone, studied it. "I don't like yelling and I don't like fighting."

"I don't yell much."

"No, thank God, and with Sara's custody at risk, you've had plenty of opportunities. I wouldn't have married you if I hadn't thought you were sensible. Instead, I would have taken my chances with the judge."

How odd that he felt so strongly about such a simple thing. "Why don't you like yelling?" she asked softly. "Did you and Sara's mother have loud fights?"

"At the end we did, and it was hell. I used to think of Melissa—of Sara upstairs, listening, but we were so angry. Both of us. I'm not blaming Eve."

She sensed that he wasn't telling her the whole story. "And there's more?" she prompted. When he hesitated, she added, "You can tell me anything. I'm your wife." She realized that for once she actually felt like one.

He hesitated again, shrugged. "Hell, it's no secret." He tossed the pebble ahead of him. It landed with a little spit of sand. "Everyone in the neighborhood eventually knew what was going on. Some of the people I do business with in earlier years also did business with my father. You can't imagine how hard I had to work to persuade them that I wasn't like him.''

Libby put her hand on his arm. He didn't seem to feel it. His eyes were again on the horizon, his body curiously still. "He gambled."

Libby let out a breath she'd been holding. "Gambled, as in he couldn't stop?" Her mind scurried along, trying to recall everything she'd ever heard about gamblers, and it seemed as if she couldn't recall a thing.

"Sure. I've read all the books about it. We were a classic case. The thing is, my mother came from a wealthy family. Very concerned with appearances. For the longest time, we—my mom and I—tried to keep a lid on things. She'd juggle bills, pay the most pressing bill collector, play the dumb society wife, anything to put people off when they called about money we owed. She was so humiliated, and I just…hated that.''

Libby squeezed his arm. She longed to do more, to bring him close to her the way she'd do for anyone who was hurting. But there was a proud, straight line to Nate's back, and she knew instinctively he wouldn't welcome her gesture. "Any kid would hate that kind of pressure. Kids need stability, a chance to be kids.''

He nodded. "But in a way, my mom encouraged him. There was something frenetic in both of them when he was winning. Some years would be good, and I'd tell myself maybe his luck could hold. My mother would always say then that my father was going to make back enough money to pay off the bills, put some aside, then stop for good.

"But then it never turned out that way. He'd buy one new car, then another. A Ferrari, a Jag, both in the same year. Hell, both in the same *day*. Furs. Jewelry. My parents would whoop it up. At night from my own room, I'd hear them having—making love. When he was winning, they didn't hide anything at all. Didn't wait till I was asleep. They were so excited about everything, all the time. So noisy.'' He shook his head.

She hurt for him. "And when he lost?" she asked softly.

"When he lost, it was worse." His voice dropped. "They yelled when they were happy. My mom screamed when they lost. She stood on the front lawn when they took her mother's silver and she screamed like a banshee."

"Oh, Nate." Impulsively, she covered his hand with her own.

Gently, he disengaged her hand, set it back on her side of the blanket. "It was a long time ago."

"Not so long ago, I think."

"A *long* time ago." His voice was very certain. "When I first went to a banker for money, to buy an old building in the warehouse district, I went to the father of one of my childhood friends. He was president of a bank, and I needed cash and a big line of credit. He said, 'Why should I loan money to the kid of the son of a bitch who bilked me out of half a million dollars?' I looked the guy in the eye, and I told him I was no gambler."

"And he gave you the money?"

"No." For the first time he smiled a little. "He gave me a *little* money, and he rode me all the time for the payments. He treated me like hell because of who my father was, and he taught me how you can be a developer without taking all the risks."

They were both quiet for a moment. He had told her so much more than why he didn't like loud voices and fighting. She studied him. He was dry-eyed, watching the waves. He did that a lot, she was discovering. She was getting to know her husband.

And she wanted to do that. Suddenly, she wanted to know everything about him. The big events that had shaped his life and the smaller things—what he ate for breakfast when he wasn't burning the blueberry pancakes, what his favorite color was, his favorite old movie, what he'd been for Halloween as a kid, his…

And, well, whether he'd be rollicking and charming in bed, or whether he'd really share the experience with her, cover her body with his own and look at her with that intensity that darkened his eyes to navy, just before he put his mouth to her ear and groaned out his ecstasy…

It's up to you. If. When. Where…

She longed to touch him. Without a thought that he might misread the signals, she put her hand on his arm again, tugged when he didn't immediately respond. He turned.

"I want to…" Her voice trailed away before gaining strength. "Just hold you." She held out her arms, gathered him to her. Under the sky, she felt his hard, unyielding body against hers. His T-shirt was worn thin, his skin hot underneath, warmed by sun and the sand beneath them.

He wrapped his arms around her, fitted the top of her head under his chin. "I figured you'd be a sucker for a story about a sad little boy. You're so good with Sara, I just…knew."

Had he deliberately tried to manipulate her? She pushed the unwelcome thought away and touched the back of his neck.

"But make no mistake. I left that sad little boy behind long ago." His voice was rough as he drew back and tipped her head up. "That boy's a man."

His mouth came down hard, fastening unerringly to hers. His tongue touched her lips, probed, and she let him in.

The sun was strong; she felt weak, almost dizzy. How quickly comfort had turned to desire. She felt the back of his neck, sensed the breadth of his shoulders, felt the solidness of his chest. He thrust his hand into the mop of her hair and held her mouth more tightly to his.

A long whistle pierced the air. Both she and Nate jerked at the same time. He started to rise. "What was *that?*"

Libby fought her way back to the present. "Ah, Sara." Her voice was shaky.

"Sara?" He was on his feet in an instant. "Is she—"

"Checking in." Libby reached up and tugged at the denim at his calf to get his attention. She threw back her head, put two fingers in her mouth and blew a blast in response.

"God." Nate flopped down onto the blanket.

She managed a shaky grin. "It's easier than screaming my lungs out. Actually, Sara's whistle didn't sound as if it was coming from too far. It's just as well we didn't get too...carried away." She was unsettled. She'd had no intention of letting him kiss her like that again, especially after they'd reached an understanding about physical intimacy. She was as he said—a sucker for a story about a sad little boy.

Once again, the unwelcome thought that he had taken advantage of her surfaced. This time she didn't push it away. She had to remember that nobody got to the top without learning to read and manipulate others.

THEY'D STAYED at the beach too long. They were late, and a sailboat depended on the wind. At the rate they were traveling, there wouldn't be much time for Libby to prepare for Tina and Trevor's arrival. Libby liked to cook, but it looked as if they'd be ordering a pizza instead. She smiled. She'd call from the car. At least now she could use Nate's cellular phone so the pizza might beat them home.

Sara stood beside Nate. "Let me trim the sails."

Nate gazed at the sky, looking a bit concerned. "The weather's changing."

"I can do it," Sara insisted.

Nate looked off to the west. A few clouds had gathered and the water was rougher now. "No," he finally said.

"Come on, please," Sara begged. "You said you were teaching me—"

"Nate—" Libby started.

"I need to move us in quicker," Nate interrupted. "There's a squall coming. Fast."

Libby pushed down a flash of concern. The shallowest of the Great Lakes, Lake Erie was famous for fast-moving storms. But the sky was hardly dark. She'd lived on this water all her life, and she saw little to indicate a big storm was coming.

"I could help you," Sara said eagerly to her father.

Nate almost physically brushed her off. "Check the straps on your life jackets, make sure they're tight," he said curtly to Libby as he started to pull in sail.

Libby checked hers and then motioned for Sara. "Just a precaution," she said as she tightened the tapes that held the life jacket to Sara's small body.

"Everybody into harness," Nate said. "Right now."

Sara looked terrified.

"Nothing's going to happen," Libby said with false lightness, giving Sara's ponytail a quick tug. Nate could have spared a word of comfort for his daughter, but as soon as they'd all attached themselves to the harnesses that would keep them with the boat in case of accident, his attention was back on the sails. He was pulling in the mainsail.

Sara looked hurt, but better hurt feelings than alarm. Libby managed a smile for Sara's sake. "Now, help me fold this blanket. It's not a glamour job, baby, but it's better than being told by the captain to swash the decks."

A tiny smile formed on Sara's face as she pulled a couple of corners of the blanket together. "*Swab* the decks."

"Whatever."

"And I do plenty of *that* at the shop."

Suddenly, the boat lurched, shuddered. A strong gust caught the sails and practically lifted the craft out of the water. Spray shot high over the bow. Libby dropped the blanket and grabbed Sara to steady her.

Sara looked scared.

The wind picked up, and in seconds, she and Sara were soaked from more spray. Libby pulled Sara against her. "There's nothing to worry about. Nate knows what to do."

"I *hate* sailing," Sara said with feeling.

Storm clouds were moving in, low and black. Nate was talking into the radio, but she couldn't hear what he was saying. So much for her lifelong experience of living next to the water. This was a different world, being *in* the lake.

She stepped over piles of line, some of it coiled, some of it not. "What can I do?" she asked as she got to Nate.

"If we were closer to the island, I'd try to duck behind it, out of the wind. But we're too far from safe harbor." His eyes were intent on hers. "We'll run with the storm, wait until it plays itself out or goes by us. It's all we can do now."

She nodded.

"Take Sara into the cockpit with you. Libby, you'll have to steer, and it's going to be a hell of a ride."

"I don't know how." She tried to keep panic from her voice.

He nodded. "You'll have to do your best. Keep her turned into the wind."

The concern in his eyes scared her. But his calm words helped. "That's all I have to do?"

"It's enough. I'm going to pull in sail as fast as I can."

Nate worked feverishly, but he couldn't get the sails in before the squall hit. The boat lurched.

"*Into* the wind!" Nate cried.

She could hardly hear him because the wind was howling. Icy rain came down in sheets, blown so hard that even the cockpit was soaking wet. Libby held on to the wheel, made adjustments. The boat jerked, caught the wind and moved.

A long streak of lightning thrust down from the clouds and found the water. In the sudden illumination, Sara's white face appeared. Sara jumped at the loud boom that followed. She clung to the boat, her elbows braced.

Nate lashed the lines for the sail, then he was everywhere, working against the storm. The wheel slipped in Libby's wet, cold hands. She'd never been so scared in her life. The big boat seemed tiny now, like a toy bobbing in an ocean.

"We're in the height of it," Nate called once. "The wind's seventy. It won't get worse."

Did he mean *seventy miles an hour?* Libby squeezed her eyes shut against the stinging spray and grasped the wheel for dear life.

"You're doing fine," Nate yelled at her.

Libby didn't know if that was true. There was only a terrifying, endless wash of gray-black water, spray and rain, clouds of vapor so thick it was like sailing into a blank wall.

Nate yelled instructions; she tried hard to comply. The wheel jerked in her hands; the boat shuddered again. Gear was everywhere, thrown about. Lines snapped. Metal shrieked. Wood groaned. The wind roared.

Sara's safety depended on her and Nate, and together they fought the storm. Most of the time, she couldn't see Nate, the rain came down so hard. Sometimes he appeared as a larger-than-life apparition, like a sailor of old, taking the boat through the storm.

After a very long time, the storm died down. Still, Nate didn't relax his tight composure as he started for the dock at Bittersweet Point. The storm had blown them badly off course. The rain still fell, now a dispiriting drizzle, as he took the wheel and maneuvered in the rough water. Libby sat next to him. The cockpit was so small, all three pairs of knees touched. Libby pulled Sara to her. Sara hiccuped and Libby held her tighter. "You're okay," she whispered. "Nate brought us in."

In truth, Nate had saved them. He'd done what needed to be done, made sure she knew what to do, had confidence that gave her confidence. He hadn't panicked, had given little sign that they were in grave danger. But Libby was no fool. She knew they could have lost their lives.

Nate slid alongside the dock. Shaking off Libby's arm, Sara got up and made her way to the side of the boat. She caught the pier and started to wrap a rope around it to secure the boat. Her shoulders were shaking.

Libby went toward Sara.

Docking wasn't easy, and the boat was rocking so hard in the rough water that they had to scramble out. On the dock, Nate grabbed Sara's arm. "Are you okay?"

Sara shook him off, too. "I didn't do anything," she said in a small voice. "I knew how to sail, and I just...sat there." Snatching her arm away, she started to cry.

Nate looked helplessly at Libby. She pulled Sara to her. "You've only had two lessons. Storms happen on this lake, and Nate knew what to do."

Sara coughed, swallowed, stood there stiffly in Libby's

arms. Libby found herself blinking back tears. She knew how hard Sara was fighting them, because what she wanted right now was to go somewhere warm with Sara and have a good cry. Her legs felt like jelly; her hands and arms ached from grasping the wheel. She wanted Nate to hold them, too. Surely, he would hug them, remind them he was the experienced sailor, that this storm wasn't really that bad.

"There's nothing you could have done, Sara," Nate said, standing apart. "The mistake was mine. I let us stay at the beach too long."

Tears ran down Sara's face.

Belatedly, his hand reached for hers, but Sara kept her own firmly on Libby's waist. He dropped his hand immediately.

Sara spoke. "But…I needed to learn. You needed me to crew the boat with you."

"Not through a storm. And we can still crew together if you want. Someday."

"I never—" her lip trembled "—want to sail, ever again."

Libby squeezed harder. "We'll talk later. Now it's time to get dry. Right, Nate?"

He looked completely out of his depth. The man who'd hauled sails and lashed rigging on a heaving deck in seventy-mile-an-hour winds looked overwhelmed by the challenge of soothing his daughter.

Nate gave them both one long look, then turned and headed for the car.

•

CHAPTER NINE

NATE LEFT the others in the kitchen and slipped out onto the sunporch. He reached into the battered refrigerator Libby kept out there for a beer. But he really just needed a few minutes alone. When they'd got home, there had been no time to talk things over, even if he'd known what to say.

Tina and Trevor had been waiting. You'd have thought that when Tina saw how bedraggled and shaken they were, she would have done the decent thing and gone home. Instead, when she'd heard their story, she'd given Nate a tight-lipped look of disapproval.

Sara had dried her tears and told about their near accident not at all the way it had really happened. The acting she and Libby did had apparently given his daughter a streak of the dramatic. She'd made it sound as if he was some kind of...hell, some kind of hero.

Tina wasn't fooled. She knew how close he'd come to blowing it, maybe even how shook he was inside. She'd glared at him and got as protective as a mother hen, sending Libby and Sara up to bathe, calling for a pizza. Then she'd got out plates and silverware, snapping everything down on the table to let him know what she thought of him.

Tina knew where every item in the kitchen was, whereas that morning Nate had to open every cupboard door to make a batch of pancakes. Tina obviously felt comfortable in Libby's house. Everyone did, apparently. Everyone but him.

Night had fallen. Through the old glass of Libby's porch, he could see the cove, then the white condominium on Bittersweet Point. The rain had stopped, but the waves were still crashing in. He was still shaking inside, remembering. If Libby hadn't had the guts to steer that boat, he honestly didn't know if they would have stayed afloat. He'd discovered something about his wife. She had courage.

He hadn't been on full alert, and a good sailor was always on full alert. Instead of keeping an eye on the weather, he'd had a good time at the beach, enjoyed his daughter, kissed his wife. He hadn't wanted to leave, to face all the problems that awaited him on shore. Once on the lake, if he hadn't been watching Libby, admiring the way the sun made her skin glow and brought out all the coppery highlights in her hair, he might have been watching the horizon instead. He'd have seen the telltale signs of a quick-brewing storm.

For him to put Sara at risk… That was unthinkable.

He'd known he wasn't husband material, but in those eight years when Sara was gone, he'd been so certain he could be a good father.

Hell.

"Nate?"

Trevor was silhouetted between the French doors.

"Trev," he acknowledged quietly.

"Don't mind Mom acting all bossy. She's really okay. Just worried about a lot of things." In the dim light, Nate could see the kid grin. "You know women."

Nate looked out at the water, letting out a long breath. "No. I don't know women." Libby, for example. She ought to be giving him hell for making a mistake. Instead, when they'd arrived at her house, she'd thanked him. Thanked him!

"I hear no man will ever understand women. You know, there's only a couple of steps down to this porch. If you could steady my chair, I could come down." Trevor hesitated. "If you want guy company."

Guy company didn't sound all that bad right now. He steadied Trevor's chair. Trevor pushed and maneuvered himself down the steps.

Trevor put his finger to his lips, warning Nate to be quiet. With a dramatic gesture, he cocked his head, listening. "Super. Mom's so busy fussing over Sara she didn't even hear me."

Right then, Nate realized how much he had missed this kid since moving to Libby's. He felt protective toward him, fatherly in a way he couldn't be with Sara, given that the stakes were so high with his daughter. In Chicago, he'd thought about Trev, about things in Harborside way more than he'd ever thought he would.

He admired the kid. How could he handle being in this wheelchair so well? Nate knew for a fact that the loss of mobility, and therefore the loss of control, would drive *him* to a bitterness that would be bone-deep.

"Anything but beer in the fridge?" Trevor pushed his wheelchair closer, maneuvered until he could pull open the door. Nate resisted the urge to do it for him. Trevor rummaged around. "Nada. Just the good stuff. I don't suppose, since there's no cola in here or anything, you could leave off being the responsible adult this once and let me have a beer."

Nate hesitated. "How old are you, anyway?"

"Fifteen," Trevor said hopefully. When Nate didn't immediately say anything, he added, "It's only six years to twenty-one.'' He sighed. "Forget it." He shut the door hard.

"Trevor? What do you need?" From the kitchen, where Sara, Libby and Tina were playing Monopoly, he could hear lots of chatter, then Tina's voice raised in concern.

"Just getting a beer," Trevor called back cheerfully. He said to Nate, "Now listen."

"A beer? You're not going to have a beer! We've discussed…" Her voice came nearer.

"Cola! A cola, Mom! Now, give a guy a minute alone, you hear? Go tell Libby how to run *her* life."

She laughed, with a warmth in her voice Nate had never heard before. "Don't take too long out there, or I'm coming to check," she warned, but her voice was not at all stern. Then her footsteps receded.

"I don't think she remembers there are steps here, or she would have come down to see what was going on, out here in the dark." Trevor rolled nearer to Nate.

Nate set his beer bottle down and then settled into a seat so that he was on a level with the kid.

Trevor shifted. "I wanted to talk to you. I got something on my mind. Had it on my mind a while." His voice was earnest, nothing at all like the teasing tone he'd taken with his mother. He turned his chair to face the water when he spoke, in a gesture that seemed eerily familiar to Nate.

Trevor cleared his throat. "The thing is, I don't want anybody to know I'm talking to you about this. My mom wouldn't like it. She won't talk about him, ever. But I think about him, all the time now."

Nate waited.

"I guess you know my dad left us."

Nate nodded.

"He left a few months after I ended up in the chair, four years ago."

Nate sucked in a breath. Lord. People in Chicago thought *he* was a tough bastard. But he had nothing on a man who walked out on an eleven-year-old kid who'd just been confined to a wheelchair.

"Don't feel sorry for me!" Trevor said in a low, fierce voice, and then he swore under his breath.

Nate knew he'd made a mistake. But the kid had picked a hell of a confidant. He was no good with kids, he was discovering. "Okay," he said quietly. "I'll try not to feel sorry for you."

"Good. My dad was there, you know, when I got checked in this hockey game and went into the wall. I think maybe Mom blamed him but it wasn't his fault, so maybe she didn't blame him. I couldn't tell because they fought so much." The words had come out in a rush.

The conversation had become very painful for Nate, as visions of himself as a kid welled, listening to the fights from upstairs, then thinking about his own battles with Eve, knowing his two-year-old daughter could hear them.

"The thing is, I never see him. I don't even know where he is."

Nate was stunned. "You don't visit?"

"Never."

"Trev—"

The kid put up a hand. "I warned you. No saying you're sorry."

"Okay," Nate said quickly, feeling completely at sea.

"Look, before my mom comes back, I want you to know some things, so listen." His eyes went back to the dark horizon. "I don't know if you've ever thought about what I can do. My mom says I can take driver's ed when I'm sixteen and the school will rent a handicapped van so I can learn. Of course we can't afford a car like that. Anyway. I can beat anyone in Super Nintendo and I was in a wheel-

chair-basketball tournament and I was *good*. Do you believe I was good?''

"Sure I do." The kid had a keen intelligence and a steely
determination that Nate both recognized and respected.

"And...the thing is..." His voice dropped. "Well,
there's this girl at school. She's not big in the chest or
anything, but she's pretty and kind of fun." His voice
picked up speed. "I kissed her some, and touched her chest,
outside her clothes one night. And I got real...hard."

If Nate had been holding his beer, he would have
dropped it. Why was Trev telling him this? If he needed to
talk to somebody about his feelings for this girl, why not
his mother, or Libby? Libby was great with kids.

Trevor never took his eyes from the horizon. "I get hard
a lot. So I know when the time comes, I...can. I think about
doing it, you know, all the time. The girl would have
to...help some, but it would...work."

Nate almost choked. Sure, ask the kid to tell Libby about
getting a hard-on for a pretty girl. Nate had once been fifteen, and he understood. God, yes. Lately, he'd been feeling
like a kid himself, aching with longing, with an untouchable, pretty girl tantalizing him, just out of reach. A girl
who was all woman, a woman he wanted to touch, to
stroke, to taste, to take. A woman who was his wife in
name only.

"So, what do you think?"

Nate needed his beer for real now. Trevor was looking
at him earnestly. It struck him that the boy probably had
nobody to talk to about this. Of course the kid needed to
know what he should do about what he was feeling. And
Nate had just been drafted for the job of telling him.

"Well," he started, feeling for the right words, "you've
got to decide when you're ready. Your body is ready, but

you've got to decide if you're ready for all the things that can come after. Pregnancy.''

"Rubbers,'' Trevor countered. "I know all about them.''

Nate cleared his throat. "Right. And you've got to use them every single time. But that's only part of what I'm saying. The time needs to be right.'' He held up his hand as Trevor started to protest. "You asked me, okay? You're too young. You're not ready and the girl won't be ready.'' In the face of the kid's curiosity, Nate felt old, jaded. Sex had once been so important. Now the men and women in his circle treated it as something casual, indulged in anytime there was attraction. The only one who felt differently was Libby.

He, too, looked out toward the horizon. "You respect the girl's feelings. You don't push her into anything. Also, Trev, you don't tell other guys how you scored or got lucky. It's private, always.''

Trevor thought about that. "I wouldn't want her to feel bad. You know, after.'' He sighed. "It's not going to happen. Not with Ann, anyway. She slapped my hand when all I was going to do was open a few buttons.''

The disgust in his voice made Nate smile a little. Maybe he hadn't done too badly with the kid, after all. He twisted off the top of his beer. He felt the oddest sense of... Belonging, maybe. All of a sudden, the sunporch felt warmer. Kind of comfortable.

"Ah, Nate?''

"Yeah?''

"Do you think, well, you came back for Sara. So I thought maybe you'd know... I figure, my dad left because of me being in the chair. Now, don't say he didn't because I *know*. But I was thinking if my father knew I could do stuff, drive a car...be a man with a girl, then maybe he'd want to see me.''

Right in that moment, Nate wanted to track down this kid's father and strangle the life out of him.

Trevor spun his wheelchair to face Nate. "My mom says you can do anything, that you've got money and lawyers. So what I want you to do is…find my father."

Nate had no idea how to respond, no idea whether Trevor ought to see his father or not. He did know that Tina Samms wouldn't like his interference. He was silent for a moment. Suddenly, this decision seemed every bit as difficult as any business decision he'd ever had to make.

Trevor waited. Nate could see the tension in his still profile as he pretended to watch the horizon. He knew then, absolutely knew, that Trevor had every intention of finding his father whether Nate helped him or not.

Abruptly, the light snapped on. Tina Samms stood in the doorway. "Trevor—" She stopped as she caught sight of Nate, and her lips pursed in disapproval. "What were you doing out here in the dark?" She cast her eyes about as if her son and Nate could be up to something on Libby's sunporch.

"Talking to Nate." Trevor's customary cheer was entirely absent. He cast a quick glance at Nate with warning in his eyes.

"About what?"

Libby appeared behind Tina, her flyaway hair glowing in the yellow light. Libby touched Tina's arm lightly. "Come on, Tina." To Nate she said, "I sent Sara up to bed. It's been a long day for her, and she kept yawning over the game."

"It's been a long day for everybody," Nate agreed carefully. He saw the protectiveness of Libby's gesture toward Tina.

Tina came onto the porch. "Trevor, I'll help you with the steps."

Nate stepped forward. "I'll do it. He's heavy."

Tina's shoulders straightened. "I've been doing it fine for four years."

Libby shot Nate a look that warned him not to interfere. Nate stood back and watched Tina struggle with the heavy wheelchair, grunting with the effort. In Nate's world, he closed a woman's car door, put a light hand on the small of her back to guide her up a flight of stairs. Polite gestures for women who expected them. He hated to watch Tina struggle, but he didn't have clue what to say. What to do. About anything.

He looked again at Libby. She was frowning at him. God, what a day this had been, really the first day they'd spent together as husband and wife. Tomorrow he had to get the crews moving at Bittersweet Point in preparation for building. There were calls from Jeff in Chicago; his answering machine was full. He and Libby had to talk about some things, things they hadn't seemed to have time for up until now. They'd yet to discuss the bills. Even the food he ate, the beer bottle in his hands, was hers.

With his mother's help, Trevor had negotiated the steps. Tina planted a quick kiss on the top of his head. Libby had already gone down the hall ahead of him, and Tina and Trevor turned their backs, closed the circle, leaving him alone on the porch.

He gave a harsh chuckle. It was hard to believe he'd had that fleeting sense of belonging. He was a weekend husband by choice. His wife didn't sleep with him by choice. His daughter apparently thought she'd failed him, out on the lake, and he *knew* he'd failed her. His wife's best friend hated him.

He couldn't wait to get back to Chicago.

"THEY WANT YOU this time, Nate. I've done my best, but they won't settle for hearing from the second-in-command any longer.'' Nate's assistant, Jeff, sat next to him at the conference table, across from his general contractor.

As contractors went, Jim Fioli was one of the best—tough, a guy who knew how to brazen it out with the workers. He was a good man to have with you in a pinch, and Nate was definitely feeling pinched.

Fioli grunted, pushing a stack of papers aside. ''The carpenters are talking about walking out in sympathy with the plumbers.''

The plumbers had no problem with Nate; they were in a contract dispute with another firm. But labor unrest had a ripple effect, touching every building project in the city. Right now the last thing Nate needed was a ripple effect.

The Iris Complex was in trouble. Buried in the paperwork he'd read on his way back to Chicago, this time Nate could see the seeds of his own downfall. He fought down a flash of panic. He'd been in tight situations before. He'd be in them again. So far, he had more reserves than any developer in the city.

He'd been up all night, crunching numbers, then all morning he'd been checking them against figures Jeff kept. Jeff's numbers were surprisingly accurate; the kid was doing a hell of a job. Now, if Nate could get the project back on schedule, he'd be okay. He couldn't afford any fines caused by delays in construction. He had an ironclad contract with Fioli; Marta had seen to that. The contractor would be the first to have to pay any fines. But Fioli flew without a net. If he folded, Nate could be next. The development business was like that. Bankruptcies had a domino effect.

Thank God there were no hitches at Bittersweet Point. He and the banker, Kevin Smithson, were seeing eye to eye on everything from the financing to the plans for an ultra-luxury resort, complete with indoor tennis courts, a lap pool, boathouses and hot tubs.

Nate decided to meet with the Iris workers at their union meeting on Friday night. He was reasonably confident he could handle them, but he wasn't looking forward to the task. Once, he'd relished the challenge. Where had all that fierce drive gone? He could still function as if he gave a damn, but nowadays everything seemed so...difficult. The air-conditioning hummed, but he was hot. He drained a cup of coffee anyway. He needed the energy.

He'd gone to Harborside the last three weekends, though this week he'd had to leave on Sunday morning in order to get back to business in Chicago. Funny how he'd resented coming back early. Libby baked bread on Sunday afternoons. Yesterday and today, he'd often found himself thinking of a shabby house on a cove, his mind conjuring curtains flapping in the open windows, a dark-haired girl chattering, a woman baking bread. A woman baking *bread,* for God's sake, and the image was earthy, sexy.

Nate looked down at a column of figures. But his mind wandered. Last weekend had been rainy, and Libby and Sara had been playing Monopoly again. For a while, he'd stood in the doorway, watching.

Then Sara had asked him to join them, so he'd sat with legs crossed on the braided rug in the living room and re-learned a game he hadn't played in twenty-five years. Libby had been lying on her stomach, intent on the game, but once or twice she'd teased him about the irony of a guy like him playing Monopoly. He told himself that he wanted to play only because he wanted to do things with Sara. He told himself he couldn't possibly be attracted to a woman who whooped when he was sent to jail, or landed on her hotel.

He'd won, of course. Then afterward, he'd wondered if

he should have let Sara win. But she was laughing over something with Libby as she put the game pieces away, so he'd decided he'd done okay.

Suddenly, he was smitten with the idea of asking Libby to move to Chicago. Why not have Sara and Libby here? He had everything they needed and more. A state-of-the-art kitchen, a housekeeper to cook in it, a pretty bedroom and matching bath for Sara, a balcony that overlooked the glittering lakeshore.

Libby could have a shop downtown. She was talented, and the naturalness of her designs would be in demand. She'd make a killing. He had contacts; they could invest in some big-time advertising. And she'd be home every night.

How would she react to the idea? She showed no inclination to move. In fact, she never even asked him how things in Chicago were going. She must not care. Well, he'd married her precisely because she didn't care, because they could have a marriage for Sara and he'd be able to keep his distance.

Hell. Nate abruptly shoved aside the stack of papers. What difference did it make, anyway? He lived in Chicago, and even *he* wasn't home every night. Last night he'd spent at the office, and the night before that, he'd been to a fancy charity auction for abused kids that had run on for hours.

He was lucky he could reserve weekends for Sara. This Friday night was Sara's play. She'd been talking about that play all week, every time he called. He'd meet with the workers at dinnertime on Friday, then he'd have just enough time to take the last commercial flight to Toledo and still make the opening curtain. He'd make everything work out.

Fioli mopped his forehead. "Damn building computers that tell you what temperature you oughta like. It's so flaming hot in here." He glanced over at the huge window, but it couldn't be opened. "Nate, I'm relieved about Iris. But I wonder how you let this labor unrest get out of hand. Not like you to let Jeff handle things like that." He shot Jeff a look. "Nothing personal, kid. It's just that some problems need the boss's touch."

Fioli stood and crumpled a piece of paper, his attention back on Nate. "Something distracting you, pal? If there is, you'd better tell me. I've got my new summerhouse in Door County riding on this deal."

With his thumb, Nate absently twisted the wedding band on his hand. "Nothing's distracting me. I've just been commuting a lot, from Ohio, where I've got another project in the works. It's been hard for me to give Iris time." Iris was a jealous mistress, he'd discovered. She seemed to resent every moment he spent in Harborside.

But Fioli wasn't listening. Instead, his eyes widening, his gaze was drawn to Nate's left hand. "Nate. Did you get *married?*"

Nate hadn't told anyone of his marriage, but he hadn't made a secret of it, either. He was wearing a wedding ring, after all. "Yes. Quietly. To an out-of-town woman. You don't know her," he added quickly, feeling oddly protective of Libby. Fioli was a good guy for business, but he was crude in his talk about women. And Fioli and his wife had an "understanding" that Libby wouldn't be able to fathom in a million years.

Fioli looked stunned. "Married. I can't believe it. You had it made for so long." He paused, thinking. "Is she knocked up or something?"

Nate started to rise, swept with an overwhelming rage. His fists balled.

Jeff put out a restraining hand, gripped Nate's arm hard and held on. Nate looked down, vaguely surprised that Jeff had the guts to rein him in. But the gesture gave him a second's pause, enough that he could answer with a controlled reply. "As a matter of fact, my wife is not pregnant. But if she were, it would be a private matter."

"Sure, sure," Fioli said quickly. "I just meant you'd do the right thing by her, you know? All that damned honor and everything. No insult intended."

Nate gave him a cool nod. He was boiling inside. It was shocking just how furious he was; he hadn't felt that way since the night the government had absconded with his only child. *Careful*, he thought. Get a grip.

Fioli gave him a grin, placating and knowing. "It's not the end of the world. As long as your wife isn't one of those romantic women, the kind who want you to spill your guts all the time and be home every night." He laughed. "As if you'd marry a woman like that. It'll work out. Men like us…"

"Jim," Nate interrupted in a deceptively low tone.

"Yeah?"

"Shut up."

Fioli flushed dark red. "Okay."

CHAPTER TEN

LIBBY HELD ON TO her program with one hand and twisted in her seat to look again for Nate. The school gymnasium was buzzing, two hundred folding chairs filled with the good folk of Harborside. On her other side, Tina was talking with Bart Portnek about costumes for the upcoming production of *Fiddler on the Roof.* All the community-theater people were here, because any occasion celebrating the arts—even a school play—brought them out. After all, there wasn't a symphony, ballet or even a professional theater troupe nearby.

"Psst! Libby! Come here!" Sara, in costume, was standing in the aisle and motioning to get Libby's attention. Libby climbed over feet and apologized about a dozen times, making a couple of promises to talk later about flowers for a wedding and the garden club picnic.

"What's up?" she asked with a bright smile as she came up to Sara. "Have you got stage fright?" That was intended to be a joke, because Sara had never had stage fright in her life.

"Naw." Sara screwed up her face. "Oh, you're teasing. Real funny." She stuck out her tongue. "I just wanted to know if you'd seen Nate yet."

Libby had been holding the seat beside her for half an hour. "He said he'd be here," she assured Sara with more confidence than she felt. This time, she'd been so sure of him. He knew how important this play was to Sara. But as the minutes dragged by and he hadn't appeared, she'd begun to wonder.

She was angry, and getting more furious by the minute, because Sara aside, Libby had been stupid, stupid, *stupid*. She'd gone to a department store in Toledo and bought a dark green dress. Flowing—but at least a solid color. And she'd splurged on a designer scent that smelled of sophistication and sandalwood, and put pearl studs in her ears. She felt prettier than usual, but oddly out of place, quivery with anticipation. As if she were a girl on a date with the handsomest boy in town.

Why had she bothered? Why had she spent one minute of her life trying to look attractive for a man like Nate?

The lights in the gymnasium dimmed suddenly, then went down jerkily. Jenna Baker's boy was spending his first semester as a stagehand. "You'd better get back," she whispered to Sara.

Sara was still looking hopefully toward the open door by the refreshment table. "Do you see him? You're bigger than me. See if you can see him."

Libby looked, but he wasn't there. "Maybe after the first act," she said, still hoping herself. "But *I'm* here." In her greasy stage makeup and garish costume, Sara looked like a little girl playing dress-up. How she would have liked to have shared this moment with Nate, asked him to pose for a picture with Sara for the camera she had in her purse. But she wouldn't admit to any disappointment right before Sara went onstage. "Go. Shoo!" She made her tone as light as possible. "And Sara, break a leg!"

Sara grinned at her words. She loved the expression, always said it felt like "real" theater when people used it.

Libby turned from the stage. Instead of returning to her seat, she stood for a few moments. From this vantage point, she could see the open doorway more clearly.

"Psst!" Sara again, and Libby dutifully turned around. The red velvet curtain billowed, and she could see only one bare arm, frantically gesturing her to come onstage.

There was a lot of giggling going on backstage. Sara poked her head out. "Mr. Gerrard said I could talk to you for a minute. I just went back to the dressing room, and guess what was there. From Nate. Red roses, a whole dozen! Everybody was wondering who they were for and I nearly died of embarrassment because they were for me." Yet her eyes sparkled with pleasure. "Do you know what they *cost?*" She paused for the barest second. "Well, of course you do. Did you know before about my red roses?"

"Not a thing," Libby said truthfully.

"And there was a card." She pushed a card out from behind the curtain.

The card said only, "Break a leg, Sara. All my love, Nate." But from the starry look in Sara's eyes, Libby knew it was enough.

That is, it would be enough—more than enough—if he managed to put in an appearance.

The curtain billowed again, sending up a cloud of dust. "Only stars of shows get red roses. And how did Nate know a real theater expression and everything? Wow, wow, wow, this is so very cool." Someone called for her, and she said, "Gotta go."

Sara disappeared behind the curtain and Libby retook her seat.

"No Nate?" Tina asked as a tape played the opening music.

Libby shook her head.

Tina made a sound of disgust. Remembering the roses, Libby felt a sudden urge to defend him. "Maybe his plane was late," she whispered.

"But he didn't bother to call you on that little toy phone

of his, did he?'' Tina squeezed Libby's hand. "Listen, don't worry about this. You'll have a good time and Sara will be great. You don't need him.''

She sighed. "Tina, he's my husband.''

"Don't remind me.''

"And he's Sara's father. He bought her roses today, and had them delivered backstage.''

That gave Tina just a moment's pause. "But where *is* he? Look. The guy wants his daughter like some kind of trophy. And now that he's got her and has you to take care of her, he takes off for his big-time life in Chicago.''

Her voice had risen, and she looked around and dropped it. "Sorry.''

Libby nodded and faced forward. The director was announcing the start of the play. Her stomach felt sour, unsettled. She could certainly see how Tina had come to her conclusions. But Tina hadn't seen him so intent and determined at the first custody hearing, hadn't seen him swallow and look away when she'd given him his first picture of Sara, hadn't seen him making pancakes with Sara, trying so hard to fit in to somebody else's life and she hadn't seen him immediately after the storm, his face wet and gray with worry about his daughter. Oh, heck, maybe Libby was reading too much into Nate's behavior. Maybe it was all wishful thinking.

She felt very alone, too, because she didn't dare admit to her best friend that she'd missed Nate this last week, that she'd looked forward to having him home, burning breakfast and making plans. And she knew what Tina would say if she confessed to the dreams she was having, hot, hot dreams of black hair and blue eyes and aristocratic features taut with desire, dreams that caused her to wake up with the sheets twisted under her.

But by the end of the play, Nate had still failed to appear

and—roses or not—Libby was furious. Sara had come out for a glass of punch, and the girl had watched and waited until Libby couldn't stand it. When the director had called the cast backstage for some instructions about tomorrow night's show, Libby was relieved.

Libby and Tina were talking to Barb Fielding at the refreshment table when Kevin Smithson came up. "Where's your famous hubby?" he asked Libby.

She flushed, and he chuckled. Barb was giving her a knowing smile, too, doubtless thinking her high color was from all the implications of being a newlywed. As if either one of them had a clue what her life was like.

"Still in Chicago, I guess," she said, and the words didn't sound as offhand as she'd intended.

"Why would he be interested in a kid's play, anyway?" Tina added.

Libby saw the looks Kevin and Barb shot one another. "He wanted to be here." No way would she have the gossip mill buzzing about a rift between her and her new husband. "And he had roses delivered backstage for Sara."

Kevin nodded. "I figured he'd want to come. The guy has a real thing for that girl of his." His eyes crinkled with good humor.

"I knew that, right away," Barb added. "Remember at the courthouse that day, Libby? He wanted Sara so bad, everybody was talking about it. Wow, he was gorgeous. And when I saw him, I knew he'd be right for you. You always did have an eye for line and form." She laughed, then did a big, fake sigh of envy for Kevin's benefit. She held out a tray of cookies to Libby.

For diplomacy's sake, Libby selected a cookie made by one of the other women, but also chose one of her own. She bit into her own cookie, made with honey and organic flour. Barb and Kevin had engaged Tina in conversation.

Libby was only half listening but heard Kevin mention Bittersweet Point.

Nate had spent a lot of time poring over documents related to Bittersweet Point. It was the biggest building project to hit Harborside. Libby had thought she had a good idea what Nate's business was like. After all, she ran a business of her own, and coped with defective inventory, taxes, fussy customers. But Nate dealt with all these things and more on a scale that boggled the mind.

"So what are your plans, anyway?" Kevin asked casually.

Tina's face had gone white. "I don't know," she finally whispered. "I thought I had more time."

"Well, you've got no lease. You must have known this was going to happen."

"But I didn't realize he was going to *tear it down.*" Her voice rose in alarm. "I thought he'd add others to it. And Trevor and I could stay until he found buyers or tenants for it."

The alarm finally penetrated Libby's fog of misery. "What's the matter, Tina?"

"Bittersweet Point," she snapped. "My home. Didn't you hear Kevin? Our banker and your *husband* plan to tear down the condominium. Put us on the street."

A bit of cookie turned to sawdust in Libby's mouth. "No, Nate's going to add to what's there."

"Kevin says he and Nate are tearing down the building."

Libby glanced at Kevin. Tina had to have misunderstood.

A slight flush darkened his cheekbones. "The style's not right. Surely you know that. On the outside, the place is ugly—"

"It's my home." A couple of people had stopped chatting and were listening.

"Nate wouldn't run you out of your home." Libby

touched Tina's hand. It was cold under her fingers. "He'd never do something like that to anybody, and especially not to Trevor."

Libby's thoughts raced. To Tina, the condominium she rented was much more than a place to live. She had her son to think about. The area was not known for choice in real estate, and most of the housing—the lower-priced housing for sure—was old. Old houses had narrow hallways and steep stairs, and light fixtures and cabinets placed high on walls. The houses Tina could afford wouldn't accommodate Trevor.

But Nate wasn't some wicked landlord. He was just a businessman...

Oh, God. She remembered some things. Some talking on the telephone she'd paid little attention to, about scheduling and groundbreaking and some kind of trouble.

Kevin looked very awkward but determinedly logical. "Even if we added on, do you know what those condos are going to cost? We're going for the upscale market—"

"That kid needs a place to live." Kurt Flanders, a beefy man with a baritone voice that carried, weighed in. "We didn't know you and Perry were planning to evict that handicapped kid."

"Challenged," Tina corrected dully. "He's not handicapped. He's challenged."

Kevin's upper lip had begun to sweat. "Nate's plans have been on the front page of the *Harborside Herald,* Tina. You *knew* what was happening."

"Yes, I knew we'd have to go *someday,* that we'd just got lucky with the rent." Her knuckles were white around her glass of punch. "We'd have to move when the other units were built and sold. But I thought I had lots of time. Just when is the wrecking ball coming, anyway?"

Libby put out a hand again. "I'll talk to him."

"And say what? He doesn't give a damn."

"He does." Her voice sounded very sure.

But did he? she couldn't help wondering. Surely he did. But heck, if he gave a damn, he'd be here now, ready to assure her best friend that she'd have a home for her son.

People she'd known all her life were muttering, the news flashing through the crowd. Most of the townspeople had supported the Point redevelopment, glad to see the mess the old developer had made being cleared up, glad to have somebody of Nate's stature taking over the job. Just last week Margaret Matwing had said how nice it would be to have something done with the crumbling break wall over at Bittersweet Point.

The lights flashed, a sign that the janitors wanted to close the gymnasium. But nobody made a move to depart.

"Bittersweet Point is bringing a hundred jobs to this town," Kevin said firmly. Slowly, the people around Libby quieted, each obviously thinking. The shop owners had been pleased about the venture, anticipating more money that would be spent downtown. The town needed the jobs, and needed the money the project would generate.

Kevin pressed his advantage. "Tina, if you'd made a move to collect all that money in child support Jonathan's been racking up all these years, maybe…"

"Leave Jonathan out of this!" Tina's voice rose again. "Trevor and I will be fine. We're always fine. No thanks to the *men* in this town."

Barb had been silent up to this time. Now she rounded on Kevin. "That was a low blow to bring up that jerk," she said with vehemence.

Libby knew she had to do something. She had to reassure her friend. She had to stick up for Nate. She had to have faith that her husband would do the right thing. She drew a deep breath.

"Nate Perry is an honorable man," she said in a loud, clear voice that commanded attention. "He doesn't realize Tina's not able to make plans right now. He'd never put her out. In fact, I promise he won't."

Near her, people nodded, then whispered. Husbands and wives turned to each other and took her statement with faith and relief. Nate Perry wouldn't do such a thing. His wife had promised. And his wife was Libby Jamieson Perry.

"It's a misunderstanding," the kindergarten teacher said to her date, and Libby could hear the word *misunderstanding* passed along from group to group. Libby says it's just a misunderstanding...a misunderstanding...yes, a...

Lord, what had she done? She'd managed to douse the flame of gossip before it had gotten completely out of control. But she'd put her reputation on the line for Nate. The reputation she'd spent a lifetime earning. If she was wrong about Nate, her place in the town was in jeopardy.

But Nate was her husband. Could she do less for her husband?

And she really *was* sure Nate had no intention of seeing Tina and Trevor forced to rent some cramped space where Trevor couldn't use his wheelchair. She had to be right, because she couldn't bear it if the man she'd agreed to share her life with could be that callous.

Married people were a twosome who took on the world as one. No matter how she'd planned things going into this marriage, somehow Nate's fate had become hers. She hoped with all her heart that she was right about his plans. And his motives.

LIBBY WASN'T SLEEPY. She'd taken off her stockings, but she was still in her new dress. She tucked her bare feet under the flowing skirt. Its long sleeves felt good in the cooler air of the sunporch. Sitting alone in the dark, she brooded.

Nate loved Sara. That much she was sure of. But it was precious little to build a life on.

Libby wrapped her arms around her calves. Was Tina right? Was the sum of Nate Perry really only the cold, hard face he presented to the world?

A key turned in the front door. Nate. Safe. Relief, totally unexpected relief, went through her. She heard his tread in the hallway. Slow, heavy. Weary-sounding.

Quickly, she got up and flicked on the light. "Nate. Can you come here?" she called before he could make a getaway upstairs.

He came, and she was waiting for him.

"Where were you?" she demanded without preamble, knowing she sounded shrill and not caring. She'd had hours to run various scenarios over and over in her mind. And each one sounded worse than the last. She wasn't just angry anymore. She'd been worried. That almost made her angrier.

He straightened at her tone. "In Chicago. Where else would I be?"

"It's a big city. Where in Chicago?"

His eyes narrowed. "In a meeting. You've never asked me before where I've been. So far, you haven't been all that interested in how I'm spending my time."

"Well, I'm your wife." Her voice was still raised.

At the word *wife* something in Nate's eyes flickered briefly. Vulnerability? Hope? Before she could tell, his expression hardened; his mouth tightened. He shoved his hands in his pockets and said coolly, "Then from now on I'll give you a schedule when I leave on Sunday nights. I'll fax you any revisions during the week. Sometimes my plans change come Wednesday."

"That's not what I mean." She bit her lip. In actual fact, she *did* wonder what he did in Chicago all week. He conducted business, she reminded herself. But she knew he socialized, too. He had a whole life there that didn't include either her or Sara. "I don't give a damn what you do on Wednesdays." That was a lie, but she felt pushed into it. "What I give a damn about is Fridays. Specifically *this* Friday. You missed Sara's play!"

Abruptly, his cool facade vanished. He leaned his head back against the wall and closed his eyes for a second. "I was in a meeting, and I missed my flight. I tried to call. Several times, in fact. But your line was busy and then just rang and rang. If you had an answering machine like the rest of the world—" He cut himself off. "My car was in Toledo at the airport, so I rented a car in Chicago. I drove."

"It's six hours by car from Chicago. Surely you knew you wouldn't make it."

"Yes," he said quietly. "I knew."

He knew. And he looked so sad.

She wouldn't allow herself to react to that sadness. This time, they were going to have a real discussion. "What are you going to do about it?"

"I'll talk to her."

"And tell her what? That you were too busy to bother?"

"Libby," he said quietly.

"She wanted you here. Instead of visiting with her friends, she spent most of the time before the opening curtain looking for you. Even afterward, during refreshments, she was still hoping. You spoiled the play for her."

Her mind's eye flashed to the roses that were in a vase in Sara's bedroom. But she wouldn't take back her words. Not even when his shoulders slumped.

Libby steeled her heart against his distress. "If you'd had your priorities straight, you'd have been here."

"Priorities according to who? *You?* I'm trying to make a living for Sara, for you and this family—" He stopped abruptly, looking suddenly confused.

Sensing that he was thinking about what he'd just said, Libby looked him straight in the eye. "Since when did Sara ask you to work eighty hours a week and make millions of dollars for her? Since when did I? You do all that just for yourself, because you're..." She stopped.

"Please." That tight line to his mouth was back. "Say what's on your mind."

You do all that because of your father, she'd been about to say. She'd heard the shame in Nate's voice when he'd talked about his insecure childhood, the note of pride that he'd been able to forge a different kind of life. Now she couldn't use something he'd told her in confidence to wound him.

She cared too much, damn it.

That thought pushed her over the edge. "We have different values in this house. Those values say that we're here for each other. We don't have much, but we share what we have. We do things together. We touch each other. What do you have in Chicago? Lots of money and all the people who want it."

"How would you know? You've never been to Chicago. How do you know what my life there is like?"

He had her there. She didn't know anything about his life, but that was by choice. "I know enough. I know that wheeling and dealing have made you an unfeeling man!"

He looked as if she'd struck him. "You're yelling," he finally said.

"You're right! I'm yelling. And do you know how I know you're an unfeeling man? Not just because you've failed your daughter, not because you've failed..." She hesitated, then said it, "Not because you've failed me, but because you're going to run a kid in a wheelchair out of his home!''

''What?''

"Trevor Samms. And Tina. I had to stand there and hear that you're going to run them out. Oh, yes, that's what was said about you in that auditorium tonight. I told this whole town that you're not going to do it, and do you know what?'' Her voice dropped but it was trembling uncontrollably. "I realized you share so little of yourself that I wasn't sure *what* you were planning. I defended you, but in my heart I wondered if my husband was going to put my best friend and her boy on the street!''

He stared at her, and she was vaguely surprised that he continued to listen. What was he still doing here, listening to her yell? He hated yelling.

To her astonishment he touched her, something he'd not done since the day they'd picnicked on the island. He reached out, touched her arm, then grabbed and held on when she tried to jerk away. His eyes were an intent, blazing blue. "What am I supposed to be planning for Trevor? Tell me what in hell you heard.''

"You and Kevin Smithson have plans to tear down the condo. Is that true?''

He looked utterly nonplussed, and relaxed his grip on her arm slightly. "Well, sure. You knew that I was redeveloping the Point.''

"We thought you were going to add more condos to Tina's. That it would take a year or more to build them all. That Tina could stay in her home until then.''

"We're tearing them down.''

At his words, shock and hurt lanced through her in equal measure. It was true, then. She had actually married a man who was everything Tina had said. What in God's name had she done? Slowly, she looked down to where his hand still gripped her forearm. A masculine hand. A hand wearing the wedding band she'd put on his finger. A hand she'd wanted on her skin. "You bastard. You really are going to put them out."

"No. Of course we're not going to do that. She'll have time to find something…"

She jerked, and her arm came free. Unable to keep back the tears, she swiped her arm across her eyes and stumbled toward the door. She pushed out into the cool dark and headed toward the water, moving fast.

If only he didn't follow. If only he responded to this messy scene by doing what he did best—withdrawing. He could head out in his rented car and be back in Chicago by dawn.

Nate followed. He didn't know what to do, what to say. Libby was far ahead. Even in the slight moonlight, she was surefooted, knowing the path to the water from a lifetime of treading it.

His strides were longer, and eventually he caught up to her. As he'd expected, she was crying.

Eve had cried when she was upset with him, and he'd never known the right thing to say to her, either. But where Libby had left the room, he'd had to listen to Eve for hours, crying, curled next to him in bed. He'd ached all over then, his eyes had burned, and he'd felt utterly helpless. He remembered the feeling well, and this time he felt the same, only more intensely. How was that possible? He'd been so careful to shield his heart. He didn't even share a bed with this woman.

For the first time, he was glad they didn't share a bed. How could she honestly believe he'd deliberately hurt a woman and her disabled kid? Well, he'd be damned if he'd let her see how she'd hurt *him,* believing he was a cold-hearted bastard. He'd expended more emotion on Libby and this family than he'd done in years. If she didn't know him by now… Damn her, anyway. She gave acceptance so unstintingly. To everyone but him.

Now Libby stood on the edge of the little ribbon of natural sand that divided the rough grass of the backyard from the lake. He stood as close to her as possible, but he resisted the urge to touch her. She'd only push him away again. "We have to talk," he said, and he hated how rough his voice sounded.

"There's nothing to talk about." In the moonlight he could see her chin come up.

"There is. What is the problem with Tina?" When she didn't immediately reply, he added, "To solve problems, I've got to know what they are."

"Sure. Ever reasonable," she retorted bitterly. "I'm worried about my friend, and you're calling it a *problem*."

He hated it when women got irrational. "Clearly, it's a problem."

She sighed finally, and he could tell she was blinking away tears. His stomach clenched.

"We all thought you were just going to add on to the condominiums, and until they were sold, Tina and Trevor could live there."

"So I gather. But my plans were never a secret. Go on."

She sighed again, but she sounded calmer now. "I think we believed that because we wanted to. Nate, that's the only place Tina can afford. She works as a seamstress, helps me in the shop, but she barely gets by."

He was astonished, and the tight knot of anger in his stomach loosened. He'd figured, with Tina and Trevor living in the luxury of Bittersweet Point, that Tina was well-off. "What about her ex-husband? Doesn't he help?" But he remembered the conversation with Trevor and already knew the answer.

"She doesn't even know where he is, but she doesn't make any move to find out, either. She's proud of making it on her own."

Nate understood pride. But it seemed that for her son's sake, Tina needed to let go of some. "The guy fathered a kid. He ought to pay to support him."

"I agree," she said unexpectedly. Okay, Nate thought. Some common ground. He wondered if Libby knew how much Trevor thought about his father.

Libby pushed a few strands of hair out of her eyes. The wind had picked up. Against her hand, the aquamarine in her engagement ring glinted. He had the strongest urge to soothe her, to pull her to him the way she did with Sara, to stroke the hair away from her eyes. To gain comfort in return.

He put his hands in his pockets.

She spoke. "Pretty soon Tina and Trevor will have more…*basic* concerns than covering old ground with Jonathan."

"They won't have to live in a rattrap." He kept his voice carefully controlled so she wouldn't know how much her assumptions had hurt him. "Look, you think I'm a selfish bastard, but in actual fact I give quite a bit to charity."

"I know," she said.

"Oh." Now he remembered all those forms he'd filed with the court. And of course there'd been full disclosure of all his assets and liabilities on the prenuptial agreement Marta had had her sign.

"So that's your solution, Nate? You'll throw her out, then give her money, like she's a charity case."

He hadn't meant it that way.

"You do that, you know." She turned to gaze at him in the cool, silvery dark. "You give to charities, but globally. Big charities, the impersonal ones. You help all kinds of people from a distance. Now Trevor will be the Disabled Kid charity, won't he? And you won't think about allowing Tina any dignity. Take the money or move into some crummy joint where Trevor can't get down the hall to a bedroom. But you've written a check. Your conscience is clear.''

She was right. Damn her, she was. But she was wrong, too. He did care about Trevor. Much more than globally. He'd no more deliberately hurt Trevor than he'd hurt Sara.

Or Libby. He had a vision of her in the kitchen, her hands in bread dough. It was an earthy image, with her pale, curving bare legs in cutoff jeans, and her hair sparkling in the light of the window.

He wanted people to care for. It was a stunning thought. For so many years, he'd thought if he only had Sara, his life would be perfect. But now this town—he cared about it somehow—in some rusty, fumbling, scary way he cared. He wanted to show his love for Sara. For Libby, he wanted to...

He cut off the thought. He was crazy to hope. He didn't even know what to hope *for*. He knew exactly why she'd married him. She'd made it clear in a thousand ways that he wasn't her idea of a husband. "What am I supposed to do about Tina?"

"Do you have to tear down the building?"

"Yes, I do." With the Iris Complex in jeopardy, it was more important than ever that Bittersweet Point stay on schedule.

"If I..." she hesitated. "If I asked you not to?"

He hesitated, too, suddenly wishing more than anything that he could do as she asked.

"As a favor to me?" she asked.

"I can't," he said finally.

"Why? Because you'll lose some money?"

If she only knew, he thought. "Yes. Because this time I can't lose money." Thank God she didn't know how tricky things were getting financially. She thought he was a failure with Sara. He knew he'd blown it tonight with his little girl. In fact, Libby had made it clear she didn't think much of him on any front. He clung to his material success, grabbed for his pride and held on with both hands.

In the dim light of the moon, he couldn't see her expression clearly. But he could tell she was studying him.

"Would you do it if I were really your wife?"

He stared at her, not sure for a second what she meant.

"You know what I mean!" She sounded impatient, disgusted with his slowness. "Will you help Tina if I agree to have sex with you?"

At her words, the anger he'd held in check flooded through him, at the same time pure lust shot through his groin.

Libby clapped a hand over her mouth, aghast at what she'd said. She had been so angry, so intent on making a point. Sensible, Nate had called her once. Sensible, she would have called herself. Sensible! How did this man bring out so much emotion? Embarrassment heated her cheeks until she figured they must be glowing in the night.

He moved a step closer. She came face-to-face with his broad chest. His voice was a tight whisper. "So you want to be a wife, do you? A tad late, but an offer, just the same."

She held her ground. Her toes dug into wet sand. The tension was unbearable. She licked her lips.

She was close enough to hear him take a breath before his hand tilted her face up. At the same time his lips came down, his other hand came around to the small of her back. He kissed her so fiercely, with such raw, aching, angry passion, that she felt herself bend backward.

So this is what it means to be swept off your feet, she thought as he lifted her to meet his mouth. His thighs molded to her legs, his arousal, hard and demanding, pressed forcefully into her belly. His breathing was uneven; she heard a low sound deep in his throat and couldn't help an answering one of her own.

She was excited, deeply excited, aroused to a fever pitch. Not only by this moment, but by the things that had gone before. The days—the nights—he'd spent in the room down the hall, the mornings when she'd spy the rumpled sheets of his bed from the doorway. The bathroom, with its lingering scent of a man and in the mornings its mirror fogged with steam. The tender way he looked at his daughter. The vulnerable, somehow yearning way he occasionally looked at *her,* and now, the hard, commanding feel of his mouth and his hips pushing against her own. All blended into splendid desire.

"So you want to be a wife?" he whispered again, this time his voice harsh with thinly suppressed desire.

"Yes," she struggled to whisper back.

"For Tina. For your friend. Because you need a favor from your husband."

No. Yes. Her mind was foggy with desire. "Yes, I—"

Abruptly, so abruptly she almost fell, he released her.

"No thanks." His voice was as cold as ice.

She stared at him, conscious of the loss of his body against hers. Her lips felt tender, her body chilled.

He turned and left her on the beach.

CHAPTER ELEVEN

LIBBY COULDN'T STAY out on the beach all night, though she was tempted. She'd sat on a creaky lawn chair and watched the waves over the water until she was as cold and miserable on the outside as she was on the inside.

The offer she'd made was so out of character that she was stunned at her own behavior.

And Nate had punished her for making it. His kiss had been calculated, she thought now, to show her that she did feel desire for him, that if he'd made love to her on the beach it would have been because she'd wanted to. Not as a sacrifice for a friend, but as a woman taking something for herself.

And he'd made no promises about Bittersweet Point.

She hadn't heard his car start around front, so she knew he was still in the house. Her house. *Their* house. It was dark. He must have gone to bed.

She dragged herself to the house. Tomorrow, she'd have to apologize for insulting him.

Of all the stupid things to say, offering herself up like some maiden chained to a rock for his enjoyment. Nate brought out her worst qualities.

She couldn't forget his promise. She was to decide about intimacy. If. When. Where. He'd been an honorable man, and she had not been an honorable woman. She'd been dishonest, because in offering herself, she hadn't really been thinking of Tina. Libby was used to thinking of herself as right and him as wrong. It was hard to believe that she had tried to manipulate Nate.

The hallway light was on. Sara's door was ajar, but the door to Nate's bedroom was firmly closed. She hesitated outside that closed door, then moved on, uncomfortable in her own home. Once in her bedroom, she took off her fancy dress and her pearl studs and put on her sunflower-patterned nightgown. Her breasts felt heavy and tender from the excitement of Nate's kiss.

She had barely gotten into bed and had not yet shut off the light when there was a quick knock on her door. Before she could even reply, Nate swung open the door.

He stood in the doorway, still in the pants from his suit, his white cotton shirt half-unbuttoned, his cuffs open.

Libby grabbed for the sheet. If he'd knocked a minute before, he would have seen her naked. Now, in her modest nightgown, she felt ridiculously exposed. Exposed as a small-town, hick woman who'd tried for sophistication and made a fool of herself.

"What do you want?" There was a quaver in her voice that she hated.

"Don't worry, I haven't come to take you up on your delightful offer." He rapped a fist on the door frame. "Hell, that's not what I came to say."

Before he could say whatever he had intended, she blurted out, "I'm sorry."

He nodded, his eyes fixed not on her face, but on the big sunflower splashed across her breasts. "Are you?"

"Yes."

He glanced into her eyes, briefly, his expression unreadable. "All right."

"You see—" she started at the same time he said, "What I want to say—"

He nodded to her to go ahead.

"This isn't working," she said miserably. "Our marriage. Our motives were good, but it's just not working."

His body went curiously still. There was a beat of silence, then two. When he spoke, his voice sounded flat, too. "Are you saying you want to end it?"

Did she want to end her marriage? The reason she'd married was still valid. Sara, asleep down the hall.

But if she ended this charade of a marriage, her house would be her own again. Not that Nate had changed anything. Her art, her threadbare quilts thrown over everything, her mom's wicker rockers—nothing had been touched. It was only his suitcase in his room, his shaving kit in the bathroom. Not really much at all.

Only his presence everywhere.

If she ended it now, there'd be no more waiting for Friday nights, telling herself she *wasn't* waiting.

No more tension with Tina.

She would explain to Sara. Libby would help her adjust. And there would be no chance of any further disappointments.

Everything could be as it was. Secure. Unchanging. Ordinary. Pleasant.

"No," she said. "I don't want to end it." Then she had a sudden, scary thought. "Do you?"

"No." He wasn't smiling, but his body seemed somehow to relax infinitesimally. "I'd only end it if I felt our marriage wasn't good for Sara."

In the end, it was all about Sara. That thought should have pleased her.

He hesitated. "Did I really spoil the play for Sara?"

"No. She wanted you there, but she had a good time. She loved the roses."

Amazingly, he cracked a smile. "Good. I'll talk to her

tomorrow. I'll tell her that no matter what, I won't miss at least my weekends with her.''

''Don't make promises you can't keep,'' she warned quickly. ''Say you'll do your best if you can't be sure you can keep your promises.''

His face tightened. ''I always keep my promises.''

Lord, they'd been making peace, and she'd managed to offend him again. ''I don't suppose,'' she said slowly, ''that you could give her more time? Spend more time here, or invite her to Chicago.''

There was a very long pause. Libby pleated the sheet she still held between her fingers like some shy virgin.

''I'd thought about inviting you both to Chicago, but this isn't a good time,'' Nate said finally. ''And I can't spend more time here. Not now.''

Her disappointment was keen. ''Oh, I see.'' But she didn't, not really.

''Things will work out. I can make them work out.'' He turned to go. ''By the way,'' he added almost casually, ''I'll think of something for Tina and Trevor. Something besides writing them a check.''

Her heart leaped. ''What will you do?''

He smiled faintly. ''I don't know. Yet. But you can tell Tina they've got time before they have to move, and even then things will work out.''

Okay. All *right*. This time, not for a moment did she doubt he meant to keep his promise. Warmth shot through her. She smiled, too.

There didn't seem to be much left to say, yet he lingered in the doorway. The fingers of one hand tapped a restless beat on the door frame. Finally, Libby relinquished her sheet, smoothed it in her lap, tried to forget that she and Nate had had a rousing fight and she had been very *un*sensible. She tried to be casual about Nate in the doorway.

Casual about being in bed, in a silly, unsexy sunflower nightgown with nothing on underneath.

Finally he spoke. "The thing is, I remembered something you said. Before. Tonight, did you really defend me to everyone who thought I was going to put Tina and Trevor out?"

She nodded.

There was a long pause. "Thank you," he said softly, and then he turned away. A moment later, she heard his bedroom door closing.

"MARTA WAINWRIGHT."

Nate had bypassed the secretary and gone straight to Marta's private line. "It's Nate," he said.

"Nate. How are you? More to the point, what can I do for you? Iris throwing a tantrum again?"

He passed a weary hand over one brow, then looked out his window, over the tops of the skyscrapers. "Always. But that's not why I called." He paused. "How easy would it be to find someone who disappeared?"

"Disappeared? How?"

"I don't know. I have his real name, age, description, social security number. I assume he'd be working as a pilot." Trevor had written Nate a letter, delivered to his Chicago address, with all that information. Nate hadn't made the kid any promises, because he still wasn't sure he should.

"If he's a pilot, he'd be easy to find. Licenses, flight plans, all that. Why?"

Nate saw by the lights on his own phone that he had two incoming calls. He let the outer office field them. He said, "Well, then, maybe he's not a pilot. I don't know how hard he's trying not to be found. The guy owes quite a bit in back child support, but I don't believe the woman's been seriously looking for him."

There was silence on the other line. "No problem," Marta finally said. The consummate attorney, she didn't ask why Nate wanted her to find a man who owed back child support. "While I'm at it, do you want me to find out where he keeps his money? Assuming he has any, that is?"

Nate smiled. "Yes. But Marta, keep this on the q.t., okay? I'm not sure what I'm going to do once this guy's found."

Again, she didn't ask any questions. "Sure."

"Good. Marta, did I ever tell you what an excellent attorney you are?"

"Every month with my retainer check." Then she laughed, an attractive, husky sound. "We do understand each other." Her voice went low, suggestive. "Anytime you want to find out how good perfect understanding can make you feel…"

"I'm married now."

She laughed again. "I prepared your prenup, remember? I know exactly why you're married, and I don't remember any old-fashioned promises of faithfulness in that document."

He was silent. He'd known an offer like this would be presented to him sometime, despite the wedding ring on his finger. Libby hadn't asked for faithfulness. Marta was right; theirs wasn't that kind of marriage. On the sexual front, at least, he didn't owe her a thing. Lately, his body had been on fire at the slightest provocation from Libby—when she passed him in the narrow hallway or the door to the bathroom, when she handed him a glass of wine and their fingers touched accidentally.

"You're almost too beautiful to resist," he said in his

best charmer's voice, but his heart wasn't in the compliment. "But, no thanks."

There was a long pause, then Marta sucked in a suddenly harsh breath. "You care for her. My God, you really do. Now listen," she added quickly. "I like you. Not just as a client, and not just as a potential bed partner. So this is both legal advice and friendly advice. Don't let this marriage thing get out of hand. That woman is not our kind."

Marta was right. He knew that. Hell, he'd come to the same conclusion countless times. But almost without his knowing it, the knowledge had lost some of its punch, even some of its certainty. "Just find Jonathan Samms," he said. "And do your best to keep Iris off my back."

NATE KEPT his promises. All of them.

The workers had started on Bittersweet Point, and the one white condominium stood in the middle of a sea of tread marks on the moist earth. The condominium was in the way. What the builders would do when they had to start construction on the sleekly rustic replacement condos, Libby didn't know. She didn't ask. And Tina didn't, either, only grudgingly acknowledged that Nate kept his promise.

Nate kept his promise to Sara, too. He was home every weekend, taking the last flight out of Chicago.

Now Libby checked the clock over the kitchen sink. Nate was due in about twenty minutes. She stuck the rest of a block of cheese into the refrigerator.

At long last, Nate and she were working some things out. Getting down to a routine of sorts. Libby cooked dinner on Friday nights. Nate cooked breakfast on Saturdays, an overcooked meal that also broke Libby's rules about a healthy breakfast. Chewy waffles. Scorch-bottom blueberry muffins spread half an inch thick with butter.

She sighed. At least Nate's concoctions were made with

organic flour. She knew, because she did the shopping, one week using her own money, the next Nate's, which he deposited in a checking account on a regular basis. It was ridiculous, he'd told her more than once, that either one of them had to cook, or that she had to clean. She cleaned during the week, while he was in Chicago, both to forestall argument and to remind herself that nothing much had really changed.

She wondered what she was trying to prove. She worked hard in the shop. Nate acknowledged that fact. He didn't want to do anything but ease things for her.

But there was no reason to get too used to what Nate's wealth would provide. Without love between them, she couldn't help wondering how long her marriage could last.

And besides, fixing up her house, cleaning it, were part of her, part of her life. She had the feeling if she gave in to Nate on these issues, she'd be giving in on more.

Would that be so bad?

She hadn't been listening for his car, she told herself. But her heartbeat picked up of its own accord when she heard the well-toned hum of his Jag. A few moments later, Nate opened the screen door of the kitchen. Over these last months, at some point that she hadn't noticed at the time, he'd got into the habit of coming around back.

"Hi," she said, looking up from the cutting board, where she was starting to chop a tomato.

"Hi," he said from across the room. He did that every Friday night, came in the kitchen door and paused there. It could be damn awkward, the way he always just stood there.

Today, he had his garment bag slung over one shoulder, a thin designer briefcase in his other hand. His hair fell onto his forehead. The sleeves of his blue broadcloth shirt were rolled up over forearms tanned from days on the water. He wore no tie any longer and his shirt was opened a button or two, showing the barest gleam of shiny, coarse dark chest hair. He'd already started to shed his Chicago clothes like an outgrown skin.

And even in dishevelment, he was perfect. How did he manage to look charming and sexy on a hot evening after a day's work and a wait at O'Hare, a drive from Toledo?

Neither one of them had ever mentioned her offer of sex or that hot kiss on the water's edge. The day after Nate went back to Chicago, Libby had put the sunflower night-gown in the dresser drawer and bought herself a new one in town. Not a sexy nightgown, just a soft-green one minus sunflowers. Maybe a tad more sheer, with a bit of lace. Looking at Nate, she felt herself blush for no reason at all.

Quickly she pulled the terry-cloth towel from the vee of her neck, where she'd put it to cover her puff-sleeved, red polka-dot blouse from spatters. She felt suddenly flushed, conscious of how carefully she'd dressed. And how silly she looked. Because with the red blouse, she wore a white skirt with so much eyelet lace that she felt awash in it. Why had she let Tina pick red, with her red hair? "A square-dancing outfit," she said lamely, indicating her clothes.

He hadn't taken his eyes off her. "I figured. Even you wouldn't wear that getup any other place." But he was smiling a little. In confusion, she looked away.

Before either of them could say more, Libby heard a familiar pounding on the stairs. "Nate!" Sara called. "I saw you drive in."

Nate took a few steps into the kitchen. Out of the corner of her eye, Libby saw his face split into a grin so wide and genuine that she suddenly wished he would smile at her that way. "Kiddo, you look great."

"I look cool," Sara corrected. Her dress was a satin-and-glitter concoction that Tina had made for her. The silver lamé sneakers from her first shopping trip with her father adorned her feet as she twirled around the kitchen, bumping Libby's elbow and sending up a splash of tomato juice. "Whoops, sorry," she exclaimed, then did a do-si-do around Nate. "What do you think?"

"Pretty." Nate cleared his throat. "As always, Sara. Very pretty." He nodded toward Libby with this last, and for a breathless minute she actually thought he might be complimenting her. But she knew better. He couldn't possibly like red polka dots and eyelet.

"Dinner will be ready soon," she said quickly.

"Have I got time for a shower?"

"Sure. Are you coming with us tonight?"

"I'd like to. I don't square-dance, though."

"It's easy!" Sara exclaimed. "I'm doing the do-si-do." She demonstrated again, folding her arms across her chest and doing a proud marching step around Nate. "Don't you dance?"

"Ah, ballroom stuff." He clarified when she frowned. "You know, like the waltz."

"Oh, the waltz. Like they do in Cinderella on Ice."

Libby caught the pained expression on Nate's face and burst out laughing

"Do you do line dancing or even rock or *anything* cool?" Sara asked.

His voice was grave, but his eyes had an unexpected twinkle. "Sara, I just don't do cool."

Sara laughed, too. "Well, I used to think you were awesomely cool, but now I know you're just a fath—" Abruptly, she cut herself off and looked away.

Just a what? Libby's hands gripped the dishtowel, and her eyes met Nate's. He had gone still. What had Sara been about to say? That Nate was just a father?

In so many ways, he was a father. He'd looked over

Sara's report card and told her he was proud of her grades. He worried about her when she was up on that horse he'd rented for her. He wanted her to share his interest in sailing, but since the storm, he hadn't pushed her. He'd been sensitive to her fear. Like a caring father.

And in so many ways, he wasn't a father. He never disciplined her. He wasn't here often enough to have to. He never hugged her. He was so very...careful.

There was a yearning in his eyes, in his expression. Sara was still turned from him, her hands plucking a bit of glitter on her skirt.

Make the first move, Nate. Take a chance.

"I gotta call Kathleen," Sara said abruptly, and turning, rushed from the room.

He'd had his chance, and he'd blown it. "Look, Nate—"

"I need that shower," he cut in, and then, following Sara, he left the room.

NATE COULDN'T BELIEVE how crowded the gymnasium was for this evening of square dancing. Libby said it wasn't as crowded as it would be later in the year when the cast of *Fiddler on the Roof,* which included Libby and his daughter, would cap the season with three performances.

The amazing thing was that he knew so many people here. He'd figured he wouldn't know a soul. Trevor was with two younger boys, showing them how he popped wheelies with his wheelchair. Now Nate recognized a carpenter from the job site at Bittersweet Point, and the heavy-equipment operator, Bart Portnek, and he even recognized the guy's wife, from the time Bart had forgotten his lunch and she'd brought some sandwiches to the job site. He recognized others. That woman who worked in the courthouse—what was her name?—and Kevin Smithson and his young wife. Amazing.

Various people spoke to him and Libby as if the two of them had been married twenty years instead of two months. A couple of people talked about the Point. Mostly they talked about the weather and if out on the lake the perch were biting.

Libby hung around until she saw he was in the middle of a group of men and then with a little wave, she took off. Sara stood off to one side with Kathleen and a group of girls. A much smaller group of boys stood in their own knot, a good distance from the girls. Each group looked at the other, tossed heads and pretended they weren't looking at all.

Nate excused himself and went over to the refreshment table. The casserole Libby had served for dinner had been some weird bean concoction. He'd never tell her, but he always ate on the plane beforehand. Kevin Smithson joined him and chose a can of cola.

"Ready for the dance?" Kevin asked.

"I guess so. Sara is excited about it."

"Are you an expert?"

Nate smiled self-consciously. "Never did it in my life. In fact, I was thinking I'd just watch."

Kevin grinned. "You want to live in Harborside, it helps if you like powerboating, acting and square dancing."

Nate liked none of those things. He didn't live in Harborside. *And* if he was learning a new skill, he learned it in private.

The lights went down and the caller took his place. A boom box played a country song. Various groups began to form squares. Most of the dancers wore jeans or denim skirts; few were as tricked out as Libby and Sara. He couldn't help a smile. Libby was unique, even in a town like Harborside.

Libby was speaking to the caller. Then she looked

around, saw Nate, headed toward him. Out of the corner of his eye, he caught sight of Sara. Suddenly, his daughter seemed to be standing alone, her group of friends hovering behind her like the chorus in a Greek tragedy.

In the kitchen earlier, had Sara really almost said she saw him as a father? After the storm on the lake, he'd almost been afraid to hope. She seemed to like him, but it wasn't enough. He wanted what Sara and Libby shared, but he didn't know exactly how to go about achieving it. He couldn't do it the way Libby did, with hugs and the right words all the time. He'd be so awkward that Sara would be embarrassed, would surely withdraw. He had to get there in his own way.

As he and Kevin watched, the group of boys huddled, talked, shifted. One boy approached his daughter.

"I think Sara's got a boy interested in a dance," Kevin said.

The boy said something, hung his head shyly. Sara flipped her hair over one shoulder, rubbed at the gym floor with the toe of her silver sneaker. Then she nodded. Careful not to touch each other, Sara and the boy got into a square made up of six other kids their age.

Watching, Nate got a lump in his throat. He couldn't blow his chance with his daughter. More than anything, he wanted to be around to see her grow into womanhood.

Libby was hurrying toward him now. "Tina's saving us a place."

Tina was saving something for him, even a spot in a square? "I'm sitting this one out."

She smiled at him. "Come on. It's not hard."

"Do it." Kevin gave him a little clap on the shoulder. "One thing I've learned, guy. If your wife wants to dance, life is a hell of a lot easier if you dance."

Near him, Trevor was making up a square with a slight blond girl as a partner.

Libby's eyes sparkled.

Nate knew he'd look foolish. But if Trevor could square-dance in a wheelchair, Nate could certainly do it.

"Okay," he said, and was rewarded with a smile from Libby that was downright incandescent. Something very tight in his chest loosened then. What the hell. She wanted him to dance, and he suddenly wanted to please her.

A guy with an electric violin had joined the caller.

"All right!" the caller shouted, clapping his hands for silence. "Everybody ready?"

There was a chorus of hoots and yells.

"Now, we've got a special treat tonight. I mean, besides John here on the 'lectric fiddle." John bowed to a smattering of whistles and applause.

"The treat I've got is a little secret I learned from a pretty redheaded gal. Seems we've got a beginner in our midst."

Nate shot Libby a glance and got a very bad feeling.

"Who?" somebody called.

"Handsome feller from the big city. I guess they don't do much square dancing in the big city." He shook his head. "So anyway, we've got a feller to teach our country ways to." John played a few bars of doomsday music on the fiddle. Everyone laughed. All of a sudden, a spotlight came on, lurched, sought, found Nate.

"I didn't think he'd make fun of you," Libby whispered back. "I just asked him to start with an easy dance."

"The lovebirds are whispering," the caller noted for the crowd. Nate had the fleeting satisfaction to see that in the harsh light of the spotlight Libby's cheeks bloomed. Around him, the laughter had an easy sound.

"Now, we're going to start with something simple.

Honor your partner." All around him the men bowed, the women curtsied. Libby went into a deep curtsy almost to his feet, her skirts pushing out around her like a parachute.

He bowed, feeling very awkward.

She put her hand in his. It was hot, a little damp.

For Nate's benefit, the caller put them through a few simple moves without music. A do-si-do like the one Sara had done. An allemande left, in which Nate forgot to do a full rotation and almost ran into Tina as a result. She gave him a tight-lipped smile, but everyone else laughed with good humor.

Then they tried it to music. The caller called out the steps a split second before the dancers were expected to perform the maneuver. It was harder than it looked. But kind of fun in its way. Swinging. Nate felt himself unexpectedly caught up in the music, the simple, insistent rhythm of the calls.

Flashing hands, a sashay of hips, then a prance back to Libby.

"Now back to kiss your pard-ner," the caller chanted. A peck to his wife's cheek, a fleeting touch of her hand. All around him, couples were whirling.

"Gents to the cen-ter."

A beat late, Nate joined three other men in the center of the square. Some guy he didn't know clapped him on the shoulder and gave him a thumbs-up sign.

The fiddle slowed.

"Your sweetheart's a cryin'." The fiddle turned a tad sultry.

Then the music stopped. "She's got a look in her eye, boys." The caller's voice had gone low, husky. "Wants that spoonin' real, real bad. What're you gents gonna do?"

"Kiss her!" the gents cried.

The music resumed. "Back to your squares, then, and do it," the caller chanted at last.

All around him, men whooped, kissed their partners exuberantly, pulling them off their feet, giving them a twirl. He looked down into Libby's eyes. Hers were shy, her lips parted. He had never been spontaneous, given to public displays of affection.

But suddenly, he ached to kiss his wife, with her perfect skin and red polka-dot blouse over breasts that were rising and falling with the effort of the dance.

He bent to her, kissed her lightly, when what he longed to do was grab her like the other husbands and act like a caveman staking a claim.

He wasn't really her husband, though. Did she want a kiss like that? She kept her hands firmly against her sides, and the moment passed. The caller sent them into a final allemande left, a swing, and then the dance was over. Everyone clapped. Nate felt so damned...disappointed somehow.

The caller blew into the microphone, and the hiss stopped everyone short. "Now, listen up, everyone. Our city feller did pretty good for his first dance, though once he did sorta step on Tina's foot, and once he was all by his lonesome tail in the middle of an empty square." The crowd laughed in appreciation.

Suddenly, Nate didn't care. They weren't laughing at him. They seemed to be laughing as though he was included. As though he was one of them.

"But he did do something very wrong."

A man from the next square called out, "What?"

"When I told the fellers to kiss their ladies, he didn't kiss his lady. Only a little peck. I think that redheaded gal deserves more than that, don't you? I mean, her just gettin' hitched." He paused. "Go ahead, son. Kiss your wife. Show us what she means to you. We'll wait."

There was laughter, a whoop or two. The spotlight, which had lost track of Nate during the dance, crept closer.

The crowd was clapping in rhythm, like at a football game. Nate was trapped. The caller couldn't possibly know that he'd touched Libby more times during the dance than at any time in the last two months of married life. Libby's eyes were wide and apprehensive, as though she expected him to turn away from her, embarrass her in front of everyone.

Show her what she means to you.

What the hell. He'd wanted to kiss her even before he'd walked into the doorway of the kitchen tonight. He'd wanted to kiss her since the day he'd *met* her.

So he did. And whatever Nathan Perry did, he did to the best of his ability. He swept a surprised Libby off her feet and into his arms like a bride crossing the threshold.

She was solid and surprisingly heavy; he had to brace his thighs to hold her. A hush fell over the crowd. The spotlight was in his eyes before he closed them. He dipped his head and captured her mouth. As her arms went around his neck, the crowd applauded.

He kissed her and kissed her, suddenly intent on proving to everyone that she was his wife. His pretty, redheaded gal.

CHAPTER TWELVE

A HALF HOUR LATER Tina Samms caught up with him. Nate was thirsty from all the dancing, and had come to the refreshment table to get a can of soda while Libby was in the ladies' room.

He hadn't had a chance to talk to Libby at all. They'd danced several more dances, joining Sara's square. In the short breaks in between dances, people kept coming up, talking.

Libby was always at the center of things, and she, well, she *sparkled*. For the first time, he truly understood why she didn't want to leave Harborside. Her roots in this town gave her life a sense of purpose, belonging. And of course she wanted those same things for Sara. Also for the first time, Nate wondered if he could give Sara those things in Chicago.

Nate himself belonged in Chicago. The feeling of purpose Libby got from this little lakeside town, he got from his business, from the steel and glass of the towers he built by the water.

Only lately, those things just seemed like…things.

Things with problems.

"Nate?"

He turned in surprise to see Tina standing next to him in a cowgirl outfit with white fringe.

"Tina," he said warily.

"Can we talk?"

"Sure." From the force of long habit, he silently offered her refreshments, and refrained from sipping his own soda until she'd popped the top on hers.

Behind him, the music was starting again, insistent, echoey-loud in the vast space. Tina headed for the door of the gym and he held it for her.

Outside on the blacktopped parking lot, he waited. For some reason, he was tense. He stood up to contractors, plumbers, bankers, politicians. But he felt so uncertain around Libby's friend. Trev's mother.

"Look," she finally said. "I just wanted to say thank you for leaving the condominium where it is for now."

He could see the words were difficult for her to say. He nodded in acknowledgment.

She took a determined breath. "I know it's hard for the workers to go around the condo all the time. It must be costing you money to leave the building up."

It was. And it was no small thing to have cost overruns at Bittersweet Point, given what he continued to lose on the Iris Complex. He pushed down the familiar tight feeling in his gut.

"I don't know what Libby said to persuade you."

If you only knew, he thought. "I didn't understand your situation," he said, his voice more curt than he intended.

"I'm not a charity case. I pay my rent every month on time." She sighed then, frowning. "I don't know why I'm defending myself. I've acted like a horse's ass."

"No, you haven't," he murmured automatically, uncomfortable with the sheen of tears in her eyes.

"I have." She studied her soda can. "I've interfered in your marriage." Her voice picked up speed. "I've said things about you to Libby, that she shouldn't trust you."

Oh, God. He'd known Tina didn't like him. He should have known she was keeping the waters churned. As if he and Libby didn't have enough problems on their own. "What did you say?" he asked.

She hesitated. Finally, she said, "I told her you were a handsome charmer like my ex-husband and that if she was foolish enough to care for you, you'd hurt her." She paused again. "I thought I was being a good, caring friend."

Nate thought about her words and felt a grudging respect. The woman had guts to face him, and she was obviously a loyal friend to Libby. "You don't even know me." Then he wondered why he was defending himself. He wanted nothing from this woman.

"Right. I don't know you, and I was wrong in at least one of my assumptions. I still wonder sometimes if you'll hurt Libby in the end, but..." She changed the can to her other hand, her head down. "Anyway, I assume you kept the condo for my son. For that, I thank you from the bottom of my heart." She swiped away the tears that had formed in the corners of her eyes and gave him a smile that was more form than real.

Nate shoved his hands in his pockets. "Tina, I'm going to have to do something about that condo someday soon. I have no choice."

She nodded. "I know."

"If you need a loan—"

"No!"

"Not a gift, a loan."

"No." This time the word came out softer. "I'll figure out something."

"I'm sure you will."

She turned away then and started back toward the gym door. He breathed a sigh of relief, glad she was gone.

She was almost at the door. He'd never understand the impulse that prompted him to speak. "Tina."

She turned.

"You need to talk to Trevor." He hesitated. "He tells me things you need to know."

She went still. "What things?"

"He'll tell you. Just talk to him, Tina," he urged. *While you still can. While you have a relationship that's sure and warm, before you're afraid to reach out to your own child.*

SARA TALKED NONSTOP from the back seat in the car going home. It was just as well, because Libby was unsettled, nervous around Nate. How could he have kissed her like that, in front of half the town? She thought back to the closed, contained man he'd been when they'd first met and couldn't believe it.

You'd think, after all this time of living—at least on weekends—in the same house, Libby would be comfortable around him. Not so. So now it was a blessing that Sara was chattering.

"Do you know they *dared* Josh to ask me to dance?" Sara said indignantly.

"Do you like him?" Libby was prepared to offer sympathy.

"He has a big nose. Though my nose is kind of big, too."

"Your nose is not big," Nate said firmly. It was the first time he'd spoken since they'd pulled out of the parking lot. Libby shot him a glance. He seemed intent on his driving. "Josh is okay."

"The dare didn't hurt your feelings?" Libby probed again.

"Well, kind of. But then I thought, well, my friends dared *me* and that's why I danced with *him*. I have to be fair and everything."

From the front seat, Libby could smile without hurting

Sara's feelings, and she did. Nate was frowning as he smoothly executed a curve.

"It was when we were playing Truth or Dare," Sara explained.

"Truth or Dare?" Nate repeated.

"Sure. When it's your turn, you have to decide which it is, Truth or Dare, and if it's Dare you have to do anything the other players decide and if it's Truth you have to answer any question they ask about your sex life."

Nate made a peculiar choking sound in his throat.

"So you picked Dare," Libby said. After all, there'd be no guilty thrill in Truth, since Sara could have no "sex life." In the dark, she Dared herself to reach out and pat the top of Nate's thigh, reassuring him of Sara's essential innocence. The moment she felt denim over taut male muscle, she was reminded of their kiss. Lord.

"It's easy," Sara went on. "Like if you picked Truth, Lib, you'd have to answer a question."

Truth. About her nonexistent sex life! She didn't dare look at Nate.

"Like…" Libby heard genuine hesitation in Sara's voice before she rushed on. "I've been thinking, you and Nate are married and I kind of know that means you do it to have babies, and that's called sex." She took a quick breath. "I didn't think anything about you two, you know, except that Kathleen's mother is going to have a baby and I've seen her mom and dad's bedroom and there's only one bed in it. Kathleen says you do it in a bed. And at our house, you know, Nate has his own bed."

There was silence in the car. Libby smoothed down her dress with suddenly damp hands. Finally, she said gently, "Do you have some questions about sex that I can answer, honey?"

Beside her, Nate cleared his throat.

"Well, I know how people do it," Sara said. "And it sounds disgusting."

"Sara," Nate finally said. "Maybe you'd feel more comfortable talking about this with Libby alone."

There was no doubt who of the three of them was the most uncomfortable. Libby felt a ridiculous urge to giggle at her suddenly old-fashioned husband, and to kiss the man silly and strip the jeans from his body as she envisioned bedrooms and making babies.

In the back seat, Sara shifted. "Well, I can understand why you two wouldn't want to do anything so weird. I was just kind of thinking, you know?"

They pulled into Libby's driveway. Nate put the car into park and was out of there like a shot.

SARA HAD BEEN overexcited by the dance and hard to settle down. But when Libby checked a half hour later, the girl had finally fallen asleep, one arm slung palm up over her forehead, as though she was having dramatic dreams.

Now Libby sat in cutoff jeans and a T-shirt, on a wicker rocker in her living room. The windows were open, and she listened to the hum of insects outside the screen and tried to relax.

Her reading light was on. She held a *Victoria* magazine in her lap, telling herself that a featured bouquet in an antique silver holder would be perfect for a gazebo wedding she had contracted. But it was difficult to concentrate on much of anything except what she'd been thinking about ever since Nate had kissed her so thoroughly in the school gym. Sex. Sex and Nate. Images. Black hair, strong and silken between her fingers. Moving bodies, silvery in the night. Nate. Nate and sex.

Cripes.

Resolutely she picked up her magazine. *Old-fashioned garden flowers work best for the look,* she read.

"Hi." Nate came downstairs and passed her on the way to the kitchen. He'd rolled up the sleeves of his chambray shirt in deference to the warmth of the night, she noted, but he hadn't changed into pajamas or whatever he wore to bed.

What did he wear to bed, anyway? She'd bet...nothing but his skin. Maybe a pair of briefs in case Sara ever came through the closed door to his room. Libby had never seen a pair of pajamas in his suitcase.

Sex. Nate.

Cripes.

Choose accent flowers in the creamy tones of old lace, unbleached muslin...

He was back with a glass of iced herbal tea in each hand.

"Thirsty?" he asked, holding one frosty glass out to her.

Sure. Thirsty. *Hungry...*

He handed her the glass and took a seat on the sofa across from her. Her nerves took another jump. He didn't sit with her in the evenings. Always, after Sara went to bed, he excused himself, and hours afterward, passing his closed door on the way to bed, she'd still hear the hum of his computer, the sound of his fax, sometimes even his beeper.

No wonder she couldn't get interested in antiques or old-fashioned flowers tonight. There was no way she could do that with her husband sitting across from her on the sofa.

Nate. Who'd kissed her tonight as though he meant it. Who'd kissed her...

As though he'd changed?

"I hope you're not upset about Sara," she said abruptly. "You know how kids talk, but I'm sure she doesn't know anything about sex beyond the basics."

"I figured that. After I'd had a chance to think about what she said."

"And I don't think we owe her any explanation about how we live. After all, she's the kid, and we're the parents, right?" She waved her magazine for emphasis.

He was looking straight at her, studying her with an intensity that was definitely unsettling. "Right."

"Just think," she rattled on brightly. "A few months ago, you might have accused me of telling her too much, being in the wrong, and you'd have used that information in the custody hearing."

His smile faded, and she was sorry she'd been blurting things out without thinking again. "Well, wouldn't you have?" she challenged.

He passed a weary hand over his forehead. "I'd have told Marta about it."

"And she would have gone from there. Morals charges." Of course, Libby thought, she herself would have made the same charges against Nate. All those women he'd been seen with around Chicago, before their marriage. The knowledge of how different she was from Nate's usual choice in women still hurt.

Nate studied his glass. "That's all past, isn't it?" When he looked up, she saw that rare vulnerability in his eyes, the expression he tried so hard to mask.

Her heart squeezed. "We have a strange arrangement. But in many ways, I guess it works."

He nodded, drained his glass. Libby tried not to examine her feelings too closely. Their marriage was nothing like what she'd contemplated a marriage to be. In many ways, it disappointed her still. Nate's continuing inability to really connect with Sara. Her own needs for real intimacy. But she and Nate got along better than she'd ever imagined. "Are you pleased with things exactly as they are?"

He gazed at her, his expression closed. "It was what I asked for, wasn't it?" There was a long pause. "Ah, are you? Pleased with how things are going?"

"Sure." What a lie, a whopper so big Libby would have disciplined Sara for telling one like it. But how could she say she wasn't satisfied, when Nate had given her everything he'd promised? Over the past few weekends, she'd dared to dream. Tonight, she'd dared... Oh, heck. Disappointed, Libby opened her magazine again, pretended to read. Nate picked up a copy of the local paper, the *Harborside Herald, Serving the Lake and the World.* The headline read, Water Commission All Wet on Drains Issue. In a minute, Nate appeared to be engrossed in the story.

Somewhere in the house, a clock ticked. Outside, there was the rhythmic whisper of waves on the beach.

"Tina and I had a talk," he finally said quietly.

"Tonight? About what?"

"The Point. Trevor. Among other things."

She nodded. "Tina said she was going to thank you. But I wondered if she really would."

"I respect the woman. I know the things she's been saying about me. She actually admitted it. Gutsy."

"Oh." Absently she fingered the magazine on her lap. Did Nate believe Libby thought those things, that she'd talked with Tina about Nate, criticized Nate? Well, she had, and suddenly some of the things she'd said seemed somehow disloyal. Some things between a husband and wife needed to stay at home, between them. That is, if he were a real husband, and she were a real wife. Confused, she shut her magazine.

He put down the newspaper. "Anyway. There's something I've wanted to talk to you about for a while. I don't want to break Trev's confidences, but I really could use some advice."

She felt herself begin to warm from the inside out. Her feelings for Nate might be confused, but this was cozy, to be sitting here talking with him like this, and the sensation was mixed with that lingering sense of anticipation from the square dance. "Okay. I won't tell him."

"Trevor wants me to find his father."

"Oh, no. Nate, you don't understand—"

"He thinks his father left because Trevor ended up in a wheelchair, and supposedly wouldn't be able to drive or have a normal relationship with a woman."

"But Trevor's doctor told Tina he can function…" She stopped as she felt the heat on her cheeks.

"I know. He told me. In some detail, as a matter of fact."

"Trevor told you all that?"

He ignored her astonishment, intent on what he was saying. "Do you think Trevor's right about why Jonathan Samms left?"

She didn't have to think about it. "I'm pretty sure that's what happened. Jonathan was very into sports and being what he called a 'real man.' He had affairs, and in a little town like Harborside, it was incredibly humiliating to Tina. But Trevor's injury, I think, was the clincher." She took a thoughtful sip of tea.

"Trevor wants to find him," Nate repeated.

"But why?"

"I'm not exactly sure. I think to tell his father that he *can* do all those things, in the hopes that he can have some kind of relationship with his old man. The thing is…" Nate stopped and looked away as though he was suddenly self-conscious, then, "Trev keeps talking about how I came back for Sara. That seems to have given him some impetus to find his own father."

"You couldn't have foreseen that."

He gave her a crooked smile. "I couldn't foresee a lot of things in this crazy town. What I'm concerned about is this. If Jonathan Samms is the bastard I think he is, how will Trev handle a rejection?"

She shook her head. "I don't know." She thought for a moment. "Maybe it's just as well that Jonathan's not been found."

Her words hung in the air for a moment. Then Nate said very quietly, "But he has."

"Oh, God. You found him?"

"Marta found him. He calls himself Jonathan Sinclair, and though he's never paid a dime of child support, he owns a charter flight service and a condo in Lake Tahoe. He also has a nineteen-year-old wife."

"Oh, God," Libby said again. "Does Trevor know you found him?"

"No. But when I saw him tonight, I almost told him. Libby, Trev is going to find his father. Maybe not this year. But eventually he'll find him, because he's determined. I know. Even when I was his age, if I'd wanted something as badly as he does, I'd have found a way." He leaned forward as he spoke.

Libby had no doubt of it. "But what will Trevor do if his father blows him off? How could he handle something like that? He's probably thinking about only one outcome."

Nate got up and went to the window. She could see his broad shoulders, then the reflection of his face in the blackness of the glass as he gazed at nothing. "I don't know a damn thing about kids. But, I've been thinking, my own father and I left so much unfinished business. He died at the track, did I ever tell you that?" He shoved his hands in his pockets. "Isn't that just like some damn soap opera, that my father died at the track of a heart attack just after he'd taken every last cent from his pocket and put it on a horse that didn't even place?''

Quietly, Libby got up and went to him. Without touching him, she stood next to him. Watching his reflection.

He spoke again quietly. ''For years, I've thought of all the things I wanted to say to him. Things like, I did okay, I made it, I'll never be like you.'' He hesitated. ''And the things for years I didn't think I'd ever want to say, because I didn't think I *felt* them. Somehow, this summer, I've been thinking about some of the stuff we did together. He's the one who first taught me to sail. He liked the water.''

''You like the water, too.''

''Yes.''

Very deliberately, she pulled his hand out of his pocket. Amazingly, he offered no resistance when she slipped her hand in his. The touch of palms—his hard, flat, hers callused—sent a wash of longing through her.

He lifted his other hand, absently made a trail in the faint dust of the sill. ''What I've been wondering, is whether Trevor doesn't have the right to *know*. Good or bad, so that he can get on with his life.''

She shook her head, sighed. ''I just don't know, Nate.''

He turned to her with a little smile. ''I thought when it came to kids, you had all the answers.''

''Maybe I've been willing to ask the questions, that's all. If I'm so great with kids, how come Trevor didn't come to me? How come he came to you?''

''Because I have money and lawyers, he said.''

''Come on.'' She squeezed his hand. ''That's not really why. He chose to talk to you. You're better with kids—people—than you give yourself credit for, Nate. I wish...'' She stopped. Quite suddenly, still conscious of his big hand linked with hers, she didn't feel like talking.

There was something about his vulnerability, his sharing,

his willingness to become involved, that did for Libby what all his money and class and perfection of form could not. She was suddenly full to the brim in feelings as heady and sweet as any she'd ever experienced.

She looked up at him and found him studying her. His eyes were fixed on her mouth, his lids half-closed.

Normally she would have looked down in confusion, in shyness. She almost did. But instead, she raised a finger and touched it to his lips. He sucked in a quick breath, but he didn't move. She'd always accused Nate of playing it safe with Sara. Of not believing in love.

But hadn't she been doing the same thing? Playing it so very, very safe? So afraid he would hurt her. Maybe he would. But how would she ever find out if she didn't take a chance?

After all, she had fallen in love with her husband.

A tad uncertainly, she traced his eyebrows with her finger. His cheek was freshly shaved, the skin satiny if she stroked downward, faintly scratchy if she brought her finger up. Through it all, he was still, and Libby almost forgot to breathe.

"Don't," he finally whispered harshly.

"Why not?" she whispered back.

His hands fisted by his sides. "I'm trying to be a gentleman here. You're making it—" he sucked in a breath as she traced the line of his lips "—damn hard."

She felt his breath against the pads of the two fingers she put across his lips to shush him. "I don't want you to be a gentleman."

As if in slow motion, he brought his hand up and covered hers. "I thought you didn't believe in it this way."

This way? Oh, *this* way. Sex without love? Was that what he was trying to say, that he didn't love her?

She knew that. All at once, she thought she knew exactly

what Nate was trying to tell her, that he always needed distance. But hadn't he shown her that he'd changed?

And did it matter? She'd be making love with Nate because *she* was in love. "Aren't you the one who told me that sex was pleasurable, natural between husband and wife?" She refused to look down, though her cheeks felt very hot.

There was silence, a long beat of silence.

Finally, he reached up to capture a lock of her hair, to run it between his fingers. "Do you know," he said in a husky whisper, "how soft this is? No hair spray, no styling gel."

"It flies all over. It's that awful red—"

He crushed a handful in his fist. "I like it."

How thrilling to hear him say so. Emboldened by the compliment, she put her hands on his shoulders and kissed him on the mouth, an openmouthed kiss that coaxed his lips to open under hers.

He gave a groan as he felt her tongue, and suddenly he was very involved, his hands stroking, then clutching her hips, pressing them intimately to his, rubbing her slowly over his arousal. Pleasure started where he was pressing, spread, returned to concentrate and grow deep within her. "You don't have to do this," he whispered finally.

"No," she said softly, "I don't. And if you're trying to say making love won't change anything between us, I know that."

There was confusion in his eyes before he closed them and kissed her again, kissed her so thoroughly that she could barely breathe.

Against her mouth, he said, "I...care about you. That's all I can say, but—"

"Stop." Before she surrendered fully to the curious combination of weakness and strength his kisses where conjuring, she had to say it. "I'm not asking for anything. You were the one who said we could...make love without becoming involved. That sex was just sex. Didn't you say that in so many words?"

He held her tightly to him as if he was afraid she'd pull away, but he looked down, straight into her eyes. "Yes. That's what I said."

The tiniest flash of disappointment went through her, because even now, she was fantasizing. But love was a gift, not something a person gave with expectations attached. "You said it was up to me. If. When. Where." She drew another deep breath. "So I'm saying yes. Now. In my bed."

Without another word, he swept her up in his arms and crossed to the hallway door. There he paused.

For the first time since her marriage, Libby felt like a bride. She felt small against his frame, tight with anticipation, very, very shy. The bare skin of her thighs touched the bare skin of his forearms. It was warm where their skin met. It was warm against his chest, where the worn chambray hid a wall of taut muscle. His heart thudded in rapid quickstep against her ear.

"Damn these small doorways," he whispered finally.

Belatedly, she looked up. Her house had a lot of narrow twists and turns. Against him, she smiled at Mr. Perfect, who was trying to do the right thing and carry her to bed but was foiled by her small, old house. "I can walk, you know."

"Right." He kissed her hard, then set her down in front of him. As she climbed the stairs, she had the sensation that he was watching her, her hips and her legs. Nate. Her husband. Tonight for the first time, he'd sleep in her bed.

She went into her room, but didn't turn on the light. In the living room, she'd been as aggressive as she'd ever been in her life. Now she needed the darkness. It had been so long.

"So very long," he whispered, his hand finding her breast, caressing. For the barest second she thought he could read her thoughts, and they were so carnal, she blushed. Then she wondered. A long time for him, too? What a fanciful notion.

But then she couldn't think at all as his hands did slow, wonderful things. In the dark, she saw the gleam of his wedding band as his hands pulled up her T-shirt. He unclasped her bra, and her breasts were in his hands, then. Her breath quickened, and she started to sway toward him.

"Sara's asleep?" He whispered the question.

She whispered, "Yes."

"I'll go close her door."

Oh. Good idea. She grabbed for the edges of her T-shirt, suddenly shy again.

He paused in the doorway. "You've got a choice. You can wait for me to undress you. Or you can get naked while I'm gone."

She didn't have the nerve to take off her clothes while he was gone. So she stood there, the edges of her T-shirt still in her hands, her bare toes digging into the worn braided rug.

When he returned, he closed and locked the door. Hearing the rusty scrape of the lock, Libby felt a moment's panic. Lord, after all this time, just after they'd reached an understanding of sorts about how they were going to live together, their relationship was about to change irrevocably.

He seemed to have no such last-minute panic. "Now, where were we?" He caught her around the waist, bent her to his powerful body and kissed her.

Over on the bed, there was a square of light from the window, but here by the door it was dark. The darkness was curiously safe and dangerous at the same time. Safe because her imperfect body was hidden from his experienced eye, dangerous because in the dark he was mysterious, larger than life. He groaned when she opened the buttons on his shirt and pushed her hands inside. Her palms were on his warm flesh.

He slipped her T-shirt over her head. "Now," he said, and he pulled her to him, rubbing her against his body so that her nipples became exquisitely stimulated by the hair of his chest. She moaned, too.

It had been so long. She'd waited so long. She'd spent so much time with him near and untouchable that she felt drawn tight, captured and tumbled by something as powerful as the storm on the lake. She started to tremble. Nate. *Husband.* Lover.

If. Where. When. *Now.* Without shyness any longer, she slipped out of her cutoff jeans and underwear and stood naked before him.

He took off his own jeans. She heard the rustle, felt his body bend, straighten, and then she was aloft again, carried and gently set down on the center of the square of light, right in the middle of her own bed.

Looming over her, he blocked the light, held her with hands on both cheeks and kissed her hard. With thoroughness and care and passion. His skin was like a blanket on the beach, warmed by the sun.

As he kissed her neck, emotion welled in her. Happiness that she'd waited for this man to come into her life. As he nipped her shoulder, happiness that he was her husband, the man who'd come back for his child. As he trailed his open mouth along the inside of her arm, she cried out at the wave of sensation that rushed through her.

Then, overwhelmed with love and sensation, she grabbed at his shoulders, swung her body and rolled on top of him.

She kissed him, touched his ear with her tongue, took a tiny nip at his neck. Then, emboldened by his harsh breath and hoarse murmurs, she closed her eyes and moved lower. Chest. Broad, hairy, male. His flat stomach.

Her chin brushed his erection, and he almost leaped off the bed. Grabbing a fistful of quilt, he groaned. Libby opened her eyes. Oh my. He was so very…aroused. Slowly, she lifted her head.

In his passion, his head had come off the bed, and now she looked into his shadowed face. The light from outdoors had washed and cleaned his features so that he was all angles and planes, a perfect melding of male form and function.

"Come here," he said in a raspy whisper, and he pulled her to him, up along his body, until when she reached him she was gasping. He rolled her to her side, facing her, and touched her between her thighs. Intimately. She gasped again. She leaned in to kiss his shoulder, to have something to press against as this incredible sensation got bigger and bigger. Without thinking, she bit down.

He jerked, moaned.

"Oh, I'm sorry!" She tried to sit up, but he grabbed her arm.

"No," he said thickly. "No sorry. Do what you want. Just…" He stopped as if there were no words.

So she lay back and let him touch her. This time, she turned her cheek to the quilt, feeling the seams of the old fabric, the valleys of tiny stitches against her face.

And when she was oh, so close, when her lips pressed so very tightly against the bedding, he pulled her hips to his. Taking her hand, he guided it to his arousal. "When you're ready," he said, and his voice sounded strained and gritty.

She was momentarily confused. They were on their

sides, facing each other, and she had expected him to come over her, take her, press against her with his power. But, no. They would share this moment, side by side. She'd never been so ready for anything in her life. She took his hard length in her hands and slipped it inside.

His breath whooshed out but he didn't move. It took her a second to realize that he wanted her to move her hips, to fill herself with him. She inched down and against him, his thighs tangled with hers, his chest pressed hard against her breasts, his arm looping around her neck as if he meant to hold on to every last inch of her. It had been a long time, but this felt right. So very right that she couldn't believe she'd shared a house with this man yet resisted him so long.

She opened her eyes, gazed into his. They were open, a shadowy gleam. "Hi," he said softly. "Hi," she said back. It was the greeting he gave her every Friday night. It was too dark to read his expression, but the one syllable now sounded as if he was greeting her for the first time ever.

Libby hadn't wanted to love this man, but she did. So she showed him love, holding back nothing. With her hands, with her mouth, with her entire being, she gave herself to him.

He had started out slowly, tenderly. But soon, inevitably, he demanded. And she was glad, for as he thrust into her, she felt her desire grow and quicken.

He groaned again at the end, harsh and fierce, and the knowledge that she pleased him fired her own passion. She saw a field of orange—poppies, daylilies, laid out under yellow sunshine so bright and hot it hurt her eyes. She shuddered in climax and held Nate tight so he could see it, too.

CHAPTER THIRTEEN

NATE WOKE to a breeze stirring the sheer curtain at the window. The night had been warm, and they'd kicked off the quilt and sheets. Now Libby lay asleep next to him, her hair damp with perspiration.

He picked up a lock of red hair that had fallen across the bridge of her nose, smoothed it back across her neck, not wanting to wake her. Not wanting to wake *his wife*.

If she awoke, this would have to end. It would have to end all too soon, anyway. After all, Sara would be up soon; his daughter was an early riser. And she'd asked those questions last night—had it only been last night? Yes. He had no idea where he and Libby went from here, and he couldn't confuse Sara further just now.

How foolish he'd been to assume he and Libby could be intimate and have it be just physical. He'd already known, bone deep, that Libby was like no other woman he'd ever met, so how could he have imagined he could have physical release without involvement?

She rolled on her back and snored a little, a tiny, ordinary-sounding, unladylike snore. He couldn't help smiling. This woman gave so much, turned a simple act like love-making into something fine and special.

He didn't deserve that. He didn't deserve *her*. He'd never been good at sharing feelings.

He let out a breath, planted a whisper-soft kiss on her shoulder and got out of bed. He might not deserve her, but he had her, and she had him. Stuck with each other. Different as night and day. And coming together with such sparks.

He picked up his discarded jeans and, forgoing his briefs, started to slide them on. Well, he and Libby were married, and they'd made love, but even in the flush of wonderment, he wasn't naive enough to think that one night of lovemaking—no matter how profound—could make up for their differences.

But it did change things. She'd been right. It did change things. She was creeping into his heart.

Did he dare let her in?

After all, he was no gambler.

Nate finished putting on his jeans, then opened the door and peered out. No Sara. Holding his shirt, underwear and sneakers, he headed down the hall to his room.

NATE HADN'T REALLY looked at her all day. Right now he was showing Sara some stupendously wonderful computer game that would only work on his supermegabyted machine. He'd brought the whole works downstairs and had set it out on the dining-room table.

Sara was thrilled with the new toy, the kind of toy that had never come into her life before Nate. Yet, in unguarded moments, her face was quiet, more content. Today, she didn't seem as careful to keep a little distance between her body and Nate's. Libby was glad of that, too. Maybe Sara, who'd gone through so much with her stepfather, was finally coming to trust Nate. Maybe Nate would somehow pick up on the change...

And maybe pigs would fly. A favorite saying of her father's, and never one to fail.

After all, Libby should know. After their night together, after they'd been as intimate as two people could be, he'd hardly looked at her. It wasn't that she'd expected hearts and flowers, but couldn't the man *look* at her?

Suddenly, as if feeling her eyes on him, he glanced up. She met his eyes. Over the blip of computer death and oblivion, they stared at each other.

His jaw tightened, his eyes stayed locked on hers. Then, as if unbidden, he smiled, a tiny smile so warm with shared secrets that she almost stopped breathing. And she knew in that moment that whatever Nate wanted to pretend, last night had meant something to him. Maybe something bigger than he knew.

His pager went off and the moment was lost. But she would never forget that look in his eyes, would hug it to herself at night when he was in Chicago and she couldn't sleep for wondering what he was doing there.

Nate pushed the button to silence the pager and stood up. "I'll use the kitchen phone."

Libby wandered into the living room. Outside, the day was brilliant. When she could pry Sara away from the keyboard, she'd suggest a swim.

She didn't intend to listen, but she overheard snatches of conversation. Nate raised his voice at one point. "Well, then for God's sake, tell them!" Finally, he said, "Yes, I get it—" and then "—all right."

A couple of minutes later he came into the living room, where she was refolding a quilt. "I've got to go back to Chicago."

"When?" She kept her voice carefully bright.

He raked a hand through his hair. "Right now."

Disappointment stabbed her. "Oh, Nate, you just got here." The memory of last night lingered. She'd been hoping for tonight... "Sara will be disappointed. I was going to suggest we have a swim and roast hot dogs after. I bought marshmallows. I actually gave in to nitrates and wall-to-wall sugar.'' Oh boy, she thought. Roasting wieners and toasting marshmallows. Just the thing to tempt Nate to stay.

"Sounds like fun." Was she imagining the wistfulness in his voice?

"Stay," she said softly.

There was a long silence. "I can't," he said finally. "Something's come up in Chicago."

There had been casual references to problems in Chicago before. Libby had ignored them, sure that Nate was in total control. Those problems had not seemed vital, anyway, not compared to whatever was going on in Sara's life, or in Tina's, not as elemental as too many bills at the end of the month. Now, maybe because she felt so in tune with him, she picked up on things. The tension in his shoulders, the tight set of his jaw.

"Problems? Real problems, I mean?" she asked with genuine sympathy.

He looked at her for another long moment. "Real problems," he agreed.

"Tell me."

"You don't want to know." He sounded offhand, but was there a note of hurt in his voice?

"Tell me," she urged again.

"I can handle it."

"Nate. I'm your wife, remember?"

It was a reminder of a hot night behind a closed door. Husband. Wife. Still, he hesitated. Finally, he said, "Walk with me?"

"Sure." He must be impatient to be off, yet he was willing to take at least some time for her. Libby called to Sara that they were going for a walk, and received only a one-syllable sound of acknowledgment.

Nate motioned for her to go ahead of him through the

sunporch door to the yard. They walked along the narrow beach, passing the boundary of her property. Next door, the Matwings, husband and wife, were deadheading the climbing roses. Libby had a quick wish that Nate liked chores. She quickly suppressed the thought, as though it was faintly disloyal.

"Funny," Nate said finally. "Nobody seems to care if people trespass."

"Nope," she agreed. "The lake's big enough for us all." But she knew what he meant. Out East, where she'd gone to school, large stretches of ocean were patrolled on behalf of owners who thought a stray jogger posed a threat. "Now," she said gently, "you have to go, and I'd like to hear about your problems."

He stopped. "Why now? Because of last night?"

Because I love you, and now I want to be your life partner, in every way possible, to share your burdens, to bring you joy. "Yes," she said, "because of last night."

He gave a harsh chuckle. "I must have been better than I thought."

"You were great," she said.

"You were…" He stopped and looked away.

She wished she knew what he was going to say. "Are you angry that I haven't paid attention to your business before?"

After a second, he started walking again. "I guess so," he admitted, sounding surprised. "I guess because it was important to me, I wanted it to be important to you."

"It is," she said, and she spontaneously took his hand. "Everything you do is important to me. But you're right. I've been so sure everything in Harborside is so superior, I've just…let you handle things."

"I *can* handle things. But my workers have finally

walked off the job at the Iris Complex. An honest-to-God wildcat.''

Libby knew that was bad.

He turned to face the water, toward Bittersweet Point, and used a hand to shade his eyes. "I'm going to go over the time limit in my contract. That means I pay fines. Fines for every day I'm late.''

Every *day?* "Do these fines amount to a lot of money?'' He shrugged, but she could read a wealth of worry into the one gesture. "Do you have enough to ride things out, Nate?'' she asked very, very quietly.

His voice was just as quiet. "How would you feel if I didn't?''

God, was he saying he didn't have the money? She couldn't believe it, but that's what he was implying. Of course, if it was a lot of money…and it surely was. Well, she was in love with the man, and that emotion had never had anything to do with the amount of money he had. In fact, that money had been a barrier, something that made him seem not quite real, and certainly it was a barrier to him being willing to share her simple life-style in Harborside.

He waited. She felt a flash of pure elation. Maybe this was the best thing that could happen.

No.

She couldn't be that selfish. Success in business was important to Nate. She couldn't wish him ill, even if she'd spent sleepless nights cursing his money and his lawyer and all the power that the money brought.

She must have taken too long to reply because he brought his hand down and turned toward the direction they'd come. "That's what I thought.''

"Oh, Nate. For Heaven's sake. *Look* at me,'' she finally said sharply, and gave a yank on his arm for good measure.

He looked, and in his eyes she saw the end of a dream. "Nate, I don't give a damn about the money, do you hear me? I never gave a damn, and I've said so often enough that you ought to believe it. What I give a damn about is you. You're my husband. My partner."

He gave a mirthless chuckle. "A partner who's about to become worth considerably less."

"Never. You could never be less to me, unless you stop trying, unless you become that closed-up man I first met. Do you know how much you've changed? You're... softer." He gave her a funny look. "Okay, bad choice of words." She tried a laugh, but it came out sounding tinny and false. She had an overriding sense that her next words were important, and a scary feeling that she wasn't up to the task of choosing them.

"You try, Nate. You're not so sure you have all the answers anymore." She thought, went on. "You're involved. You make breakfast for us all, drive Sara to her horseback-riding lessons, go along with whatever she and I have planned for the evenings. You're doing something for Trevor. Before, would you have even known he needed you? And you keep trying with Sara, even though I know she hurts you sometimes."

Too close to shore, a powerboat came speeding by. The wake sent in a few waves, bigger than before. One wet Libby's worn sneakers. She took a quick step back. "I'm proud you're my husband," she said to his back.

He took a backhanded swipe at his eyes. "Sweat," he said quickly. "It's hot."

"Right," she said, aghast that her powerful husband would shed a tear at her words, words that hadn't begun to convey her feelings.

Finally, he let out a long breath and turned. "We need to head back," he said quietly. "Iris won't stand delay."

"What will you do?"

"I'll get them back to work eventually. Then I'll assess the damage. Round up some financing. Jeff heard about a guy who's formed a new investment group. They're looking for some high-return investments, and they're willing to take high risks." His smile was undeniably bitter. "In other words, they're willing to gamble on Nate Perry and his reputation for pulling off a project in the end. Now I've got to do a bit of wooing."

"You'll do fine."

He smiled finally. "You sound confident. Got some spare cash, too?"

She took her cue from Nate, made sure her tone was light. "I'll take a hammer to Sara's piggy bank."

The tension eased somewhat. Libby was right about how he was changing. For so long, she'd denied to herself that he was changing because she was afraid she'd fall for him. But he was a good man, an honorable man.

He was the man of her heart.

They were almost back home when he spoke again. "Bittersweet Point is what screwed me up. I was cash poor when I got involved."

"Bittersweet Point? Then why *did* you get involved?"

"For Sara," he said simply. "Kevin Smithson convinced me that if I had a stake in the town, I'd get more sympathy from the judge."

Never would she have imagined that he'd knowingly make a bad business decision because of his daughter. So his motives had been right, all along, even if trying to curry favor with the judge was the wrong way to go about things. Realization of how harshly she'd judged him, realization that she loved him, twined through her. The words she longed to say, the I-love-yous, remained unsaid. She'd wait. He had business to conduct, some storms to ride out. When she said she loved him, she wanted him ready to hear it, with his heart open and free. She only hoped that day would finally come.

He stopped on the middle of her beach. Over at Bittersweet Point, the one condominium still stood, stark and ugly.

A thought struck her. She didn't know a thing about Nate's business, but... "Is there something you could do to reduce your costs on Bittersweet Point? I've seen the *Herald* articles on the Point. You've got so much going on over there. Docks, a marina, restaurants, indoor tennis courts—just so much."

"The kind of buyers we want to attract demand those amenities. I'm known for offering that type of environment. An upscale playground, my literature always says."

"Well, how about a downscale playground? A *middlescale* playground." Suddenly excited, she gripped his arm. "How about something for families? Look at how limited the housing is around here. People rent the cottages, but some of them are so shabby and inadequate. Wouldn't they buy something if they could afford it? Not something fancy, but something new and pleasant?"

He shook his head, and in spite of the problems he had, there was a spark of genuine amusement in his eyes. "Always thinking of family, Libby. Now don't get your back up," he said quickly. "I wasn't making fun of you, just...smiling a little. Okay?"

"Okay."

"Listen, I've got to go." He leaned forward and kissed her lightly on the mouth. "I really need you pulling for me this time."

"What can I do?"

"Just stand there a minute. I want to remember you like

you are today, real and genuine. Barefoot, in a yellow romper, with the wind in your hair.''

AFTER NATE LEFT, Libby and Sara got out the old charcoal grill. Sara was pleased at the idea of junk food, and she ate way too many gooey, blackened marshmallows. Libby even tried one herself. It stuck to her lips. She shuddered and Sara laughed.

But the day seemed hollow without Nate. That was a frightening feeling, because it would always be like this. She would be alone much of the time, seeing him off, waiting for him to return, building her life around two days at the end of the workweek.

Now, without him, the sun going down behind Bittersweet Point didn't seem as brilliant, the pink sky wasn't as vivid, and she didn't get that familiar pleasure when she spotted the blue heron fishing off her dock.

Sara, too, seemed quieter than usual. When Libby asked her what she was thinking about, Sara said, "Nothing." When she suggested Sara try the computer game again, she said she was waiting for Nate, because they had a tournament going and it wouldn't be fair to practice too much in between. When Libby suggested a walk, Sara claimed her stomach hurt from too many marshmallows.

So Sara sat on an old wedding-ring quilt in the yard and listlessly picked a grass blade to chew.

Libby chewed over issues instead. She wanted to help. Nate had dismissed her suggestion that the Point be turned over to families. Libby knew she was no asset to Nate in business. But the man she loved was in trouble. It didn't sit well that she was in Harborside waiting for the grill to cool down so she could scrub it, and he was in Chicago fighting for his professional life.

Bittersweet Point. She couldn't get it out of her mind.

For one thing, she knew that Nate had left Tina's condominium standing at some cost to himself. It needed to be torn down so building could begin. In fact, some of the foundations had already been dug. The sugar cube stood smack in the middle of the work.

A thought struck her. She could do something. Maybe it was more symbolic than real, but it would help. Not just Nate, either. Maybe she had a real chance to put some things right. She shot to her feet. "Come on, Sara. Let's take a little drive."

A FEW MINUTES LATER, Libby stood in the huge, hospital-white kitchen at Bittersweet Point. Tina was furious.

"How dare Nate Perry interfere with my life?" Tina's eyes were snapping. "How dare he go looking for Jonathan without even talking to me about it? And all along, he's been talking to Trevor behind my back! Trevor's *my* son."

Libby winced, but she spoke calmly. "I told you, Trevor doesn't know. Without your permission, Nate won't tell him Jonathan's been found."

During their discussion, Tina had been stamping around the island in the kitchen. Outside, Trevor and Sara shot hoops, and there was the rhythmic *thunk* of the ball bouncing off the garage doors.

Now Libby struggled with some anger of her own at the rigid way Tina looked at the world, her willingness to believe the worst of Nate.

Tina slapped her palm on the countertop. "It's not like the guy has done so great with his own kid!"

"That's not fair, Tina. Nate has tried very hard with Sara, under tough circumstances. It's okay to be angry, but it's not okay anymore to take potshots at Nate."

"Give me a break."

"He's my husband," Libby said quietly, but with a new conviction. "My first loyalty will always be to him."

"We've been friends for twenty-five years!"

Impulsively, Libby got up and looped her arm around Tina's shoulders. "You'll always have my friendship. You and Trevor are among the most important people in my life."

"But you'll choose *him* over me?"

She took a deep breath. It was hard to say her next words. "If it's necessary, yes."

"God." Tina sank into a chair. When she looked up, her eyes were wet with tears. "I never thought you'd say that."

"Who's the most important person in your life?"

She took a swipe at her eyes. "Tough question. You know who."

"Then talk to Trevor. You have to take chances, even with the people you hold most dear." She gave Tina's tight shoulder a squeeze. "Nate hasn't done anything more than talk to your son. All these months you've had misgivings about whether Trevor's really happy. You know that despite all those jokes he makes, he can't sleep. You know he sits on that deck and broods. You know what he wants and you can support that decision or you can see him grow more and more distant from you."

Tina was rigid for a second more, and then her shoulders slumped and she sobbed. Libby knelt and gathered her friend close, the way she'd do with Sara. The sobs came and came. "I just...Jonathan hurt Trevor so...he hurt me...I didn't dare...and if I admitted I needed him, even financially, then I wouldn't be standing on my own..."

"He owes this family," Libby said firmly, her heart squeezing in sympathy for Tina and outrage at what Jonathan had put her friend through. "That you need him financially doesn't say a thing about your independence.

Like Nate says, he fathered a kid and now he doesn't want to take any responsibility. So, you force him to take responsibility. With him contributing his fair share, you can afford the kind of place your son deserves. And Trevor gets what he needs emotionally.''

Tina blew her nose. ''What exactly *is* that? What could Trevor possibly need from a father he hasn't seen in four years?''

Libby shared Nate's thoughts about Trevor needing to see Jonathan, to get some perspective on his father as Trevor was coming into manhood himself.

''I don't know,'' Tina finally said, calmer now. ''I know Nate isn't the bastard I thought he was. I think I knew that long ago, just because Trevor knew, and Trevor is the most perceptive kid sometimes…'' She got up, went to the sink and filled the teakettle.

''If you thought that, why didn't you stick up for Nate, instead of warning me against him?''

Hesitating, Tina finally said, ''I've been so jealous of you.''

''Of me?'' Libby was astonished.

Tina put down the kettle and stood at the counter, her hands gripping the edge. ''Even before Nate. You had your shop. I could cope with that, even though my business was less…tangible. When Julia died, we got even closer. You had Sara and we were both single moms. And then Nate came. I thought he might hurt you. But in a way…'' Libby had to strain to hear her next words. ''In a way I was afraid. I wanted him to be a jerk because then he'd go, or you'd send him away and things would be like they used to be. You and me.'' She turned and gave Libby a watery smile. ''Two independent broads who take on the world from a little out-of-the-way place called Harborside.''

''Oh, Tina.'' Libby swallowed. ''I listened to you about

Nate." How could she not have seen this side of her friend? After all, before Sara came, she herself had envied her friend her son.

Tina's head was down. "Can you forgive me?"

Libby thought, but not for very long. Tina's words against Nate had been motivated by fear and by anger at men in general, but also by a genuine concern for Libby. Libby had felt that concern in a thousand ways, when Tina had taken over the shop when Libby was down with the flu, when Tina had gone with Libby to the emergency room that time Sara fell off her bike, when Tina had opened her home to her all those Christmases when Libby was alone, before she had Sara and Nate.

"There's nothing to forgive." She rose and held out her arms. "You're stuck with me. Friends. Buddies. Comrades-in—" The last word was lost in a poof of breath as Tina flew across the kitchen and hugged her. They clung together for a moment before Tina pulled away. "If Nate is the man you want, I'll do anything to support you. I'll even give the guy a fair shot."

Libby smiled and spoke the words in her heart. "I haven't said anything yet. Lord only knows if I'll scare the man to death when I finally do say it. But I love him."

Tina said, "Then I wish you all the happiness in the world. And the luck." To her credit, she didn't add that Libby would need it. There was a pause, then Tina spoke again. "I guess I'd better get Trevor. It's time we had an honest discussion about his feelings for Jonathan."

DEAR DAD,

I suppose you know by now that Mom found you, since you must have gotten your papers from the court about a hearing on the child support. So you'll be here on August fifteenth. Mom really, really needs the

money. She does okay with her sewing, better than
before the—

Trevor paused and bit his pencil eraser, not wanting to have
to say the word *divorce* or remind his father of all the fights
between his parents.

…better than before. She wouldn't ask you, except we
have to move. So if you could be okay about it, that
would be cool.

Anyway, I want to see you. I've wanted to for a
long time. I figure we can shoot hoops. I can do lots
of sports, you know.

Trevor crossed out the "you know" part. This letter was
much harder to write than he'd thought it would be. He got
a sicko kind of pinch right in his gut every time he thought
about seeing his dad.

For a moment he turned to his list, which had columns
of all the stuff he could do. He'd put it in his computer so
he could add stuff as he thought of it. Even using the small-
est type, the list had grown to more than a page. He'd
planned to include the list with the letter, but now he
thought maybe he should wait. Like when he saw his dad,
he could maybe *show* his dad the coolest things.

Maybe when they met, his dad would say something, do
something that would make it easy for them to hug and
stuff. His mother hugged him, and now that Trevor was
pretty much grown-up, he didn't mind, as long as his mom
only did it in private.

Will you call me when you get to town? I'll talk to
Mom so you won't feel weird or anything when you
call.

Trevor read what he'd written and frowned. The letter sounded like something a little kid would write. So he added some stuff about sports and complicated statistics about the baseball pennant race. That way his father would know Trevor wasn't going to act like a baby when they met again. After all, his father probably thought he was helpless, and he most definitely wasn't.

Trevor flexed his muscles, admiring the good big bulge of his biceps. His legs might be wasted but his arms were totally awesome.

He picked up his pencil. Now how to end this thing. Your son, Trevor? Sincerely, Trevor? Yeah, right. How dopey could you get? Yours truly, Trevor? Double barf.

Love, Trev.

CHAPTER FOURTEEN

"IT'S A GREAT IDEA," Nate said. He was sitting across from Kevin Smithson at Harborside Savings and Loan. On the mahogany conference table between them were a new set of blueprints and piles of paper, all covered with numbers. Nate had just driven in from Chicago; in fact his luggage was still in the trunk of the Jag.

"On paper your plan looks profitable. But why do you want to change the whole concept of the Point midstream?" Kevin played with his pipe. He was so young he looked rather silly sporting a pipe, especially because he'd tamped tobacco into it repeatedly but never made a move to actually light the thing.

But Nate didn't smile. "It's something Libby suggested."

Kevin raised his eyebrows, but Nate resisted the urge to defend himself. A good businessman listened to everybody, then made his decisions.

"Libby knows this area," Nate told the banker. "She said there was a shortage of vacation housing for families. So my assistant and I checked it out. She's right. Over nearer Cleveland, they're glutted with upscale developments right now. Even here, there's pressure. Look at our projected first-year vacancy statistics." Nate shoved a paper under Kevin's nose.

Kevin pushed it around with the mouthpiece of his pipe,

thinking. "But you've only got one consumer poll telling us how a family-type thing would sell."

"I don't have hard figures," Nate said, trying to contain his impatience. "That's because nobody does this kind of thing around here. Yet." It was a hell of a gamble, no doubt about it, to build a resort for people who weren't in the habit of thinking they could afford anything like a vacation condo. "Look at the numbers, Kevin. Not putting in all the add-ons means we could sell these things very reasonably. I have super marketing people in Chicago who would do up a concept when the time came to sell them. Doing it this way gives us a lot more wiggle room."

"But you still want the same amount of financial backing from the bank, even though these will cost less to build."

"Yes."

Kevin put down the pipe and leaned forward. "What is Harborside Savings and Loan subsidizing for you?"

The guy got right to the point. Nate had had several strategies figured out for handling this meeting, but at the last second he settled for the simplest: honesty. "The Iris Complex. I've got the numbers on that in my briefcase."

"Why would a little bank like ours want in on something as big as Iris?"

"Because you stand to make money."

"Make money or lose money?" Kevin countered.

"Look, you either believe in me or you don't. The time is long past since I've gone begging."

Kevin looked at him for a long moment. "You have my respect. In the end, all someone really has is his belief in a man's integrity and grit. Isn't that true?"

"Yes."

Kevin waved the pipe. "This'll have to clear the loan committee."

"Kevin, your father-in-law is president of the bank. I'm sure his floor limit is high."

Kevin was grinning now. "It does help to be a big fish in a small pond, doesn't it? Okay, friend. Let's go get a piece of cherry pie at the Shoreline and celebrate the family-condo concept."

THAT NIGHT, Nate stood in the hallway holding his garment bag and briefcase, and agreed to drive Sara to rehearsal for *Fiddler on the Roof*. Libby could pick Sara up after rehearsal, but she couldn't take Sara there because she'd promised the garden club she'd make a sunflower centerpiece for the head table at the High Summer Luncheon. Libby's part wasn't being rehearsed that night anyway.

"I'm sorry, I know you just got home," Libby said apologetically as she rushed barefoot through the house in her cutoff jeans and a faded purple T-shirt advertising floral preservative. "Sara, come on now, you're going to be late and I know Nate must want a shower after that drive in. Sara! Where are you? Now, drat that blue pitcher. I can't do van Gogh and the darn sunflowers without my blue pitcher. *Where* did I put it?"

Nate walked into the kitchen and rummaged around in the cabinet under the sink, where he'd seen Libby put the pitcher the week before. He held it up. "This?"

"Yes. Oh, how do you *do* that?" At his frown of puzzlement, she wiped the back of her hand over her sweaty upper lip. "You know, look all pulled together and perfect all the time."

Because he did all his worrying on the inside, Nate thought. He paused, then took Libby's arm and used his other hand to deliberately smooth her hair away from her hot forehead. She caught her breath at the gesture; she smelled like sun and greens. "Hi," he said softly.

"Oh. Hi." She shook her head quickly and looked up at him with a tiny, secret smile.

How he'd missed her!

"Later?" she whispered.

"Later," he confirmed, thrilled at her eagerness, the way she seemed to hunger for him the way he desperately wanted her.

Now more than ever he needed to be successful. He wanted her to be proud. He wanted to give her and Sara the security he'd lacked. He wanted his money and he wanted his family. In short, he wanted it all.

"I hate for you to have to hit the road again so soon after you got home," she said.

"I don't mind." It was the polite, charming thing one said automatically when asked for a favor. But the funny thing was, he *didn't* mind. He felt he belonged on the rare occasions Libby asked him to do something for her. Usually, everything was clean and dusted and ready on Friday nights, as though he were a guest in her house.

He frowned with a sudden thought. Libby had said this was *home*. Home. For him, too? What a warm thought. What a frightening thought, because he was dangerously close to letting her into all those places inside him that had been closed and locked for so many years he'd never thought he'd open them again.

"Sara!" she called again.

Sara came pounding down the stairs. "I'm ready." She skidded to a stop in the doorway of the kitchen and then she noticed Nate. "Oh, hi."

"Hi." As always, he got this funny lump in his throat when he saw Sara. After these months of getting to know her, it was easier to believe she was ten years old, but somehow the reality was always a tad shocking. He pulled his keys from his pocket.

"You don't have to stay at the rehearsal," Libby said as he held the door open for Sara. "I'll be done at the Legion Hall in plenty of time to pick her up."

But Nate stayed. He didn't mind sitting in the darkened auditorium on one of the bleachers, watching Sara run through a couple of songs. Several other parents were there, and they were joined by some of the adult cast. There was a low hum of whispering, as a dozen unrelated conversations went on around him. Onstage, a group was finishing "Sunrise, Sunset," a bittersweet song about time passing that made Nate shift uncomfortably. He remembered the song.

But now Sara was singing a happier tune about a matchmaker, and she and a couple of other girls came right to the edge of the stage and belted it out. Sara was the prettiest of the three, and the most talented. She definitely had a flair for the dramatic, throwing her arms out in an exuberant, totally unselfconscious way.

Hey, his kid was great. Nate was a good judge of these things. He had season tickets to both the experimental and the conventional theater in Chicago. His daughter was every bit as good—for her age—as any actress he'd seen.

He smiled as Sara hit two false notes in a row.

"Ouch," the mother next to him said under her breath.

"She's good, don't you think?" Nate asked her eagerly. "That's my daughter."

The mother smiled at him in the dark. "Sara Perry. I know who she is."

Nate nodded, unaccountably pleased that this woman—who was a stranger to him—knew his daughter, used her new last name freely. Who wouldn't love this child? This talkative, gifted child who, without even trying, could steal your heart? Who wouldn't want to throw their arms around her and...

His mind turned quickly from the thought, then came back of its own accord. With all the worries about Iris, he ought to just let his relationship with Sara ride a while.

But that was getting harder to do. As he felt his old world narrowing, pinching, he wanted to come into the new world, to be spontaneous. To hug his little girl.

But she made sure he didn't. They spent time together; she seemed happy to see him on Friday nights. But she never got really close to him. She never said she loved him. She never called him anything but Nate.

"Nate!" Sara was standing on the edge of the stage, calling him.

He walked to the bottom of the stage. Sara leaned over. "Mr. Greenfield says I can do my lines with my father. My big scene." Nate was confused. With him? "Except Mr. Murphy isn't here. Mr. Murphy is Tevye," she added by way of explanation.

Oh, the father in the *play*. Now he understood. He'd last seen *Fiddler* at a posh dinner theater in Chicago years ago, in those early days when losing his daughter had been a constant raw wound inside him. The story of a father trying to cling to tradition, yet deal with modern daughters, had been hard for a man in his circumstances to watch.

"Come on, Nate." Sara's voice was a little whiny. "I need someone to play Tevye. Mr. Greenfield will give you a script." Nate looked up to see that Mr. Greenfield was indeed going to the edge of the stage, where a long table held coffee and scripts.

Nate was no actor. The idea of strutting around the stage reading a bunch of lines was completely foreign, a public display of strong emotion—even if acting a part—uncomfortable.

"Maybe one of the other parents, or one of the boys…"

"A *boy?*" Sara was definitely whiny. "The *boys* are

shorter than me, and I have to look *up* to do this scene right.''

Mr. Greenfield came over to Sara and looked down at Nate, too. ''Mr. Perry, all you have to do is read with a little inflection to give Sara something to bounce off. Start out pushing that milk cart and then get up and walk around when your daughter makes you angry.'' He chuckled. ''I'm sure you have some experience in that area.''

Not exactly. Sara was on her best behavior on weekends. Over the phone during the week, he could sense sometimes that Libby and Sara had had a rocky day, but they didn't share it with him. It was that guest thing that they both kept up. At first, he'd liked things that way. Neat. Quiet. Contained. But now, he wished....

''Go ahead,'' one of the fathers called. ''We'll watch— and critique.'' A couple of people clapped.

Self-consciously, Nate mounted the steps to the stage. He was used to being in the public eye. But that was on his own turf. Now this stage felt too high, well-lit, exposed. He took the script and walked over to the cart, the old wooden floorboards creaking loudly. He began the scene with other characters.

Sara entered stage left and began her lines. She was Chava, the third daughter. Even so, the part was for a teenager, and Nate felt a rush of pride that the director had thought Sara good enough.

Sara/Chava leaned forward earnestly and read one of the lines that begged for her father's understanding.

Tevye was a warm, caring man, but Nate read the lines woodenly. Sara forged on. Finally, she said, ''Come on, Nate. You're ruining my ability to *conjure emotion* here.''

Nate would have laughed if he weren't so conscious of everyone watching him. He took a breath and put more emotion into his part. In fact, he strode about for emphasis, though he felt ridiculous when he did so.

"Very good, Tevye," Mr. Greenfield said genially. "I guess I won't have to make you sing 'If I Were a Rich Man' to get you in the mood, after all."

Sara strolled around the stage, in her element, although she wore a jean skirt and silver lamé sneakers instead of the peasant garb that would presumably be her costume on opening night. She talked about marrying a young man, being desperate for her father's approval. With only occasional instructions from the director, she floated around, sometimes looking earnestly at Tevye, sometimes playing for the tiny audience of parents.

And Tevye wanted to give his approval. Nate felt Tevye's love for his daughter, yet his resistance to her choice of husband. Tevye spoke to Nate's own uncertainties, his fear of his daughter withholding her love, his fears for Sara's happiness. His wishes, his dreams.

Tevye pointed out the importance of tradition.

Nate thought of how he'd maintained the status quo with Sara all this time.

Tevye reflected on his daughter's happiness as she spoke of her young man. Happiness that would be complete if her father gave his blessing. If he took a chance.

Was it time for Nate to take a chance? Could a gambler's son who hated to gamble take the risk that Sara would reject him?

Vaguely surprised at his own actions, Nate flung out his arm with a flourish as he acted the part. Tevye almost did it, almost welcomed a man into the family who went against everything he believed in.

In the end, though, Tevye stuck with tradition. Even though Nate knew the play, and therefore the outcome of this scene, he felt the agony of unshed tears in his own throat. Tevye knew his decision meant he'd never see his daughter again.

Chava's face crumpled; her body slumped. She started to back away slowly. Tevye clutched his script to his chest, then, in a last, futile gesture, held out his hand to his retreating daughter.

Chava exited stage left.

Tevye looked to the rafters and silently asked God why in a loving family, things had to be so very, very hard.

The crack of applause startled Nate. Quickly, he reoriented himself. He was in a high-school gym in the Midwest and Tevye was a figment of some writer's imagination. He felt himself flush as the applause went on.

Sara came running back out and took a deep, stagey bow. A couple of the fathers whistled. Sara turned to Nate and beamed. She grabbed his hand, held it aloft. Then she swung into another bow, this time taking Nate with her. She waved as though she were on Broadway.

And then it happened. Right there under the stage lighting, Sara threw her arms around him and said, "Wow, *gosh*, you were so terrific, Dad."

Dad. Dad! *Dad.* Nate's arms closed around her and the lump in his throat practically choked him.

And near the doorway of the auditorium, Libby stood clutching her car keys in suddenly limp fingers, not knowing whether to laugh or shout like Sara or quietly shed a tear. Or maybe she'd do all three. After all, how many times in this life did a dream come true?

TREVOR'S FATHER never called. Now Nate and Trevor were standing outside the motel where Jonathan Samms was staying while he was in town for the court hearing. Evening was falling, and hopefully Samms would be back soon. If not, Nate and Trev would be here tomorrow. Trev was determined to see his father before Samms returned to California.

It had taken Tina a long time to finally give her consent for Trevor to do this. Her stipulation was that an adult had to be with him. She probably had hoped Libby would accompany her son.

But it was inevitable, Nate thought as they waited, that Trevor had picked him. In fact, it seemed that every conversation with the kid, from those late-night talks on their respective decks at Bittersweet Point, to the one they'd had at midnight over the phone just last night, had been leading to this moment. Yet Nate still had no real idea how or why Trevor had come to attach himself to him.

Or how he'd come to care for Trev.

He shifted, incredibly uncomfortable as he anticipated the meeting to come. Whatever the outcome, it was sure to be emotional. Trevor was quiet for once, lost in thought, pushing his wheelchair forward slowly, back slowly.

Say something to ease things, Nate thought. Okay. "You can see by this place that Libby was right about her idea of a family resort." His hand swept the shabby, pink facade, where in summer the rooms of the beachfront motel were also let by the week to vacationing families. Several of those families were playing on the beach right now, and the cheerful sounds they made were starting to grate on the two on the porch. "Families would surely buy or rent something more pleasant if it was available." *Good move, Perry. This kid is waiting to see his father for the first time in four years and you're talking business.*

But what was he supposed to say? He'd already cautioned Trev about expecting too much from this meeting. *Oh, and you'd be any different? If you could have your old man back, you wouldn't be nervous? You wouldn't hope? After all, you waited eight years to see your daughter and then just assumed she'd love you.* Hell. Maybe he was an idealist, after all.

Trevor was on a forward push.

"It was Libby's idea, this family-resort concept," Nate tried again. He wished he had Libby with him. She'd know what to say, what to do.

Trevor came inching back. "Great idea," he said with no enthusiasm. Then he perked up. "Do you want to see my list?"

"Your list?"

"I've been making a list of all the things I can do." The kid's grin was back, slightly off kilter but still broad. He pulled a folded paper from the pocket of his T-shirt. Unfolding it, he said, "I've been adding stuff as I go. If when I see my dad I'm excited and forget things, I can show him."

Nate took the list. There were three columns, in very fine print. He scanned the list. *Cooking,* Trev had written, and then under that: *Sandwiches, burritos, pizza bagels. Dishes, dishwasher and by hand. Laundry—know not to put the red shirt in with anything white* and then a hand-written exclamation mark. Even here, even now, Trev could make Nate's heart lighter. He looked at the second column. *Basketball. Eighty percent free throws from the foul line. Starter on special league.*

He swallowed, hesitated and then just did what he wanted to do. Nate reached out and rumpled the kid's hair, then gave him a friendly punch on the shoulder. Trev feigned a dramatic death, then shadow punched.

"Hey," Nate finally said quietly, ending the battle by handing back the list. "Whatever happens, we'll deal with it, okay?" Trevor faced him, and it suddenly struck Nate how incredibly brave the kid was. He had no reason to believe his father had any feelings for him, but he was going to find out. To offer his love.

"He's here," Trevor said breathlessly as a sleek black rental pulled into the parking lot, crunching gravel under expensive tires. Behind the tinted-glass windshield, Nate got the impression of a large man, and next to him, a young woman. The car stopped and the driver's door started to open.

Suddenly, Nate had a premonition.

He was down the step and had his hand on the door handle just as the door slammed shut and the engine started again. Before Jonathan Samms could shift into reverse, Nate pulled the door open. He reached in and hauled a very surprised Samms to his feet.

"Stay a while," Nate said with deceptive calm. "Your son wants to see you."

Maybe because he was surprised, Samms took a step forward. Nate took advantage of the opportunity to shut the car door behind him.

Father and son looked at each other. Samms had the dark oak complexion that suggested a permanent tan. His shirt-front was open three buttons, exposing his chest hair. A huge gold arrowhead on a chain around his neck caught the light.

Trevor bumped easily down the one step, got closer to his father. Samms's eyes flickered over his son, taking in his wheelchair.

Finally, Trevor said, "Hello, Dad." A flash of a smile, quickly dying. Trev held out a hand as if to shake, then seemed to think better of it and put it on the arm of his chair.

Samms spread his legs slightly apart in an aggressive stance. "Trevor."

Pretty sure now that Samms was not going to bolt, Nate

went around to Trevor's side and put a hand on the kid's shoulder. Trev felt strong. Under Nate's hand, there were hard muscles and thick bone. Touching still didn't come easy to Nate, but he knew Trevor could use the support.

"I wanted to see you," Trevor said to his father. "I wrote you that letter. Did you get it?"

"How did your mom find me?"

"I found you. I mean, I started it because I wanted to see you."

Under Trevor's gaze, Samms's eyes shifted.

The passenger door opened, and a young woman got out. She held a bottle wrapped in brown paper. "Jonathan, what is it?" she asked in a half-vexed, half-anxious tone that told Nate that she knew very well what "it" was. Nate took in the woman's waist-length black hair, huge sunglasses, the tight tank top covering very ample breasts, and knew he was looking at Jonathan Samms's trophy wife.

Samms ignored her. "You picked a helluva time to see me, boy," he said in a hearty tone, with a big smile. "After all, your mother just spent the afternoon picking my bones in that courtroom."

Nate saw Trev's chin go up. "You owed her."

Samms shrugged. "So she says. So the judge says. But I never have paid much attention to what goes on in this one-horse town. Out-of-towners never got any justice here. In a few years, you'll find out there's a big world out there."

Once Nate would have said the same. Now he thought of his family, and his wife's friends who had become his friends, too.

"Who're you, anyway?" Samms finally addressed Nate.

"Nate Perry. Friend of the family."

"Friend of Tina's, I'll bet."

Trev said, "Oh, Dad," but Nate cut in. "I'm married to

Libby Jamieson.'' Samms's eyes narrowed at the name. ''Actually, I'm here to run interference for Trev, if he needs it. *Does* he need it?''

''From his old man? Naw.'' But Samms wouldn't look at either of them.

''Jonathan, come *on*,'' whined the woman.

''Well, the lady calls,'' Samms said with a broad wink at his son. ''But we'll keep in touch, okay?'' He started to turn.

''Dad! Wait!'' Trevor whipped his wheels forward a foot or so, moving fast despite the coarse gravel. ''I've got something I want you to see.''

Looking pained, Samms stopped. Trevor fished out his list, held it out. Samms took it and read with a frown. ''What's this?''

''All the stuff I can do,'' Trevor said eagerly. ''I thought if you were staying a day or two we could shoot hoops, or the Mud Hens are playing in Toledo, I know that's minor league but I figured you wouldn't want to drive all the way to Detroit. Anyhow, you know I'm in the chair. You can see I didn't get up and walk like we thought I might at first. But it doesn't matter.'' Trevor's voice took on speed and vibrancy. ''I can do anything, Dad. I'm getting good at guitar. I swim. When I'm sixteen, I'll be able to drive a car. The other day I went dancing.''

His father's head shot up.

''I mean, I had to do it in the wheelchair but I danced with lots of girls. They don't mind the chair, Dad. None of my friends do. I don't. That's the thing. So I was kind of thinking—hoping—if you got to know me, you…'' He took a visible breath. ''You wouldn't mind, either.''

There was a long pause. Nate tried to catch Trevor's eye, to somehow communicate his encouragement and pride in the kid.

"He can do every last thing he says, Samms," he finally said quietly. "He's also an honor student and a whiz on the computer and a fine kid. Any man would be proud to have a son like Trevor."

The late-afternoon sun beat down. Jonathan Samms wiped a bead of sweat from his upper lip. Trevor wrapped his hands around the rims of the wheels of his chair. The young woman put the bottle on the hood of the car and came to stand by Jonathan. She addressed Trevor for the first time.

"Uh, I'm Cindy."

"Hi," Trevor said.

Cindy pushed hair off her shoulders and gazed up at her husband.

Finally, Samms spoke. "Look, ah, Trevor. The thing is… Well, I live in California now, and my business is pretty busy. Flying charters in the mountains. It's rugged country, we have problems up there sometimes, and the business keeps me real, well, like I said. Real busy."

"I could come out there. To see you."

"Well, that wouldn't be a good idea. Nobody knows I have a son. That you're—" He cut himself off, then continued. "For one thing, I've got a lot of guys who work on the planes, and they're pretty macho…"

Nate got a tight feeling in the gut. He wanted so much to intervene, to save Trevor from what was coming.

Hell. What he really wanted was to punch Jonathan Samms in his tanned face, and see those perfect, upright legs crumple.

"*I'm* macho," Trevor said boldly. "As macho as I want to be."

Nate's heart swelled.

"But actually, I'm not into macho that much. Macho

guys think it's cool to hurt people." The faintest quaver crept into his voice. "Really, I think macho...sucks."

Samms fisted a hand, started to bring it down hard on the hood of the car, but at the last minute changed his mind and brought it down gently. Then rapped it once, twice. Cindy put her hand on his forearm. "Aw, God, Trevor," Samms said, and his voice had gone thick. "I didn't want it to be this way."

Hope started a faint beat in Nate's chest.

"I loved you. I did. When you were born, I must've passed out about a billion cigars. Remember how we used to toss the football? But I'm not into touchy-feely stuff. I mean, with grown-up girls I can, sure." He paused. "Oh, what the hell. What I mean is I'm no kind of father. You're old enough to have figured that out by yourself. So to ask me to get around the fact that you're crippled now—"

"I'm not," Trevor said at the same time Nate interjected, "He's not."

Trevor straightened his shoulders. "I'm not crippled. Not handicapped. Not whatever."

"I don't know the *politically correct* way to say it—"

"You don't have to know it. I'm not even a 'person with disabilities.' I'm just Trevor."

"Your dad didn't mean anything. He's not trying to hurt you," Cindy said with a kindness Nate had not expected from her.

Nate knew he had to end this fiasco of a meeting. "Trevor, let's leave and give your dad a chance to think things over." Without thinking, just wanting to get away, Nate grasped the handles of the wheelchair and started to turn Trevor away.

"No!" Trevor put his hands on the wheels and hung on tight. Nate stopped. He'd known what this meeting could bring, the heartbreak Trev could suffer. But he'd hoped against hope. And now his own heart was breaking as he saw Trev try to deal with the coldhearted man who was his father.

"Trev," Nate started.

"I said *no*. Stay out of this." He straightened his shoulders. "You said you loved me when I was born, Dad. When my legs worked. Do you love me now?" He was starting to cry, tracks of tears down a face that was whiskered with downy fuzz, the faintest beginnings of a grown man's beard.

Jonathan Samms hung his head. "Yeah."

"So," Trevor said, and his voice was high and tight with suppressed sobs. "Do you want to be my father? Do you want to do stuff together? Do you want to try again?"

Samms's other hand crumpled the paper Trevor had given him. "Like Cindy says, I don't want to hurt you. I know what I'm supposed to say." His voice went lower. "But I can't."

"Because I'm crippled."

Cindy said, "Jonathan, please," very softly.

Samms hung his head, whether in shame at himself or because of Trevor, Nate couldn't tell. "Yes. Because you're crippled. I'm sorry. Really sorry. But I can't deal with it." He spread his hands in a gesture of futility. "I never could. Everywhere we went, I knew people were looking at me because I had a crippled son."

"You bastard," Nate said, and he started to move forward. The urge that drove him was primitive, protective. So angry.

Samms quailed at Nate's advance.

With a swift move, Trevor got between them. "Give me my list." Samms looked confused. Trevor pounded on the handle of his wheelchair. "Give me back my damn *list*."

Samms looked mutely at the list he held, then he handed it back to his son. "I wish—"

"To hell with wishes." Trevor crushed the list into a ball in his fist. To Nate he said, "Let's get out of here. *Now*."

CHAPTER FIFTEEN

TREVOR BRUSHED OFF Nate's help and yanked on the door of the Jag. Trevor wished Nate would go over to the driver's side.

Trevor got the door open and hoisted himself out of his wheelchair. He bumped his elbow on the door frame getting in, something he never had a problem with. Pain shot through him, and he said, "Damn, damn, *damn,*" and finished with as many cusswords as he could think of, even the real bad ones he never used. Nate didn't correct him, and for that Trevor felt a rush of gratitude that mingled with his rage at his father.

Nate started to fold the wheelchair, but Trevor snatched it out of his hand and started folding it himself.

Thwack. Clunk. Snap.

Done. He had to let Nate load the chair into the back seat, which was something Trevor would have liked to do, but there wasn't room for him to maneuver.

Without a word, Nate got in the car. Actually, Trevor was glad Nate wasn't talking. He was very glad Nate wasn't feeling sorry for him. Yet Trevor had an urge to say the very worst things he possibly could to Nate, which wouldn't be right. But he just felt like doing something. Something like cussing out the whole damn world and then punching somebody's lights out.

Nate sat for a moment. Finally, he spoke, and when he did, he said the worst thing possible. "I'm sorry."

Trevor couldn't help it—he blew his stack. "No! Don't say you're sorry for me! Not after—after—not because—" Then to his utter horror, he burst into tears.

It wasn't a few drops of moisture coming down, like sometimes happened to guys in movies. These were sobs, terrible hoarse sobs that seemed to come from somewhere in his gut and spill out all over. "God!" he choked out, so embarrassed he wanted to pass out, there on the seat. He'd tried so hard to be cool about this. Cool with Nate. Cool with his father. He'd done so good, held everything back. But now he couldn't.

Then Nate leaned over and pulled him to him, and Trevor shook and sobbed against his chest like a little kid. His nose started to run and drip on Nate's shirt and his cheeks felt as if they were burning. He cried because his father was a jerk and his father didn't love him and his father was ashamed of him and his father really *did* leave because his son was a cripple. And for the first time in his life, he cried because he couldn't get out of the chair and walk.

Nate sat there and let him cry, and thanked God he didn't say anything more about feeling sorry for him. Finally, after a long time, when Trevor couldn't breathe through his nose and his tongue felt thick, he managed to stop. He raised his head and turned away as quick as he could so he wouldn't have to look Nate in the eye. Nate Perry had been kind of his friend and now Nate would know he was just a little kid who couldn't handle his emotions.

"Cripes," Trevor said. "Let's get out of here."

Nate started the engine. "Ready to go home?"

"Do we have to?"

"No. We can go anywhere you want."

"Can we just ride for a while?"

Nate nodded and took the slow two-laner that hugged the water going out of town. For a while they didn't talk, until Trevor said, "I don't like it that you feel sorry for me."

Nate said, "You've been through a lot. I can't help feeling sorry." His voice was kind of ragged-sounding somehow. Like his throat had been kind of tight, too, which was really weird.

"I can do anything. Any damn thing I please."

Again, Nate ignored the cussing, though his mother would have had a fit to hear how he was talking today. "I wasn't feeling sorry *for* you. I was feeling sorry that you had to go through that with your dad."

"Oh." Trevor considered that. "It was rough." He was shaking and he wanted to start crying again. "Look, can we drop it, okay? It didn't work out. End of story."

Nate nodded, and they drove for a long time. The tracks of tears on Trevor's cheeks dried, making his skin feel tight. "I guess you think my dad is a real jerk, huh?" he finally asked.

"Well," Nate said, hesitating, before adding, "Yes."

"You weren't like him. Because you came back for Sara. You loved her that much."

Nate hesitated again, then turned into the next public park. There was a gravel parking lot and a boat launch. Out on the lake was a distant powerboat heading for shore. But there was nobody else.

He turned off the engine, and in a couple of minutes Trevor had to roll down his window because it was hot with the air-conditioning off. He wondered why they were stopping.

Nate draped a hand over the steering wheel. "I don't want you to think I'm some kind of hero because I came back for Sara," he said finally. "I've had to learn a lot of things about being a good father."

"But you were here to learn them," Trevor said. "And you would never have said your kid was a cripple."

"No. I wouldn't say that to anyone. But to say it to you, somebody so incredibly special…" Nate's voice suddenly went low and fierce. "See, Trevor, there are all kinds of 'crippled,' and none of them have anything to do with your legs. The person who's crippled is your father, because he has no idea what a terrific son he has."

Trevor glanced away because he couldn't exactly look Nate in the eye. There was something about how fierce Nate was being that seemed almost too much to handle.

Nate spoke again. "You've had an accident that could have made you hard and bitter. Believe me, I know. I've been hard and bitter all my life. But you don't let life do that. You just keep yourself open. You insisted on seeing your father even though you knew it might end up like it did."

Trevor swallowed hard. "Yeah. I bawled like a baby about it, too."

"You had a right. And Trev, the day you can't cry, the day you can't feel anything anymore, well, that's the day you aren't a man anymore, either. That's what I've learned."

Trevor thought about that for a while. He thought about his mom, and teasing her. He thought about his girlfriend, Ann, who wasn't just for kissing—he really liked talking to her. And he thought about Nate, and how cool it would be if this man could be his father. Not his father, exactly, because he had a father, who was a jerk.

It seemed as though Nate was thinking stuff over, too, as they watched the powerboat maneuver back into dock. Trevor knew they'd taken Nate's baby away. But he thought maybe what Nate was saying was that you had to accept stuff like that, stuff like Trevor's father being a jerk, and not let that hard knot that was in his stomach now stay there forever.

Not be angry all the time. Like his mom used to be. She was so much…gee, he didn't know, sort of freer now, and Nate seemed to be looser, too. Heck, he was here in Harborside instead of Chicago and it seemed as if he had all the time in the world. And every time Trevor saw him with Libby, he kept smiling a goofy smile like Trevor's friend Doug's older brother when he got married to Barb Fielding's kid sister.

"Am I, like, supposed to forgive my dad?"

Nate sighed. "If you can someday. If not, what I'm saying is you still have to give other people a chance, not be so afraid they'll hurt you."

"I get it."

Nate smiled then. "I'm sure you do. Now, I bet your mom will be waiting and worrying about you."

Trevor groaned. "Better get me back. Telling her everything that happened is going to take a while." He clapped a hand to his forehead and made a sound of disgust, but he didn't really mind. His mom had been there every day since the accident and he knew she'd never cut out on him the way his old man had. He never said dopey, mushy things to his mom, but tonight he was going to tell her he loved her.

When they pulled into Trevor's road, Nate asked him for his list.

"What for?" Trevor asked, fishing out the crumpled wad of paper and handing it over.

Nate smoothed it out against the steering wheel, then folded it and put it in his pocket. "Oh, I'd just like to have it. For one thing, I was thinking we could pick some of those things you can do and do them together sometimes."

Nate wanted to hang out with him? Trevor couldn't believe it. "Like go to some games or something?"

"Sure."

"But you have to be in Chicago."

Nate got the weirdest expression on his face. Kind of sad, or maybe confused. "When this current project of mine is on track, I'll have a bit more time. We'll do things together. I promise."

Trevor's father had made promises. *I'll take you to the Tiger's game on Saturday. I'll pick you up after school on Friday and we'll shoot a few hoops together in the gym. I'll take you and Doug out to Cedar Point to play the midway games this summer for sure.* That last promise had been made at the start of the summer Jonathan Samms had packed up and left.

But Trevor knew Nate would keep his promise. It was even more cool because Nate didn't have to do this stuff, like a father was supposed to. Nate Perry was busy and important. But he wanted to spend time with Trevor.

He'd said Trevor was special. So the tears sort of wanted to come again, but this time for an entirely different reason.

"How did it go with Trevor?" Libby asked as soon as Nate had put one foot in the kitchen. Sara was at Kathleen's for pizza, and Libby had been walking the floors alone and worrying.

"Hi," he said instead of a reply.

She felt herself flushing. How could one little syllable always sound so intimate? "Hi."

He smiled a little, but it faded quickly. "I needed that. Trevor's father is a horse's ass who I could have easily killed with my bare hands."

"Oh, no. What happened?"

She took his arm for good measure. After he'd settled

himself into her living-room sofa and recounted what Trevor had gone through, Libby was furious.

"What did you say to Jonathan?"

He shrugged, his mouth hard and tight. "What was to say? Anything that prolonged the meeting or set Samms off might have hurt Trevor more." He paused. "Trev and I took a ride after, talked some."

"Will he be okay?"

He paused, considering. "He was hurt, sure. But he's an amazing kid. He's got strength and courage. We talked for a while and he seemed better."

Libby clasped her hands in her lap. She felt profound gratitude to Nate, both for being with Trevor during his confrontation with his father, but mostly for being willing to talk with him afterward. She wanted to know more, but Nate suddenly clammed up. For a second she was hurt, but then she realized that Nate was concealing strong emotion.

"You love that kid," she said quietly.

He looked her in the eye. "Yes."

Impulsively, she reached up and looped her arm around his neck, bringing his body to hers. Her heart was beating hard at meeting his, a good, thumping beat. "Thank you," she said softly.

"It was nothing," he said too quickly. But she looked up and saw that it was something. Their gazes caught, locked.

"I'm exhausted," he said finally.

"Emotional scenes do that to a person," she agreed with a smile. "Too tired for bed?"

The hard planes of his face abruptly relaxed as he smiled. A few minutes later, Libby led him up the stairs to her room. There they made love, so intense that they scarcely uttered a word as they joined their bodies and took comfort from each other in the twilight of the day.

Afterward, Libby lay on her back. Overhead, right in her line of vision, was a stained-glass dish chandelier made for her by Tina. Stained-glass making was an old hobby of her friend's.

Libby realized she'd made a decision. Looking up at the rose and blue glass, she got a lump in her throat, because even now she wasn't sure she was doing the right thing. Even to have this discussion would be the end of a dream, because once she'd hoped— No. That wasn't fair. Nate had come so very, very far. It was time to meet him halfway.

"Nate?" she ventured quietly.

"Um," he said, half-asleep beside her.

Libby focused on the ceiling. *Tina will still be your friend. And you might have to leave this house, full of your mother's things, and the shop you love so much, but you'll never lose your memories.* "Would you like me to come to Chicago?"

Beside her, he went still. When she rolled to look at him, he was sober, his eyes dark. "If you would. If you would only come with me sometimes."

The carefully controlled plea in his voice astonished her. He wanted her to come that badly? How come he'd never asked, then? She took a deep breath. "Not sometimes." Her hand stole over his, entwined. "For always. I was thinking I could sell the house and the shop, and open something there."

Around hers, his fingers tightened convulsively.

"What about Sara?" he asked quietly.

"We'll talk to her. It might not be easy, but we owe it to her, don't you think, to keep our family together?" He didn't answer, so she added, "There's something I've been thinking lately. Home isn't a place. I loved Harborside because my friends and family were here. Now half my family's elsewhere most of the time." She leaned in so that flyaway strands of hair lay on his neck, and she traced the stern, sweet line of his mouth with her finger. "You're my family now, Nate. You and Sara. My loyalty has to be to you."

He closed his eyes. Then he reached up and put a hand on the back of her head, slowly pulling her face to his. When their mouths touched, he made a sound, one note of thick emotion, and kissed her deep and hard and true.

Slowly, he drew back. "Could you come this Saturday? There's a party on Saturday night. I'd like you to go with me."

A party already. Well, that's what Chicago—and sharing Nate's life—would mean.

She took a deep breath. "Sara could stay with Tina this weekend. If you want me there, I'll be there."

"Thank you," he said softly. "It's going to be a rough one."

"A rough party?"

"Yes. It's at Charles Baker's house. He's got an investment consortium, and most of its members will be there. They want to talk over Iris." He rolled onto his back. "Libby, it's my last chance to pull this thing off. If not..."

He didn't finish his sentence, but he didn't have to. Panic stirred in Libby. Any society party would create anxiety in her, but this one... "I'm not sure my being there would help you, Nate. I'm not good at chitchat, I don't have anything to wear and I'm not beautiful and certainly not glamorous."

Nate swore softly. "You know," he said to the ceiling, "for a woman who can take a bunch of dried weeds and arrange them into a basket and make them beautiful, you don't seem to have a clue. I find you absolutely..." He turned, touched her hair and her cheek. "Fascinating."

Not beautiful. Not even pretty. Still, fascinating wasn't

bad. Of course, it had taken him a long time to get to "fascinating" and she'd only have one night to help Nate. But he'd had the courage to forge a family out of nothing. Could she do less than to face her own demons and help her husband?

"Well, this time, your *fascinating* wife will do all she can to wow them in Chicago."

A STRANGER LOOKED BACK at Libby from the mirrored wall in the foyer as Nate took off her black cape. The bright track lights should have shown a few freckles, that place on her forehead where she'd peeled earlier in the summer. Instead, the mirror showed a complexion that was velvety, highlighted with soft peach. A smudgy line of charcoal deepened and enlarged her eyes. Russet painted her lips and her mouth looked full and sensual. Not beautiful. But not bad, either.

Libby knew she looked the best she ever had. In desperation, she'd taken her one credit card, walked into the first classy boutique she'd seen and bought the dress the salesclerk recommended. It was a simple, tight black sheath. The dress was too short. It was a good three inches above the knee, over black stockings so sheer that Libby had worried about the damage her callused hands would do when she put them on. The stockings ended at the tops of her thighs. She usually wore tights, and these darn things felt downright weird.

Libby clutched the chain strap of her evening bag. The purse looked like a treasure chest for a doll. Of all the things she'd bought today, she was in love with only one of them, this glittering chest with its tiny lock and key. A box for Pandora, she thought as Nate greeted some guests who were also just arriving and made smooth introductions. Libby lingered as the others went ahead into a huge living room furnished with white leather sofas and a black lac-quered grand piano.

Nate stood behind her, gestured to the space where brightly smiling people mingled. "Welcome to Chicago, beautiful wife," he whispered.

The comment pleased her, but an instinctive denial passed her lips. "Not beautiful. Just dressed up and feeling strange."

"Hey," he said softly, and taking her hand, he drew her down a different hallway. A statue in a huge niche was built into the wall, and Nate pulled her aside, partially con-cealing her from view. The noise of the party was more distant here.

"God, you look wonderful," he said, and he bent and kissed her lightly on the neck. He'd been late arriving home from the office, and she'd been already dressed. He'd had to hurry into his tuxedo. But now that they were at the party, he didn't seem all that anxious to go in. "We'll have to get dressed up more often when you move here. You have no idea how these bare shoulders..." His voice trailed off as he used a finger to trace the thin strap.

Her skin jumped at his touch. She welcomed it, yet it made her nervous. She had an almost perverse need to point up her flaws, and she wasn't sure why. She looked up at Nate—his chiseled mouth, his straight nose.

He was perfect. "This dress is so tight," she blurted out. "The salesclerk said no panty hose, so I have these thigh-highs that kind of pinch in the wrong place..." Oh, Lord. She'd got over feeling awkward in the face of his perfection long ago. What was wrong with her?

"You don't say." His breath whispered along her neck. His voice was husky, seductive.

From behind, his hands caressed the sides of her hips,

going slightly lower as if searching for the tops of her stockings. She felt a response leap within her.

"The first time I met you, you said you'd forgotten to buy nylons." He looked down to where the black silk of her stockings met the tops of her high-heeled pumps, and his voice dropped even more. "I'm glad you're wearing them tonight."

She felt a painful squeeze deep within her middle. She remembered what she'd said, that day at the courthouse. She was surprised and embarrassed that he recalled it, too. And Nate's comment about her black silk stockings just seemed to highlight how different she was tonight.

Of course she was different. How many times did she wear a dress held up by nothing more than a couple of threads?

"You know," he whispered, "I wish we'd stayed home."

Home? His condominium had been bigger than a house, colder than a bank lobby, all sparse charcoal gray and teal and chrome. How could anyone call those huge, nearly empty rooms a home?

"Perry, there you are. Stealing a kiss already?"

Nate stepped out, drawing her to his side without a trace of embarrassment. "Randall, good to see you. I'd like to introduce my wife, Libby."

THE PARTY WAS an ordeal. Nate gallantly introduced her to nearly everyone in the packed room overlooking Lake Michigan, but everything was a whirl to Libby. Too many strange faces, too much glamour. She held her evening bag in one hand and a plate in the other, knowing she needed two hands to stand up and eat. But for some unearthly reason, she was loath to part with her treasure chest, and held on to it like some kind of talisman.

Nate had to leave her to speak with the tight knot of men gathered around the fireplace. The night was hot, and air-conditioning poured into the room. Yet on the grate, a fire was lit.

"Mrs. Perry? Libby, isn't it?"

Libby turned in surprise to find a striking redhead standing next to her. While Libby's red hair had always been an object of teasing, this woman seemed to flaunt its color—she'd chosen a dress in a shade that matched. Libby admired her brazenness, even as she looked into chilly green eyes. "I'm sorry. I know Nate introduced us, but—"

"Danielle Morgan," the redhead said smoothly, her smile coached and brittle. "So, how's married life? I just got married recently myself." With her champagne glass, she indicated a silver-haired man who was at least two decades her senior.

"Congratulations," Libby murmured.

"Oh, thank you. He's so rich," Danielle said without a trace of embarrassment. "That's why I married him, of course. He knew it. Hell, the whole world knew it." She gave a trill of laughter. Her eyes narrowed. "You, on the other hand, managed to get the best of two worlds. A rich husband. And a young, gorgeous one, too."

For a moment, both watched as Nate wove his way through the crowd. He caught Libby's eye, waved briefly, then turned away.

"Thank you," Libby said, unsure what response the comment called for.

"You know, we've all heard about Nate's marriage by now. We couldn't believe it. For a while there, everyone was talking about it."

"He does wear a wedding ring," Libby said, trying not to clench her teeth.

"Yes, and we all wonder how you coaxed him into *that*."

Libby was starting to wonder who "we all" were, but she decided it might be better not to know.

"So," Danielle continued brightly, "we wanted to get a look at the wife he's been hiding in Ohio."

Libby felt her cheeks grow hot. The cut stones of her purse bit into her palm. She put her chin up. "Well, now you've seen her."

The other woman assessed her with frank interest. "It must be the lure of the unusual. Nate has always been— shall we say—independent." She used one hand to fluff her bangs. "Of course, he's always had a thing for red-heads."

Libby's eyes flew to Danielle's hair. It dawned on her that she was looking at one of Nate's old girlfriends.

Danielle smiled wider, a slow, cruel smile. "Nate and I have been running into each other, renewing old acquaintances. If I were you, honey, I wouldn't leave him alone in Chicago all week. A man like Nate gets lonely, and there are plenty of women to console him."

Like you? Libby wanted to shriek. Suddenly, Libby felt sick. What did Danielle mean when she'd said she and Nate were renewing their acquaintance?

"Excuse me," she said tightly, and turned blindly from the window. She sensed the other woman's satisfaction.

She ran smack into a man's chest. A cracker and a stuffed mushroom flew from her plate as a tuxedoed arm reached out to steady her. "Oh, I'm so sorry," she said, and she wanted to die.

"No harm done. Are you all right?"

"Yes." Sure. How on earth had she let Nate talk her into attending this party?

"You're Perry's new wife, aren't you?"

Miserably, Libby nodded.

The man cast a sharp eye behind her, where Danielle presumably still stood. "One of the cats giving you a hard time?" He smiled, and the deep lines at the corners of his eyes crinkled.

Libby swallowed and flushed, embarrassed at how obvious this scene must appear to an experienced, urbane man like her companion.

"She's jealous. Forget her," the man said decisively. He held out a hand. "Charles Baker. I'm joining my own party late. Had some negotiations to do in the study."

Libby hurriedly set down her plate on a nearby table. This was Nate's potential new investor for Iris. His hand felt warm as she shook it, but maybe that was because her own was too cold.

"I hear you spend most of your time in the little town where Perry met you."

"Harborside, on Lake Erie. I have a business there."

The kind, rather indulgent eyes sharpened immediately "Really? What kind of business?"

As she often did when she was nervous, Libby rattled on, grateful for a good listener, grateful to get away from Danielle and all the Danielles she suddenly sensed in the room. She talked flowers, but mostly the problems with cash flow that having a business in a resort town entailed.

"I know what you mean," Charles Baker finally said, breaking in when Libby was on a roll about her plans for off-season sales. "Investing in seasonal property development has the same kind of problems."

She flushed again. Here she was going on as if she had no idea his business was much more complicated than hers. "I must be boring you," she said. She'd had secret fantasies of meeting this man and somehow impressing him, of helping Nate win Baker's confidence. Instead, she'd been talking about inventory overflows!

"So, how goes it?" Nate had come up, a glass of wine in each hand. He held one out to Libby, who accepted it and took a large, unladylike swallow.

"Just talking to your wife," Baker said. "How refreshing to meet a woman running a business. And not consulting or being on the board of directors of Daddy's company, either. Why didn't you tell me your wife ran a shop?"

Nate flashed Libby a look of surprise. She took another swallow of wine, not sure if he was pleased. Well, she'd done the best she could. She was no flirt, and if that's what Nate wanted, he would be sorely disappointed.

Nate took a sip from his own glass, then said lightly, "My wife is a woman of many talents."

Sure. The charming thing to say. Without even knowing exactly why, Libby felt her teeth clenching.

Charles Baker looked them both over. "Well, Perry, all I can say is that it took you long enough to grow up, but I'm glad you did. When a man is investing in another man, he likes to see him exercise good judgment, make good choices in both his public and his private life."

Nate went still. "Investing? Then you've decided to come in on Iris?"

Instead of answering right away, Baker turned to Libby. "My wife, Carol, is over by the windows, talking to the caterer. Why don't I introduce you? Then I think you'd best excuse your husband and me. We've got things to discuss."

"THEY'RE IN! I've got Iris licked." Only a half-dozen steps into his condominium, Nate picked her up and whirled her around.

"Wonderful." Libby made a grab for enthusiasm. After all, this was her life now.

"Charles Baker was so taken with you, said he was glad I'd picked somebody like you."

Well, at least Charles Baker had seen she was different from the Danielles. And Libby was the one Nate had married. He'd paid no attention to Danielle at that party. In fact, he'd been nothing more than superficially charming to the other women.

"Oh, baby," he murmured, and his breathing picked up. He splayed a warm male palm over her bare back.

A shiver went up her spine, despite her mood.

"This dress is…" His voice trailed off into a husky whisper. "I don't know which I want to see more, you peeling down that little bodice or you showing me the tops of those black stockings."

Heat poured within her, embarrassed heat, aroused heat. He pulled her to him, and his own arousal was blatant and demanding. His hands on her hips, he started to draw up her dress. The sensation of his hands on thin nylon, and then, abruptly, on the bare skin of her upper thighs, nearly drove her wild.

She kissed him with utter abandon, needing him, claiming him, pressed tight to his legs and chest, her fingers in the layers of his hair. She loved him. And if the price of having him was sharing his life here, so be it.

Impatient now, he shoved her tight skirt higher, to her waist. He pulled down her panties, and she kicked them off. She was frantic, desperate to make love with Nate and blot out all these confusing feelings. "Now," she said, and it was both whisper and moan.

"Yes, now." With a little hop, she wrapped her legs around his waist. The shock of her bare, most sensitive flesh on the fine weave of his trousers was like a fan on flames. He was so...hard.

Taking a couple of steps, he pressed her to the wall of the foyer. The crystal chandelier in front of her glittered in a thousand colors. She closed her eyes on the sight, but still she could see pinpricks of light against her lids. Nate's hands came between them, tugging at his own clothing. A stud or two clinked, rolled on the marble floor. His zipper came down, and then he was inside her.

Her body closed around him and she held on for dear life. Before, their lovemaking had been intense, but it had always happened lying on her bed with the door closed. There they had to be careful; they were parents. Here they were only lovers. One thrust, two. That was all it took, and she was convulsing around him.

Right as it happened, he put his lips against her ear and whispered, "I love you."

CHAPTER SIXTEEN

THE REAL WORLD came back slowly to Libby. First there was the chandelier, the high light of the foyer as she opened her eyes, then the scent of sex. She was half-dressed, jammed against the wall, held up only by Nate, who was shaking and breathing as hard as she.

He loved her. He loved her!

Warmth shot through her in a giddy rush, replaced just as quickly with cold.

Which Libby did he love? The real Libby, who baked bread and talked too much and chose sunflower nightgowns and dahlia T-shirts? Or this Libby, the one who wore black dresses that were too tight to be comfortable and balanced champagne in one hand and a plate of crudités in the other?

He moved back, and with his hands to steady her, she slid slowly down.

"Are you all right? I didn't hurt you?"

He'd never asked before, because he'd never needed to. Their lovemaking had been so hot and abandoned. So hard. He'd taken her against a *wall*, for Heaven's sake, and she had wanted it.

Her mind refused to dwell on all the times he must have made love—had sex—against the wall of his foyer.

"Sure. Yes." Unsettled, she picked up her cape from the floor and then her treasure chest from the console. She opened it and took out her credit card, lipstick and two tissues, all the tiny purse would hold. She turned to find him watching her with an intensity that was almost blinding.

"Did you hear what I said, there at the last?"

Her lips were tender from his mouth molding so hard to hers. "Yes."

"I didn't…" He swallowed. "I didn't say it only because I was caught up in what we were doing. I meant it." His eyes took her in. "I love you."

She didn't say anything. Her throat felt too tight.

He waited a beat more, and when she didn't respond, his mouth turned straight and grim. "I thought that was what you wanted to hear."

"Why did you wait until I came to Chicago to say it?"

He came toward her, his arms out. "It's just that when you said you'd come here, and then, at that party, you convinced Charles Baker to take a chance on me—"

"Wrong answer."

He stopped abruptly. Slowly, his hands fell to his sides. "What's the matter with you? This is supposed to be a celebration."

What *was* the matter? She'd volunteered to come. Suddenly, she knew the answer. "It's because you love me only this way, Nate. You love me only because I've passed the Chicago test. Because I managed not to embarrass you at the party."

"I'm proud of you."

"Are you proud of me in Harborside?"

"Well, of course, but here everything's so important—"

"More important than your family?" She felt tears start in the corners of her eyes. *More important than the happiness of the woman you just professed to love?*

"Libby," he said slowly, looking past her, taking in his surroundings. "This is who I am."

Her heart started a peculiar, irregular thump. "So in Harborside, when you came to Sara's rehearsal, when you helped Trevor through the incident with his father, when you tried the square dance, when you...when we first...that wasn't you?''

She had him. For a moment, he visibly wavered, his eyes confused. Finally, as if it didn't matter, he said, ''Sure, that was me, too.''

But it mattered. And suddenly, she was angry. All the understanding she'd tried to give him, every time she'd dared to hope, all mixed together in a powerful anger.

''You love me this way, Nate. Well, I love you *that* way.'' She looked down at her dress. ''This isn't the real me. In this dress, here in this house, I feel like a fraud. Like an actor in one of Sara's plays.'' She drew a deep breath. ''And it hurts me and makes me angry that you prefer me this way.''

Unable to bear the intensity of his gaze, she pushed past him into the living room. She stumbled a little on the unexpected step, having forgotten that his living room was sunken. Anyway, she couldn't see too well with her eyes full of tears.

''Please,'' he said, and the raw, almost desperate way he said the one word tugged at her heart.

''I made a mistake.'' Despite her best efforts, her voice quavered. ''I should never have come here. I don't wear black dresses. I don't wear lacy lingerie or sexy nightgowns. After all, you saw me one night before I bought that green nightgown. Do you remember what I was wearing?'' Her voice grew tighter. ''Yes, it's a test, Nate. Do you remember?''

''I don't take tests.'' His expression was taut and dangerous.

''You don't remember.''

Abruptly, he slammed a fist down on the table. The thick

glass of the tabletop shivered, rattled a Lalique sculpture. "You were wearing a nightgown with a sunflower as big as a dinner plate splashed across your breasts. Hell, you think I don't remember? I dreamed about taking that thing off you for a month afterward!"

Oh. For a moment she hoped—but his recollection didn't change anything, not after tonight. "You'd rather have me in a cocktail dress, impressing your friends!" Both their voices had risen now.

"I like you that way, yes. I like you in black, I like you in sunflowers, and I like you in nothing at all!" Unexpectedly, as if he'd just now realized he was yelling, his voice dropped. "I love you." Almost tentatively, as if he'd forgotten how and was just relearning the movement, he held out his hands, palms up.

At the gesture, the tears in her eyes spilled over. She was unable to hold back her pain. "I bet Danielle Morgan doesn't wear sunflowers."

"What's Danielle got to do with this?"

"You tell me, Nate."

He looked confused for a moment, before comprehension dawned. "Did she say something to you at the party?"

Oh, God. Was it true then? "Did you have an affair with Danielle?"

"Is *that* what she said?"

"Is it true?"

"No, it's not true!"

She searched his eyes. Under the circumstances of their marriage, she could forgive him, hardly blame him. But it still hurt.

He took a few steps toward her, put his hands on her shoulders. "Listen to me. I didn't sleep around on my first wife and I don't sleep around on you."

She felt suddenly limp, and she wanted someone to hold

her. Her best friend. Funny, she thought now with a touch of hysteria, that person was Nate. "You might have had a right," she whispered finally. "We were married, I should have let things happen naturally. But all my life, I've just wanted somebody to love me the way I am. For me, not for who they wanted me to be."

"Look." He spread his hands. "I admit, there were women in my life. Maybe not as many as you think." He shrugged, looked away quickly. "But I was single, and they were single. And I can't change what I did then. I can only tell you that I'm trying now."

"I'm trying, too. But I can't be what you want. I thought I could, but I...can't."

Her words seemed to hang in the air. For a long moment, they stared at each other. Libby's throat was unbearably tight.

"So," he said, and that coolness, that utter control was back in that one word. "Where do we go from here?"

"I don't know," she said miserably. "I just don't know."

NATE DIDN'T KNOW, either, but he learned one thing in the next two weeks: they couldn't go back to the way things were. In desperation, he'd fallen back on old routines. Friday nights to Sunday afternoons in Harborside, the rest of the week in Chicago.

It was terrible. How had he ever thought this was a good solution? When he was in Chicago, he thought about Harborside, wondering what *she* was doing, whether she was having a good day in the shop, what was going on with Sara. Then when he came in on Friday nights, he felt as awkward as a boy, as unwelcome as a stranger among old friends. Why couldn't he say he'd missed her, that he'd missed them?

He knew why. Because he'd offered his love for the first time in nine years, and she'd rejected him. Rejected his life.

Now it was Saturday, Harborside again, and the tension was thick. Once he would have fled to his makeshift office upstairs, or gone out for a sail. Now, teeth gritted, he endured being downstairs this hot afternoon, going over cost projections for a new project, one that was so massive in scale that it would leave Iris in the dust. A man had to keep building, and each project had to be bigger.

Sara had picked up on the tension in the house and was stuck to Libby like glue. Libby sat at the dining-room table with some ledgers from the shop. Sara sat next to her. She was supposed to be reading, but she kept interrupting. She'd gone on and on about a fight with Kathleen, then about her horse, and now she was starting on the play.

"The seam in my costume has a rip, under the arm. Nobody can see it, but I know it's there. Can you fix it?"

Libby looked up. "Sure. Later."

"If you can't fix it, Tina maybe could."

"Um," Libby said, her pencil stopping on one of a line of numbers.

Libby looked uptight. Lines marred her forehead, and she'd pulled her hair back into a ponytail as if she couldn't cope with it today. She'd said little to him. Last night, he'd snuck into her dark room like a thief, the first time he'd gone to her bed since Chicago. He'd wondered if she'd throw him out, but instead in the dark they'd held each other with bruising force. He'd whispered, "I love you," and she'd whispered, "I love you," but neither had any solutions and Nate had the terrified feeling that she'd stopped trying to find any. If Libby stopped trying...

Afterward, he'd said he couldn't sleep—the truth—and

he'd walked her beach in the dark, and then he'd returned to his own room for the night.

"I wanted to practice my lines for *Fiddler* today." Sara again.

"Maybe Kathleen would like to do that," Libby said, looking up with a frown. "You guys could make up. You always do."

"Kathleen doesn't like acting. Actually, I'm pretty mad at Kathleen. Like I told you, she—"

"Well, one of your other friends, then."

"*You're* the one in the play."

"Sara, I can't. I've got income tax forms I have to get done by midweek. I've got to work, honey."

"You're always working," Sara grumbled.

"Sara," Nate finally said. "Stop bothering Libby."

Both Libby and his daughter looked over at him in surprise. Usually he let Libby handle Sara, but the girl was bothering her, and Libby had just said she needed to work. He dropped his eyes back to his own figures.

Sara fell into a sulky silence. Nate couldn't focus. Instead he looked out the windows of the small living room. Out on the street, a couple of boys went by on bikes, followed by a black-and-white mutt that had patches of summer mange. The air was sultry, unbearably still. The clock ticked slowly. Nate rubbed the back of his neck. What was he doing here? He didn't belong here. Funny how not belonging gave him such a hurt, way inside. He pushed the thought away. Maybe a sail, after all, then an early trip back to Chicago.

Sara closed her book. "Lib, we could do one of our songs. You know, for the chorus at the wedding. 'Sunrise, Sunset.'"

"Not now, Sara." In exasperation, Libby threw down her pencil. "Why don't you go look for shells? Why don't you go in-line skating, or listen to your CDs, or go out on the sunporch and practice your lines by yourself?''

"I don't want to do stuff by myself. I'm bored." She gave a long, dramatic sigh. "It's boring in this house, boring, boring—''

"Enough," Nate snapped. "That's enough, Sara! Now go find something to do!''

She stared at him defiantly, holding her hair up above her neck. "It's too hot to do anything outside.''

He gritted his teeth. "You didn't hear me, I guess. Now I'm telling you again. Go…find…something…to do, and leave Libby alone!''

Sara leaped to her feet. "Why are you sticking up for her? You're mad at her, so why are you sticking up for her?''

Libby put out her hand, but Sara shrugged it off.

"He's not mad at me," she said. "Not exactly.''

"So why is everybody tiptoeing around this house?'' Sara faced him, but her lower lip wobbled. "Something's going to happen. I know it! And I *hate* you!''

Her steps pounded through the kitchen and sunporch and they both heard the door to the beach slam shut.

Nate raised his eyes to Libby. She stood and swore softly, and shut her ledger with a snap.

"What did I do?" Nate asked.

"For God's sake, Nate," Libby said sharply, and then she headed upstairs. A moment later, he heard the shower start.

He sat still, listening to the damn clock by himself. And then he went out the front door, fished out his car keys and got into his Jag.

He drove aimlessly, shaken. What had Sara meant, saying something was going to happen? He didn't know, but he felt it, too, an almost unbearable tension. Sara had never been angry at him before. Scared of the newness, sure. Distant, certainly. But he'd never yelled at her before. She'd never yelled at him.

I hate you.

He loved them both, but his best efforts seemed always to fail.

He got back at dusk. He wasn't sure what the welcome would be, so he went in quietly. Libby was on the phone, but she hung up quickly and came into the living room.

"Have you seen Sara?" she asked, her eyes wide with concern.

"She's not here?"

"I haven't seen her since she went out to the beach this afternoon. Her bike's still here, and I've been calling her friends. She didn't come back for dinner, Nate, and it'll be dark soon."

His gut clenched. But he made sure his voice was reasonable. "Maybe she just needed to go somewhere to cool off." After all, he told himself without much conviction, hadn't he spent the last few hours doing exactly that?

"Sure, be reasonable," she said, and her voice shook.

He was getting more scared by the minute. Libby was pretty relaxed with Sara, treated her as half grown-up. If Libby was worried... His tight stomach turned, and then he knew an old sensation, an almost unbearable fear for his daughter's safety, a sensation he was able to contain only with rigid self-control.

He made a grab for control now, but for some reason gaining it was harder than it used to be. He reached out to Libby, grabbed her shoulders and hung on for a moment. "We'll find her. After all, everybody in town knows her. People will look out for her." Thank God they were here in Harborside, not in Chicago. "Who've you called?"

"Kathleen's mom, all her friends. The Romers, who live

way down at the end of the beach. I don't know who else to call."

He didn't, either. "Stay here and wait by the phone in case she calls. I'll go out in the car and look." He didn't add that he'd just driven through town and hadn't seen a sign of Sara. Harborside wasn't that big. But there wasn't much here that could harm a ten-year-old.

Except the lake. The water.

He forced himself to remain calm. "Call Tina and see if Sara's been hanging around Bittersweet Point." At the Point, there were all kinds of machinery, pits in the dirt, lots of things that could injure a child.

That thought was bad enough. The second was worse. For the first time, he faced the idea that she might have run away, might be far away, in trouble and out of reach.

He drove every road he hadn't driven that afternoon. They were few, but it took some time because he scanned the roadside in the gathering dusk, the high weeds, the dark woodsy areas.

When he got back to the house, Libby met him in the driveway. "Tina and Trevor just got home," she told him tersely. "Trevor noticed right away your boat's missing from the dock."

Oh, God. "Sara's afraid of the boat. She'd never take it out." But he met her eyes in the dark and they both had the same thought. Sara was no sailor, but she had some experience with powerboating; every kid in Harborside had. And his boat had an inboard motor.

"Get in," he said, reaching over and pushing open the passenger-side door.

When she was seated, he headed for the yacht club.

Libby spoke. "I called the sheriff, and they've notified the Coast Guard. But I want to be there, too, Nate. I have to look. So I called Rob Johnston at the yacht club and he's going to let us borrow a powerboat.''

Nate nodded.

Unexpectedly, her hand stole between the seats, took his. Hers was icy, his way too hot. She squeezed, and the gesture brought tears to his eyes. He blinked them away. He couldn't give in to emotion. Sara might be out there on the black water. But he was aware that this time his fear for his little girl was shared by someone else. That sharing was almost overwhelming, but after a moment he released her hand. He needed to concentrate on his driving.

ONCE ON THE WATER, Nate headed for the nearest group of islands. Dark had fallen and there was only a sliver of moon. The lights on shore were a thin strand, a few other boats the barest floating glimmers.

"The Coast Guard will check these islands first thing," Libby said in a hopeful voice.

"Yes."

"Would she have enough gas in the tank, do you think, to make it to the islands?"

Libby had just given voice to one of his worst scenarios, that Sara would run out of gas and be floating helplessly on the water somewhere, or that she'd do something incredibly risky like try to raise the sail.

"I can't remember how full the tank was," he said tersely, and she was silent.

The Coast Guard was already near the largest island, moving slowly along the shoreline. That island was touristy. Crowds had spilled over from inside the bars to the tables set up by the water. Boats of every description were tied up.

Nate gave the docks a quick glance, but didn't spot his

sailboat. "I'm taking her farther in. Do you think she might go to that island where we had the picnic?"

Libby grabbed his hand, squeezed hard in hope. "Maybe she would. Yes. You know how dramatic she is, how something like going back there might appeal to her."

"But we were in a storm that day."

"But before that, we had so much fun. We were a family there."

Nate maneuvered the powerboat carefully. He remembered where the major sandbars were, but the waves shifted the bottom all the time, and you never really knew what was underneath your craft as you approached shore. Just another thing to worry about, he thought, sick with dread.

When he was in close enough, they scanned the shoreline. The island was used only by day sailors, so there were no facilities, and therefore no lights.

But... Yes! Yes! Nate's white boat was tied to the dock, its sails still furled, its mast gleaming dully.

Hands on the wheel, Nate stood. "Sara!" he called.

Libby cupped her hands around her mouth and added her voice to his. "Sara! It's Libby! Are you there?"

A small figure stood on the edge of the dock, waving. As Nate got the boat closer, he could hear her calling for Libby.

The rush of relief flashing through him buckled his knees, and he sank heavily back into the seat.

As soon as he docked, Libby was scrambling out of the boat. Sara rushed into her arms, and she held her tight. "Oh, I was so scared," Sara cried.

"Shh, baby," Libby crooned, rocking her in her arms.

Nate tied up the boat and got out on the dock.

"You're not mad?"

"I'm so glad you're all right," Libby said fiercely.

Nate's heart was in his throat, watching the scene. His

daughter's curls mingled with Libby's, and the natural way they held each other tugged at his insides. God, he loved them both. If something had happened to Sara... Unable to even fully voice the thought, Nate clenched his fists against the strength of emotion.

"I got scared," Sara said. "I got here okay, but it took so long. I didn't know how to make the boat go fast. Then when it was getting dark, I tried to start a fire, like I saw once on TV, but it didn't work." Fresh sobs shook his daughter.

"Shh," Libby murmured again. "I'm here."

"I was afraid to come home on that...*boat.*"

Thank God she hadn't tried to start back in the dark. Nate cleared his throat. "You would have run out of gas, Sara."

She raised her head for the first time and looked at him. Libby's arms were still around her. "I banged up the boat, getting it in," she said in a small voice.

He hadn't even begun to think of the perils of docking. Sara falling from the boat, hitting her head, smashing her hands between the boat and the dock. His legs started to shake.

"That's all right," Libby said soothingly.

"It was just that...when everybody was being all snotty with each other... Heywood used to do that, he'd get drunk and then we'd just kind of *know* he was going to say mean things, and me and my mom would try to be quiet. But today I thought, get it over with, get all the mean things out, and then he did yell..." She buried her face in Libby's chest.

Nate's heart hurt, a physical pain. He'd done this. Sara's running away had been his fault because he'd brought back memories for Sara of Heywood Clark. Had he yelled at her? He'd been angry, but now he didn't even remember yelling.

Libby let go of Sara, but reached out to gently stroke his daughter's bangs away from her forehead. Sara turned to look at him. Expectantly. He knew what he was supposed to say, those things Libby was saying that somehow he couldn't. The fear, the utter terror and sense of loss that he'd held at bay for the sake of the search was still there, like a fist in his chest.

"Never go out on the water alone again, Sara. You could have drowned. You could have..." He couldn't give voice to all the possibilities. "Do you know how terrified we were?" His tone was harsh. He didn't mean to be harsh. He wanted to do what Libby was doing, soothe his daughter, hold her. He'd learned to do that these last few weeks. But now he couldn't move.

And with the knowledge that he couldn't move, couldn't be what Sara needed in this moment, he knew he'd made a decision.

The right decision. The decision that was killing him inside.

ON THE WAY HOME, Nate told Sara in short, halting sentences that he wasn't angry at her. With real vehemence, Sara had vowed never to scare them again.

At home, Libby made Sara a sandwich, and then sat on her bed for over an hour. Finally, Sara fell asleep.

When she got downstairs, Nate was waiting. "Is she all right?" he asked immediately.

Libby nodded, suddenly weary. This had been a terrible day. The last two weeks had been terrible, and something had to change.

"Walk with me?" Nate asked, and his voice was so sober, his mouth so tight, that she had a very bad feeling.

He led her to the water's edge. They stood together, looking out over the water he loved, the water that could turn wicked so easily. The foundations at Bittersweet Point gleamed in the night.

"The condos are going up right on schedule," she said, nervously trying to fill the uncomfortable silence that had fallen between them.

"And they're all filled, much more quickly than our projections would ever have indicated. You were right about families needing someplace." He paused. "You were right about a lot of things. And wrong."

"Wrong?"

"Wrong about us," he said quietly. "Wrong to think we could be a family."

"Oh, Nate, I—"

"Wait. I have to say this fast. I'm no good for you or Sara. You love so easily, Libby. You touch people so easily, you go so comfortably through life."

"We love you." Her hand came out to touch his. Gently, he pulled away when she would have entwined her hand in his. He couldn't say what needed to be said, or endure what needed to be endured, if he let her touch him.

"Today proved that Sara is better off without me. I know how her stepfather hurt her, and I acted like him today."

"You're not like Heywood. For Heaven's sake—"

"I reminded her of him. And then tonight, when we found her, I couldn't touch her again. I couldn't reach out and say the right thing. What if you hadn't been with me? How would she have felt, alone and scared with a father who…" He couldn't help it; his voice started to break. "With a father who couldn't take her in his arms when she needed to be held?"

"Nate," she said, her voice breaking, too, "please let me touch you. Let me love you."

"It's better if you don't. Too much has happened to me. And I do better when I concentrate on things. I can't hurt things."

"They can't hurt you. Listen. You think you were wrong with Sara today, but you acted like a father in a real family. Real families argue, get on each other's nerves, get angry when they've been worried. Real families fight, disappoint each other, and then they make up and go on."

"I wasn't what you wanted in a husband." He faced the water.

"No," she said softly. "But you're the man I love." She paused. She was so sure she was right that Nate could be part of her life here, part of Sara's. Nate was a man who felt deeply, just held too much on the inside. She swallowed and said what she had to. "I'll come back to Chicago. I'll try again."

"You wouldn't be happy there."

"I can try," she said, her voice so very thick. *Don't start crying,* she ordered herself. If she couldn't reach Nate in the next few moments, she'd lose him. She struggled over her next words. "But I agree, we might not be happy there. I'd come easier if I knew that's what you really wanted out of life. But you've been happy here, Nate. You've fit in, you know people, they want you to be part of something. Maybe something smaller than what you're used to, but something fine and valuable and real."

He turned to her. "I'm a millionaire developer. The papers call me ruthless and coolheaded. It's what I am," he said simply. "It may not be what I want now, but it's what I've become. It's what I can handle, it's how I excel. Your way is too..." He swallowed. "Hard on the heart. And I'd break your heart and Sara's in the end."

She cried then. She couldn't help crying because he was breaking her heart here and now. "You'll have to tell Sara.

I've tried to make things easy for you, but I won't do it this time."

"Oh, God, Libby, do you think this is easy? Leaving you is the hardest thing I've ever done." He crushed her to him, holding tight, his breathing harsh and unsteady.

"You could take a chance. Why give up on us now, when it just might work out?" She was desperate to convince him, but she had no more words.

"The hurt will be worse later. For Sara. For you." He paused, but he didn't add what she'd thought he might— *for me.* Instead, he said very, very quietly, "You knew all along I'm no gambler."

For a timeless moment they held on to each other.

When he pulled away, his voice was cool, in control. "Forget the prenuptial agreement. You and Sara will have everything you need for the rest of your lives. I do want visitation spelled out, however. I just... I trust you, but I need my rights to Sara."

CHAPTER SEVENTEEN

SARA WAS ANGRY. She refused to visit Nate after he moved back to Chicago a month ago. The three performances of *Fiddler on the Roof* came and went. Libby dropped out of the chorus, unable to bear being in the play, but Sara performed like a trouper. Sara didn't, however, invite her father to be part of the audience.

Over at Bittersweet Point, Nate's condominiums were going up. The rough-sawn cedar siding fit into the setting so well that the condos were barely visible from the water. The sugar cube was torn down, and Tina and Trevor moved to town, to an old place that was awkward for Trevor. But the arrangement was temporary. Nate had offered Tina a job as live-in manager of the Point, so Tina and Trevor would be moving into one of the new units as soon as it could be completed.

One night, Tina made a casual reference to something Nate had said.

"What?" Libby asked quickly, even though the comment had nothing to do with her or Sara. She just wanted to hear his name again, know he was safe and happy in Chicago, in the life he'd chosen.

Tina repeated what Nate had said, then added, "If you want to talk to him, give him a call."

"I can't. He left me, remember? You were right all along." She couldn't help the bitterness.

"Libby, one thing I've learned is that you've got to keep

fighting for what you want. If Nate's what you want, fight for the guy. Don't let your hurt blind you to the good things in life like mine did for so long.''

Libby just shook her head

And today was the worst, the absolute worst. At the shop, Nate had served her with divorce papers. They were accompanied by a dispassionate letter from the ever-efficient Marta Wainwright. The terms were more than generous, the letter pointed out.

Libby didn't want Nate's things. She wanted Nate.

Sara came in from school, in a purple shirt and matching jeans, and in her silver sneakers. A summer's wearing had made them dingy. ''Before you ask, I don't have *any* homework. I stayed in at recess to do my math so I can help you with that harvest thing you're doing with the leaves.'' The paper leaves Libby had ordered for a fall wedding fascinated Sara. She charged around the counter, dropping her book pack midstride. ''How many can I use?''

Libby smiled a smile that suddenly felt a bit watery. Nate might be gone, but he'd left something infinitely precious behind. His daughter.

''Hey, what's all this?'' Sara picked up the papers Libby had left by the telephone.

''Sara, we've got to talk.'' Libby reached for the papers, but Sara pivoted, still reading.

''It's about the divorce,'' she finally said.

Libby said, ''Yes, but your dad wants to see you anytime you're willing. I can show you the part where it says he wants the maximum visitation—''

''Forget it. How will he have time, anyway? Trevor told me Dad has a project going that's like a whole rain forest in a hotel.'' She dropped the papers. ''Trevor also says he seems sad.''

Tina had said the same thing to Libby.

"I want him back," Sara said suddenly. It was the first time since Nate and she had had their talk and he'd packed up for Chicago that she had said such a thing.

"I do, too," Libby admitted, deciding there was no point in hiding her feelings. Sara was too perceptive.

Sara picked up a gold and rust leaf, twirling it by the stem. "I said he was like my old dad, but he isn't," she said finally. "He's nothing like Heywood."

"I know."

"I love him." Sara appeared engrossed in the leaf.

Libby choked up. Darn, she needed to do better, for Sara's sake, but nowadays her emotions lay so close to the surface.

"So how do we get him back?"

"It's not that easy, sweetheart." Libby needed to be honest. Sara needed to understand, first and foremost, that Nate loved her. "Nate loves you. He's always loved you."

"Trevor says that's why he came back."

And why he went away. "Right." Despite her best efforts, her voice was starting to thicken, so she lowered it. "You see, your dad was hurt a lot as a little boy and he didn't know how to live in a real family, and then when your mom took—when you had to go into the witness protection program, Nate lost you, and you were precious to him. So he told himself he was cold inside and nothing could touch him there. So even though Nate loves us, he thinks he's bad for us because he can't love us enough."

"But he does love us enough."

"Yes. Oh, yes. But he can't see that."

"Well," Sara said slowly, "maybe we could prove to him somehow that he does know how to be part of a family." She turned earnest eyes to Libby. Blue eyes. Nate's eyes, wide and deep with a grown-up intensity. "Remember when he tried to help me learn to sail. And he made breakfast and he helped me with my lines the night of the play rehearsal. Does he remember all those things?''

Libby nodded, but she was suddenly struck by the thought that Nate didn't know what those things really meant to her or Sara. Burned breakfasts. Carpooling. The simple things that went into making a family.

But how to make him see? Proof, Sara said, and looking down at her divorce papers Libby had an idea. She pondered for a moment, but a moment only. She hated to risk hurting Sara. But wouldn't Sara be hurt worse if they didn't take one last chance? And Sara had a special maturity that came from living with a difficult stepfather, of losing her mother, and of forging a new family with Libby. Yes. If Judge Wyatt was willing, perhaps they could prove it, after all.

NATE COULD HAVE BEEN late, because Charles Baker and his investors wanted to go over a mock-up of the new project. But even though he'd spent a hundred hours in preparation, he found himself making excuses. He was required by the court to be in Harborside for the final hearing for his divorce—and he was going to be there in plenty of time. He would see Libby again, and he couldn't wait, even though he knew seeing her only meant that the end had come.

He had to see Sara, too. He'd talked to her on the phone, but she wouldn't come to Chicago. She wanted him to come to Harborside. And Nate would, as soon as he could bear to make the trip. Maybe he'd take one of the condos on Bittersweet Point on a permanent basis, a place to see Sara if she continued to refuse to come to Chicago.

The courtroom was as he remembered it—old and majestic, with high ceilings, worthy of a big city. He wondered about the people who had built it. They must have done so with high expectations, sure that Harborside would grow someday. But it never had. Now Nate thought with a rush of unwanted sentimentality that maybe the town founders would be proud of the independent people who called it home.

The courtroom had been the beginning of his dream of a family. So it was fitting that the dream would end here. Nate clenched his jaw, searching for his self-control, his distance.

It was hard to look at Libby. She smiled at him nervously, as his own eyes took in every detail. She had on a new green suit. It seemed not her style, until he got a peep of the shell she wore underneath. Some sort of leafy print. *Okay.* His Libby.

Only not his Libby, because he was at his table with Marta, and she was alone at another table. He frowned. Why didn't she have her lawyer with her? Even though the property settlement wasn't contested, she shouldn't be without legal advice. Protectiveness rose in him, until he realized he was trying to protect her from himself.

Judge Wyatt took the bench.

Nate rose with Marta and Libby, then sat down when directed to do so. "Well," Judge Wyatt said finally, looking down over the bench with a stern countenance. "I thought when you two married that we'd seen the end of this bizarre case. Apparently, I was wrong. Ms. Wainwright."

Marta stood. "Your Honor."

"Mrs. Perry has elected to act as her own attorney today," the judge said.

"Mr. Perry would prefer it if Mrs. Perry were represented," Marta told him. "In affairs of this kind, sometimes a more…impersonal approach is better."

"I don't agree," Judge Wyatt said flatly. "Now, your petition cites irreconcilable differences."

"The grounds for divorce aren't contested, Your Honor."

"Oh, but Ms. Wainwright, they are. Mrs. Perry has chosen to fight the divorce."

Nate peered at the judge, trying to understand what was going on. The judge was smiling at Libby. Nate had a sense of the surreal. But he took the stand at Marta's direction and prepared to give testimony as to why he and Libby couldn't live together. He answered Marta's crisp questions. Yes, he had never really made Harborside his home. Yes, he'd kept his home in Chicago. Yes, he and Libby disagreed about many things. What were those things? He looked over at Libby. She was staring at him.

Actually, he thought in some surprise, they were more in sync than he'd ever imagined. Basically, they agreed on the importance of family. After all, that's what had finally made him realize how bad he was for her. They were one in their love for Sara. They both had guts. He in business, she in life. Hell, they even shared a love for the water.

He shook his head. What was he supposed to say? Irreconcilable differences. *She takes chances, risks her heart. I don't gamble.* Suddenly, that sounded…cowardly.

Somehow, he got through Marta's questions. But he fisted his hands, surprisingly shaken, when Libby got up to do her cross-examination.

"I only have a few questions, Your Honor," she said in a clear voice. Then, when she moved, her suit jacket came open. And there it was, splashed boldly across her front—a mammoth sunflower.

I like you in black and I like you in sunflowers…

He cleared his throat.

"Mr. Perry," Libby began. "Isn't it true that despite

what you testified to here today, the real reason you don't want to stay married to me is that you don't think you can be a family man?''

God, she didn't mince her words. "Yes, that's true.''

"And because you think you don't fit in here in Harborside, and in some misguided attempt to spare Sara and me some unformed, future hurt, you think it's best to get out of our lives now?''

"Objection to the word *misguided*,'' Marta said, getting to her feet.

"Sit down, Ms. Wainwright,'' the judge said. "Answer the question, Mr. Perry.''

So Nate said, "Yes.'' He had been so sure he was doing the right thing that night on her beach. Over and over in his mind in the month since he'd left, he'd heard Sara's "I hate you.'' But to try to explain today in this courtroom... Nate started to sweat.

"No further questions.''

In great relief, Nate took his seat. Marta made a short speech and then rested her case.

The judge asked Libby if she had any witnesses. Libby said she had four. "First, I call Trevor Samms.''

As Nate sat there in shock, Trevor wheeled his chair into the room and took his place near the witness stand. In a loud, clear voice, he raised his hand, took his oath and begun to tell about his father and that heartbreaking meeting at the motel.

No, Nate wanted to say. *Don't make him tell how humiliated he was that day.* But Trevor did. He testified to his anger and embarrassment. He talked then about how Nate had been there for him, how he'd sobbed on Nate's chest and Nate had driven him for miles as he'd calmed down and reconciled himself to his father's rejection. Nate wondered why the kid was making it sound as if Nate had done so much. It had been Trevor who had shown extraordinary courage.

"Mr. Perry told me that I should go ahead and feel things, that it was okay for a man to feel, to hurt, to cry."

Nate had said those things. He remembered that moment in the car with painful poignancy, so sure then—thanks to Libby—that he'd learned something about sharing feelings.

Libby took a few steps toward the witness stand, until Nate could only see the proud line of her back and the back of her head, where strands of red tangled in a fiery glow. "Do you have an opinion on what kind of father Nate Perry would make?"

Trevor turned to the judge. "Mr. Perry would make— is—the best father on earth."

"Thank you. No more questions."

The funniest thing started to happen to Nate. He could hear the roar of wind, like the breeze that caught his sails, and he could smell the fresh water–laden air that was ever-present in the unpolluted air of Harborside. Frowning, he looked up at the stained-glass windows that were sealed closed.

Then Libby said, "I call Sara Perry to the stand."

Quick as a wink, Marta was on her feet. "Sara is only ten years old, not old enough under Ohio law to make any choices about her custody—"

"Sit down, Ms. Wainwright." The judge scowled at her.

Nate got to his feet, too. What was Libby thinking, putting his daughter through this hearing? "Your Honor, my daughter's been hurt enough by this entire process. She shouldn't have to testify."

"Sit down, Mr. Perry."

"Your Honor, with all respect, we're talking about my daughter here—"

"Sit down!" the judge roared. Then, slightly softer, he

said, "Really, Mr. Perry. Sit down. I've got some things to say to you."

Nate sat on the edge of his seat.

The judge took off his glasses and leaned forward over the high bench. "When you first came to me wanting your daughter, I wondered about you. I knew who you were and where you came from, and I knew you were a man who got whatever he wanted. I couldn't help but wonder—and worry—if you wanted that little girl only to prove that nobody could take her away from you. I'm glad to know I was wrong. Because you've just demonstrated that you do care for Sara. And because of that, I'm going to let her try to knock some sense into you." He stacked a sheaf of papers. "I don't know if you're a praying man, but I am. I guess sometimes a little child really *does* need to lead them." He turned to his bailiff. "Go get Sara Perry."

When Sara was led in, her white face made Nate want to go to her immediately. She gave him a tremulous smile, and his heart squeezed painfully. Sara took the stand, and Nate didn't miss the little thumbs-up sign she and Libby exchanged. So *Sara* had something to do with planning this fiasco of a hearing?

"Well," said Sara in answer to a question from Libby that Nate had apparently missed, "he makes breakfast on Saturday mornings. It's a pretty gross breakfast," she said earnestly to the judge, before quickly adding, "But he tries."

He tries. Was that enough? Once he'd have said no way. But maybe…

"Then he drives me to horseback-riding lessons. He had his assistant do all this research into saddles, and he bought me the safest one. Not the coolest, though." Again she looked at the judge. "But he tried to get something cool and safe, too."

She testified about the sailing trip, the picnic, the storm. To Nate's utter astonishment, she said he was a hero. Then she talked about the play practice, about how he'd gotten up in front of all those parents.

He had done all those things. And they apparently meant more to Sara than she'd ever let on at the time. Hell, she wouldn't even touch him back then, and here she was saying that she remembered all those things and they were special.

"See, Judge, the thing is—"

"He tries," the judge finished for her, smiling.

"Right. I think a really, really good father tries hard. And my dad does."

That roaring was back, a good, fierce, cleansing wind. And with it Nate felt a rush of feeling so deep and true that he wondered if he'd ever known what love really was before. With that feeling came a heady rush of belonging, of happiness. He stood, his legs trembling under him. "I want to testify," he said.

"Sara's still on the stand."

"I want to testify. I want to…say some things."

The judge looked over to the other counsel table. "It's up to Libby—Mrs. Perry. It's your case, Mrs. Perry. Do you want Mr. Perry to testify?"

Libby's eyes met Nate's. He tried to communicate without words his love for her. *Please.*

"Okay," she said, and he heard a breathless note in her voice. "I had a couple of other witnesses—Kevin Smithson, Tina Samms. I was going to get the caller from the square dance, but he was out of town, and then I thought of a lot of other people…" As if realizing she was rattling on, she sat down hard.

Nate exchanged places with his daughter. Out of the corner of his eye, Nate saw Marta practically slumped in her chair. Well, he thought, if she wanted to be his attorney, she really needed to learn that things were different in Harborside.

He raised his right hand, prepared to take the oath.

The judge said, "You don't have to do that again, Mr. Perry. You're still under oath from your previous testimony."

"Give it to me anyway. I don't want there to be any doubt about what I'm going to say." The bailiff stepped forward and Nate repeated the oath.

He fixed his eyes on Libby. "I just want to say that I've learned something here today. I think it was something I should have learned a long time ago, because my wife and my daughter sure spent a lot of time teaching me. I was a slow learner, I guess. But what I've learned is what love means. Love means you take chances. You risk everything. I love my wife and my daughter and I can't imagine how I thought I could live without them."

The courtroom was utterly still. Libby sat forward in her seat, her hands clasped hard in front of her.

"And I want to live in Harborside."

Libby jumped to her feet. "Nate, you don't have to say—"

"No, Libby, I'm the one testifying here." Nate motioned to the judge.

With a grin, Judge Wyatt said, "Sit down, Mrs. Perry." Mrs. Perry sat.

"I've got a great assistant. He wants to make something of himself, and I could sell the business to him. Favorable terms. And I could use the proceeds to invest in things that are a little smaller. Resorts geared to families." At his own words, Nate felt a hundred pounds lighter. The people who depended on him would be in good hands with Jeff. And

Nate could start living again, in a little place called Harborside.

"I want to see the sunrise from our old sunporch, and walk on everybody else's beach without being accused of trespassing. I want to have homemade pie in the Shoreline and help my wife shop for organic flour and go horseback riding with my kid. I want to put in a hard day's work that means something to real people, and then sail on a hot summer's night, without worrying what'll be in my fax machine when I come back. I want to be a big fish in a little pond, I guess, like a friend of mine once said."

The judge motioned for his bailiff. "I think he wants to dismiss the case."

"You're damn right I do. I want my wife and my daughter."

He got up then, came around the witness stand, and held out his arms. In a rush, Libby and Sara mobbed him, and he wrapped his arms around them both. They were warm and alive and so much more important than any tower of steel and stone he'd ever built.

"Do you mean it, Nate? Oh, I was so afraid." Libby tucked her head against his neck.

"I'm the one who was afraid. But you both took a chance on me. How could I do less than take a chance on love?"

EPILOGUE

Ten months later:

"There it is. All finished." Nate gestured to indicate the living room in the newly completed model condominium at Bittersweet Point.

Libby looked around. The living room had been designed to be white and spacious. But with lots of prints on the walls, a few brightly colored cotton rugs on the floor, and some handmade pottery in the bay window, the effect was rather cluttered. The furniture was wicker, its cushions a green flowered print. "Nice," she said. "Was it done up by one of those sophisticated city decorators of yours?"

They both laughed. "Not exactly," Nate said. "This time I used the decorator who knows how to make a place seem like home." His laughter faded away, and he gave her a smile. That smile wasn't practiced at all, but gentle and genuine.

Libby blushed. He'd insisted she decorate the model condominium because the concept of Bittersweet Point had been her idea. "So what do you think of the decor, Nate?"

"I like it. It suits the place."

Bittersweet Point now was a sweep of rustic waterfront condominiums, set back into the woods. Simple paths made of wood chips led to the beach. There too, the area had been left natural, except for a playground area that had been built near the water's edge. The Point was crowded this time of year, because—except for the unit they were standing in—the condos had all been sold to families with young children.

The condominium on the end had a ramp and a boardwalk instead of a chip path, and the walk led right down to the water's edge. When Nate had built the unit for Tina and Trevor, he'd made sure that Trevor could get down to the beach.

Now Nate was using the condo Libby had decorated as a model for his next project. That resort was more modest than Bittersweet Point, set on a quiet, out-of-the-way island in Lake Erie. Nate envisioned it as a hub for families who liked to sail, and he planned docks and a simple clubhouse, but none of the fancy amenities that would take the cost of ownership out of reach of the average family.

He still worked too hard, Libby thought, but he was slowly learning how to relax. These days, she could easily coax him out after dinner for a swim or a walk with her and Sara.

Libby walked over to the sliding doors and glanced out. Sara had come to the Point with them, and now was out wading in the lake, in a pair of cutoff jeans. She had something in her hand, probably a new shell or rock, but her attention was focused on a gang of boys who were playing volleyball.

Nate came up behind her and looked over her shoulder. "She's growing up," he observed. His voice softened. "And I think every day how lucky and blessed I am to be here to see that. To have you and Sara—all of you—to love."

Libby's heart squeezed, both at Nate's words and the easy way he spoke the feelings in his heart. Almost unconsciously, her hand went to her stomach, a touch for their growing baby.

He planted a soft kiss on the back of her neck. "Thanks for agreeing to go to Chicago with me this weekend."

Libby held back a sigh. She wasn't really looking forward to the dedication of the Iris Complex, but Nate thought they should go to support Jeff. For all its problems, the completed Iris complex was a gleaming masterpiece, a testament to Nate's vision in design and his good judgment in giving Jeff a chance. Nate retained a financial interest in the resort but had sold most of the business to his former assistant. Everybody was happy with the results.

"I was thinking we could buy you a new dress for the round of parties after the dedication," Nate said.

"I couldn't fit into that black dress again for sure," Libby said with a rueful smile.

Nate's arm came around her, cradling her stomach, feeling the little mound low in her belly. She put her own hand there again, over his. "Maybe it would be a good idea to shop in Chicago," she conceded.

"Yes. A new dress. One with flowers." His voice whispered along her neck. "Big, humongous flowers. A dress that's easy to take off. We'll come back to our room early, and I'll tell you again how I like you in black, and big, big flowers and then in nothing but bare skin. How does that sound?"

It sounded downright wonderful. Most things these days were wonderful.

"And then when we're done in Chicago, maybe we'll take a vacation."

"Nate, we can't take a vacation now. You know how busy my shop is in the summer."

"A vacation," he insisted. "A short one. I have this great spot picked out. It's a resort with a lot of amenities. Blue sky, woods and sand and clear water, and the place we'd be staying in has all this art on the walls…"

"Sounds a lot like Bittersweet Point," she observed.

"That's because it is Bittersweet Point." Slowly, he turned her to face him. "I bought this last condo to surprise you. That's why I wanted you to decorate it."

"You bought this place? But why on earth…? We live right across the cove."

"I figure, with a baby on the way, and Sara turning into a teenager in a few years, and with my building projects and your shop, we'll want someplace to get away once in a while. Spend time alone together."

That sounded heavenly. "Yes, but…here?"

"Why not right here? After all, is there any place in the world better than right here? Better than very close to home?"

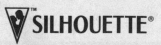